A CASE OF SOME DELICACY

KC KAHLER

Quills & Quartos
PUBLISHING

Edited by JL Ashton and Gail Warner

Proofread by Linda D'Orazio

Cover by Crowglass Design

ISBN 978-1-951033-07-1 (ebook) and 978-1-951033-08-8 (paperback)

In Memory of JanetR, this story's biggest fan

TABLE OF CONTENTS

ABOUT A MONTH AGO
I RECEIVED THIS LETTER
AND ABOUT A FORTNIGHT AGO
I ANSWERED IT
FOR I THOUGHT IT

a case of some

delicacy

AND REQUIRING EARLY ATTENTION.
IT IS FROM MY COUSIN MR COLLINS
WHO, WHEN I AM DEAD
MAY TURN YOU ALL OUT OF THIS HOUSE
AS SOON AS HE PLEASES

Mr. Bennet . Pride & Prejudice Chapter 13

Pleasing Attentions

It is a truth universally acknowledged that a single man distinguished by the patronage of the Right Honourable Lady Catherine de Bourgh must be in want of a wife.

The Reverend William Collins, having offered an olive branch to his estranged family, arrived at their estate to be welcomed by them. Mrs Bennet's enthusiasm for his visit to Longbourn vastly improved when he hinted, on the morning after his arrival, that he was of a mind to take a wife and Miss Jane Bennet held especial interest for him. Mrs Bennet, seeing a solution to the gross injustice that had contributed to her nervous condition for the last fifteen years—the entailment of Longbourn away from the female line—offered not-so-subtle encouragement to Mr Collins's burgeoning *tendre*.

Of this new accord, the five Bennet daughters were perfectly unaware, but they soon would be. Mr Collins's arrival coincided with the Meryton assembly, where he vowed to dance with each of his fair cousins. He asked Jane for the first set and Elizabeth for the second. He was a terrible dancer—awkward and solemn, apologising instead of attending, and often moving wrong without being aware of it. The moment of Elizabeth's release from him was ecstasy.

Grateful for the shortage of gentlemen, she took an opportunity to sit and rest her sore toes. Mr Bingley, a young man from the north who had recently leased the nearby estate called Netherfield Park, was standing nearby with his friend Mr Darcy. Like Mr Collins, the Netherfield party was being introduced to most of the neighbourhood on that very night. The gentlemen newcomers were near enough that Elizabeth happened to overhear their conversation. She liked Mr Bingley immediately but not his friend, for after having given offense to the entire room with his haughty, prideful behaviour, Mr Darcy gave particular insult to Elizabeth, declaring her not handsome enough to tempt him to dance. The gentlemen soon walked off, and Elizabeth remained with no very cordial feelings towards him. She decided to tell her father about it. Better to laugh at the ridiculous than to stew in anger.

Later, Mr Bingley asked Elizabeth to dance, and she was delighted with his easy and open manners. After the dance ended, her dear friend, Charlotte Lucas, sought her out.

"Is it true, Lizzy? Are Jane and Mr Collins soon to be engaged?"

The question struck Elizabeth like a thunderbolt. "Certainly not! We met him but two days ago. Where did you hear such a fanciful rumour?"

"From my mother, but *your* mother is the source. Everyone believes it is as good as settled." Charlotte elaborated on what she had heard. "Apparently, the reason for Mr Collins's visit is to choose a bride from among you. He thinks this will somehow atone for the entail. He fancies Jane."

"How can Mama expect her to marry that foolish man? And to spread such gossip! I must warn Jane." Elizabeth looked around frantically.

Charlotte gestured behind Elizabeth. "She is there, with Mr Bingley, and I suspect he will dance the next set with her. I overheard him say that Jane is the prettiest girl here."

"That is not surprising as she *is* the prettiest here, and I heard him express similar sentiments." An idea came to Elizabeth. "Perhaps we can use his preference to confuse my mother's matchmaking. You must tell her what you overheard. Surely the promise of being mother to the mistress of Netherfield would be irresistible to her."

Charlotte looked sceptical. "With five eligible daughters, I rather suspect she would settle for nothing less than to be the mother of both the mistress of Netherfield *and* the mistress of Longbourn." After a moment, she offered, "If you are certain Jane does not desire the match with Mr Collins, I shall help you interfere with your mother's plans. I see how upset you are, dear Eliza!"

"Of course Jane does not desire a match with Mr Collins. How could anyone desire such a match? To think of Jane married to that man unsettles me entirely." Elizabeth shook off the disagreeable thoughts. "While we wait for Jane to finish her dance, let me entertain you with what *I* overheard earlier this evening." She recounted the conversation between Mr Bingley and Mr Darcy. Having already enacted it for her father, Elizabeth added more flourish to Mr Darcy's proud demeanour on the second telling.

Charlotte laughed. "Lizzy, you exaggerate his mannerisms! But I do not doubt your words. Poor girl, to be only tolerable and slighted by other men! Oh look! Your father is conversing with Mr Darcy."

Elizabeth spied her father at the edge of the room, standing to Mr Darcy's side. "Ah, I imagine Papa initiated the conversation. He would not be able to resist such an opportunity, and I find that *I* cannot resist it either. I must have some sport. In the meantime, will you not inform my mother about what Mr Bingley said? If she can see Jane dancing with him as she contemplates the implications of his words, perhaps she will reconsider the desirability of Mr Collins."

❧

After devising their hurried plan for intervention, Elizabeth grasped Charlotte's hands in thanks, and they parted in opposite directions. Charlotte found Mrs Bennet standing with Mrs Philips, gossiping as usual, while Mary Bennet looked on in disapproval.

"Good evening, Mrs Bennet, Mary, Mrs Philips. Are you enjoying the ball?"

"Oh yes, it has been a delightful evening, has it not?" said Mrs Bennet. "Were you just speaking with Lizzy? I must hear about her dance with Mr Bingley."

"Elizabeth has gone to speak with Mr Bennet," said Charlotte. "I see Jane is dancing with Mr Bingley again. He is a very agreeable fellow, do you not think?"

"Very agreeable indeed! He should do nicely for Lizzy—or perhaps Lydia," replied Mrs Bennet, as if already settling the matter.

"I think he prefers his current partner. He has danced with Jane twice, and I overheard him praising her as the prettiest girl in the room."

"Jane *is* much admired," said Mrs Bennet proudly. "But Collins was there first, and it would be the most natural thing in the world for Jane to be the mistress of Longbourn. Mr Collins is quite taken with her, to be sure."

"But what does Jane think? What if she prefers Mr Bingley or some other gentleman?" Charlotte knew she tread on thin ice.

"My heavens! What would Jane think but what is best for her family? Some other gentleman? Really, Miss Lucas, you cannot expect a perfectly good eligible gentleman to be thrown away in favour of an imaginary one! No doubt other young ladies with *fewer* prospects would be glad of the chance at Mr Collins, but I assure you, dear Jane will do her duty!"

Mrs Bennet's words, intended to sting, did their job. But they also gave Charlotte a new idea to consider. At twenty-seven, she would soon be past the marriageable age. How she wished to run her own home, start a family, and no longer be a burden to her parents! If Mr Collins was the best prospect for accomplishing these goals and Jane truly had no interest in him, Charlotte resolved to bring about her own marriage. She had never been a romantic anyway.

Fitzwilliam Darcy was in a foul mood. He did not wish to be at a country assembly such as this. But Bingley had asked him most earnestly to attend, and so here he was. They entered the assembly room to hushed whispers and curious stares. Bingley was, as usual, all easiness and friendliness, which made him a favourite amongst the locals in a matter of minutes. He entreated Darcy to dance with the sister of his dance partner.

"Which do you mean?" Darcy turned around, and he looked for a moment at Elizabeth Bennet till catching her eye, then withdrew his own. "She is tolerable but not handsome enough to tempt me, and I am in no humour at present to give consequence to young ladies who are slighted by other men."

Darcy soon came to regret those words spoken without thought. As he stood watching the dancers, Mr Bennet introduced himself and explained that his estate, Longbourn, shared a border with Nether-field Park. Mr Bennet then pointed out the various members of his family: his wife, his five daughters, and his cousin, Mr Collins. He praised his two eldest daughters, Jane and Elizabeth, but ridiculed the others, admitting his wife was a vulgar matchmaker, his three youngest daughters remarkably silly, and his cousin a prancing fool. Based on his own observations throughout the night, Darcy could not disagree, but he found the source rather strange.

Miss Elizabeth soon joined the two men. Darcy was struck by the beautiful expression in her dark eyes as she looked upon her father.

"Elizabeth, my dear, have you met Mr Darcy?"

"No, Papa, I have not yet had that pleasure. I have been dancing, you know."

The introductions were made. Darcy prepared for the usual flattery and insincerity directed at him by young ladies. Refreshingly, there was no flattery, but he had the distinct impression that he was the object of a joke between Mr Bennet and his daughter.

"Mr Darcy and I were discussing our shared dislike of dancing," the former said.

Miss Elizabeth laughed. "How unfortunate you should find yourselves at a ball. I rather wonder why you have come at all." Her gaze issued a challenge.

Darcy felt he must answer it. "Mr Bingley was eager to introduce himself and his guests to the neighbourhood. I could hardly refuse."

"Lizzy, you know why *I* felt obliged to come." Mr Bennet motioned towards Mr Collins dancing with an unhappy girl—Lydia Bennet, if Darcy remembered correctly. "It is well known that I prefer to be an observer rather than a participant, and tonight I have much to observe. Of course, as an old man of little interest to the ladies, *my* disinclination to dance is far less noteworthy than Mr Darcy's."

"Indeed, I have noted more than one young lady sitting down for want of a partner, and some of them are quite tolerable." Miss Elizabeth smiled.

Darcy almost winced, considering how to extract himself from the situation. If the father and daughter would merely confront him indignantly for the insult, at least he could apologise. But their indirect teasing left him quite at a loss. Mr Darcy was not teased often, and he apologised even less often.

Miss Elizabeth ended the awkward pause by observing warmly, "Mr Bingley has won the good opinion of the neighbourhood with his eagerness to dance. We are simple people, Mr Darcy, and your friend's efforts at amiability will long endear him to us."

Darcy felt the unspoken comparison to himself. "Mr Bingley possesses that talent of conversing easily with strangers. He is well liked wherever he goes, but I find him rather too willing to befriend everyone and anyone."

"You are quite right to be discerning," said Mr Bennet. "Having a surfeit of friends is a burden on one's time. Why, if not for my peace-making cousin's visit, I would be passing a calm evening in my library, free from the bothersome demands of being sociable."

Coughing quietly, Miss Elizabeth turned away to observe the line of dancers. Rather than respond to Mr Bennet's singular way of expressing himself, Darcy followed her gaze and noticed Bingley happily dancing with the eldest Miss Bennet for the second time that night. Darcy frowned, remembering Miss Bingley had said Jane Bennet was soon to be betrothed. Once again, he would have to protect Bingley from his weakness for a pretty face.

Elizabeth made her excuses as the dance came near its end. "Papa, I must speak with Jane. Excuse me, Mr Darcy." She curtseyed and walked off.

The Reverend William Collins was delighted with his visit to Hertfordshire thus far. Lady Catherine had told him he should resolve the family quarrel, and as always, she had been correct. His reception by the Bennets and all the important people of Meryton had been quite satisfying.

Upon meeting the Bennet daughters, he found them even more handsome and amiable than they had been represented by common report, and he determined that he would follow Lady Catherine's further advice to seek a wife among them. Miss Jane Bennet, the eldest and most beautiful of her sisters, was all he required in a wife. From the first evening, she was his settled choice. The next morning, in a *tête-à-tête* with Mrs Bennet, he expressed his hopes and intentions. She could not have been more encouraging.

Miss Bennet had received his attentions with modesty and decorum, just as he would expect from the companion of his future life. How pleased Lady Catherine would be with her!

Tonight at the assembly, he danced with each of his five cousins. Though he could have eschewed the pleasure of dancing with Miss Lydia in particular, he did not wish any of the girls to feel slighted. He found her and Miss Catherine too silly and loud and altogether too prone to giggling. But such were the ways of young females. Miss Mary was quite accomplished and insightful but rather more plain than her sisters and a reluctant dancer. The two eldest Bennets, however, were agreeable, beautiful, and delightful dance partners.

As Mr Collins escorted Cousin Lydia from the dance floor, he searched for Miss Bennet. He planned to dance with her a second time, thus conveying to all assembled his intention to make her his wife. As luck would have it, she was being escorted from the dance floor by a fair-haired gentleman.

"How well you dance, Mr Collins!" exclaimed Mrs Bennet. "What a fine thing for my girls to each have the honour of such a partner."

"You flatter me, Mrs Bennet, for the honour has been mine. Indeed, I do not believe I have ever had the pleasure of so fine a set of partners. What excellent timing for my visit to coincide with this most pleasing social event. Lady Catherine de Bourgh wisely insisted I come to Hertfordshire just after Michaelmas. I do not hesitate to assume she would greatly approve of my dancing with each of my cousins at least once. Indeed, Lady Catherine would call it my duty. And I daresay neither I nor—I flatter myself—any of my fair cousins would be averse to a repeat of the now-fulfilled duty."

Just as he was about to transition this excellent speech into a request for Cousin Jane's next dance, Miss Elizabeth interrupted. "Mr Collins, have you met Mr Bingley? He has leased the estate bordering

Longbourn and is as new to Hertfordshire society, as you are. Mr Bingley, this is my cousin, Mr Collins, parson at Hunsford in Kent."

Mr Collins expressed his delight to make the acquaintance of so many illustrious people.

"It is a pleasure to meet you," said Mr Bingley with a smile. "Pardon me, but you mentioned Lady Catherine de Bourgh of Kent. I believe that she is Darcy's aunt. It is a small world, is it not?"

"Mr Darcy of Pemberley in Derbyshire?" Mr Collins asked, and after receiving confirmation, exclaimed, "How extraordinary! Lady Catherine often speaks of her nephew. Are you well acquainted with him, Mr Bingley?"

Mr Bingley laughed. "I should say so—he is staying with us at Netherfield, and he is here tonight." He looked about the room. "Though I know not where he is hiding. He has been rather unsociable."

"I left him conversing with my father in an out-of-the-way spot," volunteered Miss Elizabeth. "They were commiserating over their shared dislike of dancing. Come, Mr Collins, I shall introduce you. Surely Mr Darcy would wish to hear any news you have of his family."

Mr Collins could scarce believe his luck. As he followed Miss Elizabeth across the room, he smoothed his waistcoat, which had the unfortunate tendency to bunch about his middle. Soon they came upon Mr Bennet and a tall gentleman who looked as distinguished as Mr Collins would expect of so important a person.

"Papa," began Miss Elizabeth, "it seems that Mr Darcy and Mr Collins have a mutual acquaintance." Looking up at Mr Darcy, she continued cheerfully, "Mr Darcy, may I introduce Mr Collins, parson at Hunsford and grateful servant to Lady Catherine de Bourgh."

Mr Darcy bowed slightly, and Mr Collins bowed as low as he could in response. "Mr Darcy, it is an immense and unexpected honour to meet you! I have heard much of you from my illustrious patroness, your most esteemed aunt. I can inform you, sir, with great pleasure, that both Lady Catherine and Miss de Bourgh were in excellent health when I left them but four days ago. Indeed, Lady Catherine is always in excellent health, but Miss de Bourgh, as I understand it, is much improved since you last saw her."

Mr Darcy took a moment to digest the information. "I am glad to hear it." After glancing at the smiling countenances of Mr Bennet and Miss Elizabeth, he asked, "How long have you served as parson at Hunsford?"

"Your noble aunt bestowed her benevolence on me nearly four months ago, and I have endeavoured to serve her needs and the needs of my parishioners admirably since then. I am sure you could not be surprised at her great consideration of my every need as well."

"Oh yes, Mr Collins!" Miss Elizabeth interjected. "You must tell Mr Darcy about Lady Catherine's many helpful ideas regarding the parsonage house, such as the shelves in the upstairs closet. I daresay Mr Darcy is desirous to hear about his aunt's affability and condescension as he knows so few people here and is in no humour to dance."

Mr Collins swelled with pride that he could be of use to Mr Darcy. He was about to speak when Cousin Elizabeth added, "But I am afraid my father and I are wanted by my mother. Please excuse us— We shall leave you gentlemen to become better acquainted."

Mr Bennet took his daughter's hand to lead her away, but Mr Collins could not let her go without again thanking her for the honour of meeting Mr Darcy.

"Dear Cousin Elizabeth! I thank you for the solicitude you show on behalf of myself and Mr Darcy, indeed, of everyone around you. You are most gracious and thoughtful. Is she not, Mr Darcy?"

The corners of Mr Darcy's mouth turned up slightly as he replied, "Yes, Miss Elizabeth is compassion incarnate."

She gave a lopsided smile, which must have been an indication of her modesty. "Not at all," she said. "I consider it my duty to make newcomers as comfortable as possible. Let it not be said that Hertfordshire society is lacking in hospitality or, most importantly, friendly manners."

Mr Collins bowed over her hand. She then turned to her father, who said, "Come Lizzy, let us see where else your compassion is needed tonight," before leading her away.

Mr Collins struck up a conversation with Mr Darcy. He made sure to mention the shelves, as Miss Elizabeth had wisely suggested. But as he prepared to move from detailing Lady Catherine's improvements of the parsonage house to praising the grandeur of Rosings, Mr Darcy expressed his regrets at having to defer the conversation to another time for he wished to speak with his friend, Mr Bingley. He bowed quickly and walked away, leaving Mr Collins to reflect on what an excellent night he was having at the assembly.

Excessively Diverted

Taking great advantage of a warm spell in late October, Mrs Bennet planned a picnic at Longbourn to amuse the younger folk and forward all her matrimonial schemes.

Jane blushed while conversing with Mr Bingley amongst the late-blooming roses. Elizabeth looked on, relieved. She liked Mr Bingley very much, though she cared little for the rest of his companions. His sisters, Miss Bingley and Mrs Hurst, as well as their friend, Mr Darcy, clearly thought themselves above their Hertfordshire neighbours, while Mr Hurst seemed only to think of his food and drink. Usually Elizabeth would delight in observing, and later mocking, their haughty airs, but lately, she could spare no time to notice the many pointed comments of the two sisters nor the reserved silence and disconcerting stare, broken only by cold civility, of Mr Darcy. She had little interest in doing anything but diverting her visiting cousin from poor Jane.

The days at Longbourn since the assembly had been difficult. Mr Collins was pleased to communicate at length about his position as the parson at Hunsford, particularly when he could impress upon his listener his enviable situation as the recipient of patronage from Lady Catherine de Bourgh. Despite his earlier delight in Mr Collins's absurdity, Mr Bennet was anxious to have his library to himself again. In his library, he had always been sure of leisure and tranquillity, and although prepared—as he told Elizabeth—to meet with folly and conceit in every other room in the house, he was used to being free from them there. Thus Mr Bennet seized upon any chance to rid himself of Mr Collins's company, often at the expense of his daughters.

Jane endured her cousin's most pointed praises with equanimity, as she did all other situations. In the privacy of their night-time talks, Elizabeth spoke of her embarrassment at her mother's machinations and her disappointment in her father's wilful avoidance. Jane defended each of them with gentle words—Mama was only doing what she thought best for their future, and Papa was merely being obliging—but Elizabeth discerned that Jane said so as much to convince herself as anyone else.

Elizabeth was at turns amused at Mr Collins's ludicrousness and exasperated by it. She would sometimes provoke his effusions for further merriment. At other times, when he was showering Jane with his gallantry, Elizabeth's protective nature would awaken, and she directed the conversation to safer subjects. She was particularly proud of the few times she could elicit a discussion on the finer points of Fordyce between Mary and Mr Collins, and her efforts on those occasions were appreciated by all the Bennet girls—Mary was eager for such discussions, and her other sisters were just as eager to be free of Mr Collins's speeches.

There were other topics Elizabeth knew could be relied upon to pull the conversation away from Mr Collins while occupying her youngest sisters and distracting their mother. Thus the days were filled with enthusiastic discourse about the arrival of the militia, much speculation about Mr Bingley and his party, and, of course, many exaltations of Lady Catherine de Bourgh and her estate. Elizabeth could only be expected to do so much, after all.

When they were in company, as today at Longbourn, Charlotte was an enormous help to her efforts, giving Elizabeth and Jane respite from Mr Collins's constant ramblings. Mr Bingley—and even Miss Bingley and Mrs Hurst—unwittingly helped by seeking further acquaintance with Jane. But Elizabeth knew their paltry intervention could only distract her cousin for so long. Something had to be done to end this charade of a courtship and curtail her mother's gossiping. She must speak with her father. Mr Bennet was at that moment trying to escape his picnic guests, she observed ruefully. He slowly edged back towards the house, no doubt to hide himself in the library. She resolved to break away as soon as she could for a private conversation.

Charlotte did her best to appear interested in the grandness of the chimney piece at Rosings Park, the estate of Lady Catherine de Bourgh. She would rather hear about the parsonage house, but Mr Collins seemed determined to extol his patroness and her tastes. Almost from their first conversation, Charlotte had realised she could easily think on other topics without Mr Collins noticing her inattention.

She glanced around at the assembled picnic guests. Elizabeth, standing with Jane, Mr Bingley, and Miss Bingley near the roses, gave Charlotte a grateful smile. Charlotte nodded almost imperceptibly. She was happy to help her dear friends, but she had her own designs on Mr Collins, clumsy dancing and inane prattle aside.

Continuing her perusal, she noted Mr Darcy again watching Elizabeth. He had become rather obvious. Elizabeth had even noticed Mr Darcy's stares, but with her distraction over Jane and her overhearing that unfortunate conversation at the assembly, she believed he merely looked at her with disdain. With so much matchmaking going on, Charlotte wondered why that superb potential match was being ignored.

Thoughts of matchmaking brought Charlotte's gaze to Mrs Bennet, who returned it with an expression of displeasure. Charlotte recognised the look well—it was that of a protective mother. Mrs Bennet, not known for her great intelligence, had been the only person to guess the true nature of Charlotte's interest in Mr Collins. If his courtship of Jane Bennet ended in failure, Charlotte was resolved to position herself as his second choice. Despite Elizabeth's vehement assertions that Jane opposed the match, Charlotte doubted Jane would indeed forgo the chance to keep Longbourn within her family. Jane had always been the most sensible Bennet, and she had never directly confirmed, at least not to Charlotte, that she wished for intervention into the courtship. Such a confirmation, however, was unlikely to come from so demure and charitable a young lady.

Regardless, distracting Mr Collins served two purposes. First, it relieved Elizabeth from her assumed sentry responsibilities, and second, it positioned Charlotte to the greatest advantage should Elizabeth's assertions prove correct. Her sole regret was that she could not confide her plans in her dearest friend, but Elizabeth would disapprove of Charlotte's matrimonial calculus. Should her plans succeed, Charlotte would need to enlighten her.

Charlotte was brought back to the present by some trifling question from Mr Collins. When she answered in the affirmative, he gulped his punch before continuing his monologue.

❦

Fitzwilliam Darcy was a man distracted. To most observers, this was not unusual; he often seemed distracted when in company—staring out a window, appearing deep in thought. It was his way of avoiding the fortune hunters, social climbers, and other unsavoury characters who often sought to ingratiate themselves to him.

But no, this time he was distracted by, of all things, a country girl. In addition to grudgingly appreciating Elizabeth Bennet's fine eyes, pleasing figure, and playful manners, Darcy found her behaviour towards the ridiculous Mr Collins most perplexing. Although her manners betrayed nothing, those fine eyes—whose expressions Darcy had been studying since that first night at the assembly—occasionally revealed her true thoughts. Yet she often sought out the company of her parson cousin above all others. Why would she do such a thing?

It was rumoured Mr Collins would soon make an offer of marriage to the eldest Miss Bennet. Even with his detached aloofness in the neighbourhood, Darcy had heard of the entail on Longbourn and of Mr Collins's wish to secure a wife from among the Bennet daughters. Miss Elizabeth ought to be happy to escape such notice, letting that duty fall instead to her elder sister. But there she was, intervening in every conversation Mr Collins attempted with Miss Bennet. What could be her purpose? This most interesting question occupied Darcy's thoughts, and having little else to occupy him in company such as this, he determined to solve the puzzle for himself.

While pretending to hear what Miss Bingley was saying, Mr Darcy wondered where Miss Elizabeth had gone. During one of the few moments when he was *not* watching her, she seemed to have disappeared from the picnic guests.

Mr Collins approached and bowed with a flourish. Darcy braced himself for the inanities that were sure to come. Since being introduced—or rather punished, as would more aptly describe the meeting—at that eventful assembly, Darcy now knew what to expect from the clergyman. This only further deepened his substantial curiosity about Miss Elizabeth's seeming preference for Mr Collins's company, for she clearly thought such company a worthy punishment.

"Is it not a pleasant day for such diverting amusements?" Mr Collins motioned towards the game of battledore and shuttlecock being played by the youngest Bennets and Lucases. The giggling players had attracted an audience of smiling officers, the Philipses, the remaining Lucases, the Longs, and the Hursts. Getting no distinct reply, Mr Collins continued, "Longbourn's gardens are very fine although they are nothing to Rosings Park and, as I am told, Pemberley. Lady Catherine speaks often of your estate, Mr Darcy. I understand she has advised you in redecorating the public rooms over the years and has made recommendations to improve the grounds. As Lady Catherine has exquisite tastes, Pemberley must be very grand indeed."

Miss Bingley replied, "I am sure Pemberley's grounds need no improvements. Mr Darcy is an excellent master of that fine estate."

If not so distracted, Darcy might have found the ensuing conversation between Pemberley's fawning admirers greatly amusing. He searched for a means of escape, not only to avoid such insincere praises—Miss Bingley had never set foot on Pemberley's grounds beyond the rose garden—but also to locate a certain young lady.

At that moment, the shrill voice of Mrs Bennet could be heard nearby, "Oh! Wherever can Mr Bennet and Lizzy be? Have they no consideration for their guests? They delight in vexing me!"

Darcy seized the opportunity, amazed he could ever eagerly welcome the appearance of Mrs Bennet. "Madam, allow me to search for them so that you may continue acting as gracious hostess."

Mrs Bennet appeared surprised by Darcy's offer but accepted it. "That is very kind of you, sir. If you must coax Mr Bennet to join us, tell him that we shall soon begin the cricket. As for my daughter, tell her I demand to see her at once."

Darcy did not need to be told twice. He suspected he could find Mr Bennet in the library, though he had no idea where to find Miss Elizabeth, since she was not hovering around Mr Collins or Jane Bennet. He decided to enter the front door and ask for their whereabouts. Coming around the corner of the house, he neared the double windows that looked into the library. There he heard Miss Elizabeth's voice from inside.

"Papa, I must speak with you about Mr Collins."

Darcy recognised the opportunity to solve the mystery that had plagued him. He halted his progress without acknowledging that he was about to eavesdrop. He could just make out Miss Elizabeth's reflection in the angled pane of the open window. He could also see Mr Bennet's back, seated at his desk.

Mr Bennet turned a page in his book but made no other movement. "Please, Lizzy, Mr Collins consumes enough of our time with his company; we hardly need give him a moment more without it."

"Yes, but have you noted whose time he most consumes?"

"As long as he consumes as little of mine as possible, I am content to let the rest of you fend for yourselves." He had all the appearance of intending that to be the last word on the subject.

Moving forward into the room, Miss Elizabeth pressed on. "Papa, I find it hard to believe, with your keen eye for observation, that you have failed to grasp Mr Collins's attentions towards Jane."

"What of them?" said he, not looking up. "Jane inspires many a better man to lavish attentions upon her."

"But many a better man do not come to Longbourn with the express intent of finding a wife."

"Much to your mother's disappointment," he quipped, still reading.

"Papa, please!" Darcy watched her pause and breathe in deeply. "Would you wish for *me* to marry Mr Collins?"

Mr Bennet looked up sharply from his book. "You, my Lizzy? Heavens no. You would never accept him, ridiculous as he is."

"No, I would not," she said. Darcy audibly exhaled in relief and then ducked fully out of sight lest they had heard. Luckily he was not noticed as Miss Elizabeth continued. "But you can imagine Mama's disapprobation at my refusal."

"Naturally. However, I trust in your ability to suffer through it admirably—perhaps by increasing the frequency and length of your outdoor exertions. How conveniently you time your constitutionals to avoid your mother's morning tirades."

Mr Bennet's teasing failed to distract her. "Do you wish Jane to be put in such a situation when she has no similar escape from Mama's apoplexy?"

"I am not certain Jane would inspire your mother's apoplexy." He spoke in a detached, almost academic tone that Darcy thought irritating if not cruel.

Miss Elizabeth's voice rose. "So you would expect her to accept a proposal from Mr Collins?"

"I do not know what to expect. Jane is sensible enough to know the advantages of such a match." She made a noise that could only be described as a snort, before her father continued in a gentler tone, "Her disposition is so different from yours that I suspect she could endure Mr Collins's company with grace and even contentedness in securing her family's future."

"Why does this duty fall to her, Papa? Why should she be expected to suffer through a lifetime with that insufferable man? Might I remind you that you could barely endure three hours of his antics upon hosting him here?"

Now she stood directly in front of Mr Bennet, challenging him with her fine eyes from across his desk and in full view of Darcy's spying. But he found himself unable to move, riveted by the right-eous, beautiful anger in her face.

In her agitation, Elizabeth's attention would not be swayed from her father, and she had much more to say. "Yet you would allow Jane to endure a loveless marriage to an intolerable man, merely because she is too good, too dutiful to complain? How could you abide such a fate for any of your children, let alone your most worthy? Jane is all good-ness and serenity, but she feels just as deeply as any of us who are more open with our emotions. Like me, Jane wishes to marry for love and respect, two emotions Mr Collins is unlikely to engender in any sensible woman!"

Mr Bennet closed his book. "Lizzy, if such a proposal comes to pass and Jane refuses, I shall of course support her."

Although she was somewhat placated by this statement, Eliza-beth pressed on. "The entail complicates matters. And Mama's shameful gossiping has all but publicly announced an engagement. What if Jane feels forced to accept out of her sense of familial duty?"

"If she does accept, then she will be making a great sacrifice for her family. The decision is hers."

"No, the decision is ultimately yours. You must refuse your consent."

Mr Bennet put his book on the desk and sat up straight in his chair. His tone betrayed his vexation. "If I do as you suggest, I shall never hear the end of it from your mother."

This was just what Elizabeth dreaded hearing. It brought to the forefront of her mind long-buried thoughts about her father's inade-quacies towards his family, and the fact that these inadequacies might now be paid for with Jane's future happiness.

"Oh, what burdens you face! What great misfortunes! Why endure a few weeks of your wife's excited fretting when you can stand by and let your child enter into an unhappy union with an insensible man? Indeed, why not simply sit back and observe, with detached amusement, the inappropriate behaviour of your wife and daughters rather than trouble yourself to correct it?"

Mr Bennet interrupted sternly, "Elizabeth, you forget yourself."

"No, sir, you forget yourself and your responsibility." She was not quite yelling, but her voice commanded undivided attention. "You have known about the entail your entire life. Surely the lack of a male heir has been apparent for at least ten years. Did you then begin to exercise stricter household economy to save and invest in your daughters' security? No! Did you provide them with a proper education and the discipline to pursue their talents? No! Your indolence and aversion to confrontation allowed them to become, as you often say, the silliest girls in England. And all the while, Mama carries on unchecked, her behaviour often bordering on impropriety. Can you not see that your continued failure to act has injured us all?"

"That is quite enough!" Mr Bennet boomed as he stood. "I shall not be lectured by my daughter in my own library. I fully comprehend your feelings."

"I do not think you do." Elizabeth could not regret her words; they were the truth. But she softened her demeanour and tried to explain. "You never meant your choices to lead to this. But I shall not allow Jane to forfeit her happiness because of the follies of our family. The final decision lies with you, Father. If you fail Jane when she most needs you"—her voice broke as she gave her ultimatum—"I shall never forgive you. You must determine whether you would rather face your wife's temporary displeasure or mine, which I assure you will last as long as Jane's unhappy marriage."

Mr Bennet stood at his desk, unmoving.

"In an attempt to spare you this decision, and Jane as well, I shall endeavour to prevent the dreaded proposal from ever happening."

Mr Bennet scoffed. "Just how will you do that?"

"By shielding Jane from Mr Collins. I shall constantly insert myself into their company. I shall do whatever is in my power to protect her and to heal this rift between us." Searching his face for some sign of acknowledgement and finding none, Elizabeth concluded softly, "Please wish me luck, Papa."

Mr Bennet's shoulders slumped at her last words, but he made no other movement. As she turned to leave, Elizabeth caught sight of something at the window—the dark eyes of Mr Darcy, blinking at her in bewilderment. Then he was gone.

Stifling her gasp, Elizabeth rushed from the room, resolved to confront the interloper. She knew Mr Darcy had disdained her before, but after witnessing such insolence and hearing all of the family failings, she could only imagine what his opinion must be now. She hardly cared—what rudeness! To eavesdrop, to spy! She must find out how much he had heard and secure his word that he would reveal nothing of it to his friends.

3

Strange Bedfellows

As Darcy hurried to make his escape, he berated himself for being so lax in his concealment. The angry Elizabeth he had witnessed was intoxicating enough, but the hurt, sad Elizabeth at the end of the confrontation had wreaked havoc within him. He had wanted to run inside to comfort her, to tell her how valiant she was in defence of her sister, how selfless she was to take such a burden on herself, yet he was unable to move—and then suddenly she looked straight at him! *Blast!*

And now he must return to Mrs Bennet without succeeding in his promised task. He sped along the path, his mind racing to come up with an excuse. Although he would not stoop to the indecorous act of running, Darcy thought he had the advantage of uncommonly long legs in combination with a head start. He had not bargained, however, on his sprightly pursuer breaking into a rather unladylike run.

"Mr Darcy! A moment, please!" she called out. Her voice was surprisingly close and clearly angered.

He halted his hurried steps, endeavoured to school his features, and turned to face her. "Miss Bennet, how may I be of service?"

Elizabeth would have laughed at Mr Darcy's slightly breathless attempt at artlessness were she not so irate. "I have come to expect staring from you, but what can you mean by lurking about windows and spying on private conversations?"

He winced at the word "lurking," but did not deny it. "My apologies, Miss Bennet. I—I," he stuttered and paused. "Mrs Bennet sent me to fetch your father, and I was about to enter the house when I heard voices coming from the library window. I...you... Your voice was raised, and I was dumbstruck by the heat of the argument."

A moment of silence passed as their eyes met.

Elizabeth flushed, embarrassed afresh with the confirmation that Mr Darcy had seen her at the height of her temper. "That is hardly an excuse, sir!"

He looked away and made no reply. Sighing, she continued, "Mr Darcy, although I am sure you are shocked at my impudence, you must have deduced the very delicate nature of the conversation you just witnessed."

"I do grasp the delicacy of the subject matter, yes." It looked as if he might say more, but he remained stubbornly silent.

"Can you have the decency, sir, to promise that you will speak of what you overheard to no other soul?" She decided to come right to the point, since Mr Darcy, although visibly flustered, was being his usual taciturn self. His dark eyes, which had in the past often been steadily trained on her in what she surmised was disapproval, were now anything but steady. They darted nervously between her face and the ground. He resembled a naughty boy expecting a punishment, and she was momentarily distracted by his fine features and endearing discomposure.

At length, he met her eyes. "Of course, madam, I give you my word. I would never dream of revealing it to anyone." He paused, still holding her gaze. "In fact, I would rather offer to help you in your undertaking." He looked amazed at his own words, as if they had fallen from another man's lips.

"I do not understand your meaning."

Suddenly they heard the excited exclamation of Mrs Bennet, "Lizzy! Where have you been, you irksome girl? Mr Darcy found you at last, did he?" She made her way towards them on the path.

Mr Darcy spoke quietly and quickly, "Miss Bennet, I wish to explain myself in a more private setting. I understand that you often walk out in the morning. How early do you go?"

Was he asking her to secretly meet him alone? Elizabeth could hardly believe it, but curiosity and a bit of desperation urged her forward. As her mother's yelling became louder, she haltingly answered, "In the immediate future, I must take my walks very early, around seven in the morning, so that I can return home before... certain members of the household awake."

He seemed to catch her meaning. "And are there any particular paths you favour on a Sunday morning?"

"Lizzy! Come here at once! I shall not be ignored any longer!"

Elizabeth answered in a hushed tone, "There is a path along Oakham Stream; you can reach it from the road about a mile from here."

"I believe I shall be able to find it." Mr Darcy nodded and continued loudly, "And now I shall fetch your father as promised, Miss Elizabeth. Thank you for telling me where I might find him." He strode back towards the house, leaving Elizabeth to deal with her mother.

She shook off her confusion. "Mama, I am fetched at last. What do you require?"

"I require you to act as a gracious hostess to our guests! Wherever have you been? How can Mr Bennet hide in his library when he has duties as host? Am I expected to do everything myself?"

Knowing that none of these questions were anything but rhetorical, Elizabeth simply muttered apologies and proceeded towards the assembled guests.

"Just a moment, Lizzy," Mrs Bennet demanded. "I insist you make an effort with Mr Bingley! Stop wasting your time on that dreadful Mr Darcy who does not find you handsome. Furthermore, you must keep Charlotte Lucas away from Mr Collins! She wants to steal him from Jane; I am sure of it."

Elizabeth asked with some exasperation, "Mama, can you not see that Jane prefers Mr Bingley and Mr Bingley prefers Jane?"

"Of course he does. Who would not prefer Jane? That is why you must exert yourself. I know you can be charming when you so choose. Mr Collins will propose to Jane, and why should Mr Bingley not settle for you?"

After years of being unfavourably compared to Jane, Elizabeth endured the insulting speech fairly well. As mother and daughter returned to the guests, Mrs Bennet began, "Mr Bingley, what say you to a game of cricket?"

"Excellent! Darcy and I played at Oxford but have rarely had the chance to play since then."

"Lizzy and Lydia are our best players—you should claim Lizzy for your team. Lizzy, find out who else wants to play and arrange the teams."

"With pleasure." Elizabeth looked forward to a good cricket match despite the fact that it was all an elaborate matchmaking exercise for her mother.

❧

Mr Darcy travelled up the path towards the house, again astonished to feel relief at Mrs Bennet's timely appearance. He could not explain his strange offer of assistance to himself, let alone to Miss Elizabeth. He must invent a plausible excuse to rescind it before tomorrow morning. This was none of his business; it was a family matter and *such* a family! He ought not be involved with them any further.

Yet, for the eldest Miss Bennets, his respect only grew. Never in his suppositions and speculations about Miss Elizabeth's behaviour towards Mr Collins had he come close to guessing the truth. There was no sisterly rivalry, no mercenary scheme, no trifling flirtation. In the absence of proper parental care, she was protecting her sister from an unwanted suitor. *Extraordinary!*

He entered the front door and, finding all the servants occupied with the picnic, went directly to the library. "Mr Bennet? I am sent by your wife to fetch you."

Mr Bennet was seated at his desk with the closed book still in front of him. "Yes, yes, I know. One can hear much through open windows on both sides."

Darcy blanched. There was far too much eavesdropping going on. Surely Mr Bennet could not have heard the latter, more hushed portion of the conversation about private paths and morning walks? He cleared his throat and continued as if nothing were amiss, "Mrs Bennet recommends that I coax you with the promise of sport..." He trailed off under Mr Bennet's continued inspection.

"Mr Darcy, let us speak plainly. I know you overheard my altercation with Elizabeth, and I know she has already confronted you about your bad habit of spying. She is fleet of foot, is she not?"

Darcy made no answer, though none was likely expected.

"I have also noted your, shall we call it preoccupation, with my second daughter. I must warn you, sir, I shall not allow Lizzy to be toyed with or hurt in any manner."

Could not Mr Bennet see that she had already been hurt and by his own doing? Pushing the thought from his mind, Darcy answered with the only truth he could admit to anyone, "I assure you, I have no such intentions. One cannot stand about as silently as I do without observing people, and Miss Elizabeth is a unique young lady. I have been intrigued by her behaviour towards Mr Collins."

"You stare at my daughter out of curiosity?"

"I was curious, yes, to discover why she sought out Mr Collins's company. As I know her to be uncommonly clever, I wondered why she should bother with him. My confusion has been allayed." Darcy donned his typical mask of disinterest.

"I see. A bit of entertainment, then, observing the locals?" Mr Bennet eyed Darcy suspiciously. "Well, I suppose my daughter has already extracted a promise of your discretion, so there is nothing to do but return to my wife and those promised outdoor amusements."

Darcy was relieved Mr Bennet had dropped the subjects of staring, eavesdropping, and spying, though he believed the older gentleman was not entirely satisfied with his answers. He must be more guarded in the future.

The two gentlemen made their way out of the house to re-join the festivities, where Miss Elizabeth was organising the guests into cricket teams.

She called out, "Come, Mr Darcy, I have been told you played cricket at Oxford. As the most experienced among us, you and Mr Bingley must serve as captains."

Darcy looked from a grinning Bingley to an expectant Miss Elizabeth. "Very well. Who else is on my team?"

Bingley laughed at his friend's capitulation. "We shall have a grand time, and I daresay my team will have the advantage. Miss Elizabeth has a mind for strategy and is familiar with the strengths and weaknesses of many of the players."

"Let us not be braggarts, Mr Bingley," Miss Elizabeth cried. "The Bennets and the Lucases have often faced each other as opponents, but that is the extent of my experience. The best player of those matches, John Lucas, is unfortunately absent today." She considered the willing players. "You Lucas brothers should be split up. Do either of you have a team preference?"

Walter Lucas was fourteen, while Peter was twelve but nearly as tall as his brother. "I want to be on your team, Miss Lizzy!" the younger boy said. "You are the best girl player.".

"Such flattery certainly earns you a place on my team." Elizabeth smiled at the boy. "Lydia, we two should be split up as well. You must be on Mr Darcy's team."

"Lord, you are bossy. As long as Denny is on my team, I am satisfied," Miss Lydia bargained.

"You can also have Mr Chamberlayne while we take Mr Pratt and Mr Saunderson." Miss Elizabeth gave a dazzling smile to the young redcoats.

Turning towards the remaining Bennets and Lucases, she asked, "Well, ladies, how will you be split up? I suggest Charlotte and Mary play with me while Kitty and Maria join Lydia—beauty versus youth, you see." Amused, Darcy watched as the reaction came more slowly to certain members of her audience. Miss Lucas laughed openly, but her sister continued blinking blankly.

Miss Lydia snorted, adding, "How droll you are, Lizzy. We shall beat you right good for that!"

Miss Mary pursed her lips. "Sisters, must we ruin a friendly game with such poor sportsmanship?"

Ignoring one sister's taunt and another's reprimand, Miss Elizabeth searched for more potential players. She charmed and cajoled four more officers into joining the game as well as a youth named Henry Long. The new recruits were divided up, but now the teams had an uneven number. Miss Elizabeth looked around for one last player and frowned when she noticed Mr Collins sitting with her eldest sister.

"Jane, you must play to make the teams even."

Mrs Bennet intervened. "No, Jane must remain with the other guests. Find someone else."

"Oh, we need another gentleman actually. Mr Collins, will you not play?"

"I fear I must decline. In my youth I was quite the player, but I have not kept up the skill. I must be content with my current activity." He smiled mawkishly towards Miss Bennet.

Darcy could not abide seeing that smile nor the distress that Miss Elizabeth clearly felt. He approached the parson. "Mr Collins, my team is short a player. I would be much obliged if you joined us. In fact, you might do well to reacquaint yourself with the game as I am sure Lady Catherine will ask you to play in her annual spring cricket match. She quite enjoys the spectacle."

Mr Collins profusely thanked him for the information and the invitation in many more words than necessary. Darcy gave Miss Elizabeth the barest hint of a smile. At first, she merely gaped at him, but soon a joyful smile grew on her face—a smile she directed for the first time, he realised, exclusively at him. Darcy was sure he could endure hours of Mr Collins's effusions if the reward was such a smile. The new accomplices regarded each other surreptitiously while Mr Collins finished his speech.

Bingley exclaimed, "Excellent! We shall have ten players each. I am anxious to begin!"

※

Elizabeth and Mrs Bennet ushered the guests towards the west paddock, which had for many years witnessed the epic cricket matches between the Bennet and Lucas clans.

There were chairs, tables, blankets, and refreshments already set up on one side of the field. As Jane sat down with Mrs Hurst to watch the game, Elizabeth marvelled at how valuable an ally Mr Darcy was proving to be. Whatever his purpose for becoming involved in her family struggles, the results of his interference were undeniable. Mr Collins would spend the next several hours playing cricket rather than courting Jane.

Mr Bennet and Sir William Lucas volunteered to be umpires, as usual, and placed the stumps at each end of the square. A coin flip determined that Mr Darcy's team would strike first. Elizabeth opted to field short, though she adjusted her depth depending on the batsman. The match progressed splendidly, and everyone seemed to be enjoying themselves except Mr Darcy, who stood gravely on the side of the field flanked by Mr Collins and Miss Bingley. Under the circumstances, Elizabeth had to forgive him his gravity.

Most of the gentlemen had removed their coats within a quarter of an hour due to the unusually warm temperature of the day. Elizabeth suspected they were using restraint while striking and bowling in consideration of the ladies. As a result, the game was casual and pleasant with light banter filling the air.

Elizabeth's only point of vexation was her estrangement from her father. Serving as umpire in the past, he would often make witty comments about the play. But today he remained silent.

At half an hour into the innings, three of the batsmen had been run out or thrown out, and Mr Darcy's side had scored forty-six runs. Mr Collins joined Kitty at the stumps. Mary bowled to Kitty, who usually swung at anything. She missed three completely but caught the fourth ball late, sending it rolling gently into the grass. Kitty did not bother to run, and Charlotte quickly retrieved the ball, returning it to Mary. Meanwhile, Mr Collins, despite the shortness of the hit, had begun to run. Lydia's angry voice came from the side of the field, "Get back, Mr Collins! You will be run out!"

He froze in confusion, then turned back. Mary pretended to bobble the ball. She could have easily knocked the wicket while Mr Collins was out of the crease, but perhaps she thought it improper to embarrass a clergyman. He was thus mercifully allowed to return to his place with some pride intact. Kitty missed the next two balls, and Mr Bingley came forward to bowl to Mr Collins.

Though he bowled fast, Mr Bingley was inclined to bowl wide and give away extras. It would have bothered Elizabeth's competitive nature if he were not so jolly about it. Mr Collins managed a hit. The ball took several high bounces and then rolled deep. He was so busy watching the ball that when he finally started running, he crashed into Kitty, who had already reached his end of the pitch. She stumbled backwards to the ground, the bat flying out of her hand. Mr Collins attempted to bow and apologise, all while still running—or rather lurching—in the opposite direction.

Mr Saunderson retrieved the ball and threw it to Elizabeth, who decided that the safest course of action for all involved would be to put out the wicket before Mr Collins reached his ground. Her throw did just that, and he was out. After being helped up, Kitty chose to retire. This brought Mr Darcy and Lydia to the stumps.

Mr Bingley grinned while Mr Darcy smirked back across the pitch, lending him a mischievous quality. Mr Bingley bowled his fastest ball yet, but it was wide, very wide. Peter Lucas, the wicket keeper, had to dive to retrieve it.

Elizabeth called out, "Mr Bingley, a little restraint please. We prefer them to earn their runs, do we not?"

"My apologies. I was trying to intimidate Darcy with the sheer power of my bowling."

"Remember that I have yet to bowl to you today," warned Mr Darcy.

"Indeed! Never was there a more fearsome sight as you when you are losing a cricket match." Mr Bingley had mock fear in his voice.

"But I am not losing."

Mr Bingley bowled a slower ball, and Mr Darcy hit it with a resounding crack. It sailed over the boundary, resulting in six runs. Lydia cheered and jumped, taunting Elizabeth.

It was Elizabeth's turn to bowl. She approached the pitch, and Mr Bingley handed the ball over with a shrug. Now she would end Lydia's taunting.

Indeed, Lydia would soon be chastened, but not by Elizabeth's bowling.

4

The Silliest Girl in England

Lydia stood behind the crease, anxious to prove that she was no longer the *second* best cricket player among the Bennets. She would get no help from Mr Collins. What a laugh she had when he knocked Kitty down!

She waited for the ball, expecting it would take a strange bounce. Missing Lizzy's first throw, she huffed in frustration, but hit the next ball cleanly. It bounced between two fielders and rolled deep. With a hoot she set out to run, pleased to see that Mr Darcy was fast. They scored three runs before the ball was returned to Peter Lucas.

"Well done, Miss Lydia," said Mr Darcy. Although he was so very serious, he was quite handsome—and quite rich. What a shame he was such a bore. Lydia looked triumphantly at Lizzy, who rolled her eyes as she prepared to bowl.

The first ball took a deceptive bounce, and Mr Darcy could only block it back to protect the wicket. They did not attempt to run. But he swung cleanly at the next ball. It landed between two deep fielders before it rolled to the boundary. Four more runs!

Mr Darcy and Lydia batted through a few overs in this fashion. He usually reached the boundary, while she placed the ball well enough to score at least one run. Unfortunately, the hour time limit was soon upon them. Lydia's team had scored seventy-eight runs. The players took a break for refreshments.

Lydia sought out Mr Darcy to ask whether she could field in her normal spot: silly mid-on. Her quick reflexes often allowed her to catch or run someone out from that position.

He regarded her for a moment. "I suggest you play short instead. There are new players today. For example, Mr Bingley bats much as he bowls—he swings wildly at anything." Lydia laughed, and Mr Darcy continued, "We do not want you injured."

"I am not afraid, Mr Darcy."

"I can see that, Miss Lydia." The fleeting appearance of his dimples stunned her. "You may field as silly as you like when the batsman is someone you know, such as one of your sisters, but stay farther back when any of the gentlemen are striking. Is that agreeable?"

Lydia conceded before asking, "Where shall you put Mr Collins?"

"Deep, very deep," he answered solemnly.

She burst into giggles. "I think that is wise, Mr Darcy."

"Thank you." There were those dimples again. "Do you have any other suggestions about field positions?"

Nobody ever asked *her* for advice. "Kitty is a surprisingly good wicket keeper. Walter Lucas would do well also. And do not allow Maria to bowl unless you want six extras given away."

He acknowledged her advice and then asked, "Do you bowl?"

"Oh yes, pretty fast. But I cannot spin it as well as Lizzy." He said nothing in reply, and then she remembered something else. "If Lizzy and Peter Lucas are paired up, they will stretch what should be a one-run hit into two or three runs. They are both very quick."

"I suspected as much from the way they fielded. Miss Elizabeth seems to enjoy cricket."

"Yes, Lizzy always preferred boy games to proper girl activities. She and John Lucas were thick as thieves growing up." Lydia had always been jealous. John Lucas was the first boy she ever fancied. But he had been away for two years serving on a merchant ship.

Miss Bingley emerged from behind Mr Darcy as if she had been invited into the conversation. "Miss Eliza is a regular hoyden. It was shocking to see her leaping about and catching balls."

"She is quite an asset to her team," Mr Darcy answered.

"I do not think it proper for young ladies to play cricket amongst gentlemen."

"I disagree. Georgiana and I often played cricket with our cousins and neighbours." Mr Darcy turned to Lydia. "Georgiana is my sister. She is about your age. I taught her to play."

Miss Bingley amended her earlier statement, "Oh, playing with family is perfectly acceptable of course. But for Miss Eliza to be making a spectacle of herself among these officers and mere acquaintances, it is rather unseemly."

Lydia snorted. *Unseemly?*

Mr Darcy responded more eloquently. "Again, I disagree. If Georgiana were here, I would be happy to let her play in such a friendly match."

Miss Bingley had dominated the conversation quite long enough in Lydia's opinion. "Oh, Mr Darcy, we should love to have your sister play with us! She must be very good if you taught her." He smiled, making her quite giddy. "Does Miss Darcy have many fine gowns? And bonnets! Lord, I can imagine the bonnets she has, with you being so rich!"

Just then, Elizabeth and Mr Bingley came over. "Shall we resume the match?"

Lydia was pleased with her fielding performance. She bowled an over fairly well, and ran out Charlotte Lucas. But her proudest moment was catching out Mr Bingley, who did swing wildly at any ball that came his way.

By the time Peter Lucas and Lizzy were at the stumps together, three batsmen were out, and Mr Bingley's side had scored fifty-two runs. It was just as Lydia feared. Neither Lizzy nor their young neighbour hit powerfully, but both picked the best spots to hit the ball and ran so fast that they scored many runs. After two overs, Mr Darcy bowled again. Surely his spin would hinder Lizzy. Lydia moved even closer, certain that her quick reaction could make the difference. She wished desperately to catch Lizzy out.

Mr Darcy's first throw was wide, which disappointed Lydia. He always seemed to have such control. As she looked at him, she noticed he had rolled up his sleeves, as Denny and some of the other officers had done earlier. Lydia did not often have occasion to see men in such a state of dishabille—and certainly not gentlemen. She could not tear her gaze from Mr Darcy's forearms. They were tanned and sinewy, hinting at the strength contained therein. How had he gotten so tan? Did he roam his grand estate with his sleeves rolled up, or did he go without any shirt at all? The thought made her flush. As she watched him bowl, Lydia was struck by his gracefulness—a masculine gracefulness that she had never seen before or simply had never noticed.

Further thoughts on Mr Darcy's fine bowling form were cut short by the sudden searing pain above her right ear, and then, darkness.

Jane ran towards Lydia in a panic. When she reached the gathering crowd, Elizabeth and Mr Darcy were both kneeling at Lydia's supine form.

Elizabeth spoke quietly, "Liddy, can you hear me? Lydia?"

After a few moments, Lydia groaned and murmured, "I stood too silly." Jane sighed with relief.

"Oh Liddy!" Elizabeth cried. "Why were you not attending the match? Whatever had you so distracted?"

Her eyes were still closed, but Lydia said clearly, "Mr Darcy's arms."

Mary began coughing.

"Stop coughing, Kitty. I am the injured one."

Of course Kitty defended herself, "That's not me! That's Mary!"

Jane cleared her throat. "Perhaps if the crowd could move back a bit..."

Charlotte and her father ushered people away from the scene, leaving only Lydia's sisters and Mr Bennet standing near.

Mr Darcy asked, "Miss Lydia, can you open your eyes?"

Her eyes fluttered, but then Mrs Bennet's lamentations reached the group. "My dearest Lydia! Has Lizzy finally killed you with her hoyden's game? I knew I should not allow a cricket match today, but Lizzy insisted! Oh, speak, my poor child!"

"Mama, your yelping hurts my head," Lydia said crossly. "In the name of all that is holy, lower your voice."

"Oh!" Mrs Bennet cried in an agitated whisper. "She has been knocked senseless!"

"No, my dear, that is the most sensible thing Lydia has ever said," Mr Bennet replied. "Come, Mrs Bennet, let us summon Mr Jones for the girl. She is in capable hands for now."

As a sense of relative calm settled over the six remaining people, Mr Darcy asked again, "Miss Lydia, can you open your eyes?"

She briefly opened them, but quickly screwed them shut. "It is so very bright. It hurts my head."

The afternoon sun was quite bright and warm. Elizabeth spoke, "You may keep your eyes closed, but Jane and I shall help you into the shade. Can you sit up?"

"I think so." Her head moved off the ground before sinking down again.

Mr Darcy offered, "Perhaps I should carry her into the shade."

Elizabeth and Mary looked too shocked to respond, and Kitty started giggling.

Jane answered, "That is very kind, Mr Darcy. Please take her over to the shade of the tree, and I shall wait with her there. Lizzy, will you see to the guests? Mary, will you fetch a blanket and a drink for Lydia? Kitty, go tell Papa what we are doing."

As the middle Bennets all rushed off to do their assigned tasks, Mr Darcy carefully scooped Lydia into his arms to carry her, and Jane followed behind.

❦

Jane, Mary, and Kitty made their way upstairs after a very long day only to find Mr Collins perched at the top of the staircase, blocking the way

"My dear Cousin Jane, your diligent care of your unfortunate sister has been most commendable. I can only aspire to one day be the recipient of such loving attention as you today bestowed upon Miss Lydia."

Although Jane appreciated the praise, she dearly wished to check on her sister. A blow to the head was a serious injury. Lydia should not be left alone for very long, and Mr Collins's speeches tended towards the very long.

"I thank you, Mr Collins, but I did no more than any of my sisters would do for me. Is that not right, sisters?"

Behind her, Mary answered in the affirmative; Kitty only yawned loudly.

"Indeed, how inspiring it is to see the sisterly devotion shared amongst my fair cousins. Lady Catherine would be most gratified to hear..."

Kitty snorted and said something under her breath. Mary chastised Kitty in a hushed tone. Mr Collins was still going on about the ideal relationship between sisters, and at the moment, Jane's two sisters were of little help in allowing her to escape his undivided attention.

"...and I consider myself most fortunate to be connected with so affectionate and devoted a family of sisters."

Mary joined Jane on the top step. "Reverend Fordyce offers insight into the ideal sisterly relationship: 'When I see two sisters, both of them pleasing and both esteemed, living together without jealousy or envy, yielding to one another without affectation, and generously contending who shall do most to advance the consequence and happiness of her friend, I am highly delighted: dare I add the more highly, that such characters are not very common!'"

"That is precisely right, Cousin Mary! To see such exemplary conduct from my five cousins is indeed a delight!"

If only Jane could get away while he and Mary discussed Fordyce! While searching in vain for an escape route, she caught sight of Elizabeth peeking from behind her bedroom door. Kitty again yawned noisily, such that the sound echoed through the hallway.

Jane attempted a graceful exit. "We thank you for the sentiment, Mr Collins, and now bid you a good night. Kitty, as you can see, is quite fatigued."

Mr Collins did not seem ready to remove himself from their path. In fact, his attention was fixed on Jane in a most disconcerting manner. "Dear Cousin Jane—" he began, but was interrupted by Kitty yawning once again, making an exaggerated show of covering her mouth.

The click of a door was heard. Jane thought Elizabeth would swoop in as she had been doing lately, but instead, it was her father's aggravated voice. "What on earth is that sound? Is a goose being strangled in the hallway?" He did not wait for an explanation. "Well, girls, take yourselves and any geese present to your rooms and be quiet."

The girls scampered off to their respective doors while Mr Collins went into the guest room. After several minutes of silence, three doors were cracked open. In a flurry of nightgowns, Elizabeth, Jane, and Mary flew across the hall to Lydia and Kitty's room.

Lord, how her head hurt! Lydia could not remember what had happened immediately after her injury, but she blushed in humiliation at the memory of her foolish display. If she had only been paying attention, she could have caught Lizzy out. It would have been her greatest moment of triumph. Instead, she had done the one thing that should not be done when playing silly—she had taken her eye off the ball.

As she lay on her bed, Lydia heard a strange noise in the hallway outside her door. After a few moments, all of her sisters entered to check on her.

Perhaps the best indication Lydia's injury was not serious was the return of her natural curiosity, her desire to know all. "What was that commotion in the hallway?"

Elizabeth sat on the edge of the bed. "Mr Collins was wishing his fair cousins a good night. Do you regret not being included in his felicitations?" Lydia snorted before Elizabeth gently turned her swollen temple towards the candlelight. "Oh, Liddy, I am so sorry!"

"It is not your fault. My own inattention caused it."

"Does it hurt terribly?" Kitty asked.

"It is a dull ache now. But at first I thought I would go blind with the pain. How did I end up sitting under the elm with Jane, so far from the pitch? I do not remember."

Jane moved to sit at the head of the bed and put her arm around Lydia. "Well, Lizzy was striking and you were standing very close; you probably remember that."

Lydia listened while her sisters filled in the gaps of her memory. There were some embarrassing bits, but what was the use of dwelling on them? Besides, all of that paled in significance to one detail.

"Mr Darcy *carried* me to the elm? How wonderful! I am sure he lifted me as if I weighed nothing at all! I knew his arms were strong!"

"Lydia! You were caught gawking at those arms," Elizabeth chided.

"So? I daresay you were all admiring one or another of the gentlemen's arms."

"Even if that were the case, we would not admit as much to the object of our admiration. Mr Darcy knows you were ogling him!"

"Surely being struck insensible is ample excuse for anything I ought not to have said. I shall worry about it no longer. But I *shall* thank Mr Darcy for carrying me the next time I see him. He is so gallant!"

"He offered to send for his physician from London if Papa wished." Mary showed a hint of satisfied pride when they all reacted with astonishment at her news. "Of course it was not necessary, but it was a very generous offer."

Elizabeth grinned. "I suppose his arms were generously covered when he made it."

"Pity..." Lydia sighed. "You should have seen when he defended me to that wretched Miss Bingley by saying he would allow *his* sister to play cricket in mixed company! He is so kind, do you not think?" Lydia was quite giddy.

Jane soothed her. "He is very kind, but perhaps you should go to sleep now."

"Very well, my head does hurt. I suppose you will all go to church tomorrow without me." She pouted as she snuggled into her bed. Jane kissed her cheek before following Elizabeth and Mary into the hallway.

Only Kitty remained. "Lord, you fell like a sack of flour when that ball hit you," she said before blowing out the candle.

As she lay in the dark, Lydia's thoughts were of Mr Darcy. She did not know when she would see him again. Surely she could see Denny and the rest of the officers soon—she need only walk into Meryton to be assured a meeting. But how could she contrive a meeting with Mr Darcy? She would have to ask Mama what could be done.

5

Unpleasant Truths

Jane was hard on Elizabeth's heels when they left Lydia and Kitty's bedroom, foiling Elizabeth's hopes of slipping into bed without facing an inquisition. Surely Jane had detected the tension with their father. The question was: what should Elizabeth tell her about the confrontation or, more importantly, about Mr Darcy's proposition? Jane already knew about Elizabeth's intervention into Mr Collins's so-called courtship but insisted it was unnecessary to take so much trouble for her sake. So it was unlikely Jane would approve of meeting secretly with a gentleman in pursuit of that goal. It would be a difficult secret to keep from her sister even for one night, but a secret it must remain.

They sat on the bed together. "Lizzy, what is amiss between you and Papa? You have not spoken to each other since the cricket match."

"Please do not worry about it. We had a disagreement today; that is all."

"But you are always of like mind. What could have brought on this quarrel?"

"It should have happened long ago, but I allowed myself to be content with our camaraderie. I have been—we all have been—avoiding the unpleasant truth about Papa."

"Unpleasant truth? Whatever can you mean?"

Elizabeth sighed in resignation. "Do you not see how he neglects his responsibilities towards us? He acts as if he were a mere observer of this household rather than its head. He ridicules Mama's fits and his daughters' silliness but lifts not a finger to curtail either. He would rather avoid all inconvenience and hide away in his library."

"Oh Lizzy, that is very harsh. Pray tell me you did not say these things to him."

"I did—and much worse. I know I ought to have softened my words, but I was near fury. I hurt his feelings. I am afraid he will not forgive me."

"Of course he will forgive you. But you have not explained what precipitated this quarrel." Jane could be relentless sometimes.

Elizabeth avoided her sister's eyes. "It was a culmination of many things."

"You need not say; I already know what has brought this on. But I told you not to worry for me. I do not wish to be the cause of discord between you and Papa."

"*You* are most definitely not. It is Papa's indolence that is the cause. I cannot abide seeing you in such an impossible position. Mama is prepared to serve you up on a silver platter to a fool while Papa stands idly by. He was so glib about your future happiness today. If he will not protect you, then I must."

"I hardly need protection from our cousin. He is not aggressive or demanding."

"But he *is* terribly presumptuous. He came here thinking he merely need choose one of us to be his bride! He takes advantage of our misfortune to gain a wife who is far too good for the likes of *him*." Elizabeth leaned forward to grasp Jane's hands. "Please, you must promise you will not accept Mr Collins. Papa will at least support your refusal, but you *must* refuse. Do not listen to Mama."

Jane looked down for a moment before taking a breath. "I cannot make such a promise, not when the welfare of my family is at stake. Think of the peace of mind I shall have knowing my mother and sisters will be well cared for."

Elizabeth's eyes filled with tears. "It is unconscionable that you are burdened with this when it is not *your* responsibility. I cannot bear to think of you forced into a lifetime with that self-important toady."

Jane gave her a reproachful look for such name calling but did not bother to scold. "I admit that Mr Collins is not the sort of man I would have chosen were I free to do so. But very few young ladies— rich or poor—may marry where they wish. Lizzy, I am not saying I am resolved to marry him, but I cannot dismiss the possibility out of hand, considering our situation."

Elizabeth knew without a doubt that she must ensure Jane never faced that decision. She was too selfless and too dutiful for her own good. "Please at least promise you will think only of your own happiness without reference to anyone else. Or, if you must think of someone else's happiness, think of mine. For you know my life would be full of misery if I had to endure *such* a brother-in-law!"

Jane laughed before turning serious once again. "Oh Lizzy, I think your happiness is more important to me than is my own. Please do reconcile with Papa; I cannot bear to see you at odds with him. And do not feel you must constantly intervene with Mr Collins. If you find his company so disagreeable, by all means, remove yourself from it."

"It hardly seems fair that Mama should thrust me, her least favourite daughter, into the path of a far superior gentleman, while saddling you, the far superior sibling, with Lady Catherine de Bourgh's most dedicated sycophant. It is particularly ironic since the more estimable gentleman so clearly prefers your company to mine!" Elizabeth determined to make her sister laugh again. "Oh, Jane, how becomingly you blush! I did not even utter Mr Bingley's name!"

"Do not tease me! I shall only say Mr Bingley *is* an estimable gentleman and the most agreeable young man of my acquaintance. But, Lizzy, what of Mr Darcy? To offer to send to London for his physician like that! Surely he must rise in your opinion."

Elizabeth hoped she did not blush at the unexpected mention of Mr Darcy. "I suppose. Perhaps, as captain of the team, he felt responsible for Lydia's injury. Or perhaps cricket simply agrees with him. Before that, he could not be *tempted* to speak to anyone."

"You cling so tenaciously to that regrettable comment. I am sure he did not mean it. He is perfectly civil to me, and did he not ask you to dance at Lucas Lodge last week?"

Elizabeth rolled her eyes remembering the encounter. "Only because Sir William made it impossible for him not to."

"Well, he certainly won my good opinion today and, apparently, Lydia's as well."

"Yes, and without the benefit of a red coat. It is quite extraordinary what a pair of well-formed arms can accomplish."

Jane could not keep her countenance, and the two young ladies burst into laughter.

"I wonder how long Lydia's infatuation will last this time," Elizabeth said. "Surely Mr Darcy's grave demeanour cannot hold a candle to Mr Denny's amiability, wrapped to such advantage in regimentals."

"We shall see. I think you underestimate Mr Darcy's appeal." Elizabeth gave Jane a dubious look as her sister made her way to the door. "Good night, Lizzy. May you dream of pleasant gentlemen with pleasing arms!"

Elizabeth collapsed onto her bed. She was exhausted. Had the day's antics been performed by any family but her own, she would have laughed heartily at them. Instead, she could only groan in mortification.

She quickly fell into slumber, but her restful sleep did not last long. She tossed and turned for the remainder of the night, her thoughts rapidly trying to devise some solution to Jane's predicament. She rose earlier than usual and was out the door before sunrise.

As she paced along the shallow bank of Oakham Stream, Elizabeth was torn between eagerness to learn what Mr Darcy had in mind and humiliation at having to face him again. If she were not so desperate, she would simply decline his offer of assistance and be done with him. But after her talk with Jane, Elizabeth was resolved to seize any advantage she could to prevent Mr Collins's proposal, no matter how distasteful.

When would Mr Darcy arrive, and what would he say? Elizabeth could not keep still for her apprehension.

Fitzwilliam Darcy was not an indecisive man, but as he left Nether-field, he was torn between two possible courses of action. The proper, safe course would lead him to apologise for his inappropriate behaviour—both the spying and the highly improper suggestion to meet secretly—and then quickly take his leave of Miss Elizabeth Bennet. It was what he ought to do. How had he even come to be in such a situation—he, who always so cautiously held himself under regulation?

Yet Darcy felt inexplicably drawn to follow the improper course of action. First, there was the challenge of it—helping these two young ladies who deserved better than their circumstances would serve as a diversion. Mr Bennet was partly right about the entertainment factor.

But, if Darcy was honest with himself, he must admit to an overwhelming desire to be of assistance to Elizabeth Bennet. His mind flooded with memories from the previous day: the sound of her soft, heartbroken voice as she pleaded with her father; the glimpse of her shapely ankles innocently revealed while she ran; the music of her laughter as she joked with Bingley and the other players on her team; the gentle touch of her hand on her sister's brow as she knelt in the grass; and those eyes, always those fine eyes. At the mere thought of them, Darcy urged his mount to quicken the pace.

Darcy found the correct path and approached the sound of running water. He came to a small clearing, dismounted, and tied off his horse. Oakham Stream was a tiny brook here. Farther downstream, where it formed part of Netherfield's western boundary, it was wider with a sandy bottom. Darcy much preferred this portion of the stream, for it reminded him of a similar brook in Pemberley's woods. In the angled morning sun, he could see mist rising from the water. There, pacing, was Miss Elizabeth. She looked troubled, as if the weight of the world was upon her. In that moment, Darcy was far from indecisive; he chose the improper course of action.

He spoke her name, but she did not hear over the sound of the water. He approached her, hat in hand, and spoke again. "Good morning, Miss Elizabeth."

She gasped but recovered quickly. "Good morning, Mr Darcy. You should wear a bell around your ankle to alert unsuspecting people of your location."

Clearly, she was referring to his notorious lurking and spying, but her mention of *his* ankle recalled the sight of *her* ankles to his mind, and he actually blushed. "Perhaps I could stomp my feet as I walk. Would that serve as warning of my imminent approach?"

She looked surprised and laughed lightly at his reply. "I suppose. But a tinkling bell seems a much more pleasant sound to have associated with one's presence. Or perhaps you could follow the example of Alice, our maid, who hums incessantly."

"I assure you, any tunes I might hum would be most unpleasant to the ears. If I were to announce my presence in such a way, I would very soon find myself quite alone."

She laughed again, and Darcy nearly threw his hat into the air with the thought that he was responsible for that laugh. Instead, he asked, "How is Miss Lydia?"

She looked away uncomfortably, no doubt remembering the singular end to the cricket match. How tiring it must be to be constantly ashamed of one's family and wholly powerless to do anything about it. "Lydia is recovering. Her head hurts, but there do not appear to be any other ill effects. I am sure she will enjoy the doting of my mother over the next week."

"I am relieved to hear it." He genuinely was. Miss Lydia was just a child at that awkward cusp of adulthood. She was not the first such girl to act foolishly nor the last. Darcy of all people knew that well enough.

"Mr Darcy, thank you for convincing Mr Collins to join the cricket match. I am sure it was not pleasant to have his company for all that time. I...have you reconsidered your offer of assistance?"

"No, I still wish to help you and your sister, if I can."

"I cannot conceive why, but I shall gladly accept any help you can offer. I fear that the situation will soon reach a crisis. It is much worse than I had anticipated." All her earlier levity was gone, leaving only sadness and anxiety. She began pacing again, and he wished to put her at ease.

"Perhaps we should walk as we discuss the matter."

"Yes, I find I cannot keep still today." She stopped pacing and met his eyes. "There are some small cascades upstream."

He motioned for her to lead the way. Walking beside her, he began, "Now, tell me what has happened to make the situation worse, and then we shall form a plan of action to remedy it."

"Mr Collins is becoming more and more determined in his attentions. He might have proposed in the hallway last night—and in the presence of Kitty and Mary—were he not interrupted by my father."

She glanced at Darcy and then clarified, her voice bitter, "No, my father was not intervening on Jane's behalf. He was merely scolding the group for being too loud."

Her expression softened. "Then I spoke with Jane. I begged her to promise to refuse Mr Collins. She would not. She does not wish to marry him, but given our circumstances, she cannot dismiss the possibility. She says she will have to make that decision *if* he proposes."

Miss Elizabeth stopped walking and faced Darcy. "Jane is the most generous and caring person I have ever known. I do not make the claim merely because she is my sister. I cannot overstate her kindness, her modesty, her...goodness."

"So you fear, despite her wishes, she will succumb to concern for the future of her family should Mr Collins propose."

"Yes. A marriage to Mr Collins is bad enough to contemplate, but to think of Jane living under the thumb of Lady Catherine—forgive me, Mr Darcy, but your aunt sounds formidable—to think of Jane in that situation, it breaks my heart."

"I cannot say you are wrong about my aunt. She is meddlesome beyond your imagination. I am amazed she has found just the sort of parson who would think her meddling a blessing, but Mr Collins is such a one."

"So you see, I simply must prevent his proposal. But how am I ever to halt his suit when my mother throws them together at every opportunity with only myself and Charlotte to interfere?"

"Ah, so Miss Lucas has been intervening on your behalf."

She began walking again. "Yes, she has been invaluable, particularly when I have reached my level of tolerance with Mr Collins. She is to visit us today after church; therefore, I think we are safe for at least one more day."

"How much longer is your cousin at Longbourn?"

"He returns to Kent on Saturday."

"Six more days." Darcy could hardly believe what he was about to offer. "Would it help if Mr Bingley and I called tomorrow? I can no doubt convince Bingley to oblige. We shall ostensibly visit to inquire after Miss Lydia."

"That would be wonderful." Darcy relished the grateful smile she gave him before he caught a return of bitterness to her voice. "My mother will eagerly welcome Mr Bingley."

He could not keep a hint of disgust out of his own voice. "She has been attempting to forward a match between you and Mr Bingley."

She sighed. "I assure you I have no designs on Mr Bingley, amiable though he is."

Darcy was relieved to hear of Miss Elizabeth's disinterest in his friend. Naturally, he wished to preserve Bingley from a connexion with a family like the Bennets.

They had come to a series of small cascades where the stream spilled down some boulders. They stopped and gazed at the water. "My mother has her mind set that Jane will marry my cousin because Mr Collins expressed an interest on the day after his arrival here. She further thinks that I must marry your friend because I am the next in line, and of course, why would Mr Bingley not be looking for a wife? To her mind, security in marriage is indistinguishable from happiness in marriage. She has no concept that one might aspire to something loftier."

Darcy contemplated her words. Mrs Bennet, although more vulgar, was not so different from many of the scheming mothers of the *ton*, shamelessly throwing their daughters at wealth and rank.

"With my mother's continued encouragement, I fear Mr Collins will soon declare himself, whether he gains the appropriate privacy to do so or not."

"Is there perhaps another young lady who would wish for his attentions?" Darcy did not suppose there could be, but he had to ask.

She laughed nervously. "I realise pushing him towards someone else would make my task easier, but I would not wish him on any

46

young lady of my acquaintance, certainly not those I care about. No, interference and distraction are the only weapons at our disposal."

"Perhaps, but given his extraordinary deference to Lady Catherine's opinions and, by extension, mine, there may be another way to dissuade him." He felt her attention fully on him. "I do not have anything in mind at present, but I shall think on it."

"Thank you. Any ideas you have would be most welcome." She looked at the position of the sun through the trees. "I should return. The household will be rising soon."

As they left the cascades, Elizabeth was relieved, almost pleased, with her conversation with Mr Darcy thus far. The initial jests they exchanged had made her less anxious at the awkward situation. His subsequent businesslike manner had further relieved her unease. He acted as if it were perfectly normal for him to intervene in the courtship of a country parson he had met less than a fortnight ago, and indeed, as she conversed with him, it *seemed* perfectly normal. She had been able to speak openly of her parents and of Jane, and he had taken everything in stride, though she *had* detected his poorly concealed distaste on the topic of her mother's incessant matchmaking.

After they had discussed the particulars and formed a tentative plan, they walked back downstream in silence. But her mind was yet again assailed by questions. What could he hope to gain by involving himself in the lives of those he clearly considered beneath him? Her curiosity got the better of her.

"Mr Darcy, although I am by no means ungrateful, I simply cannot imagine why you are helping me."

He looked down as he continued walking, his hands clasped behind him. "I do not know that I can explain it fully. Perhaps I have been too long in London society. When I...overheard you yesterday, I was reminded there can be more to marriage than mercenary objectives. I am guardian to my own sister, and I can only admire your dedication to your sister's happiness."

"You can admire my dedication without assisting me."

"True, but I do not think any young lady should be placed in the position of choosing between her family's future security and marriage to man like Mr Collins, particularly when the young lady in question is pure of motive, as I now know Miss Bennet to be."

Could his reasons really be so generous? He, who would not trouble himself to speak to poor Mrs Long while sitting next to her for half an hour, would voluntarily involve himself with her cousin and her mother—two people he clearly detested? "But it is not your place to ensure my sister be spared that decision. Forgive me; I wish to better understand your motivation."

He was thoughtful for a moment. "It is not my place, but neither is it your place, Miss Elizabeth. It ought to fall to your parents, who in this case are either negligent or ignorant. If I can be of assistance to a worthy young lady in distress, then I feel I must."

Though Elizabeth had already said as much to him, it was a bit of a shock to hear him refer to her parents so dismissively. But she could not let it irritate her. Instead, she focused on the one compliment he let slip. "There is no worthier young lady than Jane."

He regarded her strangely. Something in his expression hinted at reluctance, almost conflict. She could not understand it. He spoke quietly. "I was referring to your distress." Then he continued walking down the hill.

Elizabeth was rooted to the spot, staring after him. Had he just intimated that *she* was the worthy young lady? She, who was only "tolerable" and inspired constant disapproval from him?

When she caught up to him, his demeanour was again detached and businesslike. "I also find, Miss Bennet, that I welcome the diversion this bit of intrigue will afford me. I faced a rather difficult situation this past summer, and my mind has been much occupied by it. Nothing in Hertfordshire has been able to distract me until yesterday's events gave me a respite from my thoughts."

This was more like the Mr Darcy Elizabeth had come to expect. It explained his staring and eavesdropping. He was a spectator—a *judgmental* spectator—and his favourite players seemed to be Elizabeth and her loved ones.

They arrived back at the small clearing that led to the main path.

Elizabeth wished to leave him. Now *her* attitude was businesslike. "Of course Hertfordshire society must be quite tedious to you. If it is entertainment you seek, perhaps we can arrange an exchange. I have been known to tell a good story, by local standards at least. Since I have nothing else to offer you, perhaps I can amuse you from time to time with tales of your neighbours."

He merely inclined his head.

"I walk every morning around the same time, weather permitting," she continued. "This particular spot is more often than not my destination. It is private and not too far for either of us. Is it an agreeable meeting place?"

"Yes, it is."

"Very well, if you wish to speak with me, you will know where to find me. Any ideas you have regarding a certain parson from Kent will be most appreciated. If I do not see you here tomorrow morning, I shall expect you and Mr Bingley to call during the day, correct?" She glanced at him, and he nodded.

"Now, Mr Darcy, if you will wait a few minutes before returning to the road, I shall take my leave." She curtseyed quickly and did not meet his eye before striding down the path.

As Elizabeth marched angrily towards Longbourn, she wished she had left well enough alone. Never look a gift horse in the mouth. She reminded herself that Mr Darcy's intervention was necessary, thus she must accept the humiliation of being an object of his hilarity. She tried to calm and prepare herself for the long day of vigilance ahead.

Elizabeth found Jane breaking her fast along with her parents, Mary, and Kitty. She received friendly greetings from her sisters, but her father barely glanced up from his book. Lydia was staying abed due to her injury, and Mr Collins had yet to come downstairs.

For a clergyman, Mr Collins lacked a certain eagerness to attend services. When he did finally make an appearance, Elizabeth engaged him in conversation. Between chewing his hasty meal and replying to Elizabeth's inquiries about the quality of his slumber, his expectations for the upcoming service, and his preferences in fruit preserves, he hardly had time to say two words to Jane.

At the church, Elizabeth engineered the seating to her purposes, though her mother looked displeased at the results. When the Lucases arrived, Charlotte gave Elizabeth a conspiratorial wink. With the sight of her dear friend, Elizabeth did not feel quite as daunted by the day's task. Between the two of them, they would manage. Reassured as she was, she still found herself wishing for a lengthy sermon.

Making an Effort

Lydia could not stand the boredom. Her head still hurt, but it was not bad enough to make her stay alone in bed for one minute more. She entered the sitting room to find three distinct groups of people: Lizzy and Jane were quietly conversing in the corner over their needlework, Mary sat with Charlotte Lucas and Mr Collins, and her mother sat by the window glaring at Charlotte while Kitty trimmed a bonnet.

"Lydia, my love! You should not be out of bed!" Mrs Bennet jumped up to take Lydia's hands.

"Oh, Mama, I'm so bored up there I think I shall go mad. It cannot hurt to sit downstairs, can it?"

"Kitty, get up off the settee. Lydia will sit with me."

"But I need the light from the window for my bonnet."

Her mother was unmoved. "Oh, it is a horrid bonnet anyway."

Kitty rose with a huff and sulked in the corner. Everyone else in the room asked after Lydia in turn, and she was quite pleased to be the centre of attention—pleased, that is, until the attention came from Mr Collins.

"Dear Cousin Lydia, I am relieved to see you so well recovered. Your sisters are much comforted at your improvement. Cousin Jane, in particular, has been ever so worried about your condition, and though I tried to console her as best I could, only your healthy and robust appearance can truly reassure a concerned sister. Not only do I welcome your recuperation for myself, as your loyal cousin, but for its palliative effects on such a dear lady as your eldest sister, whose worries are my worries."

Lydia was at a loss. How was she supposed to respond to such a speech? Thankfully, Lizzy jumped in and began a new conversation between Charlotte and Mr Collins. Lord! Lydia was sorry poor Jane would be burdened with that ninny for a husband. If only he were a little handsomer or a little less tiresome, it would not be so terrible. It hardly seemed fair. But there was the entail, and Mama was determined to have Mr Collins as a son-in-law. Thank goodness he had taken a fancy to Jane first!

She had not followed the conversation, but Mr Collins soon offered to retrieve a letter from Lady Catherine so he could better express some advice when Charlotte asked for clarification. When he left the room, Lydia took the opportunity to speak to her mother about another gentleman.

"Mama, you always say we must make an effort to catch a husband."

"Yes, my dear, and it is very true. How I worked my charms to catch your father, you will never know!"

Lydia winced in displeasure at the thought of it, but continued, "Well, I wish to make an effort with a certain gentleman, and I hope you will help."

Mrs Bennet leaned forward, speaking in an excited whisper, which really was no quieter than her normal voice, "Has a young man caught your fancy, dear Lydia? Who is he?"

"He is Mr Darcy."

"Mr Darcy!" cried Mrs Bennet and Lizzy in unison.

Lydia laughed at their surprise. "He is so handsome and rich, why should I not try?"

"He is certainly handsome and rich, but is he not a dreadfully dour man? I fear you would want for cheer."

"He only needs a little liveliness to cheer him, and who better than me for that? He was very kind to me yesterday. He has the most delightful dimples."

"Dimples!" Mrs Bennet patted Lydia's cheek. "If you think better of Mr Darcy, then so shall I. Perhaps he finds your agreeable temperament pleasing and has shown you a softer side of himself. I can hardly persist in thinking poorly of a man who displays such discerning tastes."

"Mama!" interjected Elizabeth. "You cannot mistake Mr Darcy's gentlemanly behaviour yesterday for anything more. He has displayed no preference for anybody here in Hertfordshire. Indeed he has shown only disdain. Please do not be so foolish as to pursue a man who clearly thinks himself better than you."

"La! Just because he does not find *you* handsome does not mean *I* should renounce him."

Elizabeth stood, her needlework falling unheeded to the floor. "A man of Mr Darcy's consequence shall despise the tasteless wiles you use for husband catching. Nothing but mortification lay there. I beg you to reconsider this folly!"

"Oh bother! You are no fun at all anymore, Lizzy. But I am determined. I shall pursue Mr Darcy and I daresay I shall be successful."

"Yes, Lydia, *we* shall pursue him for you. Do not let Lizzy's resentment dampen your enthusiasm. I wish all my girls would show such initiative. And you, the youngest!" Mrs Bennet cast her eyes about the room in mild censure. "But it is incumbent upon me to give you this small warning. You set your sights very high for a first try at a husband. Mr Darcy is a man of more consequence than any personage we have ever known. I fear for your disappointment should we not succeed."

"Oh, let us not worry about it. I am too excited! What fun we shall have—me and Lizzy as partners as we pursue Mr Darcy and Mr Bingley together! Lizzy, you must not be so vexed, or you will ruin everything."

Elizabeth looked between her mother and Lydia and then sighed and sank back down on her chair, her head in her hands. Jane patted her leg and asked, "Should someone not tell Papa of these plans?"

Kitty gave up sulking with her bonnet and laughed. "Papa doesn't care what husbands we attempt to win, so long as he hears no details."

"That is right, girls. Mr Bennet knows that such schemes are better left to me."

Mary entered the fray. "All these elaborate plans and schemes to procure that which is not meant to be procured! A lady should be the modest *recipient* of a man's attentions, not the other way around."

"Lord, Mary! I can't decide who the bigger bore is today: you or Lizzy!" Lydia expected it from Mary but not the normally high-spirited Elizabeth.

Mr Collins returned, carrying a long missive in his hands. "Ah, Miss Lucas, I am ever so grateful you suggested I retrieve this letter, for now I see that my poor synopsis could not do justice to the clarity and wisdom of Lady Catherine's phrases on the subject. Here, allow me to share her words with you..."

The groups settled back into their separate pursuits. Charlotte and Mary made up a willing audience to Mr Collins. Jane again spoke quietly to a now unhappy-looking Elizabeth. Kitty resumed trimming her bonnet, though had to squint a bit more, and Lydia and her mother spoke animatedly about a certain gentleman from Derbyshire.

On the way to his second morning *tête-à-tête* with Elizabeth Bennet, Darcy told himself that he was going to Oakham Stream to learn whether her intervention efforts had succeeded the previous day. It was a perfectly logical explanation, for if the unthinkable *had* happened, there might be no reason to call later in the day. He rounded the last turn before the clearing with breathless anticipation. And there she was.

She was not pacing. She stood perfectly still with her shoulders slumped and her gaze lowered, staring at the water. She looked utterly miserable. After dismounting, Darcy walked up beside her, and she shifted slightly.

"Has he proposed already?" he asked by way of a greeting.

She smiled briefly. "No, it is not that. Charlotte and I were successful in our efforts. I am glad you have come this morning, Mr Darcy, for it gives me a chance to warn you. And it gives *you* a chance to escape." She closed her eyes as if preparing for something very unpleasant. "There have been unexpected developments."

He waited for her to elaborate, but she seemed in her own world, eyes downcast and breath shallow. "Of what nature are these developments?"

She looked up at him. "I am sure you will abandon our scheme now. I could not blame you."

Darcy furrowed his brow at her distress.

She took a steadying breath before plunging into an explanation. "Lydia has become infatuated with you. Your...ah, the cricket game, I suppose. And...and she has spoken to my mother, who, as you know, is quite willing to help any of her daughters find husbands."

"I see."

"I am sorry, Mr Darcy. I tried to dissuade them both, but they would not listen. I can only recommend that you avoid what will surely mortify you, and do not come to call today. You can imagine what they will do, how they will act towards you."

Now that *would* be unpleasant. Lydia Bennet was just a foolish young girl who knew no better. Darcy blamed her parents' neglect more than he could blame the girl's ignorance. But he recoiled at the thought of Mrs Bennet's vulgar attentions directed at him. Through some lucky chance, he had been able to escape her notice up until now. "I had been under the impression that Mrs Bennet did not like me very much."

"You were correct in your assessment. But apparently, by gaining the approval of her favourite daughter, you have negated my mother's earlier displeasure for slighting her least favourite daughter."

Darcy winced, wishing those comments at the assembly were long forgotten. "Miss Elizabeth, I am exceedingly sorry that I ever made that comment and it was relayed to you."

She shook her head, interrupting him. "You apparently underestimate the volume of your voice, for I heard it directly from the source. But I can hardly blame you for having your own opinions."

"I assure you, that it is not my opinion at all. Bingley was infuriating me with his entreaties to dance. I...it is not remotely true." He held her gaze, for how long, he did not know. Her brow made a small crease above her nose and her eyes registered confusion. At least Darcy read it as confusion, and he *had* been studying those eyes at every opportunity.

She looked away. "Well, I thank you for the assurance, sir, but it really does not matter."

Darcy wished to change the subject. "So I am to be the new object of Mrs Bennet's matchmaking schemes."

"I do not expect you to subject yourself to them. I am quite relieved that I was able to warn you before you were thrown into such a situation."

"Miss Elizabeth, I have endured far more cunning, avaricious ladies and their grasping mothers for years and have not yet fallen prey, though it was not for their lack of effort." He looked at her gravely. "Indeed, I have managed to escape more than one plan to ensnare me in a compromising situation."

Her eyes widened in disbelief. "How dreadful! I have heard of such things, but my mother, though tenacious, would not attempt such entrapment. She has confidence that only her daughters' charms are necessary."

"So you see, I shall be quite safe—charming as Miss Lydia may be."

Miss Elizabeth's mouth fell open in a silent gasp. "But...you mean you still plan to carry out...what we discussed yesterday?"

"I am as willing as ever. I must say that I have never been pursued for anything other than my wealth. It is rather refreshing to be admired for my cricket skills."

He smiled, and she stared back, blinking several times before bursting into laughter. It felt good to cheer her. And then he laughed. There they stood on the bank of Oakham Stream, laughing together.

"And to think, Lydia used to call you 'such a bore!'" This brought another round of laughter.

Eventually, Elizabeth announced her need to return home. "I am fortunate my cousin places greater value on his leisurely mornings of sleep than he does on his courtship. Should he ever alter his priorities and exchange a couple hours of slumber for Jane's company, I would not be permitted these walks."

"A man must place limits on what he will sacrifice for love."

She laughed again, curtseyed, and walked away. He could hardly wait for the afternoon to come.

Darcy had never known a man to primp so much. Tapping his foot while waiting in Netherfield's library for Bingley to appear, he finally tossed aside the book he was holding—his attempts at reading futile —and began pacing the room. He prayed Miss Bingley would not find him; he had even less patience for her cloying flattery than usual. Finally, Bingley entered.

"I trust you are sufficiently preened."

"Darcy, listen. I do not think I should accompany you."

"Why ever not? I cannot go by myself. You know I am not easy in such company."

Bingley rolled his eyes. "You mean such company as five friendly gently bred young ladies? You are tedious at times."

Darcy was surprised by Bingley's outburst of ill humour. "Clearly, you do not object to the company. So again I ask, why should you not come?"

"I, ah, I just do not think it would be wise." At Darcy's insistent stare, Bingley sighed. "I find myself drawn to Miss Bennet beyond any young lady I have ever known. But I ought to distance myself, for she is, after all, soon to be betrothed."

Darcy was stunned. Of all the times for Bingley to show caution in his dealings with young ladies, why must it be now? Normally, he would rejoice at Bingley's rare display of restraint, but not now, for now it interfered with his own reckless yet somehow compulsory behaviour.

"I have reason to suspect that the imminent betrothal of Miss Bennet to Mr Collins is a rumour started by Mrs Bennet," he said. "Looking back to that first night at the assembly, we should have found it odd that they were discussed as 'soon-to-be' engaged. Either you are engaged or you are not—and clearly, they are not."

"Not yet. But surely it is expected."

"Perhaps. Mr Collins's intentions are perfectly obvious, but Miss Bennet's thoughts are less so."

Bingley's eyes widened. "Do you think she is the unwilling recipient of his attentions?"

Darcy's only reply was a significant look, which caused Bingley's brow to furrow with thought. "Yes, yes. He is a...unique sort of... fellow." Realisation dawned, and Bingley exclaimed, "He stands to inherit Longbourn! What a dreadful position to be in—for Miss Bennet, I mean!"

"Indeed."

After a pause, Bingley walked towards the door, calling out, "Come, we shall go then. We really ought to inquire after Miss Lydia."

Bingley was silent for much of the ensuing ride, leaving Darcy alone with his thoughts, which were invariably drawn back to Oakham Stream.

"Darcy," said Bingley as they neared Longbourn, "keep your eyes open for any confirmation of what we discussed earlier about this expected betrothal."

"I always keep my eyes open. But I caution you, Bingley, even if the betrothal does not happen, you should not attach yourself to a family like the Bennets. Do not become involved in all these match-making schemes." If only Darcy could take his own advice! Though technically, what he was doing was match-*breaking*.

"I just wish to know the truth of the matter. You may keep your counsel."

Darcy wanted to ask for an explanation of Bingley's peevish tone, but they were already at the front of the house. They dismounted, handed their horses over, and climbed the steps, each eager to see at least one of the young ladies awaiting them inside.

7

Nick of Time

Elizabeth was so tired—tired of listening to Mr Collins's inanities, tired of this terrible rift with her father, tired of keeping secrets. In fact, she realised with no little astonishment, the only person from whom she kept no secrets was Mr Darcy. No one knew of their clandestine meetings, for she could not tell Jane about such impropriety, and although she was eager for Charlotte's opinion on the matter, they had had no privacy to discuss it. Yet Mr Darcy knew all of Elizabeth's secrets. Mr Darcy, who disapproved of her family and found entertainment in her struggles. Mr Darcy, whose surprising dimples had been revealed that morning. Mr Darcy, who, via his unforeseen ability to say exactly what she needed to hear, had provided her the only bit of sanity over these last two days. Mr Darcy, whose visit she eagerly awaited now. How had this ever happened?

So lost was Elizabeth in her thoughts that she failed to notice Mr Collins's uncharacteristic silence and absorbed stare at Jane. Usually, this was precisely the moment when Elizabeth would employ him on some topic of interest. But in this instance, she allowed him to ruminate for too long—a huge error.

Mr Collins stood and cleared his throat. "If I may be so bold as to request the honour of a priv—"

"Mr Collins!" Elizabeth almost yelled his name before subduing herself. "Sir...I had hoped...you would tell us more about...Miss de Bourgh. Yes, Miss de Bourgh sounds like such an admirable young lady, and we all wish to know more of her."

"I would be most gratified to elaborate on her many charms, Cousin, but as I was saying, it is a very pleasant day out and—"

"Oh yes, do let us go into the garden where you can tell me about her! Does she play the pianoforte? Does she draw? She must have had excellent masters to teach her, for Lady Catherine would be ever so conscientious of the advantages offered by such an education."

Elizabeth was certain her volley of questions and her last observation in particular had served the purpose of engaging him on his favourite subject, but then her mother interfered. "Let poor Mr Collins finish a sentence!"

Lydia and Kitty snickered at the absurdity of such a command. Mrs Bennet ignored them. "What on earth has come over you, Lizzy? Why are you not out rambling in the woods on this fine day? Leave Jane and Mr Collins to their *own* conversation for a while, will you not?"

Elizabeth was truly in a panic.

Mr Collins suddenly remembered why he had stood up. "Oh yes, I was about to request the honour of escorting Miss—"

"Mama!!" squealed Lydia from the window. "He is come! Mr Darcy is come with Mr Bingley!"

"Oh excellent, my dear Lydia! Here, pinch your cheeks—yes, just so. Lizzy, pinch your cheeks. Go on...that will have to do."

The next few minutes were spent pinching cheeks, smoothing hair, arranging skirts, and stowing away ribbons and bonnets. Even Mr Collins checked his cravat and smoothed his waistcoat.

"Mr Bingley and Mr Darcy, ma'am," announced Mrs Hill as the two men stepped into the room, the former with a wide smile and easy greeting for all assembled and the latter with an assessing look at Elizabeth. She knew she must appear positively wild between the fright she had had a few minutes earlier and all that ridiculous cheek-pinching.

"We are very glad you have come, Mr Darcy and Mr Bingley. Is that not so, Lydia, Lizzy?"

Elizabeth would have grimaced at Lydia's enthusiastic, lash-fluttering affirmations, but she was too relieved by the sudden appearance of the gentlemen. She caught Mr Darcy's eye as she replied, "Indeed, our moods are considerably lightened with your timely call, gentlemen."

"We are pleased to be of service." Mr Darcy glanced about the room, seemingly taking stock of the players. If he sought entertainment, he was bound to get it today.

"Yes, indeed!" said Mr Bingley as he looked at Jane, who, Elizabeth noted, had an uncharacteristically flushed face. Mr Bingley paused before addressing Mrs Bennet again, "We wished to inquire about Miss Lydia's health. Darcy and I have been most concerned for her."

Mrs Bennet was pleased by this admission. "How kind of you to worry for dear Lydia! As you can see, she bears her injury well. Lydia has always been full of vigour and good cheer, never one to complain."

"Yes, but I've been ever so bored cooped up here, Mr Darcy," complained Lydia. "Oh! But I wanted to thank you for carrying me off the cricket field! I was quite astonished to hear of it from my sisters, for I do not remember a thing from when that ball knocked me down to when I sat with Jane in the shade. Lord, but my head hurt then! And you warned me about playing too silly not an hour beforehand! What a laugh!"

Everyone looked to Mr Darcy for a response. Elizabeth decided to intervene on his behalf. It was the least she could do for the poor man. "I suspect Mr Darcy is too much of a gentleman to say he told you so. But I begin to suspect something quite shocking, Mr Bingley. Apparently, my sister and your friend discussed strategy before the start of the innings, and just as Peter Lucas and I were about to overtake the lead in runs, Lydia was conveniently injured to end the match!"

Mr Darcy smirked, Lydia puffed in outrage, and Mr Bingley laughed. "I might defend my friend, for he often says that disguise of every sort is his abhorrence. But the only thing he abhors more is losing at cricket—so I can readily believe he would concoct such a nefarious plot!"

"Cousin Elizabeth, I am appalled you would suggest such underhanded tactics might be employed by Mr Darcy, the nephew of Lady Catherine." Mr Collins, aside from Lydia, was the most offended person in the room.

"My apologies to you, Mr Collins and, of course, to Mr Darcy." She cocked an eyebrow at her accomplice. "If Mr Darcy abhors disguise, perhaps I should blame only Lydia for the precipitous ending. Sadly, we shall never know who would have been victorious had the match proceeded."

"Ha! We had you beat," exclaimed Lydia. "Did we not, Mr Darcy?"

"I believe our teams were well matched, and either side could have prevailed. Miss Elizabeth arranged the players quite judiciously. It was a rewarding competition."

"Too bad Lydia ruined it," sniffed Kitty.

"Now, Kitty, you know it was Lizzy who hit Lydia." Mrs Bennet might have continued in this vein, but she seemed to recollect that Mr Bingley was present—and of course she did not want *him* to think poorly of her second daughter.

"But I do thank you, Mr Darcy, for the kindness you showed my Lydia on Saturday." Mrs Bennet looked to him for some sign of enthusiasm, but he merely inclined his head. Resigned to his silence, she added, "Kitty, ring for tea."

While Kitty obeyed, another door opened, and Mr Bennet entered the room. Elizabeth did not look forward to his petulant demeanour towards her—as if she needed another worry in this farcical visit!

"Ah, Mr Bingley and Mr Darcy. Good afternoon, gentlemen. Were you so bored at Netherfield as to seek entertainment elsewhere so soon after our eventful picnic?" The visitors replied more civilly than such a greeting deserved.

When the tea things were brought in, Elizabeth poured while Jane served. The conversation flowed easily between Mr Bingley, Elizabeth, and Jane, with eager and often awkward contributions from Lydia, Mrs Bennet, or Mr Collins. Mr Darcy spoke little, only replying when required. Mr Bennet spoke hardly a word, and when he did, it was wry or disparaging.

"I trust your sisters are well, Mr Bingley?" Elizabeth asked.

"They are quite well. They very much enjoyed the picnic. What a pleasant way to spend a Saturday! Do you not agree, Darcy?"

"It was quite enjoyable," Mr Darcy acknowledged.

"Tell me, Mr Darcy," began Mr Bennet, "which particular aspect did you enjoy the most?"

"Aside from the unusually fine weather, I most enjoyed the cricket match."

"Indeed, I daresay the cricket match was exciting enough to entertain even the most sombre amongst us."

Elizabeth knew she should not provoke her father, but she saw his sarcastic wit in a new light now. She would not let him pick on the faults of others without acknowledging his own. "Father, you forget that Mr Darcy did not just sit back and observe the match, he participated in it as a player and a captain. I am sure the other players would readily admit he performed his duties admirably."

"Oh yes, Mr Darcy was an excellent captain!" cried Lydia, unaware of any tension. "If only we could play again. You mentioned a spring cricket match at Lady Catherine's estate, Mr Darcy. Tell us, do you and your sister play in your aunt's game?"

"I have in the past, but my sister has never played cricket anywhere but at Pemberley."

Mr Bennet suddenly rose and made his excuses to return to his study, and Elizabeth silently rejoiced, though the whole situation was a source of sorrow for her.

Jane was relieved when her father removed himself from the company. He was not being agreeable. In fact, he was almost rude. She feared the antagonism between him and Elizabeth might erupt in front of the visitors.

"Is Miss Darcy at your home now?" Jane asked, trying to restart the conversation.

"No. She is in London."

"How lucky she is! She must go to a ball every night!" Lydia's enthusiasm was obvious.

"She does not. She will turn sixteen early in the New Year—far too young to be out. I could not consider her coming out for at least another two years."

Mrs Bennet and Lydia looked decidedly crestfallen at this pronouncement. Mr Collins took advantage of the pause to praise Mr Darcy's guardianship over Miss Darcy, and to extol the influence Lady Catherine had over the girl's upbringing. Mr Darcy made no reply.

Mary entered the conversation for the first time. "Lizzy, I do not believe Charlotte had a chance to tell you the news yesterday; John Lucas is to return home."

"That is wonderful news!" Elizabeth exclaimed.

"I thought John was not expected home for another year," Jane said.

"Apparently, Mr Lucas has earned sufficient fortune from his various trips to the Americas to return early."

Mary's revelation caught Mrs Bennet's interest. "What an industrious young man John Lucas is, seeking to add to his family's fortune. When is he expected back in Hertfordshire?"

"Before the yuletide. He is concluding his business in Southampton over the next few weeks," Mary answered helpfully.

"Mary and Kitty, you should call upon him when he returns to welcome him back."

Kitty sniffed. "Why should *we* go? It is Lizzy whom he will wish to see." Mrs Bennet looked displeased, but Kitty continued on unawares. "You disapproved of his 'flitting about the world on a merchant ship.' You said he shouldn't leave without getting engaged to Li—"

"Nonsense!" interrupted Mrs Bennet. "Of course John Lucas is free to go where he chooses."

Kitty shrugged. "Lizzy, tell us about when you and John climbed the ancient oaks, and he was too frightened to climb down."

"Our guests would not wish to hear such a story, and I think it paints both Jo—Mr Lucas and myself in a rather poor light," Elizabeth replied. "But it does remind me... Mr Bingley, were you aware that some of the oldest trees in all of Hertfordshire grow in the woods of Netherfield Park?"

"Indeed? We did not notice when we surveyed the estate."

"It is unlikely that you should see them from horseback. But there are about a dozen ancient oaks in the forest border that Longbourn and Netherfield share. There are also several springs on the Netherfield side." Elizabeth began to tell Mr Bingley about some of the hidden treasures of Netherfield Park.

Mr Darcy offered a suggestion. "It occurs to me, Bingley, that a good landlord should know all there is to know about his estate. Perhaps we could arrange an excursion. Would you be willing to be our guide, Miss Elizabeth?"

Mrs Bennet rarely encouraged Elizabeth's explorations of the countryside, but today was another matter. "Oh yes, Lizzy, you must show Mr Bingley anything he wishes to see."

"I am perfectly willing to act as guide. Perhaps next week?"

"I think we might do better to take advantage of the current fair weather. Bingley and I are free tomorrow if that would suit." Elizabeth nodded stiffly before Mr Darcy continued. "You mentioned that some of the ancient trees are on Longbourn's side of the border. Are any of Longbourn's other interesting features found along the route we are to take?"

Elizabeth's enthusiasm seemed to grow. "Indeed they are. Mr Collins, you might wish to come on the walk."

Jane bit back a smile as she recognised her sister's strategy—more intervention.

"It is never too early to become familiar with your estate, Mr Collins," Mr Darcy added.

"I am exceedingly obliged for the offer, Cousin Elizabeth. Of course, Mr Darcy, any suggestions you have for the proper running of an estate, I must accept with alacrity. Lady Catherine often speaks of..." Mr Collins proceeded to agree to the scheme in his usual garrulous manner, but he ended with a small request. "If I may be so bold as to suggest that our enjoyment of such an expedition can only be enhanced with the inclusion of Miss Bennet in our plans."

"Oh yes, of course Jane will accompany you, Mr Collins," interjected Mrs Bennet.

Mr Bingley smiled at Jane in a manner that made her catch her breath. He smiled often, but this was more than simple friendliness. After a moment, she noticed that Mr Collins was likewise beaming at her, though the effect was somewhat different.

"I want to come too!" Lydia cried.

"You are not yet recovered for such a long walk," Elizabeth replied.

"But it's not fair! I shall be so bored and vexed to know you and Jane are out with Mr Darcy and Mr Bingley. I can walk just as far as *you* can, I am sure."

"This is quite a bit farther than the millinery shop," Lizzy observed wryly before becoming more serious. "It is not the mere three miles along the normal roads and paths to Netherfield. This is a circuitous route through forested hills and hollows."

Lydia appealed to a higher power. "Mama! I can go, can't I?"

"Lydia my love, do you not think it will be too much for you?"

Lydia began to object, but Mr Darcy cleared his throat. "If I may, Miss Bennet seemed to provide comfort to Miss Lydia after her injury. Perhaps Miss Bennet would not mind attending to Miss Lydia's needs tonight to ensure she is well rested and able to participate tomorrow?"

"Of course; it would be my pleasure," Jane replied, though she wondered at Mr Darcy making such a suggestion.

"Indeed, Jane and Lydia should retire after tea and take supper in Lydia's room later." Elizabeth's mouth twitched as she looked at Jane. "To make sure Lydia has a calm, restful evening, they should not be disturbed."

"That is a perfect solution," gushed Lydia. "Thank you, Mr Darcy."

Mr Bingley inquired whether Kitty and Mary should like to be included, but Mrs Bennet put an end to that idea rather quickly, having arranged three pairings to her own satisfaction.

As all were now in agreement, they worked out the particulars of the scheme. When the details were settled, Mr Bingley exclaimed, "Excellent! We shall make a jolly group. And I hope we can persuade Miss Elizabeth to share her tree-climbing story on the morrow!"

"I may be persuaded when I see those magnificent trees again. I am quite looking forward to it." She paused. "I shall even forgo my usual morning walk so that *I* am not too weary."

"Oh yes, we must have our guide in top form, mustn't we, Darcy?"

"Indeed, we must."

Jane and Elizabeth saw the gentlemen to the front door when they took their leave. Mr Bingley was all enthusiasm at the prospect of seeing them so soon again. He was particularly attentive to Jane in his farewells, such that she almost missed the strange grin that Elizabeth briefly directed at Mr Darcy. Almost, but not quite.

$\approx$

"Was that not a wonderful visit?!" Lydia asked Jane for the third time that night.

"Yes, Lydia. I am happy you enjoyed yourself."

"Did you notice how Mr Darcy made sure that I would be able to come on your walk tomorrow? Made sure you were here to attend me so that I could be well rested?"

Jane nodded. She had noticed Mr Darcy's insistence on that detail. "Now, I suggest you make an effort to *be* well rested. Would you like me to read until you fall asleep?"

"Yes, please. You are the only one who can calm me down without boring me. You will make a good mother."

Jane motioned for Lydia to climb into bed and get comfortable. She did not wish to think about motherhood, for that required thinking about marriage. She read from Lydia's favourite novel for half an hour before her sister was soundly sleeping. Jane retired to Kitty's empty bed. Kitty had switched rooms for the night to allow Lydia a better chance at rest.

In the quiet darkness, Jane had time to think on the gentlemen's visit. She was sure Mr Collins had been about to offer her marriage that afternoon, and after endless hours of silent anxiety and indecision, she had determined to do what was best for her family. In that moment, she had decided to accept him.

But her resolve was tenuous at best. Elizabeth's frantic intervention had only prolonged Jane's internal struggles. She had to be sensible for the sake of her family—even though she could not escape the nagging reservation that "sensible" was merely a kinder way of saying "mercenary."

When Mr Bingley had come into the sitting room, Jane's tenuous resolve had fallen about her in tatters. How could she marry one man when she felt this way about another? It would have been so much easier to accept her fate if she had never met Mr Bingley. Every moment she spent with him made it more and more difficult to do what she knew she ought.

Whatever choice she made when the time came, someone would be disappointed in her, whether it was Lizzy, her mother, or the rest of her family.

Tomorrow, Jane would spend another day in the company of the man she was expected to marry and the one she considered the most agreeable man she had ever met. Her last thoughts of the day lingered on Mr Bingley.

Charmingly Grouped

Elizabeth was convinced Mr Darcy was a genius. For someone who supposedly abhorred disguise, he certainly had an innate talent for it. At the beginning of yesterday's visit when he said so little, Elizabeth had doubted his presence was even necessary in light of Mr Bingley's enthusiastic conversation skills. But now she realised Mr Darcy was merely being economical. He exerted himself when absolutely necessary, thus avoiding at least *some* interaction with Mr Collins and making his interference even more subtle. It was almost uncanny. Elizabeth wondered whether he amused himself in London in a similar manner.

But once again, she could not argue with his results. The day ahead was planned—from the walk, to tea at Netherfield, to dinner back at Longbourn. Jane would not be alone with Mr Collins for the entire day, and therefore could not receive his declarations. But even more ingenious had been Mr Darcy's insistence that Jane attend to Lydia's rest all evening. Unfortunately, his seeming concern for Lydia contradicted his earlier discouraging words about the suitable age for a young lady to wed; Lydia and Mrs Bennet did not quite know what to make of him.

The gentlemen arrived on horseback, leaving their mounts for the day in the care of Longbourn's stables. After some light refreshments, the sextet set out in the pairs arranged by Mrs Bennet. It seemed Lydia was quite well enough to walk five miles, but only if she could lean on one of Mr Darcy's famed arms. As Elizabeth walked next to Mr Bingley, she was fortunate to have the most agreeable partner and therefore the most agreeable conversation, yet she knew she must separate the other incompatible couples before too long. She supposed that physically pulling Jane away from Mr Collins would be too obvious, and she had no idea how to pry Lydia away from Mr Darcy.

"Mr Collins, here we come upon the smallest of Longbourn's three ponds." Elizabeth motioned for him to join her, prompting him to release Jane's arm and step forward. Mr Bingley was happy to take the place her cousin relinquished. It was almost too easy.

"Lord, why would anyone care about this tiny pond? Lydia said as she and Mr Darcy reached the edge. "It is more like a puddle."

"It may be small, but it is spring fed and therefore never dries up —even in drought."

Lydia was unimpressed with this information, playing with the buttons on her pelisse.

Mr Darcy observed, "You seem to know much about your father's estate, Miss Elizabeth."

"Oh, Lizzy fancies herself Papa's little helper, constantly reporting back to him what she sees on her walks. She visits the tenants more often than he does. What a joke!"

"I am sure Mr Bennet appreciates Miss Elizabeth's efforts."

"That is kind of you to say, but in truth, I doubt my father cares one way or the other." Elizabeth had begun to see every interaction with her father in a new light. When she thought she was being helpful to the estate, had she merely been aiding his desire to hide in the library?

She recalled herself. "Shall we proceed to the next wonder of Longbourn, gentlemen?"

Mr Collins's clear intent was to restore the earlier groupings, but fortunately, for Elizabeth could think of no way to prevent it, Mr Darcy's genius struck again. "Mr Collins, my friend here is considering some renovations to Netherfield's main staircase, and I understand my aunt has made recent improvements to Rosings' staircase.

As I have not yet had the opportunity to view these enhancements, perhaps you would be so kind as to describe them to Mr Bingley."

Elizabeth now had the pleasure of walking and talking alone with Jane through the beech trees while Mr Bingley was regaled with the grandeur of Rosings' staircase. After a quarter of an hour, Mr Collins finally felt he had done justice to the subject, leaving an opportunity for Mr Bingley to reply.

"I thank you for all of the intricate detail, Mr Collins. I shall surely keep your descriptions in mind." Mr Bingley then propelled himself ahead up the hill so that he was even with Jane and Elizabeth. He kicked a stone in front of him, scraping the ground with the toe of his boot. "I say, the ground is a strange grey colour here!"

"We are walking upon one of Hertfordshire's famous chalk hills." Elizabeth related what she knew of the geology of Hertfordshire.

Mr Bingley was delighted with everything he heard. "It seems we could not have asked for a better guide for this tour, Mr Collins. Miss Elizabeth is a veritable fount of local knowledge!" Mr Collins agreed readily and loquaciously about the superior knowledge of his fair cousin.

The constantly rearranging group descended into a wooded hollow. As the forest thinned, the ancient oaks were impossible to miss. Half the leaves had fallen already, but the trunks and branches of the giants were impressive enough on their own, even to Lydia's usual disinterest in all things natural.

"Lord, but they are big! I doubt the three of us could reach around this one together."

Lydia's enthusiasm was such that she insisted they attempt the feat. "Stretch your arms, Jane! Oh! We are almost there! If we only touch fingertips instead of holding hands, I think it can be done! Ha, there!"

Lydia proceeded to drag her laughing sisters along to similarly surround each of the gnarled giant oaks and declared that only three trees were too wide for them.

Then she eyed the gentlemen. "*You* have longer arms. Do try it and see, will you? It would be such a pity not to."

Mr Bingley easily acquiesced, and Mr Darcy tolerated Lydia's entreaties with surprising good humour. Once Mr Darcy's cooperation was acquired, Mr Collins became quite willing. The gentlemen were thus ordered about the grove by Lydia, who saved the biggest of the remaining trees for last.

"Come on, Mr Collins, you must put a little effort into stretching your arms."

After much prodding and direction, and several circuits around men and tree, Lydia was defeated. "If only you had another three or four inches between you, it would be done! What a shame Mr Collins has not longer arms. What fun this was! Did I not have an excellent idea? Lord, but this would be the most boring walk without me!"

No one contradicted Lydia's assertions, and the various members of the group began to examine the grove at leisure. Mr Bingley accompanied Jane while Mr Collins and Lydia followed Mr Darcy around. Elizabeth was left briefly in blissful solitude to admire the trees.

&#56256;

Lydia was pleased with the expedition thus far. Two miles on the arm of Mr Darcy was certainly nothing to complain about. But, lord, it was hard work getting him to talk. He always seemed to be listening intently to whatever Lizzy said. Could he actually care about rocks and sand?

"Miss Elizabeth, before we leave this grove, I feel now would be the perfect time to hear your tree-climbing story." Mr Bingley had not forgotten.

"Oh yes, Lizzy. Do tell it!" Lydia much preferred her sister's funny stories to her boring geological narration. She did the voices and inflections so well.

"Come, I shall show you the very trees involved." Elizabeth led them to a pair of oaks evenly matched in height and girth—not the largest in the grove, but still impressive.

"Do you see those branches?" She pointed up to a pair of branches about a quarter of the way up each tree. "John Lucas and I used them for a climbing race. As he is two years my senior, he had the advantage of longer limbs and should have always won. I was fast and fearless though, probably foolishly so, and I could beat him if I tried very, very hard. As I grew, I found that I wanted to climb higher." She gestured to another, more highly situated branch. "I thought it was only natural that we should make the race more difficult as we got older. John adamantly refused, insisting it was too dangerous for me."

Lizzy laughed, "This was the very worst thing he could have said to dissuade me. John did not often shy away from something daring or dangerous. To find myself willing to attempt some feat that he would not made me even more determined to prove him wrong. So the next time we had our typical climbing race—I was about eleven years old—I continued to climb after he had claimed his victory.

"'Elizabeth Bennet, you stop that at once!' John demanded.

"I ignored him. The higher I climbed, the more strident his threats became. He threatened to laugh at me when I fell. He threatened to never climb with me again. He threatened to tell Jane, to tell my father, and finally, to tell my mother. This was the ultimate betrayal. If Mama knew about my tree climbing, or half of the other activities I did with John, I would not be allowed to play with him anymore. And that was the worst possible thing that could happen.

"Finally, I reached the intended branch. In a voice shaking with emotion, I exclaimed, 'See, it is perfectly safe, John Lucas. How could you ever think of telling my mother on me? I thought we were friends!'

"John was livid as he looked up at me. 'We are not friends at all! I only play with you because there are no boys close to my age. But I would rather play alone than with a cry-baby girl who is too stupid for her own good!'

"I said, 'You are scared to climb any higher in the tree. And if you tell my mother *anything*, everyone will know that John Lucas is too frightened to climb as high as this stupid, cry-baby girl!'

"'I am not. I just do not want to encourage your stupidity.'

"'I dare you. I dare you to climb up to that branch.' I pointed angrily at the branch opposite mine.

"Of course he could not refuse a dare. John began climbing without looking down. When he reached the branch, we glared at each other across the distance.

"I regretted my actions and silently climbed down, dreading that

John would refuse to play with me again. When my feet finally reached solid ground, I expected him to resume yelling at me. But then I looked up to see John still perched at the top branch. I asked him what was wrong.

"He answered in a clear but quiet voice. 'I can't look down. It is too high. Lizzy, I *am* afraid.' This must have been very hard for him to admit.

"'Oh, well, only look at the next lowest branch or at the trunk. Do not look all the way to the ground.'

"He did not move for several minutes. I began to climb. 'I am coming to rescue you.'"

Mr Darcy barked out a laugh. Lydia stared at him with wide eyes. "Good lord, Mr Darcy, I have never seen you laugh. Jane, Lizzy—have you ever seen Mr Darcy laugh?" Jane shook her head.

"Oh, do not let Darcy's drawing room demeanour fool you. No one could be so dreadfully grave all the time." Mr Bingley, though, was staring at his friend with no little astonishment of his own.

Mr Darcy finally composed himself. "I apologise for the interruption, Miss Elizabeth. If I recall, the young girl was about to rescue the older boy from the clutches of the evil oak tree."

Lizzy continued, "I soon reached the spot where John was perched, his eyes fixed on the great trunk in front of him. 'You idiot,' he said. 'What good can you do up here?'

"'Do not be mean, or I shall not help you.'

"'What does it matter? You will tell everyone what a coward I am. Charlotte will laugh at me. I would rather stay up here forever.'

"'What does it matter if you are afraid to climb very high or, rather, to climb down from very high? My fear is much worse than yours: I am afraid of horses.'

"'Being afraid of horses *is* worse, I suppose,' he muttered.

"'Oh yes, I am quite ridiculous! Now follow me and criticise my technique as we climb down. Only look at me.'

"'I am sorry I called you stupid. We are friends, even though you are a girl.'

"I smiled at him. All was forgiven. I descended more slowly than usual, and John followed close behind. When we got to the ground, we were not alone. My father and Sir William stood a short distance away, covering their mouths to keep from laughing. John groaned.

"'Oh my Lizzy,' said Mr Bennet, 'your mother sent us to catch John putting you in danger. She was sure that he must be the bad influence on you, but I suspect it is the other way around.'

"From that point on, we always raced to the upper set of branches, and it became impossible for me to win."

"And what was your mother's reaction?" asked a chuckling Mr Darcy.

"She made me stay at home for a se'nnight to keep me away from John. It would have been longer had my father not intervened after tiring of my constant complaints. But poor John—all of our siblings heard the story often from our fathers. His only consolation was that I never did overcome my fear of horses."

Jane looked up into the pair of trees. "I never knew how high you climbed. You should have listened to John."

"If we are quite finished judging my youthful indiscretions, perhaps we should carry on with our walk. The hidden treasures of Netherfield await, Mr Bingley."

Lydia was happy she could walk on Mr Darcy's arm for another few miles. Unfortunately, he was again engrossed in Lizzy's comments, often moving up to be closer to the other two couples. Lydia did not even pay attention anymore—something about the chalk again, and an aquifer, and the large number of springs. What an awful bore!

On they walked through woods and clearings until they came to a rocky path along the side of a sloping hill. Lizzy stopped to face the group. "This concludes the tour, gentlemen. Now we need only walk along this path to be brought to the lane and then Netherfield."

Mr Collins and Mr Bingley expressed their gratitude, one long-winded and the other jovial. Finally, Lydia would have Mr Darcy to herself, and she would do her best to make him laugh—she had quite enjoyed the sight and sound of it. But after only a few minutes of walking with the taciturn gentleman, she was again foiled.

"Mr Collins, I imagine you would be interested to know I received a letter from my aunt yesterday. She is well."

"I am much gratified to hear it. How kind of you to pass such welcome intelligence to me. Do you have any other news to impart from Kent?"

The pairings were suddenly rearranged, much to Lydia's disappointment. Mr Bingley offered Jane his arm while the other two gentlemen walked together discussing Lady Catherine. Lydia had had quite enough of this new arrangement. She moved to resume her place next to Mr Darcy.

"Lydia," Elizabeth said as she took her sister's arm, "how do you fare? Are you quite well?"

Lydia tried to pull ahead. "I am well, but I wish to walk with Mr Darcy. Mama said I should, and *you* should be with Mr Bingley."

"I think we can be excused for letting our *intendeds* escape our control for one half mile out of five."

Lydia snorted but still attempted to pull ahead.

"Mr Collins and Mr Darcy are having a discussion. Do not disturb them. We still have tea and dinner to spend with the gentlemen from Netherfield."

"Let go of me." Lydia yanked her arm, pulling her sister forward. This caused Lizzy to stumble, her ankle twisting awkwardly as her foot came down unevenly on the rocky path. *Drat!*

❧

Despite his fatigue after such a long walk, the Reverend William Collins listened very carefully to Mr Darcy's words about the letter he had received from Lady Catherine.

"Lady Catherine writes to me of the engagement of a neighbour's son. Have you had the opportunity to meet the Grantly family?"

"I have met Mr and Mrs Grantly and their eldest son, but he is already married. They are a respectable family whose estate is nearby. Lady Catherine approves of them, though their rank is of course considerably lower, and their estate is nothing to Rosings. I understand Miss Grantly is so fortunate as to share a friendship with Miss de Bourgh, which is proof enough of Lady Catherine's approbation."

Mr Darcy bowed his head in response. "You are correct on all counts. I met the Grantlys when Lady Catherine invited them to dine with us during my last visit. Indeed, they are a respectable, and respectful, family. I am sure my aunt appreciates your astute perceptions in regards to her acquaintances."

Mr Collins nearly beamed at such high praise, but he remembered that the letter contained some news. If he learned this information now, perhaps he could impress Lady Catherine with his knowledge when he returned to Kent. "You mentioned that one of the sons is engaged to be married?"

"Yes, their youngest son, Mr Arthur Grantly, who has a promising career in the law, has recently become engaged. Lady Catherine and Miss de Bourgh were invited to a small celebration in the couple's honour. Unfortunately, Lady Catherine does not completely approve of the young lady."

"Oh dear, that is unfortunate." What disappointment Mr Collins would feel if Lady Catherine ever disapproved of him. "From what circumstance does this disapproval stem?"

"The young lady in question, a Miss Horton, has adequate fortune, acceptable connexions, and the appropriate education and accomplishments for her future station. Lady Catherine does not find fault in any of that. However, my aunt feels that for the wife of the third son of a family of no great consequence, Miss Horton is too handsome."

Mr Collins took a moment, but could not quite grasp the objection. "Pardon me?"

"Has my aunt never explained her philosophy on beauty and station?" Mr Darcy looked surprised that the parson did not understand, and this shamed Mr Collins.

"I see that she has not. Let me enlighten you. Lady Catherine does not approve of excessive beauty in persons of lower rank. For example, Miss Grantly is rather plain, which is one of the reasons Lady Catherine allows her to continue a friendship with my cousin. Miss Horton, however, is another matter. My aunt has decided not to make her objections known to the Grantlys. She doubts she will see much of the future Mr and Mrs Arthur Grantly; therefore, this disproportionate beauty will not trouble her often. She does not find it cause enough to upset the Grantly family over Arthur's choice, for really, in all other respects, Miss Horton is quite suitable."

"Lady Catherine is compassionate of course." This was all the reply Mr Collins could muster.

"Indeed, she is. It occurs to me, Mr Collins, that perhaps I ought not have mentioned this to you."

"Oh?" He felt unusually deficient of words.

"Yes, well, Lady Catherine would not wish her objections—since they are not severe enough to make public—to be known by anyone who might cross paths with the Grantlys. She confides in me, as I shall see them but little. If you would be so kind as to not mention this to her, I would appreciate your discretion. She may refer to the engagement of her own accord of course. It is quite possible she will discuss her opinions with you. But let us leave this disclosure to her."

"Of course, Mr Darcy, I shall not mention my knowledge to her, nor shall I let it influence my estimation of the Grantlys."

"You are very prudent, Mr Collins. I can see why my aunt has taken you under her wing."

Mr Collins could only be gratified by this observation. But as he was attempting to grasp the implications of what Mr Darcy had just revealed, he heard a commotion behind him.

"Oh Lizzy! I'm sorry!" cried Cousin Lydia, helping her sister up off the ground and onto a nearby boulder. "You twisted your ankle—are you terribly injured?"

"I...do not think so. I just need a moment." Cousin Elizabeth's face was drawn in pain.

Mr Darcy stepped forward. "May I...examine your ankle, Miss Elizabeth, to determine the extent of the injury?"

"There is no need. We should keep going." She started to rise but then sucked in a breath and faltered when she put weight on her left leg.

"Lizzy!" cried Cousin Jane. "Please let Mr Darcy look at it."

Cousin Elizabeth acquiesced. Mr Darcy knelt before her while Miss Lydia shifted anxiously behind him.

Mr Darcy reached for Miss Elizabeth's left foot, pulling it forward and resting it on his right thigh. Mr Collins looked away in embarrassment, but then he remembered that Mr Darcy of Pemberley, nephew of Lady Catherine, would never do anything improper. A pale Cousin Elizabeth winced as Mr Darcy performed his examina-

tion, feeling around her joint as she bent and rotated it at his instruc-
tion. Mr Collins tried to look at her ankle as little as possible.

"I do not think it is broken, but it is badly sprained," pronounced
Mr Darcy.

Cousin Elizabeth sighed. "I suppose it could have been worse;
this could have happened two miles back."

Mr Darcy turned towards Mr Bingley. "Charles, would you go
ahead to Netherfield and have Mr Jones fetched? And Mr Collins,
might you go ahead as well, and take the carriage to inform Mr and
Mrs Bennet?"

"I shall perform this duty most eagerly. Do not worry yourself,
Cousin; you will have the comfort of your parents as soon as
possible."

Mr Bingley was just as eager to be of assistance. "Darcy, is there
anything else I can do? Shall I prepare a room for Miss Elizabeth?"

"Yes, that is a good idea."

"Surely there is no need for all this trouble over me. Honestly, it is
nothing."

"It is no trouble at all, Miss Elizabeth," Mr Bingley assured her.
"Darcy, how will she get to Netherfield?"

"It seems I shall have the pleasure of carrying another of the Miss
Bennets." This proposed course of action shocked Mr Collins. It
seemed the others were shocked as well, for only a gasp from Miss
Lydia broke the silence.

"No, sir, it is too much!" Miss Elizabeth motioned for her sisters to
help her rise. "Jane and Lydia will help me; there is no need to take
such extreme measures. My ankle is improved already."

Miss Lydia agreed. "Yes, Jane and I shall help Lizzy walk. It is too
far for you to carry her, and she does not wish it."

"She cannot put any weight on it, and it will be much faster if I
carry her," reasoned Mr Darcy.

Dear Cousin Jane was very worried for her sister. "Please, Lizzy,
do not be difficult. Mr Darcy is right. It will be too painful for you to
walk all that way."

"If someone is to carry my cousin, perhaps it ought to be me?" Mr
Collins felt obliged to offer, though he had no enthusiasm at the
thought.

"We are wasting time arguing about this." Mr Darcy's voice now brooked no opposition, much like his aunt's. "Bingley, Mr Collins, go on ahead as discussed. The Miss Bennets and I shall work out how to proceed from here. Please make sure everything is ready when we arrive."

Mr Collins did as he was told, hurrying away from the scene. He tried to keep up with Mr Bingley but soon became winded. Mr Bingley called to him, "The sooner I send for the surgeon, the better. I shall have the carriage waiting for you when you arrive."

And so it was that a breathless Mr Collins found himself sitting in Mr Bingley's carriage, swiftly on his way back to Longbourn. He used the time to catch his breath and think back on the day. Up until Miss Elizabeth's injury, it had been a pleasant if tiring excursion. He had seen much of his future estate, and he had spent many happy moments with dear Cousin Jane. He imagined he would often repeat the act of walking Longbourn's grounds with her on his arm. But what had Mr Darcy been talking about before they were interrupted?

He must think on the conversation later, for now he had the solemn duty to inform Mr and Mrs Bennet of their daughter's injury. No doubt they would be alarmed at Miss Elizabeth's condition. He decided to work up to the disclosure slowly so as not to shock them. Yes, soften the blow with many praises about their daughter—that would be the right course of action. Luckily, Mr Collins sometimes amused himself with suggesting and arranging such little elegant compliments, though he tried to give them as unstudied an air as possible.

Every Bennet in the Country

After sending off a perspiring Mr Collins in the carriage, Bingley instructed Mrs Trent, his housekeeper, to ready a room for Miss Elizabeth.

"What do you mean, 'prepare a guest room,' Charles?" Caroline asked as they stood together in the entryway.

"We shall not allow Miss Elizabeth to be jostled about in a carriage. She must stay with us. Surely you see that."

"I see nothing of the sort. I daresay such an avid walker can suffer the consequences of her choice of activity."

"Caroline, be reasonable. She is staying, and that is final. You *will* be a gracious hostess."

She huffed in irritation. "I suppose we shall not have guests for tea then."

"Oh, yes, we shall. In fact, there may be three more people in attendance." Bingley kept his eyes on the lane in anticipation of Darcy and the Bennet ladies' arrival.

"Three more?" Caroline's voice rose in annoyance. "I thought it would be at least one less, with Mr Collins blessedly removed from our company."

"Mr Collins has only gone to retrieve Mr and Mrs Bennet. They will return to see Miss Elizabeth, I am sure."

"Are we to receive every Bennet in the country?"

Ignoring her tone, Bingley added slowly, "Mr Jones may also take tea with us. I suggest you inform the servants of the change in plans. Tea should be served in the drawing room after everyone arrives and Mr Jones has some time with Miss Elizabeth. In the meantime, please wait in the sitting room until you hear from me."

Caroline stalked off to do as he said. Bingley shook his head. He could not abide discourtesy. His sister was all that was charming in London society, but it seemed Hertfordshire did not agree with her, for she held her neighbours—even the gentry like the Bennets—in what he could only describe as contempt. He found himself increasingly annoyed by Caroline's behaviour. Darcy at least behaved consistently—he was unapproachable in both London and the country.

Bingley still stood in the doorway shaking his head when he noticed some figures walking up the lane. Darcy indeed carried Miss Elizabeth in his arms. Miss Bennet hurried beside him with a worried expression, and Miss Lydia stomped along behind. Bingley swung the door open wide as they made their way up the steps.

"Her room is not yet ready."

Darcy breezed past and into the drawing room where he placed Miss Elizabeth carefully upon a settee. She blushed and thanked him for his assistance as he backed away. Almost immediately, Miss Bennet began fussing over her sister.

"Lizzy, what can I get you? Shall I place a pillow under your foot?" She did not wait for an answer, retrieving a cushion from a nearby chair. "Mr Bingley, when will Mr Jones arrive?"

"I expect him any minute. I sent for him first thing, and Mr Collins departed for Longbourn soon after."

"My sincere thanks to you, sir, and to you, Mr Darcy. Your quick decisions have been so very helpful. I know not what we should have done without you." Miss Bennet was almost babbling as she began to lift up Miss Elizabeth's left leg to place the cushion. She winced, causing Miss Bennet to freeze in horror. Darcy took a step forward and then also froze.

"Jane, please stop fretting and sit down," Miss Elizabeth said calmly. "Here, Lydia, will you put this back where it belongs?"

Miss Lydia took the offending cushion and replaced it on the chair before seating herself upon it. After a slight pause, Miss Elizabeth added, "Now, everyone be calm. It is not as if I have never twisted an ankle before! I thank you for your hospitality, Mr Bingley, but I really must return home with my sisters. I cannot impose on you and your household as an invalid."

Before Bingley could reply, Mrs Trent announced Mr Jones. The cheery surgeon stepped into the room, booming, "What's this? Another injured Bennet girl?" He observed the patient on the settee, her legs raised before her, and then he chuckled. "Miss Elizabeth, I thought you well past the age of reckless dares and awkward scrapes!"

"I had hoped as much, Mr Jones. But I assure you I was doing nothing more reckless than walking with Lydia."

"Well, that explains it. For Miss Lydia certainly is *not* past that perilous age."

Lydia looked down at her hands. "I said I was sorry. You just would not let go of me!" Bingley did not know what this outburst was about.

"I know you never meant for this to happen. But you must think about..." Miss Elizabeth glanced at the confused faces in the room. "We shall talk about it later. For now, I think Mr Jones was summoned for a reason."

"Yes, let's get on with it. Gentlemen, I need some time alone with the Bennet sisters." Mr Jones ushered Bingley and Darcy from the room. "I shall come to you when the examination is complete," he said as he shut the door.

They stood motionless in the hallway for a moment. "The others are in the sitting room; shall we join them?"

Darcy began to walk in the correct direction but much more slowly than was normal. "Bingley, it has occurred to me...perhaps Miss Elizabeth would be more willing to stay here, as she should, if you invited Miss Bennet to stay as well."

"Yes, of course! You are a genius. Miss Elizabeth will be comforted by her sister's presence, and Miss Bennet, I am sure, can wish nothing more than to be of assistance. I shall have a second room readied directly. Go on ahead." Bingley rushed off to find Mrs Trent again and apologised sheepishly for all the changing plans. She assured him it would be no trouble.

Bingley felt a bit ashamed of himself, but he could not help it— he was glad that Miss Elizabeth had sprained her ankle. He grimaced inwardly when he admitted this horrible thought. Of course he regretted Miss Elizabeth's pain, particularly when she had been the architect of the delightful day he had enjoyed. But her injury required that she stay at Netherfield and, more to the point, that her elder sister stay to care for her.

Since his discussion with Darcy about Jane Bennet's expected engagement, Bingley had spent some time in reflection and arrived at the conclusion that she did not truly welcome Mr Collins's addresses. She was all that was proper and civil with her cousin, but after studying her expressions and demeanour, Bingley believed the lady felt nothing more than typical friendliness for the parson. Even more exciting than this conclusion was his conviction that Miss Bennet felt a good deal more for himself. She had clearly enjoyed his altered behaviour towards her over the last two days. Now she would be staying in his home, and Bingley was determined to use this opportunity to convey to her that she did have an alternative to Mr Collins if she wished.

When Bingley entered the sitting room, he heard Caroline's annoyed voice again. "A sprained ankle is hardly cause enough to take in *one* of the Bennets, let alone two."

Darcy answered her. "It is cause enough for Miss Elizabeth to avoid a rough carriage ride. Surely you of all people can sympathise after delaying our journey from Pemberley to London last summer for your much-less-severe injury." Darcy paused while Caroline struggled unsuccessfully for a reply. Bingley knew quite well to what Darcy referred. Caroline, after coaxing Darcy to escort her into Pemberley's rose garden, had foolishly tried to pluck a bloom and pricked herself with a thorn. She had caused quite a commotion at the sight of the blood, insisting it would become infected and demanding their planned departure be delayed. After two days with no sign of impending infection, Bingley had finally convinced her to travel. Darcy had not been pleased. The delay had caused him to miss a small window of opportunity to see Georgiana in London before she went to Ramsgate.

Darcy added now, obviously knowing his point had been made, "I was under the impression that you enjoyed Miss Bennet's society. Did you not tell me you would like to know more of her?"

With a look towards a fuming Caroline, Louisa agreed, "Yes, Jane Bennet is a sweet girl. But I wonder how much opportunity we shall have to entertain her if she is to be constantly looking after her injured sister."

Bingley decided to enter the conversation. "I am sure Miss Elizabeth will not require constant care. There is nothing further to discuss. The eldest Miss Bennets will be our guests for tonight, at least, and several more days if we can convince them."

A booming voice from the doorway startled the group, causing even Hurst to sit up straight. "That is excellent news, Mr Bingley. I had worried about the pain Miss Elizabeth would endure if she were to be moved now." Mr Jones had apparently finished his examination.

"What is your estimation of Miss Elizabeth's injury?" Darcy did not wait for all the greetings to be exchanged before making his inquiry.

"It is a bad sprain. She is in much pain, though she hides it well. She should not attempt to walk on it for several days, and it will be several weeks before she can resume her countryside rambles, though I doubt she will heed my advice." A worried expression crossed Darcy's face before he replaced it with his usual bland mask. He had been showing an unusual amount of emotion all day. Perhaps Hertfordshire had the opposite effect on Darcy than it did on Caroline, for now it seemed Bingley's reserved friend was *less* aloof than he would be in London. Bingley would have to observe him more closely. Of course the likelihood of *that* when Miss Bennet was in the room was not very high.

Bingley heard a tumult at the front door, causing him to abandon his thoughts. Mr and Mrs Bennet had arrived. "If we could proceed to the drawing room, tea will be served there."

They found the Bennets still in the front entryway. Darcy had little patience for the greetings and exclamations that occurred. He only wanted to return to the drawing room to make sure Miss Elizabeth was well—or as well as could be expected. But on and on Mrs Bennet's fussing went. Mr Collins's theatrics only added to the uproar. Mr Bennet immediately sought out Mr Jones and no doubt heard the prognosis, so he was no help in containing his wife. Finally, the servants arrived in the hallway with the tea things, forcing the group to move into the drawing room.

Miss Elizabeth still sat on the settee, her complexion returned to its rosy hue. Immediately after her injury, she had been pale and clammy. Later, during the walk to Netherfield—he dare not think too much about how she felt in his arms—she had been flushed. Though her colour looked better now, she still wore an anxious expression. When Mr Collins entered the room, she reached for Miss Bennet's hand. Even with her injury, Elizabeth remained chiefly concerned for her elder sister's future. She would not wish to be separated from her for even one night while Mr Collins was still at Longbourn. That worry, at least, would soon be soothed.

Miss Bingley and Mrs Hurst began serving the tea as Mrs Bennet examined her daughter. "Oh Lizzy! What a fright you gave us all! You cannot imagine the apprehension we felt when Mr Collins returned in such a manner. And then he was so reluctant to tell us what had occurred, we feared something dreadful indeed!"

"I am sorry to have alarmed you, Mama."

Motherly concern soon gave way to vexation. "How many times have I told you to watch where you are going? You've ruined all of our plans with your turned ankle. What a horrid inconvenience this must be for Mr Bingley!"

"Elizabeth has no consideration in her sprained ankles. She times them ill." Mr Bennet stood near the door as he spoke, his expression unreadable. Darcy thought his humour inappropriate considering the situation.

Elizabeth replied as if her father had not spoken. "I am perfectly prepared to end the inconvenience and return home after tea."

Bingley cleared his throat. "It is no inconvenience at all. Caroline and I would be honoured if Miss Elizabeth and Miss Bennet stayed as our guests. We would not want Miss Elizabeth to endure a rough carriage ride, and Miss Bennet's presence will be a comfort to her, will it not?"

"Oh yes! I wish nothing more than to aid Lizzy during her recovery." Miss Bennet beamed. "Thank you so much for the invitation, Mr Bingley, Miss Bingley."

"It is our pleasure, I assure you. We are delighted at the thought of hosting you both. Is that not so, Caroline?"

Miss Bingley replied in the affirmative as she poured another cup of tea, adding, "I daresay we shall all make the best out of this unfortunate turn of events. Though how lucky for Miss Eliza that her injury occurred so near to Netherfield and amongst so many friends rather than on one of her many solitary walks."

Elizabeth's face was full of amusement, but Mrs Bennet did not seem to grasp Caroline's implication. "Very lucky, indeed! I always object to her wandering off to who knows where. It is very fortunate you were with Mr Bingley, Lizzy." Then she glanced between her injured daughter and Bingley. "Of course Elizabeth should not be moved, and we must trespass on your kindness for a time. I thank you again and again. How very good of you!"

Obviously, Miss Bingley was wasting her barbs on Mrs Bennet. Instead, she said with cold civility, "You may depend upon it, madam, that Miss Eliza will receive every possible attention while she remains with us."

Mrs Bennet effused her thanks again, and then her eyes moved to her youngest daughter, who was giggling at some joke the ever-jolly Mr Jones had told. "Of course you are right that one of the girls should stay to help Lizzy. We cannot expect your household to take on such a responsibility. But, with our own guest"—Mrs Bennet motioned towards Mr Collins—"I'm afraid I cannot part with my two eldest daughters together. I require Jane at home."

An awkward silence enveloped the room. Miss Elizabeth's smile faded, and she flushed again, no doubt in mortification of her mother's outrageous behaviour.

Miss Bennet spoke first. "But Mama, I wish to stay with Lizzy. You know how I shall worry for her if I do not."

"You are a sweet girl to worry so about your sister. But really, I

87

must have you at home. Why doesn't Lydia stay here to care for Lizzy?" Mrs Bennet attempted to convince her audience that this idea had just now occurred to her. Darcy was astonished at the audacity of the woman. Bingley looked just as shocked, and Miss Bingley and Mrs Hurst were clearly disgusted, whether at Mrs Bennet's behaviour or at the idea of hosting Lydia Bennet as a guest, Darcy could not tell. Hurst continued to eat his tea cake, unmindful of the company.

"Oh yes! I shall stay and tend to Lizzy. What fun we shall have here at Netherfield!" Miss Lydia seemed delighted with the scheme.

Mr Bennet moved further into the room. "Not so hasty, Mrs Bennet. I believe Mr Bingley's original invitation should stand. Lydia, you make a poor nursemaid. Jane is much better suited to the task. Mary, Kitty, and Lydia will do tolerably well entertaining our guest at home. It is high time they took on more responsibilities." His sharp look at his youngest daughter, who had begun to protest, warned that she ought not contradict him. She snapped her mouth shut and pouted. Subtlety was not one of Miss Lydia's strengths.

Mrs Bennet, the proverbial tree from which Miss Lydia's apple fell, smiled tightly as she addressed her husband. "But you know how much I rely on Jane. And we cannot disappoint Mr Collins during his last days here in Hertfordshire by separating him from his favourite cousin."

"You rely on Jane too much. Elizabeth needs her now."

Mr Collins broke into the conversation with a smile and bow at the two eldest Bennet sisters. "Far be it from me to deprive poor Cousin Elizabeth of her dear sister's care. I wish nothing but her complete comfort."

Mr Bennet turned to Bingley. "Thank you, sir. I gratefully accept your invitation for Jane and Elizabeth." Bingley nodded in acknowledgement.

"But Mr Bennet—"

"That is an end to the matter, Mrs Bennet. Now let us enjoy our tea."

Miss Elizabeth's eyes were shining at her father. She whispered, "Thank you, Papa."

He moved to the settee, looking down on her with suspiciously moist eyes of his own. "My Lizzy, I only wish for your full recovery and your return to me happy and healthy."

Darcy was mesmerised by the look she gave her father in response to this tacit apology. She positively glowed. This should have been a private moment between father and daughter, but Darcy could not look away. In her eyes, he saw unconditional love and acceptance. Despite all the faults of the man before her—which she seemed to understand better than anybody—and despite the pain he had caused her, Elizabeth loved and accepted Mr Bennet, and believed he could be a better person. Her look expressed all this. That kind of look inspired a man to improve himself, so that he would be worthy of such love. It was the kind of look Darcy desperately wished to receive from her himself.

Darcy caught his breath. He, Fitzwilliam Darcy, was in love with Elizabeth Bennet. He loved this witty, brave, lovely country miss. He nearly staggered backwards with the realisation of it. It was so obvious now; how could he not have protected himself? Almost from the very beginning, he should have avoided her rather than seek her out everywhere he went, rather than stupidly plunge himself deeper and deeper into this impossible attachment. Of course it was impossible. Had he not just witnessed how unacceptable her family was and what degradation such a connexion would be?

Darcy knew not how the rest of the visit passed. He scarcely heard a word exchanged. He knew there must have been arrangements made for the Miss Bennets' clothes and such, but he was completely ignorant of them. Finally, Mr Jones, Mr Collins, and the rest of the Bennets took their leave. Darcy could not remember whether or not he bid them farewell.

Miss Bennet was saying something. "I think it would be best if we retired for the evening. Should we require it, we shall ring for some food to be brought to Lizzy's room."

"Yes, of course. Miss Elizabeth ought to rest now." Bingley glanced at Darcy before settling his eyes on Miss Elizabeth. "Now, how shall we get you up to your room? That is the question."

"Jane and I can manage."

"Do not be ridiculous," Bingley replied. "Mr Jones said you were not to attempt walking on it, and certainly not up a flight of stairs. You must be carried."

She sighed. "Very well, call a strong servant then."

"I shall see to it." Miss Bingley moved towards the door.

"There is no need to call a servant. I shall transport Miss Elizabeth safely to her room." Darcy could not help himself. He could not bear to think of her in another man's arms, even those of a servant. She protested, naturally, as did Miss Bingley of course. But Darcy insisted. *What folly!*

So Darcy had the very great pleasure of scooping Miss Elizabeth Bennet, the woman he loved, into his arms and carrying her up Netherfield's staircase. He deposited her in a chair in a guest room. She blushed becomingly and thanked him without meeting his eyes. Miss Bennet was genuinely grateful for his assistance. He began to see she was always genuine—Miss Elizabeth's regard for her elder sister was well-placed. He bowed to them both and wished them a good night.

As he left the room, Darcy thought about his predicament. How desperately he wanted to spend all of his time with her, to protect her, to make her happy. But he knew he could not. He resolved to distance himself from her. It seemed as if she no longer needed assistance in the matter of Mr Collins. Even if Mr Bennet had not redeemed himself today, Darcy was sure that the seed he had planted earlier in Collins's head would soon take root. He would make sure of it, and then he would end his clandestine relationship with Miss Elizabeth. He had but a few days to drink his fill of her presence while she stayed at Netherfield. It would be all he allowed himself. Then, somehow, he would free himself of this most inconvenient attachment.

Darcy returned downstairs in search of some port. He believed his consumption would rival Hurst's tonight.

10

Near and Dear at Netherfield

Jane was delighted Elizabeth and her father had reconciled. She understood quite well the unspoken apology and acceptance in the drawing room. Not only that, but Mr Bennet had exerted himself to curtail his wife's pursuit of sons-in-law. Jane could not remember him ever making such an effort. She now knew without a doubt that her father did not expect—nor secretly hope—she would marry Mr Collins. Of course he would never have asked her to do so outright, but Jane's suspicion that he harboured the secret wish for her to solve the family's problems by marrying Longbourn's heir was one of the reasons she had been resigned to accepting her fate.

But all that was over now because of dear Lizzy's courage, tenacity, and, sadly, her sprained ankle. No doubt Mr Bennet's worry over Elizabeth's welfare had partly caused him to relent in his stubbornness and resentment. When the sisters had discussed it over the course of their evening together, Elizabeth's relief was palpable. How sorry Jane was for all the anxiety Lizzy had felt on her behalf! But, finally, it seemed that Jane, Elizabeth, and Mr Bennet were in agreement: Jane would not become Mrs Collins. Only Mrs Bennet would be disappointed in this new accord.

With the lifting of these weighty worries from Elizabeth's shoulders and the boredom of being immobile, she began to tease Jane about a certain fair-haired gentleman. Apparently, Jane's usual serene countenance failed her where Mr Bingley was concerned, at least to Elizabeth's trained eyes. Jane thought at some point she must run out of blushes, but that point never seemed to arrive. When Lizzy insisted Jane at least spend mealtimes with the Bingleys and Hursts, Jane agreed, if only to escape the ceaseless teasing.

So Jane found herself sharing dinner with the Netherfield party on the day after Elizabeth's injury. Mr Bingley's manners were charming as ever. Miss Bingley and Mrs Hurst greeted Jane with much polite elegance. Mr Hurst wished her a good appetite.

Soon after they sat, Mr Bingley began, "We are delighted you have joined us, Miss Bennet! How fares your sister today?"

"Elizabeth is recovering as expected, but is already restless from being confined. She is not accustomed to idleness."

"Indeed, it must be quite a change from cricket and country walking. Louisa and I wonder how she has time for any of the usual feminine accomplishments!" Miss Bingley and her sister tittered together before sobering. "But we do hope Miss Eliza is resting comfortably despite her injury."

"She is. We are both so very grateful for your hospitality."

Mr Bingley waved away her thanks. "And we are grateful to have you here with us. You are filling in quite nicely for an absent Darcy."

"Yes, Charles, where is Mr Darcy? We missed him at breakfast today."

"You never see him at breakfast, for he eats well before you arise. You could hardly have missed him then."

"I am told he did not go for his usual ride this morning but stayed abed and rang for a tray."

Mr Bingley laughed. "My, but you do keep an eye on his activities, Caroline."

Miss Bingley looked none too pleased with her brother's teasing. Jane could understand that sentiment today.

"Charles, it is unlike him, you must own. And now he misses dinner. Is he well? Perhaps he overexerted himself yesterday. Shall I have someone look in on him?"

Mr Hurst paused in his chewing and chuckled. "I suspect Darcy merely needed a day of peace and quiet. He was quite in his cups last night."

Miss Bingley could not hide her shock. "Nonsense! I have never known Mr Darcy to be in his cups. You must be mistaken." Mrs Hurst joined in her sister's incredulity, both of them gaping at Mr Hurst.

He laughed again. "You certainly have a high opinion of the old chap. But every man overindulges on occasion, and Darcy is no different. He just hides it better than the rest of us. Last night, he was in rare form indeed. Not since the summer have I seen him in such a state, eh, Bingley?"

"Darcy would prefer not to have such matters discussed around the dinner table," Mr Bingley replied.

Mr Hurst chuckled one last time but seemed content to return his full attention back to the meal. Jane had never heard him speak so much before—and on such a subject! In the wake of his unusual burst of words, the three Bingley siblings seemed to lack the ability to carry out a more conventional conversation. Mr Bingley kept glancing nervously at Jane, while Miss Bingley appeared quite out of sorts.

Jane broke the silence, "Mr Bingley, I wonder whether I might peruse your library for some suitable reading material for Elizabeth."

"Of course! I shall take you to the library directly after dinner. I wish my collection of books were larger for Miss Elizabeth's benefit and my own credit, but I am an idle fellow, and although I have not many, I have more than I ever look into."

Now that all awkwardness was past, pleasant conversation resumed for the rest of the meal, chiefly through the efforts of Miss Bingley and Mrs Hurst. Their powers of conversation were considerable. They could describe an entertainment with accuracy, relate an anecdote with humour, and laugh at their acquaintances with spirit.

After dinner, Mr Bingley escorted Jane to the library. "I hope we find something to suit Miss Elizabeth. I must admit, I have shamefully neglected my library. Half these books were here when we moved in, and I have no idea what lurks on the upper shelves."

"I think anything by Shakespeare would suit Lizzy."

Mr Bingley looked thoughtful. "I may have one or two of the Bard's plays here somewhere. Let me think."

Mr Darcy appeared in the doorway. "Good evening." Jane did not see any indication he had been inebriated the previous night. He looked as formal and polished as ever.

"Darcy! You have made an appearance at last. Caroline will be delighted."

Mr Darcy pursed his lips. "Yes, well, I apologise for my absence today. I was behind on my correspondence. Miss Bennet, might I inquire after your sister?"

"I thank you, Mr Darcy. Elizabeth is doing well. She is frustrated with her forced inactivity, but otherwise, she is in good spirits. In fact, I am here seeking some distractions for her."

He smiled. What a change that smile played upon his countenance! "Yes, I overheard your conversation. Since I am well aware of the deficiencies of Bingley's library, I brought some of my own collection with me. I would be happy to loan a few books to Miss Elizabeth."

"That is very kind of you."

"Not at all. I shall return momentarily with a selection." He seemed oddly excited as he strode out the doorway, and Jane wondered which works he would choose.

Mr Bingley chuckled. "Darcy to the rescue again. Upon my word, he is acting strangely lately."

"Strangely? I have found him perfectly amiable. How is his behaviour out of the norm?"

"You see, he must be making an unusual effort, for very few people would describe Darcy as 'amiable.' He prefers a small group of friends who understand his reserved nature. Yet he suggested calling on your family on Monday, and he suggested the walk yesterday as well. Those two outings were a departure for him—though a most welcome departure from *my* point of view." Mr Bingley had come to stand directly before Jane during the course of this explanation. As he looked down at her with his clear blue eyes, which were now unusually serious, she quite forgot about Mr Darcy and his books.

"I...I greatly enjoyed them as well," she stuttered before recovering herself. "It has been years since I took that particular route."

"I had the impression Mr Collins was not familiar with the estate.

Has he never asked to explore Longbourn's grounds on his previous visits?"

"Mr Collins has never visited us before. Until about a fortnight ago, we had never set eyes on him."

"You've known him only a fortnight?" Mr Bingley's voice was raised in disbelief. "Forgive me, I mistakenly assumed he has been long acquainted with you...with your family, that is."

"No, there was some quarrel between our fathers. He is as new an acquaintance to me as you are, Mr Bingley."

They stared at each other for a moment. Jane could not look away, though modesty dictated she should. Mr Bingley was just about to speak again when Mr Darcy returned.

"How do you think Miss Elizabeth will like these, Miss Bennet?" He handed over four books and looked at her expectantly.

Taking a deep breath, Jane examined each of the titles. "Have you and my sister discussed literature, Mr Darcy?"

"I have not had that pleasure."

"How extraordinary! It is as if you knew her tastes. I daresay not even Papa could have chosen better." Mr Darcy's face was again transformed with a smile, complete with those rare dimples. Jane held out the copy of *Robinson Crusoe*. "With John Lucas's imminent return, Elizabeth will find this one appropriately nostalgic. It was one of the few books she could persuade him to read and discuss. She partly blames it for his adventure-seeking course in life."

"I say, this John Lucas will be a lively addition to the neighbourhood. I am quite looking forward to meeting him, aren't you, Darcy?"

Mr Darcy seemed a bit less keen on the idea. But Jane remembered his preference for smaller groups.

"I thank you for loaning these books to Elizabeth. With such engrossing reading material, perhaps she will not attempt a foolish trip down the stairs."

"She would not dare, would she?" asked Mr Bingley, laughing.

"Oh yes, she is *that* impatient. I almost wish her room lacked windows. When the rain clears and the fair weather returns, I fear I shall need to restrain her."

The two gentlemen smiled at her, and although she would happily stay and enjoy the sight, she knew poor Lizzy must be bored silly by this point. "Well, sirs, I shall return to my sister and wish you a pleasant night."

૭ઢ

Elizabeth was ready to throw her needlework across the room. This insufferable confinement dragged on and on! But she heard a knock followed shortly by Jane sticking her head into the room. "I bring you some much-needed entertainment."

"Oh, bless you. You arrived before I did something drastic."

"I shudder to think what that might have been."

"What books did you wheedle out of Mr Bingley for me?"

"None, actually. Mr Bingley is not particularly proud of his library. These came from another source entirely, and I think you will be pleased with them"

"They do not seem to be fashion magazines, so they could not have come from Miss Bingley or Mrs Hurst."

"Lizzy, such accomplished ladies must be well read."

"Oh yes, I am sure they have started many, many books; I just doubt they have finished them. Well, let me see, will you? Or are you standing just out of reach to torture me?"

Jane handed over the books, wearing what Elizabeth would have called a smug look if it were anyone but Jane. "These should keep you occupied. Mr Darcy is your benefactor, and he chose perfectly for you."

The top book was *Lyrical Ballads*, a favourite of Elizabeth's. Next came a beautiful edition of Shakespeare's *Sonnets* and then *Much Ado About Nothing*. Elizabeth had to smile at the matchmaking and eavesdropping the play contained. This was hardly a subtle choice on Mr Darcy's part. Finally, there was a well-worn copy of *Robinson Crusoe*; the classic was an old friend to her.

"He has done remarkably well. These certainly offer more allure than my needlework. Please thank Mr Darcy for me when you see him next."

Jane got a strange gleam in her eye. "Perhaps you can thank him yourself the next time he sweeps you up into his incomparable arms. You blush beautifully when he does that."

Elizabeth narrowed her eyes. This would not do at all. The memory of Mr Darcy carrying her discomposed her entirely, but she could not let Jane see that. "Are you quite certain you wish to engage in teasing with me? Look before you leap, dear sister."

"As I see it, you will tease me mercilessly regardless, so I might as well have a bit of revenge."

Elizabeth tried her best to look contrite. "You are right; I showed no mercy. But it was the only amusement I had, Jane. I promise to keep my teasing at normal levels from now on."

Jane regarded her sceptically. "We shall see. For now, I wish to tell you about the conversation at dinner."

The particular news Jane dwelt upon was Mr Hurst's revelation that Mr Darcy had been drunk the previous night. Elizabeth remembered something from their first secret meeting—Mr Darcy had talked of a "difficult situation" that occurred over the summer. And Mr Hurst revealed that the only other time he had seen Mr Darcy overindulge to such an extent was this past summer. What could have happened to him then, and why would he imbibe to excess again now? It was indeed a great mystery. But Elizabeth knew he would never share his personal affairs with her. Despite his many efforts on her behalf, her all-too-public troubles were merely a convenient distraction from his private troubles.

Of course Jane knew none of this, and Elizabeth was not eager to disclose her strange alliance with Mr Darcy, even if that alliance might now be at an end. Jane would have endless questions, some reproofs, and possibly even a few teasing comments to make if she knew. No, Elizabeth's confession would wait for another time.

The borrowed books only curtailed her restlessness until the following afternoon, when she looked longingly towards the window. There would not be many more afternoons like this before winter set in. The sunlight was clear and bright; the few clouds she could see passing by were fluffy and perfectly white. She simply must be out of doors. Surely she could limp to a bench near the house and sit happily with a book.

The staircase presented the biggest obstacle. Perhaps she could coax Becky to help her. The young chambermaid—the daughter of Longbourn's long-time groomsman, Thomas—was happy to be serving the Bennet sisters after enduring Miss Bingley and Mrs Hurst. Jane and Elizabeth were equally relieved to see a familiar face.

Yes, Becky was Elizabeth's best way to sunshine. She would be at her most persuasive when the girl came to retrieve her luncheon tray. In the meantime, Elizabeth examined the four volumes before her, trying to decide which one to bring when she made her escape.

"Shall I take your tray, miss?" Becky had finally arrived.

"Becky, how lovely to see you. I hope you might assist me down the stairs. I wish to sit outside and read."

"Oh no, miss. You aren't to walk." Becky glanced towards Elizabeth's ankle.

Elizabeth stood and walked with a limp. "Just look at that blue sky. I only need your assistance to get down the stairs. The rest I can do myself with little trouble, as you can see." She gave a dazzling smile.

Becky began to sway. "Miss Jane will be angry with me."

"Jane is never angry at anyone! You know that. Come now, it is *my* ankle."

"Well, let's see how you do in the hallway before we attempt the stairs."

Elizabeth beamed at her and grabbed one of the books off the bed. "You are a sensible girl, Becky. If you will carry this book for me, I shall put on my pelisse, and off we shall go."

The hallway presented no problem. Elizabeth's ankle was sore but steady, and it actually felt good to walk. She positioned herself at the top of the stairs with her right hand on the railing. She hopped down the first step, then the next, then the next. Becky kept even with her on her left side, one arm outstretched in case Elizabeth needed it. As well as this was going, Elizabeth's right arm and leg soon began to tire, and she really could not put more weight on the left ankle. She silently cursed the generous proportions of Netherfield's public rooms. The high ceilings certainly impressed, but the resulting staircase made a formidable foe.

About a third of the way down, Elizabeth knew she must change tactics. "Becky, I think I need a bit more support now. May I put my arm around you?"

"Of course, miss."

Elizabeth proceeded with the support of the railing and Becky. The thought occurred that she would have to climb back up these stairs eventually, but she put it from her mind. More than halfway down, Elizabeth's right leg faltered with fatigue.

"I just need a short rest." She moved to sit on the step.

"Oh miss, I knew this was a bad idea. Now here you sit, on the floor!"

Elizabeth laughed. "It is rather undignified. Let us hope no one else sees my embarrassing predicament."

She heard a distinctly male throat clearing. Mr Darcy stood at the bottom of the stairs, a smirk adorning his face. Before Elizabeth could react to this mortifying turn of events, she also noticed a very irked Jane standing next to the gentleman, hands on her hips.

"Elizabeth June Bennet, what on earth do you think you are doing?" she scolded, fierce in her protective anger. "I should have known you had some devious plan when you ordered me to go to luncheon. And now all my suspicions are confirmed. How could you drag poor Becky into your foolish schemes?"

"Jane, do not be angry. Becky and I were simply trying to commit every detail of this fine staircase to memory before Mr Bingley makes changes to it." Elizabeth knew the surest way to deflate Jane's anger was to make her laugh. Mr Darcy seemed on the verge of laughter for a moment, but Jane was not quite ready to accede. "Come, Jane,"—she patted the step next to her—"you can observe the grandeur quite well from this position."

Jane's mouth twitched before she let out an unladylike sigh of frustration. "Why did you not ask for assistance? If you really must go outside, we could have gotten a servant to carry you. You are stubborn as a mule! No, you are as stubborn as *Lydia!*"

Elizabeth gasped. "What a horrid thing to say!"

Jane sat on the step next to Elizabeth, shaking her head. "The staircase does show itself to uncommon advantage from here." The two sisters started giggling like fools while Becky shifted nervously beside them.

Mr Darcy looked on in bemusement. "If you have discovered some grand aspect of Netherfield, perhaps I should call Mr and Miss

Bingley to join you on that step. In fact, if Becky will fetch some biscuits, we might even persuade Mr Hurst to join the party."

Becky laughed, but then slapped a hand over her mouth. At this opportune moment, Mr Bingley joined Mr Darcy at the bottom of the stairs, his face full of confusion. Jane's mirth ended quickly as she hurried to stand off to the side. Elizabeth could hardly control herself —at least laughter delayed the full realisation of her humiliation.

"Dare I ask what all this could possibly mean?" Mr Bingley said.

"The Miss Bennets were just admiring your staircase."

This explanation only further confused Mr Bingley, and then he remembered something. "Oh, Darcy, I have been meaning to ask you: why did you tell Mr Collins I plan to renovate the staircase? I had not even considered it. Do you think it needs renovations?"

"I thought you had mentioned not liking the banister. But no, I think this stairway is perfect as is."

Elizabeth gaped at Mr Darcy. Disguise of every sort is his abhorrence indeed! "It is a little too steep for my tastes," she said, causing Mr Darcy to finally give way to laughter.

Mr Bingley shrugged off his bewilderment. "It is good to see you, Miss Elizabeth. Did you have any plans for beyond the eleventh step?"

"It is good to be seen, though perhaps not under these circumstances. My intended destination was a garden bench as near to the house as possible." She turned to Becky and reached up for the book. "Thank you for your assistance. I am sorry to have taken you away from your duties for so long."

Becky, looking relieved to escape the strange situation, curtseyed and hurried up the stairs.

Mr Darcy began climbing the steps. "I know just the bench for you, Miss Elizabeth. Please allow me to take you there."

"Oh no! Call a servant as Jane said." Elizabeth looked frantically towards Jane, who only reacted with an uncharacteristic smirk. Perhaps Elizabeth *had* taken her teasing a trifle too far. Even Jane had her limits.

As all this crossed Elizabeth's mind, Mr Darcy arrived at that cursed eleventh step and bent to easily lift her up. "Why bother a servant when I am already here and perfectly capable?"

If being caught sitting on the stairs was embarrassing, being carried by Mr Darcy through the halls and rooms of Netherfield for the third time was absolutely mortifying. Elizabeth blushed of course, and she caught Jane's amused expression over Mr Darcy's impressive shoulder. She stared down at the book she still clutched in her hand.

"Which of my books did you think appropriate reading material for your afternoon in the fresh air?" Elizabeth snapped her gaze up to Mr Darcy. This was even more awkward if he insisted on conversing with her—as if she needed to be reminded of their unnerving proximity or his fluid strength. Or the gold flecks in his eyes. Or the pleasing angle of his jaw. *Stop that!*

"I...I thank you for the loan of your books. They are all excellent choices, but here I have *Robinson Crusoe*, an old favourite."

He said nothing in reply to her great relief. After what seemed an eternity, Elizabeth found herself deposited on a bench in a lovely spot in the garden. As she recovered from her embarrassment, Mr Darcy spoke with Jane. Elizabeth realised with dread they were likely arranging for him to transport her back up to her room. Oh dear, this escape plan had been flawed indeed. But she decided to put it out of her mind and enjoy the crisp air and bright sunlight while she could.

11
Correspondent's Confession

Fitzwilliam Darcy had never been jealous of anyone in his life. Yet now he was intensely jealous of a man he did not know. Why had he loaned Miss Elizabeth that blasted book? It had seemed a harmless enough choice at the time—but no, of course it would be associated with *him*. And worse yet, why did she have to prefer it to the other books he had loaned her? Jealousy was just a dreadful feeling. It was also completely ridiculous, considering Darcy had no intention of any future with Miss Elizabeth Bennet. Why should her old friend not return home and claim her? The two obviously had much affection for each other. But just thinking about the possibility sent Darcy into either blind rage or profound misery. Or both. He found it difficult to endure company in such a state, so he determined *not* to think about said possibility.

Another dangerous topic for reflection for entirely different reasons was how perfect she felt in his arms. Darcy could not meditate on that very great pleasure while in company either, lest his imaginings make him unfit to be seen. A safer focus for reverie was her laughter and her smile. In those he found pure delight. And what joy he had experienced this afternoon—at the staircase of all places.

Darcy sighed. He was not making much progress in his letter. Anne would laugh at him when she read it. But at least she could understand falling in love with someone unsuitable. Yes, that much she could certainly understand.

"What do you do there so secretly, Mr Darcy?"

Darcy looked up to behold four female faces plus Bingley awaiting his answer. He really should have chosen someplace more private to write this letter, but he found that he preferred to stay in the sitting room, where a certain young lady had hobbled after spending more than an hour on a garden bench. "It is no secret; I am writing a letter to my cousin."

"Oh, the viscount or Colonel Fitzwilliam?" Miss Bingley let the Bennet ladies know the extent of her knowledge about Darcy's family.

"Neither. The recipient of this letter will be Miss de Bourgh." Darcy enjoyed the brief pinched expression that crossed Miss Bingley's face. The Miss Bennets merely looked respectfully curious.

Mrs Hurst replied on behalf of her sister. "What comfort correspondence must provide her, confined as she with her poor health."

"I am happy to report my cousin's health has improved over the last year." Darcy suspected this improvement was due to Anne finally seeing a competent physician. Lady Catherine held some rather old-fashioned opinions on health and diet, and thus, had previously chosen a physician who would agree with everything she said. Naturally, such a physician had been no help to Anne.

Miss Bingley reacted to Darcy's disclosure. "That is excellent news. How wonderful for your family. Tell me, will Miss de Bourgh finally be out in London society? She has such limited experience among the *ton*. I fear she might be overwhelmed. Louisa and I would be happy to ease her way."

In truth, Anne had no desire to mix in London society even though she might now be able to do so. But Miss Bingley probably could not grasp such an idea. "A generous offer, but Lady Matlock and Lady Leland will take on that task, if necessary. They have connexions and influence enough to provide anyone a thorough introduction to society. You have never met Lady Matlock or her daughter-in-law, have you?" Darcy knew perfectly well that she had not, despite her best efforts. But his patience where Miss Bingley was concerned had been stretched rather thin lately. If she teased him again about a certain pair of fine eyes, Darcy could not vouch for his behaviour.

"I have not yet had that pleasure. Perhaps when we all return to London, I shall have the chance."

"Perhaps." He readied his pen again, hoping to curtail the conversation.

Mrs Hurst surmised that Darcy was quite finished with the subject, so she raised a new one. "Tell us, Miss Bennet, will your family have the opportunity to travel to London soon?"

"We have no such plans in the immediate future."

"What a pity. London during Christmastime is not to be missed. The festivities, the culture! Have your relations in London never invited you to partake?"

Miss Elizabeth, who had been observing up until now, answered. "Christmas in London must be festive indeed, but our young cousins delight in spending Christmas in the country with us."

"Christmas with young children is the best sort of Christmas," Bingley said. He turned towards Miss Bennet. "How old are your cousins?"

"Thomas is twelve, Michael is ten, Emily is nine, and little Cecilia is six."

"Good heavens! Wherever do you all sleep when they come to visit? You must be very crowded." Mrs Hurst seemed genuinely perplexed by the sleeping arrangements, though she could have expressed herself more tactfully.

"The boys have Jane's room and we girls have a merry time splitting up the remaining three rooms among us. We switch the arrangements around every few nights for a little excitement." Miss Elizabeth had such adorable mischief in her expression. Darcy could picture her, clad in her nightclothes, giggling and playing with a small girl. A sweeter vision he had never had. He sighed again, perhaps a little too loudly, for all eyes suddenly turned to him.

"We seem to be keeping you from your letter, Darcy. Just say the word, and we shall endeavour to be silent. Though, really, you can always go wherever Hurst goes to write his many letters."

"Not at all. I was enjoying the discussion, I assure you."

Bingley looked at him strangely. "All this talk of Christmas and children must remind you of Georgiana."

"Yes, it does, in a way. Though Georgiana cannot remain a child, much as I might wish her to." Darcy heard the wistfulness in his own voice. He had not meant to sound so morose. Miss Elizabeth caught him in the compassion of her gaze, and he could hardly tear himself away when Miss Bingley spoke to him.

"Perhaps *you* wish her to remain a child, but I am sure dear Georgiana cannot wait to be out in society, going to balls and dinner parties. What young lady would not wish for that?"

For all her assertions that she and Georgiana were "dear friends," Miss Bingley knew nothing of his sister. Georgiana had been dreading coming out even before last summer's disaster. Now she was positively terrified.

"Lizzy was very reluctant to come out, I remember," offered Miss Bennet. "What was it you said, Lizzy? Why should you talk to other gentlemen when none of them could say anything half as witty as Papa nor half as outrageous as John Lucas?" Darcy tried not to flinch.

Miss Elizabeth laughed. "Yes, I wished to remain a rambunctious girl. Then Papa told me that if I came out, he would finally have someone sensible to talk to in company. Flattery was the surest way to convince me. So out I went."

"And Charlotte and I were glad to have you with us. You must admit that you enjoyed it the very first night. And you absolutely adored dancing. You still do!"

"Yes, I suppose I am not quite as unique as I fancied myself." She stood up tentatively. "Now I think I should start my long journey upstairs and rest a bit before I make the return trip for dinner. Mr Darcy will have one less person to distract him from his letter. Excuse me." She curtseyed with surprising grace and limped towards the door.

"Wait, Lizzy, I shall help you." Miss Bennet took her sister's arm, and they walked on together. Before they left the room, Miss Bennet threw a glance back in Darcy's direction. She need not have bothered; he would have acted regardless.

He waited a moment or two and then began gathering his papers. "I believe I shall retire to my rooms to finish this letter. Excuse me."

Darcy strode into the hallway to find the Miss Bennets nearing the stairs. Miss Elizabeth appeared as if she would stubbornly climb them herself.

"Might I offer some assistance, Miss Elizabeth?"

She stiffened and shot her sister an accusatory glare. "I suppose this already was arranged between you. Why should you ask me?"

"Lizzy, please be a little more gracious. You know you cannot climb these steps in your condition."

Miss Elizabeth looked as if she might argue the point, but then she sighed. "I am sorry. This is very frustrating. I thank you for your trouble, Mr Darcy, particularly for keeping these uh, measures as... covert as possible."

"It is no trouble. And the others need not know the extent of your incapacitation." Both young ladies smiled at him, one appreciative and one reluctant. "Miss Bennet, if I may ask you to hold these papers for me..."

"Yes, of course."

Darcy positioned himself and Miss Elizabeth waited with an air of resignation. And then he was carrying her light and pleasing figure up the stairs. He paced himself to prolong the experience.

Miss Bennet began a polite conversation. "Mr Hurst seems to write very many letters. Are they all business matters?"

"No. Believe it or not, he and his mother exchange letters every few days." Darcy had never quite grasped how a man like Hurst could have such a close relationship with his mother.

Miss Elizabeth giggled. When Darcy caught her eye, she blushed crimson. "Pardon me."

"You simply must share whatever thought amused you."

"Well...I was wondering what he could write about so often."

"And did any ideas occur to you?"

"Yes. I think Mr Hurst must send his mother a complete account of every meal served to him, course by course."

Darcy could not help the laughter that escaped him, and Miss Bennet joined in. All too soon, he was in Miss Elizabeth's room, and he had to release her.

He turned to Miss Bennet. "Shall I come half an hour before dinner?"

"Yes, thank you so much, Mr Darcy." She returned his letters to him.

Miss Elizabeth let out a sound of exasperation. "I am right here, and I can hear you, you know."

"I know very well, Lizzy. I also know that you wish to eat dinner in company tonight. You will have to endure my interference, for I shall not let you attempt those stairs by yourself." Miss Bennet could be stern with the proper motivation—that of an obstinate, sulking sister.

Darcy bowed to them with a smirk. Back in his own room, he read over what he had already written to Anne and began writing again.

I cannot imagine how you endure seeing your C. so often. It has been only two days since I realised the depth of my feelings for L. and I can hardly control myself. I am delighted with every new revelation about her, enthralled by her every expression. What sorrow yet what relief I shall feel when I leave this place, and her, behind. Then perhaps it will be easier to recall why she is unsuitable.

A knock on the door interrupted Darcy. "Enter."

Bingley came in and shut the door behind him. He appeared decidedly uneasy. "Darcy, I...well, I wanted to make you an offer."

Darcy raised his eyebrows in unspoken inquiry.

"You seem...I am not sure how to describe it, but...I offer myself as a good listener. Heaven knows you have listened to me drone on about my problems and have given me much good advice. I know you are not comfortable exposing your feelings to others, and I do not wish to pry but... You seemed to overcome whatever difficulties worried you this summer, but now you are even less...yourself." Bingley held his palms up, signalling his inability to express himself any better.

Darcy paused to collect his thoughts. "I thank you, Bingley. I cannot...that is, talking about what troubles me would not be best. But I appreciate your concern. Is my melancholy so obvious?"

"Is it melancholy? Sometimes you seem quite gleeful but then an air of despair follows, and then, of course, your typical indifference covers all." Bingley was more perceptive than Darcy had assumed.

"Do not worry yourself. It is perhaps not obvious to those who do not know you as I do."

"Good, good. I do not wish to lay my troubles open for all to see." Darcy knew not what else to say.

Bingley studied him for a long moment. "Forgive me, I must ask this. You are not... That is to say, you do not...admire Miss Bennet, do you?"

"Miss Jane Bennet?" Darcy could not keep the surprise from his voice. "I think her an admirable young lady, of course. But I do not, you know, *admire* her." This conversation was very uncomfortable.

Bingley's relief was palpable. "Right, right. Well, I have kept you from your letter again. My offer stands, if you should reconsider." He already had the door open, seeming eager to remove himself from all this awkward hesitance. Then he was gone, and Darcy was left alone. He was already looking forward to dinner and the trip downstairs in particular.

High Animal Spirits

"Hurry up! Your precious Fordyce extract will wait." Lydia had been waiting to go to Netherfield for two days, and she would not wait another minute. "If you dare say something about patience being a virtue, Mary, I shall scream."

Kitty snickered. "You are very nearly screaming already."

Mary hid a grin, which only angered Lydia more. "You are delaying us on purpose! How can you do that to poor Mr Collins? You know he has many calls to make before he leaves tomorrow." Lydia could not care less about Mr Collins. In fact, after two days with him at Longbourn without the protective presence of Jane and Lizzy, she was ready to haul his trunk out to the carriage herself.

"Lydia, I can stop my work any time, but Mama was not yet ready to leave."

"She is ready now, so put your pen down this instant."

The tumult of four pelisses and four bonnets being donned soon followed. Mr Bennet came into the entryway. "Must you take all the girls with you? You do not want to overtax Mr Bingley's hospitality."

"Mr Bennet, I shall not be moved on this. You have insisted we not visit Jane and Lizzy for two days, and so we have not. But now Mr Collins must take his leave of the Bingleys and the Philipses. You would not deprive my sister of a visit from her nieces, would you?"

"Very well, but heed this, Mrs Bennet: under no circumstances are you to cajole or accept an invitation for any of our other daughters to stay at Netherfield."

"Yes, yes. I shall do as you say, but it is really quite vexing. You have no consideration for my nerves!"

"Papa, *please* let us go now." Lydia feared her mother's pouting would soon lead to a full-blown attack of "nerves." Then she would never get to Netherfield!

"Off you all go then. I shall not be accused of depriving Hertford-shire of Mr Collins's proper farewells. Give my regards to Jane and Lizzy."

Mr Collins droned on and on during the carriage ride. Thank-fully, just as he paused for breath, Kitty turned to Lydia and asked loudly, "I wonder what news Aunt Philips will have of the officers today. It has been too long since we've seen Denny and Saunderson, has it not?"

"I suppose. They are great fun." Lydia had an entirely different gentleman on her mind.

Kitty nodded. "*Much* more fun than dull old Mr Darcy. I do not see how you endured an entire day with him. At least Mr Bingley—"

"He is not dull! He is distinguished!" Lydia glared at Kitty. "*You* would not understand."

"I must agree with Cousin Lydia on this matter. Mr Darcy is a gentleman of great eminence. Lady Catherine has told me much about her illustrious nephew, his estate in Derbyshire, and his house in town. For example..."

Kitty whispered, "Now you have got him started again, you ninny."

Lydia wished Mr Collins would give even more details. For the first time since making his acquaintance, Lydia found herself in complete concurrence of opinion with her cousin. Mary listened to all that was said with her usual air of detachment, while Kitty began humming quietly. They soon arrived at Netherfield. Lydia would not have to settle for second-hand information anymore; she could see the man himself! She nearly leapt from the carriage. It was a pity it had begun to rain lightly; she would not be able to walk with Mr Darcy through the gardens now.

The footman went to announce them. After a few moments, Miss Bingley and Mrs Hurst came from the back of the house, followed by Lizzy, who was limping and leaning on Jane's arm. Lydia felt a pang of guilt at the sight of her. But then she remembered Lizzy had been rewarded with a stay at Netherfield, making her pursuit of Mr Bingley that much easier.

Miss Bingley greeted them in a manner that seemed outwardly friendly but still made Lydia want to pinch her. "How wonderful for Miss Eliza to see *all* her sisters. And Mr Collins too! Please do come into the drawing room. It is more spacious than the sitting room."

Soon everyone was settled in the drawing room.

"Miss Bingley," began Mrs Bennet, "the purpose of our visit today is twofold. First, we wished to check on our dear Lizzy. And second, Mr Collins wishes to bid farewell to your party, as he will be leaving us tomorrow."

"Indeed, Miss Bingley and Mrs Hurst, let me express my great delight in making your acquaintance. Your company throughout my stay has been a great joy, and your hospitality, particularly towards dear Cousin Elizabeth at the time of her injury, has been most generous."

Miss Bingley and Mrs Hurst replied in kind, though again, Lydia detected that vague sense of superiority from them.

"Mr Collins hoped to take his leave of Mr Bingley, Mr Hurst, and Mr Darcy, as well," said Mrs Bennet. "Are they out today?"

Miss Bingley looked towards the window. "They went shooting after luncheon, but I suspect they will return soon due to the rain." Lydia hoped very much for that to be true. This visit would be pointless if she did not see Mr Darcy.

Miss Bingley continued, "Poor Mr Darcy. I had hoped he could at least find some amusement in sport. Not much else here in Hertfordshire interests him, you know."

Mrs Hurst turned towards Mr Collins to explain. "He is here to help my brother with estate matters."

Miss Bingley chimed in again, "Oh yes, how very generous he is, giving up London's superior society to lend his expertise to Charles."

Mr Collins nodded in vigorous agreement. "I suspect Mr Darcy is much like his aunt in this respect. I shall tell Lady Catherine in what great esteem her nephew is held by his friends."

"Indeed, Mr Darcy is our family's *most* valued friend. I hope Charles learns quickly as I am sure Mr Darcy longs to return to the people and places he prefers."

Lydia could not let this go on. "He enjoyed the picnic well enough, *and* our walk the other day. The entire outing was *his* idea."

Miss Bingley smiled. "One must find amusement where one can." Oh, what Lydia would not give for just one good pinch!

As Lydia contemplated how to respond, Lizzy joined the discussion. "I suppose one must. My sisters and I are pleased Mr Darcy chose to spend his leisure time with *us* for the day."

Well done, Lizzy! Lydia must ask her how to do that—how to say something civil, but in such a way that the meaning was actually sharp and insulting. She could see how such a skill would be useful in dealing with the likes of Miss Bingley. Lizzy was the only one who could instruct her—Jane was too good, Mary too pious, and Mrs Bennet too awed by finery and elegant manners. Kitty lacked any insight at all into the hidden significance of conversations. If you wanted Kitty to catch your meaning, you had to tell her directly.

Lydia's thoughts had distracted her from following the conversation, but it now centred on Lizzy's recovery and how she and Jane had spent their days at Netherfield. Lydia scarcely believed that Lizzy had eaten only one meal, last night's dinner, with the Netherfield party. How could she waste such a wonderful opportunity to catch Mr Bingley? If Lydia had stayed at Netherfield, her quarry would not have escaped so easily.

Footsteps in the hallway indicated that the quarry had returned. *Bless the rain!*

Mr Bingley burst into the room. "How delightful to see you all! Please excuse my dishevelled appearance, but I wished to greet you immediately. Darcy and Hurst will be along after they've righted themselves a bit."

A round of polite conversation followed. It was an absolute bore to Lydia. Finally, Mr Hurst and Mr Darcy entered, the latter looking the perfect gentleman, despite being caught in the rain. Yet more civil greetings were exchanged, and the two gentlemen seated themselves.

Mr Hurst surprised Lydia by speaking. "Mrs Bennet, your daughter must be greatly comforted by a visit from her mother. I take it you have inspected Miss Elizabeth's progress?"

"Indeed I have, sir," was her answer. "She is yet too injured to be removed. We must trespass a little longer on Mr Bingley's kindness."

"Removed!" cried Mr Bingley. "It must not be thought of. My sister and I shall not hear of her removal."

Mrs Bennet was profuse in her acknowledgments before adding, "You have a sweet room here, Mr Bingley, and a charming prospect over that gravel walk. I do not know a place in the country that is equal to Netherfield. You will not think of quitting it in a hurry, I hope, even though you have but a short lease."

"Whatever I do is done in a hurry," replied he, "and therefore, if I should resolve to quit Netherfield, I should probably be off in five minutes. At present, however, I consider myself as quite fixed here."

"That is exactly what I should have supposed of you," said Elizabeth.

"You begin to comprehend me, do you?" cried Mr Bingley, turning towards her.

"Oh yes, I understand you perfectly." Perhaps Lizzy *was* flirting a bit—though surely not enough in Lydia's opinion.

"I wish I might take this for a compliment, but to be so easily seen through, I am afraid, is pitiful."

"That is as it happens. It does not necessarily follow that a deep, intricate character is more or less estimable than such a one as yours."

"I did not know that you were a studier of character, Miss Elizabeth. It must be an amusing study."

"Yes, but intricate characters are the *most* amusing. They have at least that advantage."

"The country," said Mr Darcy, "can, in general, supply but few subjects for such a study. In a country neighbourhood, you move in a very confined and unvarying society." Lydia could not abide Miss Bingley's barely concealed sneer.

"But people themselves alter so much that there is something new to be observed in them forever," replied Elizabeth.

"Oh yes!" cried Lydia, wanting to have a part in the rapid conversation. "We are constantly surprised by people we have known for our entire lives. Why, who could have thought that Jacob Goulding would run off with the governess?"

Lydia thought too late that perhaps it was not yet proper to speak of the incident.

Kitty, at least, saw no impropriety in the subject, which did not reassure Lydia. "La! I'd almost forgotten about jowly Jacob Goulding! But surely the militia coming is the most exciting event to happen in Meryton since then." Kitty looked at Mr Bingley. "Well, and your party's arrival, I suppose," she added.

"Yes, we have had excellent company this autumn! And my girls are so popular with the officers, much as I once was." Lord, Lydia hoped Mrs Bennet would not tell one of *those* stories.

"Mama, has Charlotte Lucas been to Longbourn since Jane and I came away?" asked Elizabeth suddenly.

"Yes, she called yesterday with her father. The Lucases are very good sort of girls. It is a pity they are not handsome! Not that I think Charlotte so very plain—but then she is our particular friend."

"I find Miss Lucas to be a very pleasant young woman," said Mr Collins. Lydia remembered how grateful she was to Charlotte for occupying Mr Collins for nearly an hour yesterday.

"Oh! Yes, but you must own she is very plain. Lady Lucas herself has often said so and envied me Jane's beauty." Mrs Bennet looked around the room before adding quickly, "and Lizzy's wit and Lydia's vivacity. I do not like to boast of my own children. It is what everybody says."

"In this case, I must agree with the commonly accepted estimation of my fair cousins. It is not often that I find such rumours to be not only confirmed but exceeded entirely." Mr Collins grinned at Jane and Lizzy during this speech but spared a look at each Bennet girl. Lydia wanted no part in such simpering compliments from the prattling parson. *Poor Jane!*

"Mr Bingley," Lydia said, hoping to change the subject, "when you first came into Hertfordshire, you promised to hold a ball here at Netherfield. It would be the most shameful thing in the world if you did not keep your promise."

He smiled. "I am perfectly ready, I assure you, to keep my engagement, and when your sister is recovered, you will, if you please, name the very day of the ball. But you would not wish to be dancing while she cannot."

"Yes, it would be much better to wait till Lizzy is well, for she does enjoy dancing." Lydia would feel very guilty indeed if Lizzy missed a ball because of her ankle.

With one of her goals for this visit accomplished, namely pressing Mr Bingley to give a ball, Lydia decided to concentrate on her second goal. It would be a challenge with Mr Darcy being so taciturn, but Lydia felt she was equal to it.

§

The Reverend William Collins had much to consider. Choosing the companion of his future life had proved more difficult than he had anticipated. When he arrived at Netherfield to say goodbye, he was determined not to show any sign of particular admiration to Cousin Jane, nothing that could further elevate her with the hope of influencing his felicity. Surely, though such an idea had been suggested previously, his behaviour during the last day must have material weight in confirming or crushing it.

He thanked heaven he had been constantly interrupted before he could declare himself more formally and that he and Mr Darcy had shared the private conversation about the Grantlys. Today, Mr Collins would display just the right amount of attention to his eldest cousin.

He had neglected the conversation for too long with his ruminations. At that moment, his cousins were much excited by the prospect of a ball upon Cousin Elizabeth's full recovery.

"I shall do my very best to hasten the advent of the ball," said she, "and in so doing, delight Kitty and Lydia."

Mr Collins took this opportunity to show his affectionate concern for his second-eldest cousin. "I hope, as I am sure we all do, that the wait for that happy day will be very short indeed, but you must not risk prolonging your injury by overexerting yourself too soon, dear Cousin."

"Yes, Lizzy, you must not rush home," agreed Mrs Bennet. "Ankle injuries are not to be trifled with."

Miss Bingley was ever so gracious in her agreement. "We all anticipate Miss Eliza's full recovery so that she may return to the well-worn paths around Longbourn."

Miss Elizabeth smiled sweetly. "How can I help but heal with such sincere good wishes?"

Cousin Lydia sounded impatient. "I think it is obvious we *all* want Lizzy to heal so that she can go for her walks again, and dance at the ball."

Miss Elizabeth laughed. She was quite fetching when she did. "Thank you, Lydia, for so succinctly summarising a good five minutes' worth of conversation. Let us speak of my injury no more, please. It is hardly proper to give such undivided attention to my ankle."

Mr Collins did not know whether to disapprove of her impertinence or be charmed by it. Mr Darcy suddenly rose from his chair and stood by the window. So, disapproval must ultimately be the correct reaction, though most everyone else seemed to be charmed.

"Does it still rain, Mr Darcy?" Cousin Lydia asked.

He did not turn towards the room when he answered, "Yes, very lightly."

She seemed not to care one way or the other, for she was already on to a new topic. "Will you dance more at your friend's ball than you did at the assembly?"

"He could not dance any *less*," said Cousin Catherine.

"Oh, he most certainly could," warned Miss Elizabeth. "He could turn *his* ankle."

Mr Bingley laughed. "Now we must spend a good five minutes discussing Darcy's ankles. Excellent!"

Mr Collins resented that the nephew of Lady Catherine should be teased in such a disrespectful manner. "Mr Darcy, if you have any letters for Lady Catherine or Miss de Bourgh, I would happily convey them to Kent."

He still faced the window. "I thank you, Mr Collins, but at present I have no letters to send to Rosings."

"Darcy labours over his letters for days and days. He studies too much for words of four syllables. Do you not, Darcy?"

Mr Collins decided to intervene again. "A man of undoubtedly profound thoughts does himself credit when he expresses them as clearly and eloquently as possible. I spend many hours composing and refining my sermons."

"Mustn't you deliver a sermon in just two days' time?" asked Miss Elizabeth.

"Indeed, I must."

"And has its quality not suffered due to your stay with us? We must not keep you from your important work any longer."

"I thank you for your affectionate concern, dear lady. Although my cousins offered manifold distractions over the course of my visit, Mr Bennet will attest that I did not escape my duties entirely while in Hertfordshire. I toiled in Longbourn's library. I even shared parts of tomorrow's sermon with Cousin Mary and Miss Lucas and found their insights most enlightening."

"Charlotte always offers the most practical advice. And Mary's knowledge of religious texts is unsurpassed. I daresay you could not have consulted any two better ladies in Hertfordshire."

"I shall not disagree with you, Cousin Elizabeth. Would that I always had such a resource to rely on when in need of inspiration. Of course Lady Catherine often offers her insightful recommendations." Mr Collins congratulated himself for seizing every opportunity to compliment his patroness in front of her nephew.

"Mama, mustn't we leave now to visit Aunt Philips?" asked Cousin Catherine.

Mrs Bennet agreed with regret. "Unfortunately, we must take our leave of you all. We plan to make several calls in the course of the afternoon so Mr Collins can bid farewell to all his friends."

The carriage was called, and Mr Collins used the resulting commotion to bid farewell in turn to Mr Bingley, Miss Bingley, Mrs Hurst, Mr Hurst, and finally, Mr Darcy.

The gentleman replied with much solemnity. "Mr Collins, when my aunt expressed the sort of man she required to fill the position of parson at Hunsford, I doubted she should ever find him. But now, after having made your acquaintance, all my scepticism is overthrown."

"I thank you for your fulsome estimation of my qualities. It is my solemn vow to continue serving your esteemed aunt to the very best of my abilities."

"I am glad to hear it. Lady Catherine is perhaps a demanding patroness, but you can be assured of the rectitude of her opinions." He bowed to Mr Collins. "Please give my regards to my aunt. I know your eloquence will do them justice." Mr Collins bowed low in response, avowing to express Mr Darcy's regards admirably, but when he rose from his bow, the gentleman had already retreated back to the window.

Mr Collins approached his two eldest cousins, who were engaged in animated conversation with their sisters. He cleared his throat, and the many voices in the room quieted.

"And now my dear cousins, I cannot express how much I have enjoyed our time together over these last weeks. I thank you both for your many kindnesses and your many attentions during the course of my visit. It is an honour and a delight, not only to know you both, but to claim a family connexion to you. I consider myself most privileged indeed."

Mr Collins was struck again by the classic beauty of Miss Bennet, who rose and replied first. "Mr Collins, you are too kind. You are to be commended for taking the initiative to end the estrangement between our families. We wish you a very pleasant journey home." She reached her hand out to him, and he took the liberty of kissing the back of her fingers as he thanked her for her sentiments.

He turned to Miss Elizabeth, who was, by necessity, still seated. "Dear Cousin Elizabeth, I am particularly grieved to be leaving you in such a state, when I know you to be so active a young lady. But, alas, my duties call me away."

"Believe me, Mr Collins, we all appreciate that your duties call you away from us." Her generous smile distracted him from the sudden bout of coughing suffered by one of his younger cousins.

"You are gracious indeed. But I leave with comfort in my firm belief that the next time I see you, you will be restored to perfect health." He reached for her hand, which she offered, and he kissed it.

"I...thank you, Mr Collins. A safe journey to you, sir." She looked past him. "Mary, please give my regards to Charlotte. It seems like ages since I've seen her."

The visitors congregated at the door except for Cousin Lydia, who lingered near the window, behind Mr Darcy.

Miss Catherine exhaled audibly. "Come along, Lydia! I wish to have as much time as possible with Aunt Philips."

Miss Lydia trudged across the room. "Be quiet, Kitty!"

At the door, Mr Collins turned and bowed one last time to the assemblage in the drawing room. When he boarded the carriage, his two youngest cousins were arguing.

"I *told* you he was dull," Miss Catherine said.

Cousin Lydia defended Mr Darcy once again, this time with a pout. "How could anyone get a word in with all this talk of ankles and sermons?"

After a long visit with Mrs Philips to hear all the comings and goings of the militia's officers, the party boarded the carriage again to visit Lucas Lodge.

"Now, girls, we cannot make such a lengthy call at the Lucases' as we did at the Philipses'. We must not linger too near to dinner. Mr Collins, I caution you not to be drawn into a long conversation with Charlotte Lucas, as you often are."

"Have no fear. I shall only briefly thank Miss Lucas for her very pleasing company over the course of my visit."

And so he did. Miss Lucas returned the compliment courteously, as usual. Yes, Miss Lucas was indeed a very pleasant young lady. But for the watchful eye of Mrs Bennet, Mr Collins would have kissed her hand when they parted.

Back at Longbourn, Mr Collins looked about the room he had occupied for nearly three weeks to make sure he had not forgotten anything while packing. His trunk sat at the foot of the bed, ready to be hauled to the carriage. But first, he must speak with Mrs Bennet.

He found her in the sitting room with his youngest cousins, who excused themselves soon after he entered the room.

Mrs Bennet motioned for him to sit near her. "Mr Collins, your visit has flown by. We are very sorry to see you go."

"My dear Mrs Bennet, I am sorry to be leaving the bosom of my family after being so graciously welcomed back into it. Truly, madam, I am inexpressibly overjoyed by not only our reconciliation, but also by the kind reception given to me by you, your husband, and your lovely daughters. It is my greatest hope that this visit is only the propitious beginning to a deep and permanent bond between us." Mr Collins had rehearsed this speech earlier in his room, and he must admit, he delivered it splendidly.

Mrs Bennet seemed to agree. "If it were so, we would be most honoured, my dear Mr Collins. Pray, do not forget your new friends when you return to Kent. You simply must come visit us again. All my girls desire it—especially Jane."

Mr Collins decided not to address the issue of Miss Bennet at this time. He needed to come to some decisions before he could remark on any one of his fair cousins specifically. But he was gratified that the desired invitation was so easily procured. "It is my fondest wish to return to you all very soon if you will have me."

"Have you? Why of course we shall have you, Mr Collins!" cried Mrs Bennet. Then she placed her hand on his arm as she spoke in a low voice. "Let me assure you, you are always welcome—just as soon as you are able to return, please do so. If it pleases you, I shall write to you when Mr Bingley sets the date for his ball, that you may come and dance with my girls again."

"Oh, dear madam, you do me great honour. Indeed, if it is at all possible, I shall come to you again for Mr Bingley's ball."

She could barely contain her excitement. "Excellent! Now, let us not spoil the surprise for the girls by mentioning this to them. I would not want to get their hopes up if we do not succeed. I shall reveal our happy scheme just before you arrive. My girls will be astounded—what a good joke! It is just the sort of thing that Mr Bennet would do, but now *I* shall be the one with the surprise! Do remember, however, if you cannot come for the ball, you are very welcome another time, sir."

With their plans settled and the carriage ready, Mrs Bennet ordered that Mr Collins's trunk be loaded. Mr Bennet and the three girls gathered at the front door to bid him farewell. Mrs Bennet—with a wink to Mr Collins—said how happy they should be to see him at Longbourn again. He knew that the ruse must be performed now.

"My dear Madam," he replied, "this invitation is particularly gratifying because I unquestionably wish to continue our relationship now that I know the pleasure of intimacy with my Longbourn family. I most certainly shall be very grateful to accept your hospitality again in the near future."

"But is there not danger of Lady Catherine's disapprobation, my good sir?" asked Mr Bennet. "You had better neglect your relations than run the risk of offending your patroness."

"My dear sir," replied Mr Collins, "I am particularly obliged to you for this friendly caution, and you may depend upon my not taking so material a step without her ladyship's concurrence."

"You cannot be too much on your guard. Risk anything rather than her displeasure. If you find it likely to be raised by your coming to us again, stay quietly at home, and be satisfied that we shall take no offence."

"Believe me, my gratitude is warmly excited by such affectionate attention. As for my fair cousins, although my absence may not be long enough to render it necessary, I shall now take the liberty of wishing them health and happiness, not excepting Miss Elizabeth and Miss Bennet."

Mr Collins boarded the carriage then and was on his way back to Kent. The rocking of the carriage made him sleepy, and he settled himself in more comfortably. He had much to think about. He surmised he had perhaps three or four weeks in which to reach some decision, when he might return to Hertfordshire for the ball. He could not explicitly ask Lady Catherine for her advice because he was not to mention what Mr Darcy had divulged privately. But he could ask her which qualities were to be most valued in a parson's wife. He must compose his query carefully before he broached the subject with her. And he would do so, just after he took a bit of a nap.

13

Deduction and Denial

Charlotte Lucas simply had to speak to Elizabeth. They had barely had any private conversations over the last fortnight. Mr Collins's visit had kept them very busy. But this was precisely why she must speak with Lizzy. Charlotte was always most observant of people's tone, in how they spoke, and what their expressions revealed. The last two times she had seen Mr Collins, she observed some notable differences in his behaviour and manner of address.

Based on her observations and discussions with the parson, Charlotte believed something had occurred to drastically alter his intentions towards Jane Bennet. Yet Mrs Bennet still seemed unaware of any change in the parson's preferences, and Mr Collins did not appear offended, so clearly, Jane had not refused him. Charlotte expected a large, public debacle—it could hardly be avoided considering Mrs Bennet's disposition. She had been prepared to take advantage of said debacle by finally putting her own plans into effect. But Mr Collins had gone back to Kent without proposing to anyone. How had Lizzy done it?

Charlotte decided a trip to Netherfield was necessary to see Elizabeth and Jane. Her parents had the carriage for the day. Walking the two and a half miles would be no problem, but she could not go alone. Maria was off visiting Longbourn, eager to see her friends without Mr Collins's stifling presence. John was not expected for another few weeks. Only Walter and Peter, her rambunctious young brothers, remained. Charlotte would have to bribe them with the promise of some treats purchased in Meryton, not only to walk with her but also to behave while at Netherfield.

The three of them set off in high spirits. Walter and Peter ran ahead or lagged behind, depending on what silly game they were playing. Charlotte kept a moderate pace and carefully avoided the muddy areas. Her brothers, however, soon outstripped her. They waited for her in the last field, with the house in view. Peter's trousers were spattered in mud up to his knees, and Walter's were scarcely any better.

She exclaimed, "Did you purposely jump into all the puddles!?"

"No, but it was hard to avoid them," Walter said.

"*I* avoided the mud well enough. You cannot go into Netherfield looking like that!"

"*You* walk at a snail's pace. And we don't care to go in anyway. We will wait outside for you."

Charlotte threw up her hands. "Just make sure you stay within sight of the front door. I do not want to search for you when it is time to leave."

She reached the door soon after leaving her muddy brothers. The footman asked her to follow him to the sitting room, where he announced her. Charlotte did not see Jane or Lizzy—only the Bingley siblings were present.

Mr Bingley greeted her first. "Miss Lucas, what a delightful surprise!"

The usual niceties followed. Charlotte felt she should at least make some polite conversation with the mistress of the house before asking to see Elizabeth. Of course, with Mr Bingley's help, polite conversation was a very easy task. He mentioned Lizzy, and Charlotte had her opening.

"And now we come to the main reason for my walk to Netherfield today. Might I see the Miss Ben—"

"You walked here? Alone?" Mrs Hurst interrupted.

"Not alone. My brothers, Walter and Peter, came with me."

Mr Bingley was perplexed. "But where are they, Miss Lucas?"

She laughed. "They remained outside as they are not fit to be indoors. Upon my word, they must have walked through every muddy puddle on the way here. They prefer to be outdoors, in any case."

Miss Bingley tittered. "In that respect, they are much like our Miss Eliza. She insists on going out into the garden to read despite her ankle and the season."

"I can well believe it. Lizzy would wish to take advantage of every sunny afternoon before the chill sets in. Is she in the garden now?"

"Yes, with her sister. Allow me to escort you to your friends. You must be rewarded for your long walk." Mr Bingley seemed quite eager to go into the garden himself.

He offered his arm and led Charlotte out into the garden.

They turned a corner around a short hedge to find Jane and Elizabeth sharing a picturesque bench. Lizzy raised her eyes from her book at the sound of their approach.

"Charlotte!" She made as if to rise.

Jane placed a restraining hand on her sister's shoulder before rising herself to embrace Charlotte. "Dear Charlotte! I am very happy to see you, but I doubt my joy can compare to Lizzy's elation upon seeing you. She has been mentioning you constantly."

Charlotte laughed and walked towards Elizabeth's beckoning hands. "It does seem an eternity since we have spoken. So I did something of which I am sure Lizzy would approve: I walked here just to see her."

"That is the mark of a true friend!" Elizabeth pulled Charlotte down to sit next to her on the bench. "I am so grateful for your exertion. But did you come alone?"

"Through a bit of bribery, Walter and Peter served as escorts, though their clothing has suffered some mud for their efforts. Lord knows how they are occupying themselves now."

"They can at least come into the garden if they wish. Shall I find them?" offered Mr Bingley.

"You need not bother. They can find endless amusements with just rocks and sticks, it seems."

He laughed but persisted. "Perhaps Miss Bennet will join me on a walk as it seems she has lost her seat. If we come across the young Masters Lucas, I shall invite them into the garden."

Charlotte did not protest further, for she suspected her brothers were merely the excuse Mr Bingley used to invite Jane on a walk. The lady accepted the invitation, as well as the offered arm. Charlotte began to suspect that the true matchmaking genius in the Bennet family was Elizabeth.

The two friends were soon left alone. "I have so much to tell you!" they declared in chorus.

Laughing, Elizabeth urged Charlotte to begin. "I suspect my tale will be much longer."

"Very well. But first let me ask, how is your ankle? I heard accounts of your injury both from Lydia and Mr Collins."

"Oh, it is just a sprained ankle. Though the timing, as it turned out, has been rather fortuitous, considering my cousin's departure schedule. Pray, tell me your impressions of his behaviour over this last week."

"This is why I came to you today. How did you do it, Lizzy? I am almost certain Mr Collins has reconsidered his intentions towards Jane."

"What makes you say so? Please give me all your little insights. You have such an eye for reading people."

"Well, did you ever observe how Mr Collins often referred to Jane as either 'dear' or 'dearest Cousin Jane.'"

"I think he referred to all of us as 'dear cousin' at one time or another."

"I never heard him refer to Mary, Kitty, or Lydia as such. Only you and Jane share that honour, but Jane most often received the appellation. I remember this quite precisely. His use of 'dearest Cousin Jane' began, I believe, at the picnic, and he employed the term constantly on Sunday."

Elizabeth grimaced. "I can just hear his voice saying it. But I assume you raise this subject for a reason other than discomfiting me."

"Indeed, I do. When I saw him on Thursday, and yesterday as well, he did not once refer to Jane as either dear or dearest. But *dear* Cousin Elizabeth's injury was much talked of—he was beside himself with worry over your suffering." Charlotte added the last merely to get a reaction.

"Stop that!" Elizabeth grimaced again before continuing, "If I understand you correctly, as of Thursday, Mr Collins did not consider Jane his dearest cousin any longer."

"I cannot say what he thinks, only what he wishes to convey. You know he very carefully chooses his words, and sometimes I think he even has his comments composed in his head before he utters them."

"I did sometimes feel as if he had rehearsed his speeches!" Elizabeth nodded. "So you believe my cousin purposefully ceased referring to Jane as 'dearest' or, to a lesser extent, 'dear.'"

"Yes, that is my feeling."

"Yesterday, he did not distinguish Jane with any special attentions. He kissed my hand as well as hers." Elizabeth graced Charlotte with another scowling grimace before continuing. "What else of his behaviour tells you he has abandoned his hopes for Jane?"

"I think his carefully altered manner of address is the most important indication. But, in addition to this, as of Thursday, his conversations were less filled with glowing praises of Jane specifically. Instead, he praised the entire Bennet family or, sometimes, you or Mary. Previously, he often spoke of Jane as if he were already engaged to her, though he never said so directly. I cannot tell you how many times he mentioned that Lady Catherine would 'approve' of 'dear Cousin Jane.' This all changed as of Thursday."

"Oh, it does sound promising. If you are convinced, then I shall rely on your assessment," Elizabeth said with a satisfied smile. "But I must tell you, if Jane received a marriage proposal from Mr Collins *now*, she would refuse him. So much has happened since the picnic."

"Can you be referring to her obvious regard for Mr Bingley?"

"Yes, in part. I am gladdened to have you confirm my observations. It is evident to me that Jane is in a way to be very much in love. Lord, how she blushes! It is so unlike her. And I think he returns the sentiment."

"I agree. But you must tell me all that has happened. How did Mr Bingley come to know that the betrothal rumours were false?"

"I do not know. Now that I think of it, I believe his behaviour may have changed soon after the picnic. He and Mr Darcy..." Elizabeth trailed off, her brow furrowed. After a brief pause, she shook her head. "Mr Bingley and Mr Darcy visited Longbourn on Monday to inquire after Lydia's cricket injury."

"I doubt Mr Bingley would act on his preference for Jane while under the impression that she was already spoken for. Perhaps Jane herself discredited the rumour and encouraged Mr Bingley."

Elizabeth laughed. "You know she is far too demure to do such a thing."

"Lizzy, please answer my questions forthrightly! Then did Jane discourage Mr Collins somehow without giving offense?"

"No, I suspect that honour goes to—Mr Darcy!" Elizabeth announced the name with dramatic flair. "Mr Darcy!" Charlotte sputtered.

"Indeed! I believe he said something to Mr Collins on our walk with the express purpose of dissuading my cousin's suit. Whatever he said must have been successful."

"But how? Why?"

"I know his involvement in my family's private affairs strains credulity. Yet he is deeply involved. He and I are conspirators, and I have been unable to confide our plot to anyone else, even Jane. It will be such a relief to tell you everything and get your opinion."

"Please, relieve us both and reveal your tale, then. I can hardly wait to hear how this has all transpired!"

"It started at the picnic. I followed my father into the library."

Elizabeth told Charlotte everything—every detail she could remember about her intervention into Mr Collins's matrimonial plans. The words spilled forth from her in a torrent. Elizabeth needed this anchor in the real world. In revealing all to another person, the experiences Elizabeth had shared over the last se'nnight with Mr Darcy became both more real and less intimate. She ended her tale with Mr Bennet's restraint of his wife's manipulations and Jane's resolution to refuse any proposal from Mr Collins.

"I hardly know what to say, Elizabeth. This is most extraordinary!"

"Please share all your impressions with me. I am eager for another perspective."

Charlotte sat in silence for a few moments while Elizabeth waited for the dispassionate analysis she had come to expect from her friend. Charlotte would never judge her for what were, by any social standards, inappropriate and perilous actions—issuing angry ultimatums to her father, secret rendezvous with a gentleman in secluded woods, misleading her entire family.

"First, I am very pleased you reconciled with your father after such a heated quarrel. Second, I am happy Jane now knows her own mind and will not let other concerns influence her decisions regarding her future. Third, I agree that Mr Darcy must have said something to deter Mr Collins from Jane on that fateful walk. It would explain our observations of your cousin's altered behaviour. Mr Darcy is a very clever man."

"Oh yes, I am convinced he is the cleverest man I have ever known." Elizabeth thought this was an obvious point.

"Why did he offer to help you, to become a part of a surreptitious alliance?"

"I told you—he seeks entertainment, distraction. There is no theatre in Meryton, you know," she quipped.

Charlotte regarded her for a moment. "Will you tell me of Mr Darcy's behaviour since the walk—since your injury?"

"Well, I did not venture out of my room on Wednesday, so I did not see him. But Jane saw him briefly after dinner. He loaned her some books for me. Oh! Mr Hurst revealed at dinner that night that Mr Darcy had been inebriated the previous evening!" Elizabeth proceeded to tell Charlotte her suspicion that Mr Darcy suffered some misfortune during the summer.

"I cannot speculate on what happened to Mr Darcy before he came to Hertfordshire," Charlotte said thoughtfully. "On the night he was in his cups, Mr Darcy witnessed your reconciliation with your father. Is it safe to assume he understood the implications of your father's unusual actions?"

"Yes, for as I said, he is very clever. I have not been able to discuss any of this with him of course, since I can hardly escape for a secret meeting." Elizabeth indicated her ankle.

"What happened after that? When did you next see Mr Darcy?"

Elizabeth was less eager to share the last few days with anyone, namely the trips up and down the stairs. But they were hardly a secret. She decided to treat her stairway transportation only as a necessary consequence of her injury, and she chose her words carefully when recounting recent events.

Charlotte listened in silence and then smirked. "Has he carried you up and down the stairs every time?"

Elizabeth had expected some teasing about this. She knew it would pass quickly. Charlotte was far too interested in obtaining details to spend much time on ridicule. All the same, Elizabeth rolled her eyes. "No, today I made the trip downstairs by myself for the first time. I would have done so sooner had not Jane been constantly conspiring with Mr Darcy. I surprised everyone by joining them for the midday meal. Then Jane and I came into the garden, and here you found me."

Charlotte was not quite ready to let it go. "How exasperating it must have been to lack control over your own movements. I can only imagine how you sulked!"

"At least my ankle is healing and I shall soon be my own person again. But all in all, I would say I handled it rather well. I only snapped at Jane twice, I think."

"And did you ever snap at Mr Darcy?"

"Yes, once." Elizabeth admitted.

"How did he react?" Charlotte asked, barely containing her mirth.

"He had no time to react—Jane was already scolding me for my ingratitude."

Charlotte laughed, and Elizabeth waited in ill humour. "Are you quite finished now? Why are you so interested in every nuance of Mr Darcy's behaviour?"

Charlotte sobered. "I have a suspicion. In fact, I've had a suspicion for some time, and am only trying to confirm or deny it. But Mr Darcy is a difficult man to read. He is very reserved."

"I must agree. Sometimes he is so haughty and aloof, like today at luncheon, and other times, he is quite an engaging conversationalist. I find myself puzzled by his moods. So, what is this suspicion of yours? It is not like you to be so cryptic, Charlotte."

"I think Mr Darcy admires you."

The friends locked gazes for a long moment. "He said he admired my dedication to my sister's happiness."

"No, you know what I mean. I think he admires you as a man admires a woman. Perhaps he is even in lov—"

Elizabeth protested before the sentence was finished. "No! We all know he does not find me handsome."

"You said he apologised for that comment—that he was only frustrated with Mr Bingley's entreaties to dance."

Elizabeth sighed. "Lay your case before me then. Though I am sure you will not convince me of something so ludicrous."

"You know he stares at you quite a bit. It was particularly obvious at the picnic."

"I told you, he must find me more entertaining than anyone else in Hertfordshire. He is a spectator to the follies of my family. I noticed his staring too, but I assure you, I certainly did not feel admiration or even approval in his gaze."

"I always found his gaze inscrutable. But I now think it must have been fascination."

Elizabeth laughed nervously. "Call it fascination if you like. It does not change the fact that he looks down on all of us, including me. We are amusing in our foibles and struggles."

"If it is only entertainment he seeks, why do his eyes not more often find Lydia or your mother? I daresay there are any number of others who are far more amusing to watch."

"How can I possibly guess why he chooses me as his object? I hope you base your outrageous suspicion on more than just his staring and eavesdropping."

"I do. He has gone to much trouble and acted out of character to help you. Aside from his uncharacteristic exertions to speak with Mr Collins, he has knowingly placed himself at risk for marriage rumours—not only by allowing himself to be the object of Lydia and your mother's aspirations, but also by meeting with you secretly. You said he has been the target of entrapment schemes before. He must trust you completely to meet with you, or perhaps he would not mind being discovered in this case."

"Charlotte, you make me laugh. He knows I am not looking for a husband. He heard me state to my father quite vehemently that I would only marry for love."

"Even before he heard you make that statement, I am sure he knew you were not out to catch a husband. Perhaps this is part of his enthrallment."

"This is preposterous." Elizabeth, disturbed by the conversation, wished to speak on some other subject.

But Charlotte would not oblige her. "This week, my father received a reply to a letter he had sent a friend in London. He informs us that Mr Darcy became master of a great estate when he was just two and twenty. Since that time, he has been one of the most sought after—and most reluctant—bachelors of the *ton*. And no wonder: he comes from a storied family with good connexions, yet both his parents are deceased, so he is sole master of a great fortune, *and* he is handsome! Imagine, Lizzy, how different you must be from what he is accustomed to in London. Just compare your behaviour to all those rapacious ladies flattering him constantly."

"Like Miss Bingley," Elizabeth murmured, her mind dwelling on what Charlotte had revealed. She knew Mr Darcy was guardian to his sister, but she had not considered how that situation came about. To be guardian of a young girl and master of the family estate at such a young age must have been a great responsibility.

"Precisely," said Charlotte.

Elizabeth shook her head. "Your so-called evidence is very thin indeed, and there is a flaw in your logic. Mr Darcy has long been successful at avoiding matrimony. I see nothing to indicate he has changed his mind. So he must not be violently in love with me, as you suggest."

"One can be in love without intending to wed. Whether or not he acts on his inclination is entirely up to him, as I know *you* will do nothing to encourage him."

"Now you sound like my mother. I do not understand your insistence that all Mr Darcy's actions be attributed to some unlikely love for me. You, who pride yourself on *not* being a romantic."

"And I do not understand *your* insistence that they be attributed to some ignoble desire for amusement."

"Because he said as much!"

"But he gave you other reasons—reasons you seem bent on ignoring." Charlotte paused. "It seems a lot of trouble to take on for a mere fleeting distraction."

"The rich can afford to be eccentric and do as they please."

"You are so convinced of your own opinion that you will not listen to anything else. John always said that when you made up your mind, you were like a dog with a bone."

Elizabeth was happy to seize onto this new subject. "*He* would know."

"You cannot seriously still believe you were in the right about his choice. It has been over two years!"

"He gave up a great opportunity. What I would not give for the chance to attend Cambridge—and he just threw it away."

"John is not you. You know he was never studious. He always wanted to experience things for himself rather than read about them. He did horribly at Cambridge when he was there."

"But he could have done better. He does not lack intellect, only discipline."

"Why do you presume *you* know what is best for John, or for Jane? What if she had decided to marry Mr Collins? Would you have accepted her choice?"

"You cannot possibly think I have done wrong intervening *there*. Jane should not have to make that sacrifice, and I am perfectly content with my role in ensuring she did not."

"Many people marry for security. It is as valid a reason to wed as is love, and I daresay it is a more common reason."

"Marrying for security may be common, but Mr Collins is a very uncommon sort of man! It is much better Jane was spared making that choice."

"I trust Jane to know her own mind and make her own decisions. She is as rational as you are." Charlotte gave Elizabeth a pointed look. "I also trust John to know his own mind and make his own decisions. He did so, and from all indications, he chose well for himself. He has obtained experience and maturity, not to mention great financial success, yet you still cling to your old opinion on the matter."

"Perhaps his decision to serve on a merchant ship was not wrong.

I suppose I shall have the chance to see when he arrives. But he will always wonder what might have been, had he chosen differently."

"No, his decision was absolutely correct, and he does not wonder at all about what might have been. Only *you* are unwilling to accept it. You are quick to form opinions yet slow to reconsider them. It is high time to let go of this particular bone."

Elizabeth did not like how close this discussion had come to an argument. She could tell that Charlotte was in earnest. "I shall accede this much: I shall bury this particular bone for now. But if I do not see some of this great 'maturity' you speak of when John arrives, I shall dig it right back up!"

Charlotte smiled. "I suppose that is a great concession coming from you, Lizzy, and I shall take it."

They were quiet for a moment. Elizabeth thought she heard footsteps approaching, but before she could confirm it, Charlotte spoke again, "I brought with me what I suspect will be the last letter we receive from John before he returns to us. He answered the riddle you sent in my previous letter."

"Oh, do let me see this letter. I must examine the mature handwriting and marvel at John's riddle-solving acumen!"

Elizabeth stretched her hand out for the letter, but Charlotte was no longer seated. She was curtseying. Elizabeth looked up in confusion to see Mr Darcy, with a book in his hand, bowing stiffly.

"Good day, Miss Lucas, Miss Elizabeth. Forgive me, I did not know Miss Lucas was... That is, I did not know this bench was occupied."

"Mr Darcy, I fear you must regret showing me your favourite spot in the garden. I have quite taken it over and allow no one else to enjoy it."

"Nonsense, I am happy to share it with someone who appreciates it. I shall leave you to your visit and find myself another bench."

He turned to leave, and before Elizabeth could consider her words, she called out, "Wait! Mr Darcy, do not go yet, please."

He turned to look at her with a guarded expression, and Charlotte regarded her quizzically. "I have been catching Miss Lucas up on all that has happened since I last spoke to her. I...I have no secrets from Charlotte."

Charlotte's head bowed as she examined the gravel path. Mr Darcy met Elizabeth's eyes for a long moment before his cheeks turned a pinkish hue, and he, too, looked at the ground. Elizabeth was astonished—she had made him blush!

"Forgive me. I know this is awkward and quite improper; I just do not know whether I shall ever have another chance to ask you what I must. I rely on Charlotte's perception and trust her completely, Mr Darcy. She will not reveal anything that is told to her in confidence."

Elizabeth's companions raised their heads to consider each other for a moment. Mr Darcy's posture relaxed slightly. "It is I who is sworn to secrecy, not you, Miss Elizabeth. I shall trust in your judgment. What did you wish to ask me?"

"Thank you." She let out the breath she had been holding. "I am a selfish creature, and I simply must know what you discussed with Mr Collins on our walk, just before my misstep. Charlotte and I are convinced that whatever you told him changed his intentions towards Jane."

"If you must know, then I suppose I must tell you. Please be seated, Miss Lucas, and I shall explain." He paused, waiting for his audience to settle themselves, and then he began pacing. "I simply informed Mr Collins of some news regarding a family he is acquainted with in Kent, the Grantlys."

14

Her Favourite Lucas

When Darcy finished his explanation, two incredulous ladies gaped at him. He had not expected to be spending his afternoon thus. From his window, he had seen Miss Bennet and Mr Bingley walking in front of the house, which meant that Miss Elizabeth was most likely alone in the garden. He had planned to sequester himself away, but the temptation was too great. Like the lovesick whelp that he was, Darcy had grabbed a book and made his way to the spot where he thought she would be, hoping for a few minutes alone with her. Instead, he found Miss Lucas on a visit, and somehow, he had found himself talking openly about his manipulation of Mr Collins.

Miss Lucas recovered first. "Extraordinary!"

"I *told* you he is the cleverest man I know." Miss Elizabeth's words combined with the hint of pride in her voice made Darcy feel ridiculously pleased. "Only the cleverest of men could turn Jane's beauty into a *dis*advantage for her marriage prospects!"

Miss Lucas asked, "But is it true? Does Lady Catherine truly disapprove of 'excessive' beauty?"

"Let us say that Lady Catherine holds many similar opinions, so it is not out of the realm of possibilities."

Miss Elizabeth laughed with her friend. "Oh, Mr Darcy, I pity anyone who is unfortunate enough to be the victim of your wicked intellect."

"But what of your own wit, Miss Elizabeth? A few of the comments you directed at Mr Collins yesterday made it difficult to keep one's countenance."

Darcy savoured her unaffected laughter again.

"I was quite impatient with my poor cousin yesterday. He has an uncanny talent for taking all fun out of a conversation. Whenever Mr Bingley and I tried to tease you, the dauntless Mr Collins came to your rescue."

Darcy considered Miss Elizabeth's teasing a sweet torture, much like his assumed role as her stairway transport. The mischievous tilt of her mouth now told him that he would again be the object of her teasing.

"But I find it difficult to accept that you, of all people, could not keep your countenance," she continued. "You are not easily amused. You smile so rarely that every little smirk is like some hard-won prize."

This was reassuring to hear, for Darcy had thought he grinned at her like a fool far too often.

He was, in fact, trying *not* to grin like a fool when Miss Lucas cleared her throat. He soon felt some of that shrewd perception. Her knowing gaze observed him—there was no challenge or jealousy in it, merely frank assessment.

"Not all people are as lively as you in company, Lizzy. But I do wonder; how will Mr Collins act when he returns to Hertfordshire?"

"Returns?" Miss Elizabeth asked.

"Yes," Miss Lucas continued, "he repeatedly referred to the next time he would see us. I assume your mother would gladly invite him to visit again."

"Oh yes, any eligible bachelor will be given free access to Longbourn's guest room. I would not be surprised if Mr Collins visits us again. But if he is resolved not to have Jane, and Jane is resolved not to have him, there can be only tedium in his company."

"But Mr Collins is clearly on the hunt for a wife, and there is still the matter of the entail. You may find him ridiculous, but his intention to marry one of you displaced Bennets is, at its heart, a decent one. I think he may set his sights on you, Lizzy." Miss Lucas looked at Darcy rather than her friend when she made this prediction. He had never thought the foolish parson would dare aspire to such a superior woman, but now Darcy could see the logic in Miss Lucas's prediction.

"Oh yes," Miss Elizabeth replied, "I have it on good authority that I am only tolerable. Lady Catherine can hardly be offended by me!"

Darcy winced. He attempted another apology, but she waved it away and was already speaking again. "If Mr Collins does indeed transfer his steadfast affection to me, he will be quite surprised at how very impractical I can be."

"Your mother will be absolutely horrible if you reject him, Lizzy. You will never hear the end of it."

"I am already a constant disappointment to my mother. It hardly signifies."

"I wish there were some way for you to avoid all that unpleasantness."

"Unfortunately, a young lady has no control over who proposes to her. But this is all hypothetical, is it not? My cousin's second visit may never come. I shall not trouble myself over it. For now, Mr Darcy and I should indulge in some much-deserved boasting for one proposal successfully averted." She smiled brightly at him, and he was powerless to stop his answering grin.

Darcy, aware that the exchange was being observed with keen eyes, attempted to redirect the praise. "I believe Miss Lucas offered her assistance before I ever stumbled into the situation."

"*I* was the only person to stumble in all of this! I think *you* rather lurked your way into the situation." Miss Elizabeth feigned reproach. *Sweet torture!* Then she turned her warm smile towards her friend. "But indeed, Charlotte's patient interference was invaluable. I suspect she knows more about your aunt than you do by now, Mr Darcy."

Miss Lucas nodded solemnly. "I am particularly knowledgeable about the chimney piece at Rosings."

Darcy found the freedom of open conversation with these two ladies rather refreshing. He could tease too. "I believe all three of us are very well informed about the shelves in the parsonage's closet."

Darcy referenced Miss Elizabeth's cruel punishment on the night of the assembly with his own air of reproach.

She giggled. He hoped no one could hear his heart pounding in his chest.

Over the rush of blood in his ears, he just caught the last part of what Miss Lucas was saying. "I can hardly believe all the trouble so many people have gone through to *prevent* a proposal. Most young ladies do all they can to encourage one."

"What a silly generalisation, Charlotte. Some single ladies are quite content with their situations. You, for example, have three kind and dutiful brothers. You can be assured of security in the future whether you marry or not. You could live your whole life perfectly contented at Lucas Lodge."

"I believe the future Mrs John Lucas will have something to say about that."

"Ha! You need not worry about objections from *her*."

Darcy wondered what that meant. Did John Lucas have an understanding with some young lady? Why was it not spoken of, and why did Mrs Bennet consider him an eligible bachelor? Perhaps it was some secret attachment known only to Miss Lucas and Miss Elizabeth. Darcy felt all the air rush out of his lungs. Could John Lucas and Miss Elizabeth already have an understanding between them? He did not take the time to consider his words or his somewhat frantic tone. "Who is the future—?"

Bingley's voice interrupted. "We found the lads, Miss Lucas. Oh, Darcy, I thought you had business to occupy you."

The little area with the bench was becoming rather crowded with the return of Miss Bennet and Bingley. Glad of the interruption now that he had control of himself, Darcy bowed to the lady in greeting before answering. "I decided to take a short respite from my pursuits." He did not need to explain his presence further, for the sounds of an approaching uproar distracted everyone.

"Mr Bingley, you really should have left my brothers where you found them," Miss Lucas said with some dread in her voice. "I fear for the safety of your finely manicured garden."

"But you would not keep your brothers from me, would you?" Elizabeth complained. "You know how I enjoy their company."

"You only like Peter because he compliments you constantly."

She laughed. "Peter is one of the few people who prefers my charms to Jane's. How can a young lady not be moved by such blind devotion?"

The lads in question now ran headlong into Bingley's back with a muffled "Oof." Luckily, Bingley was solid enough to withstand the onslaught. He only laughed.

"Walter! Peter! You can forget about receiving any treat in Meryton to reward such coarse behaviour!" Miss Lucas sounded very much like a cross older sister.

"Now, there's no reason for that, Miss Lucas," said Bingley. "I was standing in a most inconvenient spot."

While the elder of the two lads hung back next to Bingley, the younger boldly stepped just in front of the bench. He bowed in a most gentlemanlike manner towards Miss Elizabeth, though the muddy spatters all over him detracted from the effect somewhat. "Good day, Miss Elizabeth."

She replied formally, "Good day, Master Peter. I cannot thank you and Walter enough for escorting dear Charlotte to visit me. I have been most eager for her company."

Peter looked her over. "Charlotte said you were injured. Did Miss Lydia hit a cricket ball at your head?"

Everyone laughed, even Darcy, before Miss Elizabeth replied, "No. Although that would have been a much more exciting way to injure myself, I merely turned my ankle during a walk."

Peter seemed to have no response to this disappointing answer. He turned towards Bingley. "The weather is fine today. Might we play cricket now, Mr Bingley? You and Mr Darcy can be captains again."

Walter Lucas spoke for the first time. "You dolt. There aren't nearly enough people to play."

"Mr Bingley's two sisters and that Mr Hurst fellow could play with us," replied Peter defensively. "And I bet we can catch Tommy before he returns to Longbourn."

Miss Lucas decided to intervene. "Peter, we haven't the time for a cricket match. And poor Lizzy could not play, she could only watch."

This last piece of knowledge seemed to make an impression. "I am sorry, Miss Lizzy. I forgot how much you would hate not being able to play."

"You are quite forgiven, Peter. I do not blame you for trying." She looked towards her sister then. "But what's this about Tommy being nearby? Did he come to see Becky? I should have liked to say hello."

Miss Bennet held up a piece of paper in her hand. "He did see his sister briefly, yes, but his purpose was to deliver a note to us. Mama has declined our request."

Miss Elizabeth set her mouth grimly and held her hand out for the note. "Yes, I am sure she cannot spare the carriage at all. But she can spare *us* easily enough, it seems."

After a brief perusal of Mrs Bennet's reply, she looked up. "Mr Bingley, might we trouble you for the use of your carriage today? I am quite healed enough to ride home now and need not impose on you any longer." Darcy did not know whether he felt relief or disappointment at the thought of Miss Elizabeth leaving, but he again hoped no one could hear his pounding heart.

"Today?" Bingley seemed rather alarmed by the prospect. "No, no. You know it is no imposition at all. I...we enjoy having you as guests. You must stay longer, please. Tonight's dinner was planned with the assumption of your presence, in any case."

The two Miss Bennets shared a long look before the elder spoke. "It would be rude for us to leave so abruptly. But tomorrow, we must return home. There is no justification for prolonging our burden on you and Miss Bingley."

"Nonsense. My sisters greatly enjoy having female company apart from each other. We shall be bereft without you." Bingley looked to Darcy for some assistance, but Darcy thought it best not to speak for fear of what he might say.

Miss Elizabeth was kind but firm in her reply. "Come now, Mr Bingley. It is a mere three miles to Longbourn, and you know my mother counts you in her debt for a dinner. You are welcome to call on us at any time as neighbours and now, we hope, as friends." She swept Darcy in her gaze as she spoke the last. "Just ask Walter and Peter how very often the Lucases and the Bennets visit each other, invited or not."

"Miss Catherine seems to be visiting Maria every day," said

Walter, with a hint of impatience in his voice. "Charlotte, mustn't we leave soon to ensure we reach the shops in Meryton before closing?"

"You think you will still receive a treat, do you?"

"You promised!"

"Miss Lucas, what say I loan you the use of my carriage for your trip home, so long as Masters Walter and Peter get their treats?"

"I would never dream of sullying your fine carriage with these muddy ruffians."

Peter swiped his finger over one of his muddy knees and held it up for all to see. "It is quite dried on now."

"There, you see. My carriage will be absolutely unsullied. I insist, Miss Lucas."

She acquiesced, and Bingley, with cheerful enthusiasm, excused himself to call for the carriage. Peter spoke in a low voice to his sister and Miss Elizabeth, who smirked at Darcy over the boy's shoulder.

"Ask him yourself, Peter. He is not so very dour as he appears, I promise," she said.

The youngest Lucas turned to him. "Do you have a pack of foxhounds, Mr Darcy?"

Darcy was taken aback by the odd question. "No. We breed and train land spaniels at Pemberley."

Peter considered this and then nodded in approval. "And do you drink very much wine?"

Miss Elizabeth brought a hand up to cover her mouth as Peter and Walter waited expectantly for an answer. Thankfully, Miss Lucas put an end to it. "I think it is time we went round the house to the carriage, brothers."

"I believe even *I* can make it all that way if I can lean on strong Lucas arms," added Miss Elizabeth, standing. The boys obliged, Peter quite happily, and Walter with slightly less zeal.

Darcy offered one arm each to Miss Bennet and Miss Lucas. The two threesomes began walking towards the front of the house. Darcy did not speak, but rather listened to the group ahead of him.

"Peter, you are growing far too quickly."

"But I am nearly thirteen, Miss Lizzy."

"I know, but I do not look forward to being the shortest of all the Bennets and Lucases."

"I very much look forward to being the tallest of them all. Mama says I shall even be taller than John."

"I daresay you will be taller than John. Perhaps you may be as tall as Mr Darcy."

Darcy felt ridiculously pleased again, though he kept his face indifferent as Peter peered at him over his shoulder. The groups soon turned the corner towards the front of the house. The carriage had just arrived and farewells were exchanged. Then the Lucas siblings boarded the carriage and were gone. Bingley and the Miss Bennets chatted amiably as he led them up to the front door. Miss Elizabeth and Miss Bennet continued up the main staircase to dress for dinner. Miss Elizabeth managed the deed on her own two feet, Darcy noted with some regret.

As he dressed for dinner, he tried to convince himself that he welcomed the Bennet sisters' departure. He could now begin putting a certain fine-eyed beauty out of his mind and, hopefully, out of his heart. He had one last evening to enjoy her company.

Darcy sighed as his valet carefully tied his cravat. He knew he was behaving like a lovelorn fool. He found comfort in the fact that no one else knew of his dilemma. No one, that is, except perhaps Charlotte Lucas.

"Sir, your arms, please," Higgins, the valet, held up Darcy's coat.

"Pardon me. My mind was elsewhere." Darcy lifted his arms into the sleeves.

"If that is all, sir…"

"Yes, thank you." As his valet left him, Darcy mentally prepared himself for his last evening in company with Miss Elizabeth. He knew he would no doubt dine with her again before he left Hertfordshire, but not in so intimate a gathering. He would most likely never speak freely with her again, as he had today. He would never be alone with her again. He would never hold her in his arms again. Much as he wished it otherwise, he knew what duty demanded of him.

Darcy gave himself one last inspection in the mirror, and he was struck by his despondent expression. He looked himself in the eye. "Enough of that. Make some excellent memories tonight. They must last you forever."

15

Depending Upon His Own Judgment

Charles Bingley had spent the happiest week in his recollection. But the angelic Miss Bennet had returned home, and he was bereft. Had it been only three days? It felt like an eternity. In contrast to Miss Bennet, his sisters' voices were grating, their opinions disparaging. He could not spend his time with them. They only suffered by comparison, and he did not wish to think ill of his own sisters. Rising early to avoid breaking his fast with them seemed a wise approach.

Bingley sank down across the table from Darcy, who neither acknowledged him nor commented on his early appearance. Darcy had been more reticent and irritable than usual lately. Bingley had known his friend to be reserved, even severe, in society, but now that he was in company again with only close acquaintances, he should have been at least slightly more companionable. Instead, the opposite was true.

Bingley could not remember his friend being a livelier raconteur than on the last night the Miss Bennets had been present. Miss Elizabeth and Darcy had left the whole room behind when discussing literature. No one, least of all Bingley, could keep up with their many quotes and references.

That Darcy disappeared, however, the moment the Miss Bennets pulled away in Bingley's carriage on Sunday. Since then, Darcy had resumed his morning rides. He returned from them looking like a Lucas boy—windblown, dishevelled, and muddy. The rest of the time, he buried himself in books and correspondence. Sometimes, he just stared out the window, and he seemed to be imbibing a bit more than usual as well. One would think *he* was the one pining for a beautiful young lady. But perhaps the Miss Bennets had served as a distraction from whatever was troubling Darcy, and now he was returned to his former cares.

Bingley had already offered his help; to bring it up again would be even more awkward. But he had his own melancholy to consider. He would like some of Darcy's advice, and perhaps getting his friend to speak on one topic would ease the transition into other matters.

"Would you object to my accompanying you on your ride this morning?"

Darcy shrugged. "I suppose not. But my ride will be vigorous, I warn you."

"I believe I shall be able to keep up."

About an hour later, Bingley had to admit that the ride was indeed vigorous. He followed behind Darcy, letting his friend choose their route over fields and along lanes. They came to a halt at the bank of Oakham Stream. Darcy dismounted without a word and, while his mount drank, stared upstream into the woods.

Bingley came to stand near his brooding friend. "I believe I shall call at Longbourn today to inquire after Miss Elizabeth. Will you come with me?"

Darcy continued to stare at the stream for a few moments. "I think it would be best if I did not. In fact, I think it would be best if *you* did not either."

"Why ever not? It is common courtesy to check on Miss Elizabeth. And I thought you would welcome the distraction."

"Have you not noticed that Mrs Bennet is an unabashed matchmaker, and she has been trying to match each of us with one of her daughters?"

"She is harmless, Darcy. All mothers wish their daughters to make good marriages. Besides, I believe I would be quite content to be matched with one of her daughters."

Darcy finally looked at Bingley for a long moment. "You speak of Miss Bennet."

"Indeed, I do. She is utter perfection."

"It is just like you, Bingley, to rush into an attachment. You hardly know her."

Bingley had expected Darcy to urge caution. "There, you are wrong. I know she is the sweetest, kindest, most generous, most beautiful young lady of my acquaintance. You forget how much time I have spent with her, particularly in the last week."

"And do you think she returns your regard?"

"She is certainly not indifferent to me." He glanced away from Darcy's doubtful look. "I admit she does not show her emotions overmuch. *You* can hardly be a critic there. But even you must own that her manner towards me is very different than towards any other—Mr Collins, her erstwhile suitor, included."

Darcy looked down at the running water of the stream. "I concede I did detect a difference in her behaviour towards you, yes."

Bingley was elated to have his own viewpoint confirmed. "My angel blushes only for me. Had you noticed?" He remembered her last blush, when he had said his goodbyes and helped her into the carriage, his hand lingering on hers longer than was necessary. Oh, yes, Bingley greatly enjoyed her blushes.

"Wipe that lovesick grin off your face." Darcy's harsh voice was an unwelcome intrusion. "There is nothing objectionable in Miss Bennet. She is, as you say, kind, generous, and beautiful, and her conduct is all that it ought to be. But, Bingley, her family, her fortune, her connexions... One uncle in trade and another a country lawyer? No dowry to speak of. And the behaviour of her parents and her sisters..."

"Enough! You really can be the most reprehensible snob sometimes. Do you realise how very much you sound like Caroline at this moment?" Bingley paused as he took in Darcy's shocked expression. He had never spoken so forcefully to his friend before. "Miss Bennet is a gentleman's daughter, a gentleman's granddaughter—which is more than Caroline can claim. I do not forget where my fortune was made. That same fortune allows me to marry without a concern for my bride's dowry, and I am grateful for that freedom. The Bennets are a prominent and well-respected family in Hertfordshire. What care I for silly sisters and vulgar mothers? Who amongst us does not have a family member who disappoints us or embarrasses us?"

Darcy remained silent, spending several minutes considering Bingley's impassioned speech. He took on a conciliatory tone. "Bingley, I am merely trying to protect you from your own impetuosity. I raise these objections for you to consider. If you are still firm in your position—and I begin to see that you are—then I shall speak on them no more."

"I love her, Darcy. I wish nothing more than to spend my life with her if she will have me." As soon as Bingley voiced the words, he knew them to be true. He knew not what reaction to expect from his friend though. They had never discussed such weighty personal matters before. Would Darcy diminish his feelings, deride them, or accept them?

Darcy took a deep breath. "*Will* she have you? Have you declared yourself?"

"It would not have been proper while she was a guest in my house. This is one of the reasons I wish to call at Longbourn today: to determine her willingness without such strictures on my behaviour."

"You surprise me with your restraint. But you were right not to act while she was under your protection. What are the other reasons you wish to call at Longbourn?"

Bingley grinned. "Her voice, her eyes, her smile, her face, her blush, to name just a few. Nay, do not laugh at me. I miss her terribly. I miss everything about her. Perhaps if you ever fall in love, you will understand."

Darcy sobered and returned his gaze to the stream. "I daresay I shall understand."

"You will come with me to Longbourn then?"

Darcy deliberated, still looking at the water. Several emotions played over his features before he answered. "I am sorry, but I prefer not to encourage Miss Lydia's pursuit of me. In any case, I have much business to attend to here."

Darcy had not worried about Miss Lydia's infatuation last week. Bingley bit back this observation. He did not wish to quarrel. "But I cannot go alone."

"Caroline was the hostess. She should be the one to visit the Bennets. Perhaps it is time you accustom her to the notion of sharing more than a friendship with Miss Bennet."

Bingley groaned, and Darcy barely smiled. "I do not envy you your task. Be as forceful as you were with me, and she will be persuaded, or at least, she will see that you are resolute. She has, in the past, perhaps expected you to yield too much to her influence."

"She has, for I *have* yielded. But Caroline will soon see that no one will dissuade me from Miss Bennet."

"Forgive me for sounding superior, but I think you have changed for the better. I have never known you to stand so strongly for yourself. Is it because of Miss Bennet?"

"I cannot believe my luck at finding such a woman and finding her unattached. How can I not strive to be the best man I can be for her?"

Darcy again became thoughtful. He took the reins of his horse in hand. "Shall we return to the house? A very difficult conversation awaits you."

The ride back to the house was just as invigorating as the ride away from it. When they arrived, Bingley and Darcy adjourned to their separate rooms for baths.

About two hours later, Bingley wished he was still soaking in that bath.

"Charles, you cannot be serious," Caroline said after nearly choking on her wine. Bingley was wise to wait until most of the meal had been eaten before broaching the subject. Only Hurst was still eating, as the servants knew to give him larger portions.

"I assure you, I am in earnest."

"But that family! The mother alone ought to send any potential suitors running, not to mention the sisters! You can do so much better, Charles."

"I have no wish to 'do better.' You can say nothing to disparage Miss Bennet. The faults of her family are no better or worse than any other family and entirely out of her control."

"You know very well that the faults of her family are worse than *many* other families." Caroline looked decidedly red about the face. She was not taking the news well.

Louisa spoke up in a calmer tone. "Charles, we all know Miss Bennet is a dear, sweet girl. I cannot blame you for admiring her. But you must consider her position in society, her fortune, her connexions. When seeking a potential spouse, there is more to consider than beauty and sweetness of temper."

Bingley nearly laughed at the idea that Mrs Reginald Hurst was lecturing him about how to choose the correct spouse. "Indeed, there is, Louisa. There is compatibility, shared interests, the ability to hold a conversation beyond two sentences. There is also mutual respect and affection. All of these I have found in abundance in Miss Bennet."

Reginald Hurst belched and muttered apologies.

Caroline made a disgusted sound. "Mr Darcy, please help us talk sense to our poor brother. Surely you agree with us!"

"We have already discussed your reservations. He assures me that the strength of his feelings outweigh these secondary concerns. I trust him to know his own heart. And I trust his friends and family to accept his decisions and rejoice in his happiness."

Sometimes, Bingley had to step back in awe of his friend's ability to express himself. When Darcy decided to speak, you could be assured that he really *said* something. He did not prattle on for the sake of hearing his own voice.

"But you would not attach yourself to the Bennets, would you? It would be insupportable!"

Bingley was surprised to see anger flash across Darcy's face, but his voice was calm when he replied, "I am not Charles. Only he can determine that which will bring him happiness."

Caroline turned back to her brother, obviously disappointed in Darcy's reaction. "This is just what that horrid Mrs Bennet hoped for, and you have stupidly fallen into her trap! She has been throwing all of her daughters at any eligible man—Mr Collins, you, Mr Darcy! The impudence! And what's worse, those girls throw *themselves* at any eligible man."

Bingley began to protest, but Caroline waved him off. "Perhaps not Miss Bennet, but I am convinced that shameless Miss Eliza's twisted ankle was just part of a plot to throw the eldest Bennets into your company. They hoped to charm you both!"

Darcy rose from his chair and went to the window, turning his back to the table. Caroline continued her ever-more-shrill speech towards his back. "At least Mr Darcy had sense enough not to be taken in. But you, Charles, you need not always be so obliging!"

"I shall make a start at being disobliging right now, Caroline, by advising you to hold your sharp tongue. You will not speak ill of Miss Bennet or Miss Elizabeth in my presence again." Bingley was surprised by the steely nature of his own voice, and Caroline appeared no less shocked.

"And what of Mr Collins?' she sputtered. "You seem to be forgetting him in all this mooning over Miss Bennet."

"Mr Collins has gone back to Kent. There has been no engagement announced, not even a formal courtship. Clearly, the rumours about a match between them were just that: rumours. And lucky for me, for I am free to *moon* over Miss Bennet to my heart's content, and I shall begin directly, when you and I call at Longbourn this afternoon."

"I shall do no such thing! We only just rid our house of the Bennets; why should I go seek them out?"

"*My* house, Caroline. Though I allow you to be mistress here, it is my house. Now perhaps you would like to reconsider your plans for this afternoon and accompany me, as my sister and the gracious hostess you are, to Longbourn to inquire after Miss Elizabeth's health." Bingley recognised that he was making some unnamed threat, but if he could bluff his way through this confrontation and then speak with Darcy, all would be well. He kept his face unreadable as his two sisters regarded him intently. They were trying to determine his resolve.

Louisa blinked first. "As I have said since making her acquaintance, I should like to know more of Miss Bennet. It is no surprise you feel the same way. She is a lovely, sweet girl. Caroline and I were just lamenting her absence earlier."

Caroline spoke through a tight mouth. "Yes, Miss Bennet is all that is lovely. I should very much like to see her this afternoon."

"Excellent! Be ready to leave in one hour, please," said Bingley, happy to return to his normal cheerful tone.

16

The Nature of Things

Elizabeth watched from the front window as Mr Bingley handed his sister into their carriage. She could not help but recall the last time she had been helped into that very carriage. It was on Sunday in front of Netherfield, and the manner in which she was assisted was quite a bit different. Mr Darcy had literally lifted her quite easily with his hands on her hips. His gold-flecked dark eyes were intent on her as he did so. It was disconcerting, to say the least, and she had hoped her blush could be dismissed as a normal reaction to the chilly air.

She did not know what to think about Mr Darcy after her discussion with Charlotte. She could never repay him for all of his assistance; that much she did know. But the man himself was a puzzle. Sometimes conversing with him was easy and natural. Other times, he was silent and brooding, often wearing that disapproving mask she had become accustomed to in the earliest days of their acquaintance. At those times, Elizabeth found herself wishing to draw him into the conversation, so that she might provoke one of his rare smiles. She enjoyed his smiles. But more disturbing was the great disappointment she had felt when the carriage had come to Longbourn today and *he* had not emerged from it.

Now that Mr and Miss Bingley were gone, Mrs Bennet found

herself in the rare position of needing to scold Jane. "Jane, how could you agree to walk in the garden with Mr Bingley, let alone linger so long with him? You know he is meant for Lizzy."

Elizabeth spoke up cheerfully. "I hereby relinquish any claims on him. He and Jane are much better suited."

"Nonsense! Jane is for Mr Collins. Everyone knows that."

Elizabeth was about to make some disparaging comments, but Jane spoke first. "Mama, I am not for Mr Collins. I shall never be for Mr Collins."

Mary looked up from her book, her pen frozen above her extract. Lydia and Kitty watched too, their hands continuing to work at the ribbon, though they made no appreciable progress retrimming their bonnets. There was something about Jane's posture, her tone.

Mrs Bennet may not have noticed this subtle difference in Jane, but she certainly realised she had been directly contradicted. "Of course you will. He fancies you, Jane. I am sure he will offer for you when he returns to Hertfordshire. If not for Miss Lizzy and her ankle, you might well have been engaged to him already."

"He never declared his intentions to *me*. He never asked my permission or Papa's permission to court me. He has gone without speaking of it, and it is just as well, for I would not have welcomed his suit. I shall never marry Mr Collins."

Mrs Bennet's rate of breathing increased. "What is this nonsense you speak? Of course you will have him. It is your duty! The entail! Jane, do you want us all starving in the hedgerows when your father is dead?" This, to Mrs Bennet, was always the last word on any subject.

"It is not my duty. I have always wished to marry for love. I do not love Mr Collins, and therefore, it would be mercenary for me to accept him. In any case, no offer of marriage was made, and Mr Collins has left us. Soon, the rumours of a betrothal will die down. I wonder how they ever started. I suppose people simply assumed too much too quickly."

The silence in the room was only broken by Mrs Bennet's whimpering and keening. Elizabeth sat in awe of her elder sister—her obvious resolve, her subtle reprimand of her mother's gossip-mongering. There was a new glow about her, a self-assuredness. Indeed, that must have been *quite* a stroll in the garden.

Mrs Bennet finally broke into a wail, "What is to become of us? No one has consideration for my nerves! Such flutterings and spasms! All I wish is to see my daughters well married and secure, but everyone is against me! Ungrateful children!"

The Bennet daughters knew well what was to follow if they did not act: hours upon hours of howling and bawling. Normally, Jane would comfort Mrs Bennet with her calming presence, but since Jane herself had provoked their mother's "attack" this time, the girls did not know how to proceed. Jane moved towards her mother, hoping to soothe that which she had roused.

She was immediately rebuffed. "No! You have been poisoned against me, my sweetest Jane." Mrs Bennet turned on Elizabeth. "This is *your* influence! You ungrateful, meddlesome girl! You have been sabotaging my every effort at matchmaking! I care little for *your* security—you can foolishly throw away a wonderful gentleman like Mr Bingley as you wish. If that were your only offense—"

"Mama!" Jane interrupted in a cross voice, which further shocked everyone in the room. She returned to her normal serene tone before continuing, "Do not blame Lizzy for this. It is *my* doing, and mine alone. You cannot make any two people fall in love just because you wish it. It would have been so much easier if I could love Mr Collins, but I cannot, and as he is an honourable man, he deserves better."

Mrs Bennet returned to whimpering. Jane changed the subject. "I am very happy you invited Mr Bingley and his party to dinner on Saturday. How will you arrange the seating to encourage conversation?"

Mrs Bennet wiped at her eyes and sniffled. "L-Lydia must sit next to Mr Darcy, of course. Her vivacity will liven him up." Elizabeth felt a surge of protectiveness for Mr Darcy come over her, and it troubled her.

"Yes, of course. And what will be served? How many courses?" Jane asked. Elizabeth could see that she was successfully manipulating their mother, another first.

"I...I must speak with Cook about it." Mrs Bennet rose from her seat. "You really will not have Mr Collins?"

"No, I simply could not. I am sorry."

"Mr Bingley seems very fond of you, does he not?"

Jane blushed and looked down. "I believe he is."

"And you are fond of him?"

Jane swallowed and looked around the room. Elizabeth knew that to admit such a thing in front of her talkative mother and sisters would be a great leap for Jane, who guarded her emotions very closely. "Yes, I am."

Mrs Bennet shot a reproachful look at Elizabeth. "Then Jane will sit between Mr and Miss Bingley at dinner. I have so much to plan! Cook! Cooook!" Her voice trailed off as she exited the room.

Nobody moved for some time except Mary, who began writing furiously again, as if the interruption had set her behind on her extract.

Elizabeth could contain her praise no longer. "Well, *that* went much better than it might have. Jane, you handled her splendidly! If Papa took lessons from you, we might see more of him!"

"Wait," Kitty interrupted with a shake of her head. "Jane is for Mr Bingley now? But what about all of Mama's efforts to match him with Lizzy?"

"Kitty, Mama is not the final authority on who will marry whom. It was perfectly obvious, even on the night of the assembly, that Jane and Mr Bingley...enjoyed each other's company."

"I did not notice anything."

Lydia laughed. "Of course *you* did not. You always miss such obvious things. Sometimes I wonder whether you have eyes and ears."

"But everyone was talking about Jane and Mr Collins. How was I to know that it would be Jane and Mr Bingley instead? Why did no one tell me?"

Elizabeth tried to be gentler with Kitty than Lydia had been. "Because it was not certain. It is indelicate to speak about potential engagements and courtships before they are official. If you ever have questions about such things, do not blurt them out when other people are present. Wait until you are alone with any of us to ask."

Kitty nodded. "Thank you, Lizzy. I shall ask you or Jane."

"You may ask Mary too. She can advise you about these matters as well as Jane or I."

"What about me?" Lydia demanded. "I could see that Mr Bingley mooned over Jane just as well as you could."

"Yet you went along with all of Mama's schemes for him and for Mr Collins without question." Lydia appeared unhappy with this observation but did not contradict it. Elizabeth addressed her two youngest siblings. "Do you see how much trouble the gossip about Mr Collins has caused poor Jane? She and Mr Bingley could have been courting properly all this time if only he knew the rumours about a forthcoming betrothal were false."

Jane began to protest but was interrupted by Lydia. "Mr Bingley is *much* better than Mr Collins, Jane. I am happy for you."

Jane blushed again. "Lydia, Lizzy, nothing is settled. Nothing has even been spoken, really."

Elizabeth seized the opportunity for teasing. She spoke to her younger sisters again. "Oh, but it will be soon, I am certain. He is half in love with Jane already. You should have seen them at Netherfield together. They were all bashful blushes and quiet *tête-à-têtes*."

"Do tell us all about it, Lizzy!" cried Lydia. "I suppose, for Jane's sake, it is better that Papa insisted on her staying at Netherfield instead of me. But oh! How I wish I could have stayed too! I should have turned *my* ankle. Mr Darcy would have carried me around all week, and he would be half in love with me by now!"

Elizabeth shot an alarmed look at Jane. Had she told the others about Elizabeth's trips up and down Netherfield's staircase in the arms of Mr Darcy? Jane shook her head slightly, indicating she had not revealed that bit of information, but then she grinned. Elizabeth reconsidered her plan to reveal all the romantic details of Jane's Netherfield stay to Kitty and Lydia for fear of some sort of retribution from her much-altered sister.

"But Lizzy, tell us about Mr Bingley's behav—" Kitty stopped suddenly, a terrified look coming over her face. "But who must marry Mr Collins now? Mama insists he is coming back."

"Not I—I am for Mr Darcy! And not Jane either. It must be one of you three!" Lydia announced before Mary's persistent scribbling distracted her. "Good lord, do you extract the entire book? I cannot understand why you should continually make extracts from books you already know from memory."

Mary placed her pen down and folded her hands, muttering about the devil's workshop.

Elizabeth brought them back to the subject at hand. "None of us must marry anyone if we do not wish it. Papa would never force us into a marriage. Mama may carry on about one couple or another, but we need not oblige her. If we did, Jane would have married that fat Mr Burns who wished to court her when she was sixteen." Kitty and Lydia snorted at the memory.

Elizabeth continued, "And Mama certainly has no sway over the gentlemen involved, otherwise John Lucas would have proposed to *me* two years ago. These gentlemen have minds and wishes of their own; they are not simply trophies to be won or prey to be trapped." Elizabeth did not mention Mr Darcy, but she knew by Lydia's frown that she had already made the connexion.

Elizabeth looked at each of her younger sisters in turn before continuing. "Choosing to marry is the most important decision of a lady's life. You need not settle for the first man that asks you. I wish to share common interests with my future husband, to find mutual respect and affection with him. We should all strive for such a marriage."

"Your sister is wise, girls." All five ladies turned to see Mr Bennet standing in the doorway. "Many people come to regret imprudent marriages made under the influence of silly infatuations or monetary concerns. I wish better for my children. I shall never force you to accept any man, no matter how rich he is or how your mother carries on." He glanced at Mrs Bennet's empty chair. "I can offer you that much at least, if not a very secure future. I leave it up to each of you to find the best way to balance your security with your happiness. I hope you find both."

Elizabeth was quite sure Mr Bennet had never spoken so seriously to Lydia or Kitty before. She sent her father a warm smile. Her relationship with him since her return had been somewhat tentative as each discovered its new limits. They spoke more openly now, rather than just the superficial witty banter they had shared before. Mr Bennet would always prefer retreating to the quiet of his books rather than confronting his wife, but he was making some effort to improve his youngest daughters. Elizabeth acknowledged and accepted his nature now, yet she continually encouraged the positive steps he was taking.

Mr Bennet could not speak seriously for long, however, and his normal wit soon intruded. "As I understand it, one of my daughters has made a significant movement in the direction of both security *and* happiness today. The very embodiment of security and happiness wrapped up in one five-thousand-pounds-a-year package, a man called Mr Bingley, was spied through my library window walking out with my eldest daughter. Though my eyesight is not all that it once was, Jane and this Mr Bingley looked quite cosy, even under the eager eyes of their chaperones. So Jane, shall I make an effort on Saturday to converse with your Mr Bingley, or would you rather I discourage him?"

"Papa…" Jane sighed. "He is not *my* Mr Bingley." Jane's cheeks were the reddest Elizabeth had ever seen them.

"Not yet," Kitty corrected.

Jane recovered slightly. "I should hope you will be friendly and polite, and thank him for his kindness to Lizzy."

"Indeed, I shall. I see you are being tight-lipped, Jane, something I greatly appreciate in any of the six females who share my house, so I shall tease you no more. Instead, I should like to speak with Elizabeth, if I may steal her away from you all for a moment."

He offered his hand to help Elizabeth rise and walk with him into the library. He closed the door behind them. and they settled in their chairs.

"Now, Lizzy, tell me your impressions of this momentous visit today."

"Mr and Miss Bingley seemed at odds somehow, though they talked and laughed as if there were no tension between them. It was very peculiar. I believe Mr Bingley's visit was a declaration of sorts about his intentions towards Jane."

"But you detect dissension from the fashionable Miss Bingley? How can anyone disapprove of Jane?"

"Miss Bingley disapproves of everyone in Hertfordshire. We are not rich or connected enough for her. But I think she is resigned to her brother's decision. She was the one to suggest they walk in the garden, a suggestion Mr Bingley seemed to appreciate."

Mr Bennet considered this for a moment before observing, "Mr Darcy did not accompany his friend today."

Elizabeth dreaded the subject but kept her voice indifferent. "No, apparently he had estate matters to attend to." She added with a roll of her eyes, "Lydia was quite disappointed by his absence."

He chuckled, though Elizabeth knew his levity was as forced as hers. "It is just as well. A prominent man like Mr Darcy may find amusement among normal people for a while, but he will go back to his great estate, his important family, and his superior society, and forget all about his few months spent among *us*. Anyone who hopes for more from him is bound to be disappointed."

This was not the first time Elizabeth had heard similar speculation about Mr Darcy. Logic told her it must be true, though deep down... "I must agree with you and with Miss Bingley, who said much the same to me while the others were walking in the garden. Of course she has her own special way of elevating Mr Darcy and diminishing everyone else."

"Oh dear, we find ourselves in agreement with Miss Bingley. Will wonders never cease?"

They shared a smile before Elizabeth broached a delicate subject. "Papa, as you know, the Netherfield party is to dine here Saturday. Will you speak to Lydia about her behaviour towards Mr Darcy? I doubt Mr Bingley would mind her antics, but there is no need to give his sisters further reasons to disapprove of us."

He sighed. "I shall speak to her as best I can, Lizzy. But I do not wish to cast Mr Darcy as the forbidden fruit. It would be much better if she simply becomes bored with his taciturn nature."

"But he is not always taciturn, Papa. When the mood strikes him, he can be quite a lively conversationalist." Mr Bennet eyed her, and she wished she had kept that opinion to herself.

"I very much doubt the mood will strike him to converse energetically on any topic Lydia may bring up. But I suppose we shall see on

Saturday. In the meantime, I shall speak to Lydia. Please send her in when you go."

Elizabeth rose and kissed his cheek, which he accepted with some surprise for it was an unusual gesture. "Thank you, Papa."

As she left the library, Elizabeth repeated to herself: *We shall see on Saturday.*

17

The Effect of the Meeting

Fitzwilliam Darcy stared out his window, not seeing any of the countryside stretching before Netherfield. For the last ten days, he had thrown himself into physical and mental exertion in an attempt to rid his mind and heart of a certain young lady. He had not had much success, but Darcy blamed circumstances beyond his control rather than any lack of determination on his part.

First, it was Bingley. When not singing his angel's praises directly, he somehow managed to relate everything back to Miss Bennet no matter how unrelated the subject. Naturally, with a certain young lady's sister's name constantly in the ears, Darcy could hardly help thinking of the young lady herself. Bingley and his Miss Bennet had come to an understanding of sorts, though an unspoken one for now. Bingley was confident she returned his feelings, and Darcy knew it was only a matter of time before his impulsive friend formalised the understanding by asking for a proper courtship. For only the second time in his life, Darcy envied someone. His jealousy of John Lucas was merely a blind, mindless reaction to that man's past and possible future with...a certain young lady. But Darcy's envy of his own friend was quite different. He envied Bingley's freedom to choose whom he wished as well as his somewhat foolhardy resolve to ignore all other concerns but those of the heart.

The second reason for Darcy's failure to remove a certain young lady from his thoughts was quite simple. He had dined with that very same young lady less than a week ago in her home. Miss Elizabeth's company had been as ever delightful despite the behaviour of her mother and the singular concentration of her youngest sister on him. He had even allowed himself the pleasure of one unencumbered conversation with her, a supplement to their previous literary discussion. This time, Mr Bennet participated to some extent—when he had not been eyeing Darcy suspiciously—but it did not detract from Darcy's enjoyment. On the contrary, her father's participation only lent a further sparkle to Elizabeth's fine eyes. During such a conversation, he could completely forget about Mrs Bennet's bewildered stare and Miss Lydia's petulant pout, and he paid no heed to Bingley's foolish grin, Miss Bennet's serene smile, and Miss Bingley's scowl. Miss Elizabeth was seated nearly as far away as possible at the table, but to him, it was as if no one else were in the room. If only...

Darcy checked his thoughts. It would not help at all to dwell on the impossible. He resolved not to think about dinner at Longbourn or any of the other precious memories involving Elizabeth Bennet, at least until he left Hertfordshire. Then he could relive them all—which he knew he would—without fear of slipping in his resolution. He was scheduled to leave in four weeks' time, but Darcy began to doubt his own abilities to withstand temptation for that long. Perhaps he should hasten his departure to town. He could not leave before Bingley's ball, however, which would take place in a se'nnight. He owed his friend that much.

There was a knock on the door. With his permission, a footman entered bearing a letter from Rosings. Darcy sat down to read, happy for a distraction. It began in the usual way; Anne asked after his and Georgiana's health, and commented on news she had received from other members of the family. But then she moved on to the topic that had lately filled their letters to each other: unsuitable attachments.

How did you enjoy dinner in company with your L? I saw C. last week. It will likely turn out to be the highlight of my November. Melancholy seized me so fully afterwards, that Mother declared I was relapsing and nearly called back that old fool apothecary, Mr Mortimer.

What a lovesick pair we make, Cousin. After reading your last letter, I must admit to a shameful sort of satisfaction that you now suffer in love as I have for the last half year. At least we can commiserate over our impossible attachments. Thank goodness you sent Tess and Roger to us from Pemberley. There is nothing as invaluable as a loyal servant except of course, a pair of them! I have never been more grateful for their help in exchanging our secret letters. Who else could understand my struggle as you can?

I must admit to another bit of mischief. I have been applying to Mr Collins for information about all the young ladies of Hertfordshire. (He is only too happy to oblige, as you can imagine.) I had quite given up discovering your secret, for none of the charming L.s he described, given names or surnames, seemed likely suspects. But then, clever cousin, an idea struck me: nicknames! Have no fear; your secret is safe with me. It is only fair that I know the identity of your beloved since you are actually acquainted with mine. Mr Collins seems to have a fondness for your L., although I am sure the qualities that attract you are quite lost on him. I occasionally must stifle giggles when he relates some comment of hers without truly understanding it. I should very much like to meet your L.

I hesitate to write this, but have you considered following your heart? I find myself dwelling on the possibility more and more often. You love your L. I know you do not make such a declaration lightly, nor would I. In my case, I spent the first few months determined to ignore and overcome my feelings. I believe this is your current resolution. Let me make a prediction: you will not succeed. You and I are similar creatures. We have been spoilt by our parents, who allowed, encouraged, almost taught us to be selfish and overbearing; to care for none beyond our own family circle; to think meanly of all the rest of the world. Now, we have each fallen in love with those of whom we would think meanly. Mark my words: we, both of us, love rarely but deeply. Are we to suffer a lifetime of regret and loneliness simply because we value our station over our hearts?

I know I sound quite unlike myself. Perhaps it is the lingering melancholy from my recent encounter with C. But consider. You have been eagerly pursued by all the right sorts of ladies for these five years. They had large fortunes and good breeding. Some even had titles. Has any one of them in all that time inspired just a fraction of the emotion that your L. inspires in you after only a month? Should such a rare spark, such an extraordinary connexion, be thrown over merely for society's expectations? I begin to think that it should not.

I fear it is too late for me. I have rebuffed C.'s subtle overtures before, and he need hardly guess why when he hears Mother speak. But you, Fitzwilliam, still have a chance to seize your happiness. Think carefully about what it is that you truly desire and what truly matters most. Dear Cousin, I pray you find your happiness. Know that I shall always support you and Georgiana in all your decisions.

Yours in commiseration,
Anne

Just when Darcy most needed reassurance from the one person who perfectly understood his dilemma, Anne sends him *this* advice. Just when he needed to be reminded about principles, obligation, and duty, she undercuts all his resolve. He threw the letter down in disgust.

There was another knock on the door.

"Enter!" he bit out, turning to see a hesitant Bingley standing in the doorway.

"Good God! What is the matter?" cried he, with more feeling than politeness. Then recollecting himself, he asked, "Have you received bad news?"

"No, not bad exactly, just...unexpected. I..."—Darcy looked down at the letter—"I prefer not to discuss it."

He could feel Bingley staring at him for a long moment. "Forgive me for interrupting. I came to inquire whether you wished to ride into Meryton with me, but obviously, you wish to be alone." Bingley pivoted and reached to close the door behind him.

"Wait. Thank you, I would like to accompany you if you do not mind. I...it will be good to get outside." Darcy smiled faintly at his friend. He knew he should not let his frustration get the better of him.

Bingley blinked at him and then the ready smile returned. "In half an hour, then?"

"Yes, I shall be ready."

They rode towards Meryton in silence. Darcy felt a pang of guilt, knowing his moodiness was the likely reason for Bingley's uncharacteristic quiet. As they approached the outskirts of the village, he turned to try to make some conversation, only to behold the most ridiculous grin on his friend's face. He followed Bingley's gaze to a group of people, five women and two men. The air rushed out of him. Elizabeth was among the group.

"I hoped we might catch them," Bingley said. "I knew they were to visit their Aunt Philips today. I see Miss Elizabeth was able to walk all the way."

Darcy snapped, "Why did you not tell me they might be here?"

Bingley looked intently at him. "Because I knew you would not come. The only time that damnable forlorn countenance has lifted from you in the last fortnight was when we dined with the Miss Bennets. I do not know what troubles you, but I feel compelled to cheer you somehow." He motioned towards the five ladies.

Darcy closed his eyes. "*This* most certainly will not cheer me. I shall go back to the house."

"You cannot! They have seen us."

Just then, Darcy heard the excited exclamation of Miss Lydia, "Mr Darcy!" she cried. Bingley shrugged at him before springing forward.

Darcy cursed under his breath as he urged his mount to follow. When they reached the group, Bingley jumped down from his horse immediately, and Darcy did the same. He congratulated himself for not yet glancing at Elizabeth. He was determined not to stare at her; so he kept his eyes trained directly before him. Bingley had already taken Miss Bennet's gloved hand in greeting. Miss Lydia stood out in front of the group, waiting for Darcy's greeting.

"Miss Lydia." He bowed to her, and then he quickly turned to greet each of the others behind her, from left to right: Miss Bennet, Miss Mary, Miss Catherine, and Mr Denny. His eyes at last rested on Elizabeth. It seemed as if time stood still. She smiled at him and murmured her greetings as she curtseyed. He was transfixed. A movement next to her intruded on Darcy's consciousness. The second man had moved closer to Elizabeth. This annoyed Darcy, and he looked at the man, only to have the wind knocked out of him a second time.

George Wickham was there, standing next to a certain young lady.

§.

The Bennet sisters left their Aunt Philips's house and walked along the main thoroughfare of Meryton.

"Let us go to the milliner's before we return home," Kitty said.

Lydia readily agreed. A trip into the village would be wasted without a visit to the millinery shop. The pair hurried ahead of their sisters. Before entering the shop, however, Kitty spied Mr Denny and another man walking towards them.

Mary, Elizabeth, and Jane caught up just as Mr Denny addressed them. He then entreated permission to introduce his friend, Mr Wickham, who had returned with him the day before from town and, he was happy to say, had accepted a commission in their corps. This was exactly as it should be, Lydia thought, for the young man wanted only regimentals to make him completely charming. His appearance was greatly in his favour. Though not quite as pleasing to Lydia as one Mr Darcy, Mr Wickham had all the best parts of beauty—a fine countenance, a good figure, and very pleasing address. The introduction was followed up on his side by a happy readiness of conversation.d The whole party were still standing and talking together very agreeably when the sound of horses drew their notice, and Darcy and Bingley were seen riding down the street.

"Mr Darcy!" cried Lydia. What a delightful surprise!

Mr Bingley rode towards the group, with Mr Darcy close behind.

Both gentlemen dismounted, Mr Bingley with a look that was positively gleeful. He took Jane's hand and bowed over it in greeting. Mr Darcy had not said anything yet, so Lydia stepped forward from the group, hoping for a warm welcome similar to Mr Bingley's for Jane. Mr Darcy bowed towards her and said in his deep voice, "Miss Lydia." Then he turned to greet Jane, Mary, Kitty, Denny, and Lizzy. Lydia was disappointed that he had not smiled at her, but now felt a little better about it, for he had not smiled at anyone. If anything, he looked distracted.

Lydia was about to introduce him to Mr Wickham when his eyes shifted and were suddenly arrested by the sight of the stranger. Lydia, happening to see the countenance of both as they looked at each other, was all astonishment at the effect of the meeting. Both changed colour, one looked white, the other red. Mr Wickham, after a few moments, touched his hat—a salutation which Mr Darcy just deigned to return. What could be the meaning of it? It was impossible to imagine; it was impossible not to long to know.

Mr Darcy looked absolutely livid as he gathered his reins. He could not leave so soon! Lydia reconsidered her initial favourable opinion of Mr Wickham. She turned her back to him and stepped towards Mr Darcy.

"Mr Collins is coming to stay with us again."

He paused, glanced at her, and then glanced behind her. Lydia's statement had succeeded in drawing another man's attention as well.

"Mr Collins is coming back?" asked Mr Bingley.

Mr Denny and Mr Wickham bid the group farewell and departed quickly. Lizzy came to stand beside Lydia. Mr Darcy dropped his reins, much to Lydia's relief.

Lizzy addressed Mr Bingley. "My cousin will be with us again on Monday."

"Monday? It seems rather sudden."

Kitty laughed. "He and Mama were scheming to surprise us! Can you imagine? We would still be ignorant of his impending arrival if not for Mary."

Both gentlemen looked at Mary, who appeared decidedly uncomfortable under their scrutiny. "I simply noticed some peculiar menu requests for meals next week."

"Don't be so modest, Mary." Lydia turned to Mr Darcy to explain. "Mr Collins raved about the boiled potatoes when he was here before, and Mary saw that my mother had ordered boiled potatoes for nearly every meal! Mary informed Lizzy of her suspicions, and Lizzy and Papa confronted Mama, who admitted everything and whined about her good joke being spoilt. She had planned not to tell any of us about it until the very day Mr Collins appeared on our doorstep!"

"And what was the reason for this subterfuge?" Mr Darcy asked her. She felt a flush of success that her story had interested him.

"Mama claims she did not want any of us to get our hopes up that Mr Collins might come to Mr Bingley's ball before it was confirmed. What a laugh!"

"Mr Bingley," interjected Lizzy, "I hope you do not mind the addition of one more to our party on the night of the ball."

"No, of course not. He is family, after all. What is one more guest among so many?" Mr Bingley looked down for a moment before continuing. "In fact, I am happy to have run into you all today, for I have a question regarding the ball. Might I request the honour of the first set with Miss Bennet?"

Jane blushed and nodded her acceptance. Lydia thought the scene a very sweet one.

Mr Bingley beamed as he turned towards the others. "And as I see that your ankle is well enough for walking, I assume it will be well enough for dancing, Miss Elizabeth. May I request the second set?"

Lizzy laughed. "Oh yes. I intend to teach my irksome ankle a lesson over the next week with ample walking and much dancing. I gratefully look forward to our set."

Mr Bingley proceeded to ask Mary, Kitty, and Lydia each for a dance on the night of the ball. What an agreeable fellow! When he had five dances secure, he turned to Jane again. "Would it be too much to ask you, Miss Bennet, for the supper set as well?"

Jane returned his gaze. "I shall be honoured, Mr Bingley."

The group fell quiet, and the silence was a bit awkward for all but the two people gazing intently at each other. Mr Darcy seemed to be very interested in the gravel on the road.

Mr Bingley finally roused himself. "Now, if we can only persuade Darcy to dance, my ball will be a complete success!"

Mr Darcy appeared decidedly uncomfortable under the scrutiny of the group. "No doubt I shall dance, though I cannot promise that it will be very much."

Lydia hoped that continuing to talk about dancing would urge Mr Darcy to ask her for the first set. "But you dance so well, Mr Darcy! We all saw you at the assembly. Why should you dislike an activity you perform with such skill?"

Lizzy interjected, "Lydia, you make the neatest stitches of any of us, and yet you despise your needlework."

"Good lord, you cannot seriously compare needlework to dancing!"

"How can any of us account for our preferences and inclinations? Society expects certain activities from each of us, that we may come to resent those very activities."

Mr Darcy stared at Lizzy as she finished speaking. Then he gathered his reins and cleared his throat. "If you would excuse me, I must return to Netherfield. Bingley no longer requires my company, and I have much business to occupy me." He bowed towards each of them as he said his goodbyes. With a parting glance at Mr Bingley, he mounted and rode away.

Mr Bingley sighed and shook his head. "I am not so eager to depart from your company, ladies. Will you allow me to escort you home?"

They agreed promptly, and the sextet made their way out of Meryton. Kitty never did get to the millinery shop.

Lydia kicked a stone on the road as she walked back to Longbourn. She should have been pleased after unexpectedly meeting Mr Darcy. Instead, she was frustrated. He was even more reticent than usual. Lydia would have doubted such a thing possible before today. She kicked another stone. It skipped in front of her and ricocheted off Kitty's heel.

"Ouch!" Kitty yelled, causing Jane and Mr Bingley to stop and turn. Kitty spun around and glared.

"Lydia is very sorry, Kitty. She did not mean to strike you." Lizzy elbowed Lydia.

"Yes. Sorry, Kitty."

Kitty harrumphed. "If you must kick stones, I insist you walk in front."

"I shan't kick any more, I promise."

The group continued on, with Jane and Mr Bingley leading the way towards Longbourn, followed by Mary and Kitty and, finally, Lydia and Elizabeth.

"Lizzy, will you teach me about literature?"

Her sister started to laugh but stopped when Lydia caught her eyes. "Literature? What has brought on this sudden interest?"

"I wish to be able to speak about literature. It seems the only thing that interests Mr Darcy. If I am to catch him, I must learn." Lydia thought this a brilliant plan. Surely, if she put so much effort into catching a husband, she would be successful.

"I am happy to help you learn literature if your aim is to improve yourself. But you ought not play at being studious simply to catch a husband."

"But becoming Mr Darcy's wife *would* improve me. If I must discuss books with him to do it, then I shall. By the time of the ball, I hope to be able to speak about literature as you do."

Lizzy stifled more laughter. "The ball? It is but a week away. You could not possibly become well versed in literature by then, even if you spent every hour from now until the first dance set reading."

"Must I read so very much? Can't you just tell me about these books?"

Lizzy laughed outright. "A man as clever as Mr Darcy would quickly discover that you were only pretending. You saw at dinner how easily he returned all my best barbs."

"I suppose such a clever man would want a clever wife," said Lydia glumly. She sighed and kicked another stone, which skipped past Kitty just barely.

Elizabeth took Lydia's arm. "Mr Darcy has very high standards for whom he considers an accomplished lady." She turned her nose up and said in a mock deep voice, "'The improvement of her mind by extensive reading' is only the most important of these standards."

"Did he say that when you stayed at Netherfield?" Lizzy nodded.

"What else did he say?" This could be very helpful information indeed.

Elizabeth sighed. "One thing at a time, please. I shall pick out two books for you to read this week—two books I know you will enjoy. We shall make a start there. At the ball, you can ask Mr Darcy if he wishes to discuss them."

"But may I discuss them with you first? I do not wish to make a fool of myself."

"Yes, you may, if you will make me a promise. If you enjoy those two books, you will read two more that I recommend after the ball. The improvement of your mind *is* a worthwhile pursuit, whether or not any man ever knows about it."

"Very well. Do you think Papa would discuss these books with me too? Perhaps he will not think me so silly anymore."

"Yes, we three will discuss them together, and Papa will know that you can be witty too, Liddy"

"I should like that." Lydia looked up at the thinning canopy for a moment. "Lizzy, did you notice the strange interaction between Mr Darcy and Mr Wickham?"

"I most certainly did. How could one not notice? Except for Kitty, of course."

"Of course. And perhaps Jane and Mr Bingley." Lydia motioned towards the much-absorbed couple ahead of them. "But what can it mean? They must have been previously acquainted."

"Yes, but I cannot imagine what would cause such a cold greeting. Mr Darcy appeared positively furious. It is very strange."

"Very strange," agreed Lydia.

The group approached Longbourn. They all entered the front door, but Mr Bingley immediately asked to see Mr Bennet and disappeared. The girls went into the sitting room.

"Jane, where has Mr Bingley gone?" asked Lizzy.

Jane turned to embrace her. "I am the happiest creature in the world! Mr Bingley has asked permission to court me formally, and I have given it. He now speaks to Papa. 'Tis too much!, By far too much; I do not deserve it. Oh! I am so happy!"

"Oh Jane, you deserve it more than anyone!" cried Lizzy, before releasing Jane so that all of her excited sisters might embrace her.

"You will have the most wonderful time at the ball now!" added Lydia. "Everyone will know that Mr Bingley is courting you. Everyone will know that he has fallen madly in love with you."

Jane soon went to find their mother, who would no doubt receive the news with much satisfaction. Despite her disappointment in what had happened in Meryton, Lydia would not give up on Mr Darcy yet. No doubt she would be in company with him more often now that Jane and Mr Bingley were courting. She could not let herself be discouraged, for she had two books to read. At the ball, surely he would reward her efforts.

18

A Most
Determined Talker

Lydia guffawed as she read near the window. Elizabeth had known that Sir Toby Belch would be to her sister's liking. She envied Lydia's ability to so effortlessly recover from disappointment, for *she* could not forget yesterday's events in Meryton with such ease.

Elizabeth had been exceedingly happy to see Mr Darcy; she must admit the truth of it to herself at least. Despite the warnings from her father, from Miss Bingley, from the very man himself, Elizabeth had allowed herself to become attached to him. Perhaps it was simply a consequence of the unique experiences they had shared. The secrets between them lent an air of intimacy, which Elizabeth's confession to Charlotte had not curtailed. When Mr Darcy chose to engage in conversation—for it was seemingly impossible to compel him to do so—she found the resulting discussions more stimulating and thought provoking than any she had ever had before.

Yet, she now realised, it was a mistaken feeling of intimacy, for she knew very little about Mr Darcy. He never talked about himself, never revealed anything of his life. She grew weary of the mystery: his inscrutable gaze, his maddening silence. So Elizabeth had been quite pleased to meet Mr Wickham. With his ready smile, agreeable manners, and effortless conversation, *this* interaction was refreshing in its simplicity. Yet—and there *was* the inevitable "yet"—perhaps the ease of his smile made the expression less valuable. Perhaps his dark eyes lacked the depth of another's. Perhaps conversing with him was simply a way to pass time pleasantly rather than a true exchange of ideas.

Elizabeth chastised herself. It would be most unwise to begin comparing every man she met to Mr Darcy. When had *he* become the ideal? With his moods, his haughtiness, and his inability to be pleased by anyone around him? No, Elizabeth was determined to return to her previous preferences. Mr Wickham was precisely the sort of new acquaintance in whom she would have delighted. So she *would* be delighted with him even if—or perhaps because—he and Mr Darcy were at odds. They were as different from each other as possible.

Elizabeth and her sisters were to return to the Philipses' tonight. Her aunt had promised a nice, noisy game of lottery tickets with some of the officers and a little bit of hot supper afterwards. The prospect of such delights was very cheering to Kitty in particular.

"How is your book, Lydia?" Kitty could scarcely keep the ridicule from her voice.

"It is very entertaining. You should read it when I finish rather than retrimming one of your bonnets for the tenth time."

Elizabeth found Lydia's newfound scholarly superiority very amusing, and if the hidden smile on her face was any indication, Jane did as well. Of course Jane had done *nothing* but smile for the last twenty-four hours.

Kitty was unimpressed. "Perhaps you should make extracts of your favourite passages. Then we can compare your penmanship to Mary's."

Mary was, at that moment, making yet another extract. Elizabeth began to wonder whether Mary's pastime was more than it seemed.

Lydia rolled her eyes. She apparently did not wish to engage in further taunting.

Kitty, deprived of her sparring partner, changed the subject. "I am so looking forward to tonight. I hope Aunt Philips extended the invitation to Mr Wickham. Surely if Denny was invited, and he must have been, his friend would be as well."

Lydia glanced at Elizabeth. "He is pleasant enough, I suppose. But I would much rather Mr Bingley and Mr Darcy be invited."

"Ha! Mr Darcy would not play lottery tickets. He would stand in the corner and say not a word to anyone."

The undeniable truth of this statement silenced Lydia, who made a great show of lifting up her book to resume her reading.

&.

As the men joined the women later that night at the Philipses', the handsome, agreeable Mr Wickham was the happy man towards whom almost every female eye was turned, and Elizabeth was the woman by whom he finally seated himself. He immediately fell into conversation, and although it was only on its being a wet evening and the probability of a rainy season, she remembered her earlier pledge to be delighted with him.

There was no danger of Lydia's engrossing Mr Wickham, for she was extremely fond of lottery tickets, eager in making bets and exclaiming after prizes. Seated between Elizabeth and Lydia, Mr Wickham was therefore at leisure to talk to Elizabeth, and she was willing to hear him. What she chiefly wished to hear she could not hope to be told—the history of his acquaintance with Mr Darcy. However, her curiosity was unexpectedly relieved when Mr Wickham began the subject himself. He inquired how far Netherfield was from Meryton and, after receiving her answer, asked in a hesitating manner how long Mr Darcy had been staying there.

"About a month." Unwilling to let the subject drop, she added, "He is a man of very large property in Derbyshire, I understand."

"Yes," replied Wickham, "his estate there is a noble one. A clear ten thousand per annum. You could not have met with a person more capable of giving you certain information on that head than myself, for I have been connected with his family in a particular manner from my infancy. My father was steward for the late Mr Darcy, and I grew up alongside this Mr Darcy."

Elizabeth could not but look surprised.

"You may well be surprised, Miss Bennet, at such an assertion after seeing, as you probably did, the very cold manner of our meeting yesterday. Are you much acquainted with Mr Darcy?"

"As much as I ever will be, no doubt," Elizabeth deflected. "I have spent four days in the same house with him, and I think him a very difficult man to know." Her choice of words was an attempt to coax Mr Wickham into an explanation of his relationship with Mr Darcy. "He is not liked overmuch in Hertfordshire. Everybody was disgusted with his pride upon his first appearance amongst us."

"I cannot pretend to be sorry," said Wickham. He looked at her with a sad smile. "We are not on friendly terms any longer, and it always gives me pain to meet him. His father was one of the best men that ever breathed and the truest friend I ever had. I can never be in company with *this* Mr Darcy without being grieved to the soul by a thousand tender recollections. His behaviour towards myself has been scandalous, but I verily believe I could forgive him anything and everything rather than disgrace the memory of his father."

Elizabeth listened with all her heart. She found her insatiable curiosity about Mr Darcy shameful, particularly when she suspected Mr Wickham of having ulterior motives in his revelations. Information from a questionable source was still information at least. The delicacy of the subject prevented further inquiry, but she inquired anyway. "As I understand it, his father died some five years ago?"

"Yes, and before he died, the late Mr Darcy bequeathed me the next presentation of the best living in his gift. He was my godfather and excessively attached to me. I cannot do justice to his kindness. He meant to provide for me amply and thought he had done it, but when the living fell, it was given elsewhere."

"Good heavens!" cried Elizabeth, truly shocked. "But how could that be? How could his will be disregarded? Why did not you seek legal redress?"

"There was just such an informality in the terms of the bequest as to give me no hope from law. A man of honour could not have doubted the intention, but Mr Darcy chose to doubt it—or to treat it as merely a conditional recommendation."

Elizabeth's scepticism increased at this convenient ambiguity, though she carefully worded her reply so that he might continue his tale. "Such disgraceful behaviour would deserve to be publicly exposed."

"It will not be by me. Till I can forget his father, I can never defy or expose him."

She paused to consider the contradiction of Mr Wickham's noble words. He *had* exposed the son to her that very night. Then she caught Lydia's furious look behind Mr Wickham. She had been eavesdropping. Elizabeth shook her head once, hoping to discourage Lydia from causing a scene.

Unbidden, Mr Wickham continued on about his former friend. "It surprises me not that he should display such pride to the good people of Hertfordshire—almost all his actions may be traced to pride. He can be a conversable companion if he thinks it worth his while. Among those who are his equals in consequence, he is a very different man from what he is to the less prosperous. His pride never deserts him, but with the rich, he is liberal-minded, just, sincere, rational, honourable, and perhaps agreeable, allowing something for fortune and figure."

Elizabeth would have agreed easily with these last observations were it not for Mr Darcy's behaviour towards *her* at certain times. Surely he had not thought to gain anything by helping her—other than entertainment perhaps.

"He has also brotherly pride and affection, which makes him a very kind and careful guardian of his sister; and you will hear him generally cried up as the most attentive and best of brothers."

"What sort of a girl is Miss Darcy?" Elizabeth still could not contain her curiosity.

He shook his head. "I wish I could call her amiable. It gives me pain to speak ill of a Darcy, but she is too much like her brother—very, very proud."

Lydia turned to them with a false smile on her face. "Pardon me, I could not help but overhear your conversation. Mr Darcy mentioned his sister to me. As I understand it, Miss Darcy is only fifteen years old and not yet out. What kind of a man would declare to perfect strangers that a defenceless, orphaned girl at least ten years his junior is too proud?" Lydia eyed him without mercy.

Mr Wickham blinked at her, his face paling as it had the previous day in the street. "I apologise if I have shocked you. I have an open, unguarded temperament and have been known to speak perhaps too easily on all manner of subjects."

"Indeed! I have heard you readily speak about *this* subject to young ladies with whom you are barely acquainted. If it 'gives you pain' to speak ill of a Darcy, you certainly had your share of pain tonight!" Though she kept her voice at a normal level, Lydia's eyes were sparking.

Elizabeth prayed that her overexcited sister would control herself. "Lydia, Mr Wickham means no harm. Let us not spoil this pleasant evening over what is surely a misunderstanding. Think of Aunt Philips." Her eyes beseeched Lydia for calm.

"*Means no harm*? I am sure he means precisely that! And after Mr Darcy has been so kind to me—to you as well!" Lydia stood with her head held high. "It seems I have lost my enthusiasm for the game. I leave you to your conversation." She walked off towards Mary without looking back.

Mr Wickham turned to Elizabeth, looking very grave. "Oh dear, this is another of Mr Darcy's traits that I hesitate to mention in mixed company, but you must be warned for the sake of your young sister."

"What do you mean?"

"Well, when Darcy is amongst people whom he does not consider...of much consequence, he sometimes...he sometimes amuses himself with some poor young lady who is flattered when he grants his much-sought-after attentions." At Elizabeth's incredulous look, Mr Wickham continued, "Oh, he does nothing to compromise her, nothing so reprehensible. He simply leaves her pining after him, nursing her disappointed hopes."

Elizabeth considered how to respond to this latest accusation but was at a loss. Could there be any truth in what Mr Wickham had told her? Could it all be pure fabrication? If so, Mr Wickham certainly had a cruel and vivid imagination. No, she suspected there were grains of truth in his words. But which parts?

As she contemplated all she had heard, the voice of Aunt Philips carried above the din of the room. "Upon my word, Mr Collins was so much struck with the size and furniture of our apartment that he declared he might almost have supposed himself in the summer breakfast parlour at Rosings, the estate of Lady Catherine de Bourgh."

Mr Wickham's attention was caught; he asked Elizabeth in a low voice whether her family was very intimately acquainted with the family of de Bourgh.

"No. We only know of them through my cousin Mr Collins. Lady Catherine de Bourgh has lately given him a living."

"You know of course that Lady Catherine de Bourgh and Lady Anne Darcy were sisters; consequently, she is aunt to the present Mr Darcy."

"Yes, I did know of the relationship."

"Her daughter, Miss de Bourgh, will have a very large fortune, and it is believed that she and her cousin will unite the two estates."

This information made Elizabeth gasp. Mr Wickham gazed at her. "Ah yes, of course his prior arrangement with Miss de Bourgh would not be known here. It might interfere too much with his amusement."

Elizabeth had heard quite enough. She rose. "Excuse me. I believe I should speak to my sister now."

He grasped her hand and smiled at her. "Of course; I hope I have not distressed you or Miss Lydia. That should be the very last thing I desire."

She pulled her hand back. "Do not trouble yourself, Mr Wickham. No doubt Lydia will forget all about Mr Darcy when he leaves Hertfordshire. She is not built for melancholy." She left him there and crossed the room to Lydia and Mary.

Lydia immediately addressed her. "So you finally wearied of his horrible lies. I do not understand *how* you could have listened to him for so long. You do not believe anything he said about Mr Darcy, do you?"

Elizabeth shook her head, but in her mind, she could think of but one thing: an afternoon spent in the sitting room at Netherfield where Mr Darcy wrote a letter to his cousin Anne de Bourgh.

19

A Fine Figure of a Man

The Reverend William Collins arrived at Longbourn on a rainy Monday afternoon. He was received with much civility, particularly by Mrs Bennet and Miss Bennet. Very soon after partaking in tea with his guest, Mr Bennet returned to his study while the Bennet ladies took up their individual pursuits.

Mr Collins was pretending to read a book, but in reality, he contemplated the blessed state of marriage. He had spent the last fortnight in similar contemplation. Yes, his days of bachelorhood would soon be at an end. When he left Hertfordshire the last time, he had been undecided between three young ladies. He had now, based on his own preferences, Mr Darcy's intelligence, and consultation with Lady Catherine, made his choice. He only had to be sure that he was not—through the raising of expectations during his last visit—honour bound to offer for Miss Bennet.

The prospect of marriage to the young lady was by no means disagreeable. On the contrary, she had been Mr Collins's first choice until the fortuitous conversation with Mr Darcy in which he was advised that Lady Catherine would disapprove of Miss Bennet's exceptional beauty beyond her rank. During his time back in Kent, Mr Collins had the privilege of dining at Rosings with the Grantlys, including the youngest son, Arthur Grantly, and his betrothed, Miss

Horton. The young lady in question was indeed handsome, but if he must compare the two, Mr Collins must conclude that Miss Bennet's extraordinary beauty eclipsed Miss Horton's. Lady Catherine would think her far too beautiful to be a country parson's wife.

Thus two young ladies remained from which Mr Collins would choose the companion of his future life. He did not think he flattered himself to own that each of them had conveyed an interest in him. Of course the position of Mrs Collins was quite a desirable circumstance, both in his current situation and his future one. Mr Collins did have a preference of his own, though he appreciated the varying fine qualities in each of the young ladies. Miss Lucas was kind and modest. She was an exceptional listener, but she also shared her sound and practical opinions when asked for them. Miss Elizabeth was kind, too, and a very caring sister. She had a liveliness about her to which one could not but be drawn even if it occasionally neared impertinence. Though not a classic beauty like her elder sister, Miss Elizabeth was very handsome. This perhaps held more weight for Mr Collins than it ought. But if he must give up exceptional beauty to please his patroness, did he not still deserve a pretty wife?

"Lizzy!" Miss Lydia cried, breaking Mr Collins's reverie. "I have finished the first book you recommended!"

"That is excellent, Lydia. I am surprised you did it so quickly. Perhaps, if you are not completely weary of reading, you will have time to finish the second one before the ball."

"Oh, I shall, especially if it continues to rain. But may we go speak with Papa about this one first? Do you think he will take the time to discuss it with us?"

"*Twelfth Night* is one of his favourites, and I secured a promise from him that he would discuss it with you. Let us make him keep his word now, shall we?" Cousin Elizabeth held out her hand, which Cousin Lydia took with a grin, and they entered Mr Bennet's study together. The scene only confirmed to Mr Collins that Miss Elizabeth was a very caring sister indeed.

He returned to his own book without actually reading it. He was confident he had made the right selection. Although the decision was ultimately his, Mr Collins had been pleased to obtain Lady Catherine's advice yesterday at tea, and what she had said provided the final impetus for Mr Collins's choice of bride.

"I trust that upon your return from Hertfordshire *this* time, you will have, if not a wife, at least a betrothed, as I advised," she had said.

"That is my intention, Lady Catherine."

"Good. I would generally commend a man for taking care and deliberation before making a decision of such import, but I see no reason to delay. As you have described them, these three eldest Bennet sisters sound like good, respectable girls. They are at least a gentleman's daughters, and they are in a very precarious position. I greatly approve of you making one of them the future mistress of that estate, entailed as it is away from the female line. Anne, of course, will never face a similar predicament, but I have imagination enough to sympathise with their plight."

"Indeed, Lady Catherine, your elevated rank has not blinded you to the condition of others. What insight, what compassion you show to all around you, even to those whom you have never met!"

She had nodded and taken a sip of tea. "I have a letter for my nephew, if you will be so kind as to deliver it, Mr Collins."

"I shall perform this service most eagerly, Lady Catherine."

"I wish you a pleasant journey then. Do take care in packing your trunk. I have told you before the best method, have I not?"

He was brought back to the present when Mrs Bennet came to sit next to him, wringing her hands. "Oh Mr Collins..."

He put his book down and saw that only Miss Mary remained in the room. It had quite escaped his notice when the others left. Mrs Bennet continued, "I hope I do not distress you, but I must inform you as soon as possible of some news. Mr Bingley and my Jane have entered into a formal courtship. Apparently, they developed tender feelings for each other during the time Jane spent at Netherfield nursing Lizzy. I hope you are not terribly disappointed. I know Jane catches many a young man's eye, but who can ever predict these sorts of things?"

She ended her nervous speech and waited for his reply with much trepidation. Mr Collins was of course relieved that he was not honour bound to Miss Bennet. Yet he also felt a sting of bitterness that she should move on so quickly. Regardless, this was, for his purposes, very welcome intelligence.

"Have no fear, Mrs Bennet. I rejoice in my cousin's happiness and in your good fortune. It is a very good match, and Mr Bingley is a most amiable gentleman."

"You are too good, Mr Collins. I have been so worried that you might have been inadvertently injured in all of this."

"Do not trouble yourself, madam," he replied in a quiet voice. "My heart *has* been touched but by another of your fine daughters." He lowered his voice to a whisper, "Miss Elizabeth."

"Dear me! How happy I am to hear you say so! You have my complete support, Mr Collins., I do not know of any prepossessions *there*. The upcoming ball will be a great opportunity for romance, do you not think? Lizzy loves to dance." She winked at him, and he had to smile despite the unseemliness of such a gesture.

"Indeed, madam, I shall not waste the occasion."

Mrs Bennet left him alone on the settee with one last wink.

Later, after all the daughters of the house had returned to the sitting room, Mrs Bennet said, "Girls, I am afraid, with all this rain, we must send out for the shoe roses for the ball."

This statement began an enthusiastic conversation about the ball, particularly between the youngest Miss Bennets.

After a little while, Mr Collins cleared his throat. "I shall hope to be honoured with the hands of all my fair cousins in the course of the evening, and I take this opportunity of soliciting yours, Miss Elizabeth, for the two first dances especially, a preference which I trust my cousin Jane will attribute to the right cause and not to any disrespect for her."

Miss Elizabeth looked surprised, a testament to her modesty, but she accepted with grace.

"I wonder," Cousin Lydia said, "how many sets Mr Darcy will dance."

Miss Catherine snorted in a rather unladylike fashion. "I should guess only two sets, one each with Miss Bingley and Mrs Hurst."

"Certainly not! He will at least dance with me and with Jane, now that she and Mr Bingley are courting. Do you not think, Lizzy?"

"I can hardly say what Mr Darcy will do, Lydia."

Mr Collins broke into the conversation, "I suspect the letter I carry for Mr Darcy must be delivered on the night of the ball, for the roads are far too muddy now."

Miss Elizabeth gazed at him for a moment. "Do you carry a letter from Miss de Bourgh for her cousin?"

The question confused him. "Mr Darcy and Miss de Bourgh do not exchange letters, as far as I know. The letter is from Lady Catherine, and I promised to deliver it to her nephew personally." Mr Collins related this with pride.

Cousin Elizabeth looked at Miss Mary. "Mr Collins, we are very curious about Miss de Bourgh. We have heard wonderful things about her and her accomplishments. Will you tell us more about her?"

Mr Collins was happy to oblige. He hoped that the future Mrs Collins and Miss de Bourgh might become friends. He told them about the daughter of his patroness for some time, and all his cousins save Miss Catherine seemed quite interested in the subject. Finally, he thought he had done Miss de Bourgh justice.

Cousin Lydia turned to Cousin Elizabeth, "Lizzy, where is the second book you have chosen for me?"

"Do you really wish to start it so soon?"

"Oh yes, I intend to finish it before the ball, as we discussed."

"Very well, come to my room. While I search for it, I shall tell you a bit about it."

As the two young ladies left, Mr Collins realised he must make an increased effort to compliment Miss Elizabeth's wit and vivacity over the next few days. He would be most attentive. And on the night of the ball, his behaviour towards his dearest cousin would make his preference obvious for all to see. Then he would ask her to be his wife. It was a very good plan indeed.

Mr Collins turned to Cousin Mary. "Miss Mary, which of Fordyce's sermons are you studying today?"

Darcy paced through the crowded rooms of Netherfield, partly out of impatience and partly out of a desire to avoid Miss Bingley. He knew she expected to dance the first set with him, though he was being most disobliging by not asking her. No, if he were to dance the first set with anyone, it would be with a certain young lady. What could be taking them so long? Despite the crush of guests already present, Darcy cared only about one who had not yet arrived. But suddenly, he knew she was there. He neither saw nor heard her, but rather heard the voice of her excited mother, and for the third time in his life, Fitzwilliam Darcy was thankful for Mrs Bennet's appearance. Bingley, too, immediately brightened at the sound and bolted towards the door. This gave Darcy an excuse to look in that direction.

She entered on the arms of her eldest and youngest sisters, but they were merely faceless blurs to Darcy. He could see only her, looking more beautiful than any woman ought. By God, Anne must be right. This breathless euphoria, this desperate longing—how could any man withstand it? He should accompany Bingley to London in two days and stay there, fleeing like a coward. But perhaps he would not. He wondered at his wavering resolve. Perhaps he would stay here and...what, precisely? He did not know. All he knew was that he wanted to dance with Elizabeth Bennet tonight.

He began to walk towards her. Miss Elizabeth laughed at something Miss Lydia said and then beamed at the approaching Bingley. She relinquished Miss Bennet's arm to him, watching with open pleasure at her sister's happiness. Then her eyes glanced around the room, seemingly seeking something. In a matter of seconds, they found Darcy, and she smiled. If his step faltered just an instant, he could hardly blame himself. He continued to stride purposefully towards her, holding her gaze, but before he reached her to claim his dance, two things happened nearly simultaneously.

Miss Lydia spied him, and she began to step forward. But Miss Elizabeth held fast to her arm and spoke some low but forceful words in her ear. Miss Lydia halted in indecision, then visibly checked herself and nodded slightly. As Darcy attempted to decipher this interaction, he noticed movement at Miss Elizabeth's other arm. Mr Collins insinuated himself where Miss Bennet had vacated and was, at that moment, elbowing Miss Elizabeth in an awkward attempt to offer his arm to her. She accepted it with clear reluctance, and he smiled at her in a way that was sickeningly familiar. Mr Collins had often directed that mawkish smile at Jane Bennet before he was dissuaded from pursuing her.

Finally arriving at the group, Darcy greeted Miss Bennet first, as Bingley proudly had her out in front of the rest of the Bennets. She curtseyed, and he bowed. "Good evening, Miss Bennet. Your arrival has been much anticipated. Mr Bingley even held up the start of the dancing, causing much agitation among the guests."

"Oh dear! I am sorry. You have no idea how long it takes eight people to prepare for an occasion like this. Mr Bingley, you should not have altered your plans for me."

Bingley grinned like a fool. "But I would wait all night for the opportunity to dance with you. Now that you are here, I find I do not wish to wait any longer. Let us go tell the musicians to begin." Bingley led Miss Bennet away.

Darcy attempted brief polite greetings to the other Bennets, but he was interrupted by Mrs Bennet's grating voice. "Mr Darcy! What a dashing figure you cut in your formal attire! I daresay you are even more dashing than the officers! And I thought regimentals could not be improved upon!"

An acceptable reply to such a greeting escaped him. He was saved from formulating one by the arrival of Lieutenants Denny and Saunderson. The former addressed Mrs Bennet with a gallant bow. "What is this I hear about improving upon regimentals? Who dares such blasphemy?" He kissed her gloved hand.

Mrs Bennet tittered and batted her lashes. "Oh Mr Denny! You know I meant no disrespect. In my youth, I had quite the eye for a man in regimentals, I assure you! But Mr Darcy is so very tall and his garments so well-tailored that one cannot help but notice his fine figure. My, how flattering breeches are to male legs!"

Had Darcy not been so determined to dance with Elizabeth, he doubted he could endure the further inspection of his...person by her mother. Fortunately, Mr Bennet's timely intervention spared him.

"Come, Mrs Bennet, leave the rapt admiration of fashions and figures to the young people. Let us examine the available libations." He directed her away from the group. Darcy thought the consumption of spirits by Mrs Bennet would only make matters worse.

However, he thanked heaven for her present removal and vowed to avoid her for the rest of the night.

Mr Denny turned to the youngest Bennets. "Miss Lydia, Miss Catherine, may we solicit the first two dances from each of you?"

Though her sister accepted with alacrity, Miss Lydia shot Darcy a pleading look before accepting in turn. That foursome engaged in lively conversation as the officers escorted the girls away, leaving Darcy's task a much easier one. He now had only one ridiculous obstacle left to overcome.

The obstacle released the arm of a certain young lady and genuflected solemnly. Darcy could barely keep from rolling his eyes, an expression that did not go unnoticed by Miss Elizabeth. She curtseyed to him with a grin while her cousin held himself prostrate. Darcy could have quite happily stared at her for the rest of the night, but it was not to be. Mr Collins finally rose to his full height.

"Mr Darcy! I am honoured to see you again and pleased that I bring you nothing but propitious news of your dear aunt and cousin. I left both of them in excellent health only two short days ago. I have the further honour of delivering to your hands a letter from Lady Catherine." Mr Collins produced a missive from inside his waistcoat and handed it to Darcy with a flourish.

Darcy hid the letter away in his coat. Lady Catherine never wrote anything of particular interest, and he had much more important matters to address. If only Mr Collins would suddenly disappear or, perhaps, bow again. "Thank you for relaying news of my family, Mr Collins. I had not expected to see you in Hertfordshire again so soon."

"But how could any man stay away when he knows such inducements await him?" He again directed a mawkish grin at Elizabeth. This time she could barely keep from rolling *her* eyes.

"Indeed." Darcy found himself maddeningly unable to speak the words he desperately wished to speak. The murmur of the crowd indicated that the music would soon start. *Ask, you fool!*

Mr Collins again offered his arm to Miss Elizabeth. "If you will excuse us, I do not wish to miss one moment of this special dance with my dearest cousin."

With a look of resignation and a barely perceptible shrug, Miss

Elizabeth accepted the proffered arm. *Blast!* She had already promised her first dance to this fool. Darcy could only watch helplessly as the woman he loved was led away by a buffoon.

He cursed himself for not seizing his opportunity to secure a dance the way Bingley had in the street in Meryton last week. Bingley! She had promised her second set to Bingley! *Blast!* All of Darcy's nervous excitement transformed into ire. He stalked the edges of the room as the couples took their places. Miss Bingley spied him and began to approach, but the look on his face as he turned abruptly away seemed to make her abandon her pursuit.

The music began, and Darcy watched in ill humour. All four of the occupied Bennet sisters danced well, but Darcy was most attentive to a certain young lady. Miss Elizabeth moved through her turns gracefully except when interaction with Mr Collins was necessary. No partner could make *him* graceful. Darcy winced along with her when Mr Collins's poor dancing skills claimed a casualty in the form of the lady's sore toes. *Blast!* If only he had spared her this mortification!

"Good evening, Mr Darcy." He turned with a scowl to behold Miss Mary Bennet standing beside him.

He attempted to control both his scowl and his shock and made an effort to be friendly. "Good evening, Miss Mary. I am sorry, I did not greet you properly in the excitement of your family's arrival." In truth, he had not even noticed her.

"I took no offense. I, too, was caught up in the goings-on." She fell silent as she watched the dancers, and he could not keep himself from again watching one dancer in particular. At length, she spoke again. "All my sisters are engaged for the first two sets."

Darcy suddenly felt some compassion for her—to be the plainest of five sisters must be a constant burden, particularly at a ball. Mary Bennet was not unattractive, but compared to her sisters, particularly the eldest, she seemed plain. "May I have the honour of the next dance?"

Her gaze snapped to him. "Oh! Do not think I mentioned it in order to beg for a partner. You are very kind, and I thank you, but like you, I prefer not to dance. I have already promised Mr Collins and Mr Bingley each a set, and that is more than enough dancing for one night for my tastes. Will you be horribly offended if I decline your gracious offer?"

"No, not at all. I understand better than you realise. In this we are kindred spirits."

"Indeed, we are. I see that you take great interest in observing people, as I do. I only mentioned my sisters' dance cards because... well, because two of my sisters in particular are eager to discuss a matter of some import with you, and the subject will require the modicum of privacy that is afforded by a dance."

He stared at her, dumbstruck.

"Forgive my forwardness. As an avid observer, I see and hear many things, but I am no gossip, I assure you. The important matter I mentioned involves the gentleman whose acquaintance we made in Meryton just last week, on the day you and Mr Bingley met us unexpectedly."

His scowl returned along with a seething rage. *Wickham.*

"You obviously know which gentleman I mean." Miss Mary did not seem offended by Darcy's change in demeanour. "We met him again at my Aunt Philips's house the following night. He had some conversation with Lydia and, especially, with Elizabeth."

His stomach lurched with the knowledge that Wickham had spent any time at all with Elizabeth. He could only imagine what had been said. His eyes again found her on the dance floor, confirming that she was well and unharmed (aside from the aforementioned toes of course).

"Both my sisters are eager to share the particulars with you, but I would recommend you seek the story from Elizabeth. She heard more than Lydia and is less prone to fits of melodrama. In such a public setting, I think you will appreciate Lizzy's poise and discretion."

He turned to really look at Mary Bennet for the first time. "I thank you for the information. I shall seek to secure a dance with Miss Elizabeth at her earliest convenience." He knew not why he added, "I had planned on it already."

She inclined her head and began to move away, but he halted her with one last statement. "If you should change your mind and wish to dance more than two sets, I shall be honoured to be your partner, Miss Mary."

She smiled as he bowed to her. "I shall keep your generous offer in mind. Now I suggest you seek out either Mr Collins or Mr Bingley, for they will trade partners for the next set."

"Thank you," he called again to her retreating form. *Most extraordinary!* But he had no time to contemplate Miss Mary Bennet, not when he must intercept her sister as soon as possible.

Darcy closed in on the dancers for the final notes. The room erupted into applause. He easily found Miss Elizabeth among the crowd, for she was most eager to escape, though Mr Collins insisted on escorting her from the dance floor. She pointed and fixed her eyes on something in particular as they made their way through the throng. Darcy followed her gaze to Miss Lucas, who stood not too far from him. He seized the opportunity and greeted the young lady first.

"Good evening, Miss Lucas. I am happy to see you again." Darcy really *was* happy to see her. He knew her to be a sensible and considerate young lady based on their unconventional discussion in Netherfield's garden.

"Good evening, Mr Darcy. Oh look, Elizabeth is coming this way too." She smiled at him and then at the approaching couple. "With Mr Collins," she added.

Darcy had almost forgotten how perceptive she was. He had apparently lost his ability to conceal any of his thoughts and emotions. Or perhaps he had only lost that ability where Elizabeth Bennet was concerned.

"Miss Lucas!" exclaimed Mr Collins when he arrived. "I am delighted to see you again."

Bingley and Miss Bennet arrived at the small group as well, and a few moments of enthusiastic greetings followed. Darcy took advantage of the confusion to position himself as close to his object as possible. As Mr Collins held forth on the horrors of muddy roads, Darcy took his chance. "Miss Elizabeth," he said quietly, "I hope to have the pleasure of dancing with you this evening."

She looked surprised. "Indeed, Mr Darcy? I had thought dancing was a punishment to you. However, my third set is yours. I should hardly dream of refusing you for fear of discouraging your uncharacteristic desire to dance."

Success! At last he had secured his dance. "I believe you know that I am not entirely opposed to dancing, merely that I dislike dancing with strangers. I should very much enjoy dancing with *you*. I look forward to it."

Surprise flashed in her eyes again—those fine eyes. He held her gaze while a slow blush overspread her cheeks. Darcy had no desire to ever look away.

"I...I thank you," she stammered, finally looking down.

Aside from the annoyance of Mr Collins's continued presence, Darcy thoroughly enjoyed the ensuing conversation amongst the small group. With Miss Elizabeth, Miss Bennet, Miss Lucas, and Bingley present, Darcy realised these were the people he most favoured in Hertfordshire. The evening had taken a decidedly positive turn. He only need wait through one more dance set, a mere half hour. This may very well be the best ball he had ever attended.

20

Tolerably Encouraging

Charlotte Lucas had been watching the various Bennet girls and their admirers since they arrived. It was *most* diverting. She must tell John about it. Unfortunately, his planned return in a fortnight did not allow him to witness all this romantic intrigue for himself.

Jane and Mr Bingley were completely absorbed in each other; it was a blessing considering the sour looks coming from *his* sisters. Mr Darcy watched Elizabeth like a hawk from the edge of the room, looking decidedly displeased. Mr Collins, meanwhile, showered his attentions on Lizzy. When Lizzy was not avoiding her dance partner's missteps, she stole glances in Mr Darcy's direction. Lydia may have been the most amusing of all. She took pleasure in her dance with Lieutenant Denny, laughing and talking, but if there was any lull in the conversation, her head would whip around in search of Mr Darcy, who, invariably, would be staring at her sister. Mary prowled the edges of the room, a female version of Mr Darcy, only lacking the glower. Then there was Kitty, who was completely oblivious to it all and therefore enjoying herself in blissful ignorance. Most diverting indeed.

The dance would soon end. Charlotte caught Elizabeth's weary eye and nodded. Yes, Charlotte could serve her own purposes and provide some welcome relief to her friend by distracting Mr Collins tonight. Based on his obvious attentions, she predicted that Lizzy would soon be the recipient—and the rejecter—of a marriage proposal. Charlotte need only make herself helpful and available to both of them over these next few days. She again wished that she could share her aspirations with her friend, but Lizzy would only argue with her and try to convince her to be happy as a spinster. No, if Mr Collins wanted a wife so badly, Charlotte was content to fill the role.

"Good evening, Miss Lucas. I am happy to see you again." Charlotte was suddenly addressed by Mr Darcy.

"Good evening, Mr Darcy. Oh look, Elizabeth is coming this way too." She smiled at him and then at the approaching couple. "With Mr Collins."

A flash of displeasure crossed Mr Darcy's face. Ah, perhaps Charlotte could help her friend in another way tonight. She would distract one unwanted suitor but encourage another suitor who needed a little push. Something must be done; the poor man's staring was becoming almost indecent. Elizabeth was certainly not indifferent to him, but she was, wisely, being cautious. How could a most excellent match be made when one person was wracked with indecision and the other with wariness? Perhaps jealousy could serve as impetus for Mr Darcy to act.

Lizzy and Mr Collins had arrived. "Miss Lucas! I am delighted to meet you again."

"And I am delighted to see you, Mr Collins. I am so pleased you were able to return to Hertfordshire for the ball," Charlotte replied before briefly embracing Elizabeth in greeting. Her expression told Charlotte that she had news to share in private.

Jane and Mr Bingley, the very picture of a besotted couple, arrived too. More greetings were exchanged, and Charlotte attempted to give Lizzy a moment of respite. "Mr Collins, when did you arrive?"

"On Monday, and I was received with much warmth from my dear relations." He smiled fondly at Lizzy.

Charlotte tried again. "Monday? Did you travel in all that rain? How dreadful!" This approach worked, for Mr Collins had many observations to share about the differences in weather between Kent and Hertfordshire, as well as many complaints about the muddy roads.

"Well, Mr Collins," said Mr Bingley cheerfully, "you have arrived safely despite your troubles and can now enjoy an evening of dancing amongst the beautiful ladies here." He never took his eyes off of Jane.

"Indeed, Mr Bingley, and I am very much looking forward to the next dance with dear Cousin Jane, if you can be persuaded to give her up for half an hour."

Mr Bingley laughed. "Well, I suppose I must. But at least I have the consolation of Miss Elizabeth's company for that half hour."

Lizzy finally joined the banter. "Mr Bingley, I doubt your dancing skills can live up to my sister's glowing praises, but you will have your chance to prove yourself to me in a few moments."

Mr Bingley looked ecstatic. "I shall put my best effort forward. Now, if we may somehow persuade Darcy to dance, I shall be completely triumphant tonight. How might we convince him?"

Mr Darcy replied, "There is no need to convince me. Miss Elizabeth has graciously promised her third set to me."

"Excellent!" cried Mr Bingley, with an incredulous look.

"You do my dear cousin a great honour, Mr Darcy." Mr Collins perhaps felt the distinction too strongly, apparently considering this a tribute to *his* importance rather than to Lizzy's.

"On the contrary, it is my honour," Mr Darcy said seriously. Then he added, "I hope to be honoured similarly with a dance from Miss Bennet tonight."

Jane demurely agreed to dance the fourth set with Mr Darcy while Mr Bingley beamed with pride. The second set would soon begin. The newly re-arranged couples moved off to take their places, leaving Charlotte with Mr Darcy again. They watched the dancers lining up and then he turned to her. "Perhaps you will favour me with this dance, Miss Lucas, if you are not otherwise engaged."

"I thank you, Mr Darcy. I am not engaged."

He offered his arm, and they followed in the steps of the others. Charlotte glanced around at her neighbours. Most were turned in her direction with obvious curiosity, but two faces in particular stood out. Lydia, standing up with Mr Saunderson some distance away, gaped at Charlotte and her illustrious partner, and Miss Bingley looked absolutely enraged. She was paired with Augustus Goulding (known locally, rather unfortunately, as Gussy, and the only remaining eligible Goulding after Jacob's scandalous elopement with the governess). The music began, and Miss Bingley was forced to impress the room with her fine dancing skills. As hostess, she danced first.

"I saw your sister, Miss Maria, here, but what occupies your brothers tonight?" Poor, taciturn Mr Darcy sought distraction in conversation to keep from staring at Elizabeth.

Charlotte obliged. Perhaps it was time to test out her jealousy theory. "Walter is extremely pleased to have the house to himself tonight. But Peter tried desperately to convince my parents that he should attend the ball. He even promised to fetch punch for any of us should we become thirsty from our dancing exertions."

Mr Darcy laughed, a most pleasant sound. "I cannot imagine why he would wish to come so very badly."

"Can you not? He knew Lizzy would be here."

"Ah," he managed to say as his eyes were naturally drawn again towards Elizabeth. She and Mr Bingley were just about to take their turn, following Mr Collins and a now slightly limping Jane.

"But if Peter *had* come tonight, he would be very distressed. I imagine it cannot be easy to watch another man pursue the woman you admire, even if the rival has no hope of success."

"I imagine not," he said, watching his friend move through the turns with Elizabeth.

Charlotte continued smoothly. "In fact, Walter had a similar preference for Jane Bennet just a couple of years ago. Every time she received any suitor's interest, Walter felt it keenly. But, he has moved past those feelings. I hope Peter can do the same, for it is an inevitability that Lizzy's charms will induce ever more suitors to pursue her."

"I imagine so."

"Yes, my two younger brothers are simply too young to form an alliance with any of the Bennet girls. I should very much like to call them my sisters. Lizzy and I in particular share an intimate relationship as if we were already sisters." Charlotte thought she had said enough. Mr Darcy was a clever man—there was no need to belabour the point.

They were silent for some time as they went through their turns together. Charlotte felt all eyes upon them, but Mr Darcy was mindless of the attention, appearing deep in thought. He was a superior dancer despite his reluctance.

"I have heard much of your eldest brother, Miss Lucas. When will he return?" Mr Darcy asked, proving that Charlotte had indeed said quite enough, for she had never mentioned John explicitly.

"We expect John in a fortnight. He is finishing some business in Southampton and London. In fact, this is meant to be a surprise to my parents, but I suppose *you* are unlikely to spread the news. John is most likely buying a house in town."

"Then he has been successful in his business ventures."

"He has. Of course he cannot afford to buy in the most fashionable parts of town, but we Lucases shall be quite content regardless. I am very proud of my brother."

"As you should be."

All conversation was at an end until the conclusion of the set. Mr Darcy then offered his arm to her. They moved towards a group forming from various Bennet and Bingley siblings and their dance partners. Caroline Bingley brightened considerably when she saw Charlotte and Mr Darcy approaching.

Gussy Goulding grinned at Charlotte, revealing his missing tooth up front. "Miss Lucas! I did not see your family arrive. Pray, how do you do?"

"Very well, Mr Goulding, and you?"

"Oh, I am very well. But I am missing the antics of your brother John. I shall never forget his behaviour at our ball just before he left on his adventures. Poor Jenny worked for hours and still could not save the rug."

Charlotte laughed. "I am very sorry for Jenny's trouble. But do not suppose that John would behave similarly now. All those expecting the same reckless youth to return will be rather disappointed."

"That is a pity. I was very much looking forward to livelier Christmas gatherings with his return." Gussy winked at Charlotte. "Speaking of punch, may I fetch some for you, Miss Bingley?"

"No, thank you, Mr Goulding."

"What about you, Miss Lucas? Would you like some punch?" Charlotte accepted his kind offer.

"I believe I would benefit from some refreshment at the moment," said clever Elizabeth to no one in particular.

"Dearest Cousin! How negligent of your comfort I have been! Allow me to fetch you some punch this instant," replied Mr Collins with much urgency.

The two gentlemen walked off together in search of punch, and Charlotte whispered to Mr Darcy, "Peter's presence would have been superfluous, poor boy."

He barked out a laugh before getting himself under regulation again, and he shot Charlotte a reproachful look. She smiled at him. Lizzy, Jane, Mr Bingley, Mrs Hurst, and Miss Bingley watched the exchange with varying expressions: curiosity, disbelief, disdain. Mr Hurst looked disappointed that he had missed his chance to visit the refreshments.

"It is wonderful for you, is it not, Miss Eliza, that Mr Collins should return to visit his dear relations so soon? Louisa and I were saying to each other how very much he belongs with you all at Longbourn."

"We do our best to make everyone feel welcome in our house, Miss Bingley," said Elizabeth in a guileless tone. "We Bennets have no false pretensions or affectations of superiority."

Charlotte tried not to smirk. Miss Bingley seemed to be regrouping to land another barb when Mr Collins and Mr Goulding returned, punch in hands. Charlotte thanked Gus for his trouble.

"I apologise for the delay, dearest cousin. I ran into Miss Maria Lucas and felt the need to greet her properly."

"I quite understand, Mr Collins. You should not neglect your friends." Lizzy sipped her punch and said nothing more.

"Has anyone seen Miss Mary recently?" asked Mr Collins. "She promised me the third set."

"Perhaps you had better go look for her."

"But I hesitate to leave you, Miss Elizabeth."

"I am perfectly well, Mr Collins. I should not wish my sister to be disappointed at missing her dance with you."

"Of course not. You are a most caring sister. I shall find Cousin Mary now and seek you out after the third set."

Lizzy avoided a reply by again sipping her punch, and Mr Collins made his exit with a solemn bow.

Then Kitty, Lydia, and Maria arrived with Lieutenants Denny, Saunderson, Pratt, and Chamberlayne. Kitty introduced Gus to the officers as "Gussy Goulding" and did not realise she had done so. Gussy did not seem to realise it either. After all the niceties were accomplished, Kitty and Maria fell again into giggles with the officers, but Lydia pushed her way further into the circle with purpose.

"Mr Darcy! You have played a joke on us, I think, pretending that you would not dance tonight. But I saw you and Miss Lucas dancing the last together, and I am convinced that you enjoyed it."

"I asked Miss Lucas on the impulse of the moment, but I confess, I did enjoy our dance."

Charlotte began to return his compliment but was cut off by Miss Bingley. "You dance superbly, Mr Darcy. It really is cruel of you to do it so rarely. I hope the impulse will strike you again tonight."

Lydia and Miss Bingley hung on his every word. "I daresay it will." This reply left much to be desired. Elizabeth stared intently at her punch.

The musicians readied their instruments for the next set. Lydia asked in desperation, "Will the impulse not strike you right now, Mr Darcy?"

"It already has." He turned towards Lizzy. "This is our dance, Miss Elizabeth."

Lydia gasped and Miss Bingley glared. Elizabeth shared a strange look with Lydia for a moment, but then accepted Mr Darcy's arm. "Indeed, it is. I only hope I shall do you credit and not put you off dancing for the rest of the night. I should not wish to be blamed for depriving everyone else of the privilege of seeing you dance."

"You can have no fear of that, Miss Elizabeth."

They walked away together, and the group that remained sorted itself into couples for the dance. Charlotte wound up promising her next two sets to Mr Denny and Mr Chamberlayne, respectively. But she was most anxious to speak with Elizabeth, hopefully privately.

21

Finding Him Very Agreeable

As she walked towards the dance floor on the arm of Mr Darcy, Elizabeth was preoccupied with the task at hand. Prior to the ball, she and Lydia had agreed that Elizabeth would be the one to warn Mr Darcy about Mr Wickham's falsehoods. Lydia had reluctantly conceded that she might become too agitated to carry out the task discreetly herself, and in exchange for this concession, Elizabeth unequivocally promised to explain how Lydia had defended Mr Darcy and his sister against Mr Wickham's insults. Lydia remembered all this, surely, but her countenance revealed wounded feelings nonetheless when she discovered Mr Darcy had asked Elizabeth to dance. There was nothing Elizabeth could do about it except keep her promise.

It was a delicate subject to broach under any circumstances, let alone in her current nervous state. They took their places and stood for some time without speaking a word. Elizabeth began to imagine that their silence was to last through the two dances.

"I am afraid we must have some conversation, Mr Darcy. It would look odd to be entirely silent for half an hour together."

He smiled slightly. "Indeed. I had hoped you would start the conversation. Your talent for it certainly exceeds mine."

"I suppose you are much better at listening, particularly through open windows." She could not resist the chance to tease him again.

He took it well, laughing quietly. This exchange eased Elizabeth's tension considerably as they began their turn, and she felt an odd sort of calm, a strange rightness, in dancing with him, even in silence. They moved through the steps in perfect harmony with each other. When their hands met, his grasp was firm and warm through her glove. When their eyes met, she wondered that she did not miss a step, for everything but those gold-flecked dark eyes would fall away from her awareness, including the movement of her own limbs.

When they had gone down the dance, he asked her whether she and her sisters often walked to Meryton. This was the opening she needed. She answered in the affirmative and added, "When you met us there the other day, we had just been forming a new acquaintance."

His jaw clenched, but he said not a word. Elizabeth knew she must go on. "Mr Wickham is blessed with such happy manners as may ensure his making friends quickly, but after a long conversation with him, I find I do not wish to remain friends."

"I am relieved to hear it. I speak from personal experience when I say that he is not the sort of friend one wishes to keep. I hope..." He paused until she met his eyes, his expression so very earnest. "I hope you were not subjected to anything untoward during the course of your conversation."

"I confess that his choice of subject matter—and the liberty with which he spoke about it to a new acquaintance—shocked me." Elizabeth feared they would never reach the heart of the matter if they continued to speak in such veiled, cautious language. "I shall come directly to the point, for Lydia and I agreed you must be warned. His chief topic of interest was *you,* and he had no shortage of uncomplimentary things to say."

"I thank you and Miss Lydia for your concern. I am well aware of his grievances against me."

"I must also tell you that Lydia was your staunchest defender against what she termed 'horrible lies.'" His jaw unclenched a bit. "She took particular umbrage to some unflattering statements about Miss Darcy."

The effect of her last statement was profound; if Elizabeth had ever thought Mr Darcy's countenance foreboding before, she had been gravely mistaken. "He dares to malign Georgiana!" he hissed.

She stepped towards him, placing her fingers on his sleeve, and spoke softly but urgently, "Please, sir, I should not have mentioned it in so public a setting. He said only that she is too proud. Nothing more, I promise you."

He looked into her eyes for a long moment. She had never seen his expression so unguarded, and what she read there—agony, rage, fear—nearly broke her heart. He finally looked down at her hand, composing himself, and she stepped back into her place. He glanced around. "I am not able to reveal too much, but I must warn you about his character so that you and all your sisters might be on your guard."

He spoke with such gravity as to hold special weight in Elizabeth's consciousness. She pondered how best to decipher his meaning, but he abruptly changed the subject. "Tell me, Miss Elizabeth, have you resumed your morning walks now that your injury is healed?"

She eyed him. Could he again be suggesting they meet secretly in the woods? Could she again be considering doing it? "I have, though I go a bit later now to account for the shortening days."

He nodded before she added quietly, "I also walk out later to avoid rather than intercept one member of the household. It appears I have attained far too much success in my efforts to distract a certain gentleman's interest."

"Perhaps I could reveal more of my aunt's deeply held opinions to further influence him. Although, in light of our previous discussion, I cannot imagine why he thinks his new object would be any more acceptable than his first under that criterion."

She shook her head. "I appreciate your attempt at flattery, Mr Darcy, but everyone knows his first object is the real beauty. He is keenly aware of what he has given up."

"Utter nonsense," he grumbled, looking towards Mary suffering through her dance with Mr Collins.

"In any case, I thank you for your offer to intercede again, but I think it high time the gentleman in question experiences rejection first hand. Perhaps then he will cease making assumptions about his own significance in young ladies' affections."

"I would not count on it, Miss Elizabeth," he quipped.

They silently moved through the next dance together, again in a harmony that Elizabeth could not help but notice. Afterwards, they watched as first Lydia and Mr Bingley and then Jane and Mr Goulding went down the dance. Elizabeth remembered the nearly equal excitement and anticipation her two sisters felt while preparing for the ball, though Lydia vocalised it far more. Now, how differently they appeared in visage. Lydia's usual vivacity dimmed with her disappointment, though Mr Bingley's jovial spirit could do naught but cheer her a bit. Jane, on the other hand, veritably glowed in happiness.

"I wonder, Mr Darcy, had you known the repercussions that would follow from your first interference into my family's romantic affairs, would you have so readily agreed to assist me?" He turned to her in question, and she added simply, "Jane and Mr Bingley."

"Yes, of course I would," he assured her with some degree of surprise in his voice.

"But I am sure expectations for his prospects were...a bit higher."

"Those concerns are of little consequence now. I could never disapprove of anything or anyone that brings such felicity to my friend."

She wondered whether he *had* ever voiced concerns about Jane's low connexions and meagre fortune to Mr Bingley. Surely Miss Bingley and Mrs Hurst had done so. No matter—there could be little question as to Mr Bingley's intentions after tonight. "I have never seen Jane happier either," she said fondly. "I could never tell an adequate number of amusing tales to repay the service you rendered *there*, intentional or not."

"You give yourself too little credit."

She puzzled over his ambiguous reply as the dance ended, and he offered her his arm. They met up with Jane and Gus Goulding, Lydia and Mr Bingley, and Mary and Mr Collins. Lydia's questioning look moved from Elizabeth, who nodded, to Mr Darcy, who smiled and bowed slightly. Lydia beamed in response.

Elizabeth wished for a sudden loss of hearing, situated as she was at the dinner table between her mother and her cousin. Better yet, she wished each of her voluble neighbours would suffer sudden (but temporary, she supposed) laryngitis.

Ever since Mrs Bennet's outrageous statements about Mr Darcy's...attire, Elizabeth had attempted to avoid her mother lest she might hear more. When they sat down to supper, therefore, she considered it a most unlucky perverseness that placed them within one of each other, but deeply was she relieved to find her mother talking to Lady Lucas of nothing else but her expectation that Jane would be soon married to Mr Bingley. Thank goodness the pair was already in a formal courtship, otherwise Mrs Bennet's bragging would be excessively premature and tasteless indeed.

It was an animating subject, and Mrs Bennet seemed incapable of fatigue while enumerating the advantages of the match. Mr Bingley being such a charming young man and so rich and living but three miles from them were the first points of self-congratulation. It was, moreover, such a promising thing for her younger daughters, as Jane's marrying so greatly must throw them in the way of other rich men. This last observation was accompanied, much to Elizabeth's horror, by a pointed look at Mr Darcy. She finally ended her commentary with a significant look towards Mr Collins and Elizabeth. "And I am certain my other daughters will follow Jane into similarly advantageous marriages, some sooner than others." She winked at Lady Lucas.

Directly to Elizabeth's right—for cruel fate did not afford her the shield of even one other body there—sat Mr Collins. The only lucky circumstance in the seating arrangements, though luck probably had nothing to do with it, was that dear Charlotte sat to Mr Collins's right and thus occupied the parson for some of the time. Had Elizabeth been sitting near someone with whom she wanted to converse, Charlotte's distraction would have been even more appreciated. As it was, Elizabeth would take whatever relief she could get.

She tried to let her mind wander, thinking back to her last dance partner, Captain Carter, who currently sat next to Lydia some distance down the table. He and Mr Collins had exchanged their supper set partners before taking seats. Lydia might perhaps now regret her hasty accession to the substitution, for though she would have been forced to sit next to Mr Collins, she would also be in closer proximity to Mr Darcy. *Mr Darcy...*

Elizabeth pushed the distracting thought away and tried to think about her dance with Captain Carter. But, although enjoyable enough, their dance had been completely unremarkable. So she thought about her dance partner prior to the last one, Gussy Goulding. Despite his reputation for clumsiness earned through a propensity towards sometimes disfiguring injuries during his awkward adolescence, he actually danced better than Mr Collins. But again, that dance left her with nothing worth pondering now, even if her toes did survive the set unscathed. Gus was currently chatting amiably with everyone around him while seated next to Charlotte on the far side and almost directly across from Mr Darcy. *Mr Darcy...*

"Dearest Cousin, are you quite well?"

Elizabeth was almost happy to have her train of thought interrupted by Mr Collins's inquiry. But she realised she had been unconsciously staring at Mr Darcy across the table. She could not look away fast enough now, even as she blushed at his questioning gaze.

"Forgive me, Mr Collins. My mind was elsewhere. What did you say?"

"I just remarked on my success in dancing with each of my fair cousins tonight. Now that my duty, however pleasant it was, is fulfilled, I can give way to my...fancy for future dances."

The chances of Elizabeth enjoying the remainder of the ball were very grim indeed. She took a spoonful of white soup. How best to reply?

"Mr Collins," said Mr Darcy, speaking for the first time during the meal. "My aunt mentioned a new phaeton in the letter you kindly delivered to me tonight. Have you seen it?"

"Indeed, I have, Mr Darcy. It is a splendid conveyance, I assure you, perfectly suited to Lady Catherine's elevated rank..."

Charlotte leaned back in her chair to peer at Elizabeth behind Mr Collins and then smirked. How Elizabeth wished to speak with her! At least Elizabeth was again free of Mr Collins's attentions for the rest of the meal. The same could not be said of Mr Darcy, however.

When supper was over, the dancing resumed. Mr Denny approached Elizabeth, reminding her of their promised dance, and she was only too happy to escape Mr Collins for another half hour. Upon the conclusion of the dance, she indicated a wish to speak with Charlotte, and Mr Denny obligingly escorted her towards her friend, but they were intercepted by Mr Collins.

"Dearest Cousin, you are a superior dancer. Might I have the honour of the next with you?"

As Mr Denny bowed to them and moved away, Elizabeth considered her options. The very notion of dancing again with Mr Collins made her toes cry out in protest. "I thank you, but I fear I might overstrain my healed ankle by dancing anymore tonight."

His alarm was great. "Cousin Elizabeth! How very thoughtless of me! Allow me to assist you. You simply must be seated."

When she was seated, in vain did she entreat him to stand up with someone else. He assured her that as to dancing, he was perfectly indifferent; that his chief object was to recommend himself to her, and that he should therefore make a point of remaining close to her the whole evening. "But sir, you must at least dance with Charlotte. The Lucases are very important friends to us at Longbourn, and you know Charlotte is particularly dear to me."

"If this pleases you, I shall be very happy to dance with Miss Lucas." He left her to approach Charlotte, and Elizabeth felt not a little guilt at subjecting her poor friend's toes to such a punishment. But this might be the last half hour she would have to herself.

As the dancers took their places, Mr Darcy approached. Her astonishment was great when he applied for her hand again. "I am very sorry, Mr Darcy, but I cannot dance again tonight."

He looked down at her feet. "Have you reinjured your ankle? Do you require assistance?"

"No, although just a few moments ago, I *did* use my ankle as an excuse to forego another dance with Mr Collins. A sincere concern for my toes actually prompted my refusal. Either way, I am not at liberty to dance any more tonight."

She thought she might be rewarded with a smile, but instead he said gravely, "Then I wish I had asked you five minutes earlier. I trust you will still be able to take your morning walks?"

"Oh yes, refraining from dancing is just a precaution against further injury, you see. At least that will be my explanation should anyone question my intent to walk." She paused. "Besides, I shall not try to walk tomorrow after our late night. I shall be quite ready to do so on the day following, however."

He nodded, saying nothing more. She looked towards the line of dancers and saw Lydia standing up with Henry Long.

"Mr Darcy, I wonder whether I might ask a favour of you tonight." He waited. "Lydia prepared for tonight's ball in a fairly unusual way. She read two books in the last week. Well, one and three-quarters, if truth be told."

"In preparation for a ball?"

"Yes, you see, she deduced, reasonably so, that the likeliest way to tempt *you* to speak is to discuss literature."

He smirked. "I see."

"She asked me for advice on how to become more...of an authority on literary works. I recommended two books and offered to discuss them with her before the ball. In exchange, I extracted a promise that she would read at least two more books after the ball. Whatever her motivation, I most heartily approve of her desire to improve her mind through reading. Do you not agree?"

"Of course. What, then, is the favour you ask?"

"I fear if she fails in her efforts, she will be discouraged, not to mention, terribly disappointed. Would it be too much trouble for you to speak with her tonight? About books, I mean?" She felt foolish the moment the words were spoken.

"I do owe Miss Lydia my thanks. Perhaps I might ask her to dance the next?"

"Oh! She would surely be overjoyed if you do, but I would urge caution in giving her *too* much encouragement."

"I shall be encouraging in a brotherly sort of way. I excel at brotherly encouragement." He grinned, complete with dimples.

She laughed. "As Lydia has no brother, let us hope she recognises it as such. I must further caution you not to smile at her like that."

His brow furrowed as the dimples disappeared. Elizabeth was sorry she had said anything. "My sister always tells me I ought to smile *more*."

"Well, yes, but not if you wish to escape the notice of the fairer sex. Remember when I told you that every smirk is like some hard-won prize? Imagine what a flash of those dimples means to a young lady."

He looked rather stunned and pink around the cheeks. But this was nothing to Elizabeth's full blush after realising what she had said. The aforementioned dimples really did have quite an effect, making her say aloud all manner of idiotic things.

The fluttering of a handkerchief above the crowd caught Elizabeth's attention. She knew who was attached to that handkerchief.

"Mr Darcy, I did not apologise for my mother's earlier behaviour, but I think the best way to make amends is to warn you that she now comes this way. Perhaps you had better go back to haunting the edges of the room."

He did not need to be told twice. The urgency of the situation was quite apparent to him. "Thank you, Miss Elizabeth. Though I regret our conversation must be cut short, I quite agree with you."

He bowed to her and strode away, leaving Elizabeth alone to answer when her mother exclaimed, "Lizzy, why is Mr Collins dancing with Charlotte Lucas? Why are you not dancing with him? Where did Mr Darcy go?"

Elizabeth silently lamented the very poor prospect that she might enjoy the rest of the evening. At least Jane and Lydia would be happy, and Kitty was perfectly happy as well. She could not tell whether Mary enjoyed herself or not. But beyond all this, and beyond worries about Mr Collins, Elizabeth could not help but think upon her next morning walk with anticipation. Where had all her caution gone? She lost it somewhere during her third dance, no doubt.

Books in a Ballroom

Lydia was not enjoying the ball at Netherfield. No, that was not entirely true. She was enjoying herself—after all, she had been asked to dance every set so far, and Denny, Saunderson, Pratt, and Chamberlayne were such good fun. But she had hardly even spoken to Mr Darcy. He had danced three sets tonight: one with Charlotte Lucas, one with Lizzy, and the next with Jane. But then he retreated to the edges of the room, skipping the supper set entirely. Lydia was sure of this because she caught glimpses of him during her miserable dance with Mr Collins. Luckily, she escaped her cousin just before the meal, sitting instead with Captain Carter and the jolly collection of officers she, Kitty, and Maria so enjoyed. She did not even mind terribly that Mary King, ghastly freckles and all, had somehow ingratiated herself into their group.

When everyone had finished eating, Henry Long approached and asked her for a set. (*Drat!* Another set claimed, and still no closer to her goal!) He then proceeded to ask Maria and Kitty for subsequent sets. His bashful, stammering request revealed that the third of the three young ladies was his real object of admiration. He was a good sort of boy, just a few months older than Kitty, all lanky arms and legs. Kitty was completely insensible to young Mr Long's preference, and Lydia decided it best her sister remain uninformed until *after* the promised dance. Kitty tended to blurt out the most bizarre things when nervous. Within the past hour, she had tried to compliment Mrs Hurst's feathers, saying they must have been plucked from the tail of a sizeable bird. Lord, how Lydia and Maria had laughed! Mrs Hurst only trembled in indignation, making those very feathers quiver on her head.

The assembled guests moved back into the ballroom, and the musicians readied their instruments. Lydia danced her promised set with Captain Carter. She tried to spy Mr Darcy but could not find him. When the set was over, she saw her mother and Aunt Philips nearby.

"Mama," she said after Captain Carter delivered her to Mrs Bennet, "have you seen Mr Darcy?"

"No, my dear Lydia, not since supper. Has he not asked you to dance yet? Teasing man! Perhaps he thinks you are too occupied by the officers. You must separate yourself from them, agreeable as they are, for a little while at least."

"Yes, perhaps I shall." Lydia scanned the crowd for a tall, well-dressed figure. "If Jane and Mr Bingley were more inclined towards conversation tonight, I would stay near them in the hopes of intercepting Mr Darcy."

"Dear Jane! She has caught Mr Bingley, I am certain of it! You must not bother them. If I do see Mr Darcy, I shall raise up my handkerchief like so to catch your attention." Mrs Bennet demonstrated the signal while Aunt Philips nodded in approval.

Lydia proceeded to answer any number of silly questions about her dance partners and her meal. Mrs Bennet seemed to be a bit in her cups, with her cheeks red and her handkerchief raised every now and then to cover her hiccups just a moment too late.

"I knew you would be asked to dance every set! With your agreeable temperament, who can resist you? And Mrs Long has the impudence to boast of her nieces' success tonight! As if those two could hold a candle to any of my girls!"

Henry Long came to claim his dance, and Lydia hoped he had not heard Mrs Bennet going on about his family so. They danced and chatted together. Lydia learned that he would go off to Oxford next fall.

"Are you looking forward to it very much? To leaving here and seeing something beyond Meryton?"

"Not particularly. I should much rather stay with my friends. Though I know I ought to be grateful for the opportunity, I cannot imagine spending so much time reading what was written by dead men in dead languages."

Lydia laughed. "Make sure to tell Kitty that when you dance with her. She will agree with you."

Some alarm crossed his face, and then he smiled, embarrassed. Lydia could only laugh again and shake her head. Out of the corner of her eye, she caught sight of a fluttering hankie above the crowd. Her attention immediately fixed on the tall man whose presence elicited this signal. He was speaking to Elizabeth; Lydia watched as he quickly strode away. She lost him in the crowd, but when she found him again, she was surprised to see him looking right at her. When would this dance end?

It ended in approximately a quarter of an hour, in truth, but it felt an eternity to Lydia. She took Mr Long's proffered arm, considering how best to approach Mr Darcy where she had last seen him at the edge of the room. She need not have bothered, for the pair's progress through the crowd was suddenly halted by the gentleman himself.

He bowed to them both. "Miss Lydia, may I have the next dance?"

"You may!"

He bowed again and quickly retreated. *Drat!* Why was he constantly striding away? No matter, she would dance the next with Mr Darcy!

She spent the next ten minutes in giddy giggles with Maria and Kitty while Mr Long looked on awkwardly. Kitty grudgingly admitted she was wrong in her prediction that Mr Darcy would only dance two sets the entire night. "Perhaps Mr Darcy is inebriated, for I cannot account for the change in his behaviour any other way."

Unfortunately for Kitty, the gentleman in question—looking decidedly sober—had just appeared at her side. "Miss Maria, Miss Catherine," he greeted. The latter's mouth hung open while the former burst into laughter again.

Lydia was torn between laughing at Kitty and being mortified by her. She opted for escape instead. "Mr Darcy, have you come to claim your dance?"

"I have." He held out his arm, which she happily took, and they moved towards the dancers.

After they took their places, she asked, "Are you enjoying the ball, Mr Darcy?"

"I am," he replied, far too gravely for the sentiment. "And you, Miss Lydia?"

"Of course. All ladies, young and old, enjoy a good ball."

"I am not sure your generalisation applies to one of your sisters." He nodded towards Mary standing in the doorway.

"Oh, do not let her fool you. She loves to observe all these people interacting with each other. In many ways, Mary is like my father. He observes so that he might ridicule, while Mary observes so that she might disapprove."

"She does not appear to disapprove. She rather seems to be committing everything to memory."

Lydia considered. "She does have a remarkable memory. She can quote any passage from the Bible or from *Fordyce's Sermons*. Whenever we need to know the date of someone's birth or anniversary, Mary will know it—not just within our own family, but every prominent family in and around Meryton." They had discussed Mary quite long enough. "When is *your* birthday, Mr Darcy?"

"In September." She waited for him to inquire when hers was, but instead he said, "I understand that I owe you my thanks, Miss Lydia, for...your defence of my character."

"Lizzy explained what occurred at my Aunt Philips's house then?" Lydia longed to tell him all about Mr Wickham's lies and what she had said in reply, but she knew she must not do so here, where anyone might overhear.

"Yes. I thank you and applaud your discernment." She glowed in happiness at his praise. "Superficial charms can often conceal a base character, particularly to one as young as yourself."

"I am not so very young."

He showed the first hint of a smile. "When is your birthday?"

She beamed. "In June."

"Then you are near six months younger than my sister, and she is twelve years my junior."

This would not do at all. Lydia contemplated how to get the conversation back to more accommodating subjects as they went down the dance together. My, but he was a splendid dancer!

After a few moments of standing together in silence, she said, "Lizzy tells me you travel with a collection of books."

"When I visit Bingley, I must, for he is not a great reader."

She laughed. "No. The last time he came to Longbourn he called Netherfield's library a 'pitiful façade' in comparison to Papa's library."

He smiled, though not enough to reveal his dimples, unfortunately. "I can well believe it. At least Mr Bingley readily admits his flaws." He paused. "Are *you* a great reader, Miss Lydia?"

"Not especially. But I have lately read two books recommended by my sister." Lydia was terribly nervous now that her efforts over the last week might be discussed. She could easily converse on any number of silly subjects, but she did not wish to appear silly when she attempted a more serious topic.

"Indeed? Which books?"

"The first was *Twelfth Night*."

"I trust you enjoyed it. Most people who read it do. It is even better to see it performed."

"I can imagine—especially the physical comedy of the Fool and Sir Andrew. Have you seen it performed in London?"

"I have, twice actually." He paused, and Lydia felt woefully inept in the face of his much greater experience and understanding. Then he asked her, "Which is your favourite character?"

"Sir Toby, I suppose, for pure entertainment. He is clever and jolly, but also a bit cruel, I think."

He nodded in agreement. "And what think you of the heroine?"

"Viola deserves her happiness. She is the only character to consider the feelings of others throughout the play."

"That is true. The others are occupied only with their own melancholy, their own ambitions, or the singular pursuit of revelry."

Lydia's mind cluttered with the words of both her father and Elizabeth during their discussions in the library, but she could not think of what to say next. In her indecision, she allowed the conversation to falter. They were quiet for several minutes.

"What was the second book you spoke of?" he asked suddenly.

"Oh! *Robinson Crusoe*. Though I have not quite finished it."

He did not seem to approve of the second choice as much as he had the first. "You say your sister recommended these books?"

"She did. Papa said Lizzy's mind must be full of the imminent return of John Lucas, who my mother feared would drown in a shipwreck. I think Elizabeth just meant to satisfy my craving for the dramatic and exotic. She knows I am not one to finish a dull book."

He smiled slightly, but appeared completely preoccupied. Silence overtook them again, an occurrence that was altogether unusual for Lydia. Eventually, Mr Darcy spoke again, "Your family and the Lucas family are very close. Have you always been so?"

Lydia felt much more comfortable discussing her neighbours, so she happily seized the subject. "Yes, for as long as I can remember. Sir William bought what is now called Lucas Lodge just after John was born. Jane was an infant at the time also. Mama and Lady Lucas therefore had much in common, as did Sir William and Papa. Charlotte, John, and Jane spent much time together, and then came Lizzy and Mary. Just a few months separate Maria and Kitty in age as well. Poor John was the only boy for the longest time."

"I can imagine you did not want for playmates."

"To be sure. And we all became quite good at cricket, except for Maria. She is hopeless."

He smiled. As the set ended, Lydia could not be quite satisfied with her performance. She had shared more conversation with Mr Darcy than ever before, yet she had frozen up when discussing the books. He had smiled several times but never enough to reveal his dimples. She took his arm again and he led her to where Lizzy, Mr Collins, and Charlotte Lucas were standing together.

Lydia offered a small shrug at Elizabeth's questioning gaze. "Lizzy, you have not danced the last two sets. Why ever not?"

"I do not wish to overstrain my ankle."

"Your ankle? But it hasn't bothered you in ages!" Lydia then noticed Lizzy's pleading look, accompanied by a glance at Mr Collins.

"Oh... Of course dancing might put a strain on it. Better not to risk further injury."

"You are very wise, Cousin Lydia. One cannot be too careful when it comes to such matters. I could not bear to see dear Cousin Elizabeth suffer again." He looked towards Lizzy with the most simpering expression.

"Mr Collins," said Mr Darcy, "have you finished dancing for the night as well?"

"Indeed, I am completely indifferent to dancing. I wish only to make myself valuable to my dear cousin's comfort for the remainder of the ball."

"You do yourself credit. I wish I could refrain from dancing further, but I have not yet danced with our hostess, and as you know, it is a courtesy, a duty almost, which ought not to be overlooked."

Mr Collins looked guilty. "I suppose my mind has been too occupied, for I have been remiss in this duty."

"It is not too late, Mr Collins. I plan to ask Mrs Hurst for the upcoming set, and then Miss Bingley for the next. Perhaps you could do the reverse."

Mr Collins worried his brow. "But Cousin Elizabeth, dare I leave you for so long in your vulnerable state?"

"Sir, you certainly must observe this civility with our hostess, as we have no other gentleman in our party who could fill the role. I have friends and family enough here to look after me. Be sure to tell Miss Bingley how very much I enjoyed the ball."

Mr Collins bowed low over her hand and Lydia held in her laugh at Lizzy's expression. Mr Darcy then bowed slightly to each of them, saying, "Thank you for the dance, Miss Lydia."

Lydia watched in confusion as the two gentlemen walked off together, but Elizabeth soon addressed her. "Did you impress Mr Darcy with your newfound literary prowess?"

She sighed. "I clung to generalities, like a coward. I feared I might say something foolish if I attempted more."

"Nonsense! You articulated your views perfectly well with me and Papa. You must only gain confidence with further study. Besides, you promised you would read two more books."

"Yes, yes. I shall keep my promise. But I wish to finish *Robinson Crusoe* first."

"Excellent! I am so proud of you."

"Oh shush!" Lydia blushed at the sincere praise and then said sternly, "Now Lizzy, did you tell a fib about your ankle to our cousin?"

"You cannot blame me, can you? You and Charlotte know only too well a second dance with Mr Collins might result in permanent injury to my toes."

"He's just dreadful!"

The three of them giggled over the horror of dancing with Mr Collins, and then Gussy Goulding came to ask Lydia to dance. She danced the set after that with Mr Pratt and the final set with Denny again.

The Longbourn party were the last of all the company to depart and, by a manoeuvre of Mrs Bennet, had to wait for their carriages after everybody else was gone. Mr Bingley and Jane were standing together, a little detached from the rest, and talked only to each other. Mr Collins plagued poor Elizabeth with repeated inquiries after her health and comfort. Kitty yawned loudly, and Mary and Mr Bennet watched it all. Mrs Hurst and her sister scarcely opened their mouths except to complain of fatigue. They repulsed every attempt of Mrs Bennet at conversation and, by so doing, raised Lydia's ire.

While Mr Collins gave a long speech to Mr Darcy, who, for some reason, sought conversation with the parson, Lydia addressed Miss Bingley. "I congratulate you, Miss Bingley, on the elegance of the entertainment. Your hospitality has induced even those who normally dance little to dance much tonight."

Miss Bingley raised her chin so that she might peer down her nose at Lydia. The adjustment was necessary, as they were about the same height. "Indeed. Some of the early pairings were unusual, but I believe everyone ended the night as they ought." She referred, of course, to her being Mr Darcy's last partner of the night.

"I hope you did not feel slighted by Mr Collins's late application for your hand. He corrected his error as soon as Mr Darcy reminded him it is an expected courtesy to favour the hostess with a dance."

Miss Bingley narrowed her eyes. "Not at all. Like all your family, your cousin's manners cannot possibly fail to impress."

Lydia shrugged. Miss Bingley would have to do better than that. "How kind of you to say so."

Miss Bingley turned away towards Mrs Hurst, and Lydia winked at Elizabeth's grin.

*

"Oh, no one knows what I suffer! Ungrateful girl! Who will keep her when Mr Bennet is dead? Not I! Not I! I cannot keep her when I am starving in the hedgerows myself!"

Lydia wished for a sudden loss of hearing, or better yet, she wished her mother would suffer complete laryngitis. Even from downstairs, she could hear every fretful exclamation. How was she to finish her book with all this uproar? After a late night of dancing, today should have been a day for rest and relaxation. As such, Lydia had slept later than anyone. When she had come downstairs, she learned that Mr Collins had made an offer to Lizzy, and Lizzy would not have him. Mrs Bennet had appealed to Mr Bennet's authority to compel Lizzy into the match, but Mr Bennet had been most unaccommodating.

While Mr Collins was present, making everyone uncomfortable with his resentful silence, Mrs Bennet had directed a stream of peevish complaints at poor Lizzy. Then Charlotte had come to visit. Upon her arrival, Mrs Bennet renewed her inventory of grievances, seeking a more sympathetic ear in their neighbour. Probably wishing to give her friend relief, Charlotte had invited Mr Collins to Lucas Lodge for dinner. When the two left together, all the Bennet girls were glad of it.

But they soon wished Mr Collins would return. His removal had unleashed a new level of agitation they had heretofore never witnessed in their mother. Sensible that any attempt to reason with or sooth her would only increase the irritation, her daughters left Mrs Bennet to Hill's experienced care, and the pair removed above stairs. That had been over an hour ago, and in that time, Mrs Bennet's lamentations had lessened neither in volume nor frequency. Nor had any sign of the much-wished-for laryngitis made itself known.

"I have done with her from this very day! Oh Hill! My salts, my salts! My poor nerves!!"

Lydia slammed her book shut and spoke over the racket. "Hadn't someone better go try to quiet her?"

"You mean someone who is not yourself," said Kitty.

Lydia whined. "I just wish to finish my book."

"How much longer can she possibly carry on this way?" Even stoic Mary showed signs of annoyance.

"I shall try to calm her," offered dear Jane. She really was too good, though she scaled the stairs like a woman condemned.

The four girls were quiet for some time, hoping for a cessation of the wailing. It finally came. Instead they heard plaintive whimpering, a vast improvement indeed. Hill came down the stairs for a much-deserved reprieve.

Lydia turned to Lizzy and spoke quietly so that she might not be heard upstairs or through the library door. "Where is Papa? He has not shown himself all day."

Elizabeth sighed. "Do not expect to see him for some time."

"How can he let Mama abuse you so?"

"He supported my refusal. I should not imagine two acts of such bravery in one day."

Lydia wished to have her suspicions confirmed. "During Mr Collins's first visit, you purposefully deflected his attention from Jane to yourself, did you not?"

Lizzy paused for a long moment before admitting the truth to three sets of attentive eyes and ears. "Yes. I did everything in my power to separate Jane from Mr Collins, and I rejoice in my success."

"But you would not have done so had you known he would turn his hopes towards you," Kitty stated the obvious.

"I certainly would. You know Jane is too good. She may have felt an obligation to accept him. I am a much less dutiful daughter." Lizzy smiled wryly.

Lydia was taken aback. "But what you have endured for your kindness towards Jane! You were plagued by Mr Collins at the ball so much that you even had to stop dancing too early. You love to dance! And now you must face all of Mama's ire without any hope of relief from Papa."

"I am quite willing to suffer through Mama's disapprobation if it saves Jane from a loveless marriage to a prancing fool. And my small sacrifice is doubly rewarded in seeing Jane so well matched with Mr Bingley."

"Oh Lizzy. I begin to think *you* are too good."

Elizabeth waved away the praise. "You had best take advantage of the lull to read your book."

Lydia silently resolved to help shield her sister from their mother's further ill humour. She felt it was the least she could do after all of Lizzy's assistance with her first foray into literature.

Just as Lydia found her place in *Robinson Crusoe*, Mrs Hill announced from the doorway, "Mr Bingley."

He stepped into the room, his eyes fruitlessly seeking Jane.

"Mr Bingley," said Lizzy warmly. "How wonderful to see you. My mother is feeling a bit under the weather today."

Just then some pathetic keening reached their ears from upstairs. Mr Bingley appeared confused, "Oh, I am sorry to intrude. I had wished to speak with Miss Bennet."

"It is hardly an intrusion, I assure you. Please sit and we shall fetch Jane for you. Lydia, may I speak with you?"

Lydia followed her into the hallway. Lizzy whispered, "I am sorry, but you must go up. Bring Hill if you wish. My presence would only make things worse."

Lydia nodded, "What shall I do?"

"Send Jane down, and for pity's sake, do everything you can to control Mama's exclamations. Mr Bingley's attachment to Jane is strong, I suspect, but every man has his limit."

Lydia giggled, and the sound carried up the stairs.

"No one knows what I suffer!! No one takes my part!!"

Elizabeth winced, "Go now, before it gets worse. I will send Hill up directly."

Lydia climbed the stairs. She would not fail Jane or Lizzy.

23
Tormenting a Respectable Man

They were dancing together again. It must have been the last set, for most of the guests had already departed. In fact, there were no other dancers, only Darcy and Elizabeth.

He reached for her hands—where had his gloves gone? More importantly, where had *her* gloves gone? It was as if she had read his thoughts during their first dance and discarded the despised things sometime in the interim. Oh, but the feel of her hands thrilled him! How perfectly they fit in his, how soft was her skin. How he wished to never let her go.

He did not let her go. There was no one left to witness them as he spun her across the room onto the balcony. She stood with him in the moonlight, her bare hands still in his. She smiled a smile full of ease and warmth. The expression on her face, the look in her eyes—it made his knees weak and his breath short. It was an expression she reserved only for her most cherished loved ones. His fondest, most precious wish was that she look upon him thus.

And now she did, in the moonlight on the balcony. He stepped towards her. Closer. She tilted her face up to him. Closer. He felt her warm breath on his lips, and still, her fine eyes held him in a trance.

"Lizzy," he whispered as he closed his eyes and moved forward the last fraction of an inch.

His lips met nothing.

His eyes flew open and he looked around frantically. His breath was short for an entirely different reason now. He was alone.

He leaned over the balustrade and saw her far below, standing on the ground. Heights never bothered him before, but he was terrified now. If she had not been there, staring up at him, he would have stepped back and never looked down again.

"Come down," she said. "Please."

"I shall," he said, desperate to get to her. He turned to leave the balcony.

There was no door. No window. Nothing.

He went back to the railing. Thank God she was still there. He heard footsteps but saw no one else in the night.

"Must I jump?" He did not like the sound of those footsteps.

"Yes."

"But it is very high."

She turned her head in the direction of the approaching intruder.

He whispered as he gripped the rail, "I am frightened." But she did not hear. He stood frozen in fear, racking his brain for another way, and all the while, the footsteps continued.

"Please," she said again, looking up at him once more.

The footsteps got closer and closer as Darcy gathered his courage. A man's voice called from the darkness, "Lizzy."

Darcy swung one leg over the railing as Elizabeth took a few steps back. "Wait!" Darcy pleaded.

"Lizzy," the voice called again. She turned and began walking towards it.

"No!" Darcy yelled as he swung his other leg over the railing. He must reach her before this newcomer did. He jumped.

He fell for the longest time, his stomach in his throat. But he knew he was too late.

Darcy jerked awake in the armchair as if he had landed there. He had dozed off in the library after a short night plagued by similar dreams. He cursed under his breath.

Someone whistled, "Rough slumbers, old boy? I had thought of waking you, but sometimes that's worse."

Darcy looked up to see Hurst swirling a glass of port. "What time is it?" he asked thickly.

"Nearly time for dinner. I think you need one of these more than I do." Hurst moved across the room to pour another glass.

"Bingley has not returned from Longbourn?" Darcy took the proffered glass and swallowed half of it.

"He has, but he went upstairs in high dudgeon after some words with Caroline. My mother always said those siblings were prone to the most ridiculous histrionics, but I thought she only meant the females."

Darcy sat up. Did Bingley argue with Miss Bingley or did his foul mood precede the altercation? If Bingley's visit had not gone well, it only meant one thing: rejection. Darcy could not believe it.

He gulped the rest of his port. "Thank you, Hurst. I needed that." He rose and moved towards the door. "I shall see what has upset him."

Hurst shrugged, muttering, "Young people in love..."

Darcy climbed the stairs and knocked on Bingley's door.

"Yes, I know dinner is soon, Caroline," came the testy answer.

Darcy turned the knob and swung the door open. "Darcy! You look awful!"

He ignored Bingley's greeting. "Hurst told me you were distressed when you returned from Longbourn."

"Oh! No, not really. It is not what you think. I was a bit miffed, yes."

"What are you talking about?" Darcy did not have the energy to decipher Bingley's mysterious statement.

"The situation at Longbourn prevented me from proposing."

Darcy motioned impatiently for more explanation.

"The whole house is in an uproar. Ja—Miss Bennet was very worried about her sister and exasperated by her mother."

"I do not understand."

"Mr Collins proposed to Miss Elizabeth this morning and was refused. Mrs Bennet has taken to her rooms in an aggravated fit of self-pity, while Mr Bennet has sought refuge in the library, leaving the girls to bear the brunt of her nervous...condition, not to mention Mr Collins's wounded pride."

"But she will not be forced into the match?" Darcy asked, alarmed.

"No, Jane told me the last thing Mr Bennet did before disappearing was refuse to force the marriage. But you know how he is: an odd mixture of sarcastic wit and caprice. He supported Miss Elizabeth's refusal in such a manner as to vex Mrs Bennet as much as possible. I was not present for the worst of it, and what I saw, or heard rather, was bad enough. None of the girls dare to even raise their voices above a whisper, for fear of Mrs Bennet renewing her verbal abuses of Miss Elizabeth."

"Why does Mr Bennet not *do* something?" Darcy asked crossly.

Bingley shook his head sadly, "I have no idea. But under the circumstances, I could not ask Jane to marry me. She was too tired and anxious. It must wait until I return from London. I shall retrieve the ring, in any case."

Darcy slumped into one of the chairs before the fireplace, rubbing his eyes. Bingley took the facing chair.

"Have you decided to accompany me to London then? You do not look fit for the ride, quite frankly."

"No. I shall remain here for now." Darcy had an appointment to keep in the morning and was now even more determined to keep it. She might need to talk, and he was quite willing to hear her. He also must know precisely what Wickham had told her. He had not decided how much he should explain about *that* man. But surely Elizabeth could be trusted with Georgiana's secret.

"Good. Perhaps Caroline will stop pestering me now. She wanted us all to leave for London tomorrow, to stay through the New Year. Can you imagine? I realise she did not know the purpose of my call at Longbourn today, but even so, I am publicly committed to Miss Bennet already!"

"Did you clearly inform your sister of your intentions?"

"Yes, repeatedly. But she insists I ought to take a few months away from here to carefully consider, or reconsider, as the case may be."

"The time for consideration is long past. You have committed yourself by honour, and I daresay, by inclination."

"I have no regrets whatsoever, Darcy, no wish to reconsider. I am perfectly content with my choice. Had I not acted when I did, it might have been Jane who received a marriage proposal from Mr Collins this morning! Then how great would have been my regret?"

"Indeed." Darcy stared into the fire.

"Now, what has you in such a foul mood? Too much dancing last night? Or too much drinking?" Bingley had apparently pulled himself from his "miff."

Darcy's lips turned up slightly. "If I *were* in a foul mood, I would credit it to too little sleep last night."

"Ah. I had very little sleep as well, but I suppose men in the throes of love do not need to sleep as mortal men do. I believe I could have flown to Longbourn today."

"Sometimes you really are the biggest fool, Bingley."

"I know. One of us must be every now and again, and it certainly will not be the staid, sensible, dutiful Mr Darcy."

Darcy had no reply to this. Sense, seriousness, responsibility—he had always been proud of these traits in himself. But now *he* was a man in the throes of love as much as Bingley was. What is love but a throwing over of sense and seriousness? And in his case, duty? Darcy had not embraced it, and therefore, his nights were tormented, while down the hall, Bingley enjoyed the sleep of a man without regret.

Darcy knew what the dream meant. Jealousy, indecision, fear—these were the new traits he saw within himself. And they were wholly foreign to him. Not that he had never been afraid before. He had been. But it had never dictated his actions, or his inactions. Such indecision was wrapped up in the fear. At first, he had been afraid of society's judgment. But the deeper he fell into this love, the more another fear grew. It was now so large it dwarfed the other. He knew Elizabeth would reject anyone she did not love. He feared revealing his feelings to her, for she had the power to crush him. He feared risking himself.

But fear and indecision can only last so long. At some point, he would choose; either he would confess to her and take his chances or he would leave Hertfordshire as planned and recommit himself to sense, seriousness, and responsibility.

As for tomorrow, the decision was already made. He would meet her, and he would enjoy every minute of it. Perhaps it was a mistake. Dancing had only appeared in his dreams *after* he had danced with her. But he could not regret it. The first half of the dream was heaven. He would gladly dream it again, even if every awakening was as jarring as the one he had had twenty minutes ago. He would gladly dance with her again. And tomorrow, he would gladly meet with her again, alone. So much for sense and responsibility.

"Shall we go down for dinner?"

"Yes, let us face your sister," Darcy said.

Elizabeth rose just before the sun. She lay for several minutes savouring the quiet of Longbourn. She heard no wailing, no whimpering. Her mother was asleep. When she awoke, would today be a repeat of yesterday's drama? Elizabeth did not mind so much for herself—she was often the target of her mother's complaints, though yesterday was an extreme example—but she hated how disruptive Mrs Bennet's behaviour was to her sisters. Poor Lydia had barely finished a chapter all day. And poor Jane! Aside from the brief respite afforded by Mr Bingley's visit, she had spent most of her day trying, often in vain, to calm Mrs Bennet.

Elizabeth went to her window, looking out at the sunrise. She could not contain her excitement. How early would he come to Oakham Stream? What would he say? They no longer had any secret agenda to accomplish, but he clearly wished for privacy to speak to her. He must have more to tell her concerning Mr Wickham. She could not imagine, could not let herself think, that it might be more than that. She remembered the way he had distracted Mr Collins at the ball for her benefit, the way he had danced with Lydia at her request. And of course she remembered their dance. In truth, her mother's noisy lamentations could hardly disturb Elizabeth's reflections on the subject; such thoughts had filled her mind since the end of the ball. It made her feel doubly guilty. Jane, Charlotte, and even Lydia, were trying so hard to shield her, when all the while she had this secret delight, this hidden sanctuary.

She quietly went downstairs. No one stirred yet. She retrieved her boots and sat at the back door to tie them.

"Good morning, Lizzy." Mr Bennet's quiet voice startled her.

"Good morning, Papa."

"I am happy to see the cold will not keep you from escaping the situation here."

"You know me better than that. But..."—she paused, not knowing whether she should say anything further—"but I do wish the others had some means of escape too. I am sorry to have caused such turmoil here."

He shook his head sadly. "You have done nothing wrong, Lizzy. I thought perhaps we should give your mother one day of free... expression. And frankly, I did not wish to further provoke her under the circumstances. I am sorry you all suffered through it while I hid behind the thick door of the library. But if your mother has not yet calmed, I shall not let today follow yesterday's course. Do not think too poorly of your dawdling papa."

"You know I do not, and I am exceedingly grateful you supported my refusal. But now, we both must deal with the consequences, unpleasant as they may be, without burdening everyone else in the house." She wished to lighten the mood, adding, "Besides, if you wish for Lydia to continue her literary exertions, she must have a bit more quiet."

He smiled. "Then, by all means, I shall see that she has it. Once again you have done what I should have long ago. Your influence has greatly improved her."

"She only needed a little encouragement in the right direction and perhaps a little motivation that none of us could have supplied."

"What motivation is that?"

"That of a handsome, rich, eligible gentleman who values a rousing literary discussion, of course."

"Ah, the venerable Mr Darcy. Well, I suppose his coming here will have one lasting positive effect, as long as Lydia does not repudiate her scholarly advances when he departs."

"It is up to us to make sure she does not." Elizabeth said, not wishing to dwell upon a certain gentleman's departure.

"That's my determined Lizzy, putting me to shame again. Now, what ideas have you about improving Kitty's disposition?" Though delivered in a jesting tone, Elizabeth knew her father's wish for advice was sincere. He genuinely wanted to improve his previously neglected daughters.

"Jane and I have a few thoughts. Perhaps later today you will invite us behind that thick door to discuss it."

"Depend upon it. Now, I see you are eager to be out of doors. I shall delay you no longer. Be sure to keep warm." He held her coat up for her.

She was indeed eager to leave the house, though he could hardly guess why. She slipped her arms into the sleeves and buttoned herself up. "I may be later than usual."

"But," he said with mock surprise, "do you not wish to break your fast with your mother and your cousin?"

She pulled her gloves on. "Goodbye, Papa."

"I shall instruct Cook to keep some food warm for you whenever you return."

She grinned at him as she turned towards the door. And then she was outside, hurrying towards the road, her mind full of cheerful thoughts. Her father continued his slow progress towards better managing his family, and Mr Collins would depart for good tomorrow, with no further desire to find a wife among them. Jane and Mr Bingley's courtship was going splendidly, John would be returning in a matter of weeks, and the Gardiners would be visiting shortly after that.

But most importantly, Elizabeth was on her way to meet Mr Darcy. She arrived, her spirits high, at the small clearing on the bank of Oakham Stream and stood watching the water flow over the rocks for a few minutes. She had a most amusing tale to tell about her first marriage proposal. She could laugh about it now that it was over. She did laugh.

"The future Mrs Collins, I presume."

The deep voice, sounding so formal, yet ripe with a suppressed smile, signalled that Elizabeth was no longer alone. She was laughing gaily as she turned to face him, and the sight of him there, as tall and imposing as ever, yet now so *welcome*, made her giddy with the feeling of shared camaraderie and mutual success. She had never felt such a communion of spirit with anyone before—not Charlotte, not John, not even Jane, really. With any of those three, in such a giddy moment of triumph, Elizabeth would have embraced them, and that instinct quite overtook her.

A laugh still on her lips, her arms were suddenly about his upper arms, her hands on his back, and her cheek pressed up against his chest before she even knew what she had done. "What a story I have to tell you, my brilliant accomplice."

Only when she felt his large hands on her back did Elizabeth realize the impropriety of her actions. Her mirth died in her throat, and she froze in mortification. She became keenly aware of Mr Darcy's person—the tautness of his arms under hers, the feel of his shoulder blades beneath her gloved palms through the layers of his clothing, the rise and fall of his chest. He sighed quietly.

After a moment more of tense confusion, Elizabeth withdrew. Her eyelids lowered onto reddened cheeks, she murmured, "Forgive me. Forgive me." She could not raise her eyes to his as she stepped away. "I quite let my glee overrun my faculties."

Elizabeth felt a brief, light touch on her upper arms before he stepped back and cleared his throat. "Please, do not worry yourself. I quite understand your celebratory enthusiasm. A huge weight has been lifted off your shoulders. I am relieved to see your spirits so high. Bingley's account of the atmosphere at Longbourn yesterday... well, I know you had a difficult time of it."

Regaining some of her composure, she still could not look him in the eye. She stared at his top coat button instead. "Oh, I am accustomed to my mother's disapproval and was only too happy to finally put an end to Mr Collins's aspirations for a Bennet wife. I honestly do not want to imagine how differently things might have turned out without your help. I cannot thank you enough, Mr Darcy."

"The only thanks I require is the disclosure of this story you mentioned."

"Yes, I am quite eager to share it with someone at least once. I suppose it is horribly indiscreet to do so; even Mr Collins deserves *some* compassion. But you are already sworn to secrecy, and I owe you some amusing stories." Now she raised the level of her gaze to his chin. She could go no higher. Instead, she turned back to the water. "Shall we walk? It is too cold to keep still."

He motioned for her to lead the way, and she carefully kept her distance as she moved past him. Elizabeth gathered her jumbled thoughts while they walked upstream.

"Let me set the scene," she began. "After a very late breakfast, Mr Collins found me, together with my mother and Kitty, in the breakfast room. He began by asking my mother for the honour of a private audience with her fair daughter."

Elizabeth proceeded to relate, in as much detail as possible, the ensuing marriage proposal, complete with Mr Collins's stated reasons for marrying, not the least of which was the helpful advice of Mr Darcy's own aunt.

"Good God! You imitate Mr Collins's formal cadence perfectly," the gentleman interjected between laughs. "I readily believe my aunt meddlesome enough to dictate the qualities he should seek in a wife."

"Do you wish to hear more of his thoughts on your esteemed aunt?"

"Oh yes, please do continue. I have not heard nearly enough about my aunt through your cousin."

She laughed and continued but was soon interrupted again. "Wit and vivacity tempered with silence and respect? He is a bigger fool than I suspected," he grumbled.

"Do you not think, were I ever to be in Lady Catherine de Bourgh's munificent presence, that I would be cowed into respectful silence?" He looked doubtful. "But you have interrupted me again. Mr Collins was not yet finished with his addresses, and I have not even gotten to my reply, or replies. As it turned out, one would not suffice."

"Now you have really piqued my curiosity. *I* shall be cowed into respectful silence and endeavour to disrupt your account no further."

As they walked slowly upstream, Elizabeth continued with Mr Collins's thoughts on her dowry (or lack thereof) and then finally got to the multiple refusals she was forced to give. Mr Darcy's silence could not last through the parson's thick-headed failure to grasp her rejection. Amusement must win out. He laughed a full, generous laugh, with his head thrown back. He found the phrase "true delicacy of the female character" particularly humourous, and Elizabeth found his laughter particularly pleasing.

"But I am not finished. There are still two more refusals to be given."

"Two more?" he asked, truly incredulous. "How can any man be so deluded about his own desirability?"

"You will hear his reasons for doubting my sincerity directly. It seems that, despite 'manifold attractions,' I am unlikely to ever receive another offer of marriage. You see, my portion is so small that it undoes the 'effects of my loveliness and amiable qualifications.'"

Mr Darcy was no longer amused. His pace increased considerably as they walked up the hill. "Was there ever one so obtuse and insulting as he? You ought not to have been subjected to his insensitive ramblings—wholly mistaken ramblings! I should have intervened at the ball to spare you this."

"Mr Darcy, please!" He stopped and turned back, looking angry. She continued, "I assure you, my self-esteem is intact. I had thought allowing his intended courtship to reach its natural conclusion would afford him a bit of much-needed humility when he was finally refused. It seems I underestimated how well Mr Collins thinks of himself, for he has simply credited my refusal to some fault in *me* rather than himself. But his opinions are nothing to me, and I did not require your protection from them. You have done enough to help with my problems already, considering you...well, you should not take such trouble on my account."

He stared past her into the trees. "Come now, and let me at last finish my tale. I am not accustomed to so many interruptions." At her gentle rebuke, his countenance softened, and he offered his arm so that they might continue walking. Though she had come this far without his assistance, she took the proffered arm.

She was happy to see the return of his smile when she mentioned the "usual practice of elegant females." She then told him about her father's singular way of supporting her refusal.

Mr Darcy could not keep from smirking at it, but then he shook his head. "Your father could have put an end to all this days ago. And though I commend his ultimate decision, he should have taken more care in pacifying your mother. Bingley tells me she was quite vocal."

"Poor Mr Bingley. Lydia tried her best to soothe my mother during his visit, but she does not have Jane's talent for it. As for my father,"—she shrugged—"he took my part when I needed him to. He is making small steps to better fulfil his duties. That is all I can ask, is it not?" She looked up into his eyes and was caught there again, like she had been during their dance. They had stopped walking, though she could not remember when. With some effort, she looked back down at her hand on his arm and pulled away.

"Now, diverting as my romantic conquests may be, I suspect there is another reason you asked to meet today. I think you wish to discuss Mr Wickham."

He sighed, seemingly reluctant to take on the new subject. He searched her face. "Yes, you are correct. But I fear you may be too chilled to continue."

"No, I am perfectly fine as long as we keep moving."

"Very well. But you must not hesitate to tell me if you are cold."

She nodded, and he presented his arm again. They began to walk back the way they had come. After a long moment, he began, "Perhaps I shall know better how to start if you share what he told you at the Philipses' house."

"Of course. He sat between Lydia and myself..."

24

Like a Glove

While Darcy enjoyed walking with Elizabeth on his arm, he worried that she was cold. She had been warm when he *first* found her, laughing to herself as if she had not endured hours of verbal invective after fending off an unwanted marriage proposal. Her resilience amazed him. He immediately wished to share in her good humour.

But her reaction to his greeting went much further. Even through multiple layers of clothing, the feel of her in his arms, so alive and joyful yet so fragile, nearly undid him. How could this country miss throw *him*, the staid, reserved Fitzwilliam Darcy, into such extreme emotions—and after so little time?

He was as discomposed as Elizabeth was when she pulled away from him. If she had not been too embarrassed to look at his face, she would have known then and there that he was hopelessly in love with her. If he only knew her thoughts. Was she discomfited merely because she forgot herself? Or could it be more than that? Did she regret embracing him? Was she put off by his response? He could not blame himself for returning the gesture. In fact, it had taken all his strength of will not to press her closer and closer to himself.

But he could not dwell on it now; she was speaking on a much less pleasant subject: Wickham. "He sat between Lydia and myself. His powers of conversation are considerable. After perhaps a quarter of an hour spent on various topics, he asked about you. He said he had been connected to your family since infancy. He spoke very highly of your father, but…" she paused and stole a glance at Darcy.

"I can guess what followed: he was promised a living, but I cruelly chose to ignore my father's dying wishes and gave the living elsewhere."

"It cannot be true!" she cried.

"No, of course not, although parts of his tale are truthful. What he fails to reveal is that between my father's death and the living falling open, he requested, and was given, a generous sum for its value. He took the money and no doubt gambled it away." He watched her expression as shock gave way to disgust. "He is a most profligate spender."

"As well as a prolific liar. How can you let him continue defaming your character to strangers?"

"People who know me will know the truth. Others may believe what they wish. I have no need to expose my private affairs to the world to defend myself against *him*."

"But Mr Wickham has every charm of air and address, and he related his story with such sincerity. I fear most people, upon hearing the account from him, *would* believe him."

"You did not."

She shook her head. "This may pain you, but I may well have believed him if my acquaintance with you had not progressed beyond what it was only a month ago. You did not make a very agreeable first impression at the assembly, and for most people of Meryton, that is the only impression they have of you."

Darcy thought back to the assembly. "I do not recall anything amiss or offensive in my behaviour that night."

She looked at him askance, and he coloured. "I know I can never apologise enough for my comments, but my offense against you could not have been overheard by everyone."

"I was not referring to that offense specifically," she replied, leaving Darcy confused. Before he could ask what she meant, she continued, "You might be surprised at how many of my friends and neighbours have complimented my remarkable imitation of *your* formal cadence."

"You repeated *that* to others?"

"I am sorry for it now because I worsened the neighbourhood's opinion of you. But yes, I told the story with great spirit, as you can well imagine."

"Am I to understand that everyone here knows I said...what I said? Even your parents and sisters?" His mortification was beyond words.

"Yes, precisely."

"It is a wonder I have been received civilly by anyone! And that you should repeat such insults about yourself; I am astounded."

She shrugged. "I am quite accustomed to being compared unfavourably with Jane. Even through childhood, I could not possibly measure up to her in beauty or goodness. You did not really say anything untrue, though your manner *was* insulting."

Goodness? Was there anyone as brave and selfless as she? He stopped walking and turned to her. "I cannot tell you how much I regret my stupid, hurtful words. I assure you now, truthfully, you are one of the handsomest women of my acquaintance."

His declaration left her quite speechless. She looked into his eyes for several moments, but then she turned away. It was so odd; most young ladies would consider such a statement from him a huge triumph. But he had clearly made her uncomfortable.

He cleared his throat. "You mentioned my giving another offense, separate from those infamous remarks, on the night of the assembly. To what were you referring?"

She clasped her hands in front of her, still refusing to raise her eyes to his. She took a breath before replying, "You carried yourself with much haughtiness and disdain for those around you. You would not speak to anyone but your own party. In short, you were above being pleased. Everyone was disgusted by your pride and found you most disagreeable. We may not be as fashionable or clever as those you mix with in London, but we know when we are held in derision."

She finally looked up at him again, and he saw in her expression a dare, a challenge to dispute her assertions.

"I am ill qualified to recommend myself to strangers," he said stiffly.

She would not be put off with this paltry explanation. "Why is a man of sense and education, who has lived in the world, ill qualified to recommend himself to strangers?"

"I certainly have not the talent that some people possess of conversing easily with those I have never seen before." He kicked a stone on the ground before him, unable to meet her gaze.

"You are shy!" she finally exclaimed.

He winced. "That is part of it. I am, by nature, shy."

She boldly reached for his arm again so that they might continue walking. She spoke more quietly, coaxing him to explain himself. "What is the other part of it? Why do you so assiduously avoid becoming better acquainted with others?"

He took several steps with her before trying to answer. "I find it difficult to trust anyone outside of my close circle. Those who seek a friendship with me in town are usually after something, fluence, connexions, marriage, what have you. I know that sounds arrogant. I have been...injured in the past. I also must protect Georgiana from the insincere social climbers who might seek her acquaintance solely as a means to earn mine."

He risked a glance down at her and saw only compassion.

"But you must know that Hertfordshire society is different from that in London. The people here only wanted to welcome you with pleasant conversation. They are seeking nothing further from you. Well, perhaps mothers are always seeking husbands for their daughters, but you yourself said that the mothers in town are much more scheming than even my mother, which is no small feat."

"You are correct, of course. Perhaps with a little effort, I may improve the neighbourhood's opinion of me. Do you think it possible?"

"Absolutely. You changed *my* opinion, a very difficult task indeed. And at the ball, you made a great start with everyone else by dancing with the local girls. As I said on your first night among us, we are simple people and can be won over easily enough. Then, if Mr Wickham shares his tale with others so liberally, they will already be predisposed to disbelieve his accusations against an honourable man."

Blast! Wickham! They had reached the clearing where his horse waited. Her hand trembled on his arm. She must be cold by now. "In your eagerness to chastise me for my rude manners, we have neglected the subject of Mr Wickham. I have more to tell you of him, but I fear you must return indoors. You are chilled."

She laughed. "It is only my hands, really. No doubt I deserve the discomfort for being such an impertinent scold."

He grasped her hand with his free one. "Your gloves are too thin. You should have a fur-lined pair."

She removed her hand from his, much to his disappointment. "What a dreadful extravagance, here in Hertfordshire's normally mild climate!"

"Perhaps. But they are standard in Derbyshire. Georgiana has several pairs."

"I can well believe that you protect her from all manner of threats, including the weather."

With Wickham so prominently on his mind, he could not help but think of the time he had failed to protect Georgiana. His face fell.

She put her hand back on his arm. Her empathy never ceased to amaze him. "I am sorry. I have affronted you. I tease too much, I know. I am like my father that way."

"No, your teasing is a mixture of sweetness and archness; you can never affront with that. But I have failed to protect Georgiana most wretchedly. She suffered a blow last summer due to my negligence."

"Last summer," she murmured as she searched his face. "But it could not be your fault."

"It most assuredly was. I am her guardian. May I...do I ask too much—will you meet me here tomorrow so that I might tell you about it?"

"You need not share any painful memories with me."

"But I wish to. I could use some female advice."

"Ah, yes. Well, I always walk out in the mornings," she said with a grin.

"And I often enjoy a morning ride," he answered with his own grin. Then he was again mesmerised by her eyes, her rosy cheeks, everything. He knew not how long he stood there looking at her.

She shivered again and averted her gaze. "I should go."

"I shall bring my extra gloves tomorrow. Though I am sure you would only need one of them for both your tiny hands."

She laughed and walked away, shaking her head. She turned back suddenly. "You should expect a call from Mr Collins today. He wishes to be of service to you by carrying any letters you have for Rosings with him when he leaves tomorrow."

"He is overcoming his heartbreak at your rejection by throwing himself into his duties, I suppose."

She looked at him sourly. "I take it back. You deserve every bit of my teasing." She turned with a huff back towards the road.

They had been together for nearly two hours, and he could have stayed with her there on the banks of Oakham Stream all day but for her shivering. Darcy cursed the cold as he rode back to Netherfield.

He entered the house and went directly to the stairs.

"Mr Darcy! You have taken a very long ride today and in such cold! I am amazed at how very hardy you are sometimes, yet so refined! A true gentleman!"

Darcy paused reluctantly halfway up the stairs. He had feared that Miss Bingley's flirting and flattery would increase when her brother was not there to observe it, but he did not expect it to begin so soon. "Good morning. I take it that Bingley has departed already."

"He has, just half an hour ago," she answered. "It is a pity you did not wish to accompany him to London today; we could have all gone and taken the opportunity to do some shopping in town."

"I had no need for such an abbreviated trip to London."

"But you could have seen Georgiana, and I would be happy to help you shop for a Christmas gift for the dear girl."

"Thank you, but I have already purchased several gifts for her."

"Of course you have! You are an excellent brother! If dear Georgiana were not such a kind, gentle girl, I might fear that you spoil her. You are so fond of each other. Do you not wish to see her?"

This had gone on long enough. "I always wish to see my sister, but she is quite content with Lady Matlock and Lady Leland. They expect me in three weeks' time, as planned. Now, if you do not mind, I wish to change."

"I look forward to sharing luncheon with the refined gentleman under all that dust," Miss Bingley replied, boldly perusing his person as he turned to climb the rest of the stairs.

He arrived in his rooms just as Higgins sent Becky out on some task. The valet could not keep his reproachful look quite contained. "Your bath required more hot water, sir. It should only be a few minutes."

"Thank you for seeing to it. My morning rides in the future will no doubt be of varying lengths. Perhaps you should wait until I return to order a bath."

"Very good, sir," Higgins replied impassively.

Darcy used the time to finish his reply to Lady Catherine, which he would give to Mr Collins. That way, she could not claim the post misdirected it.

I am as happy as you are at Anne's improved health, Aunt, but do not make any such announcement. Please speak with Anne about this yourself, or at least wait until I can speak with you both in person. I assure you, any premature announcement about my engagement will be denounced and retracted at my demand. Such a public display would reflect very poorly on all of us.

That should serve to keep her quiet for a few more months, although her last letter was quite demanding on the subject. The time had come to finally disappoint Lady Catherine's aspirations for the joining of Rosings and Pemberley. It had been far easier to let her believe what she wanted as long as no engagement actually existed. He and Anne had postponed the confrontation partly because of Anne's poor health but also because they each found the rumours about the match useful. Whenever said rumour circulated, Darcy received less marked attentions from the fairer sex.

He added a few more paragraphs in response to what she had written, and then he signed, sanded, and sealed the letter. One unpleasant task was completed. Now he must endure lunch and dinner with Miss Bingley and a visit from Mr Collins. He would try to spend as much time as possible alone, or at least with Hurst, for the rest of the day.

❧

Elizabeth spent the day in equal parts recollection of that morning's *tête-à-tête* and anticipation of the next morning's conversation. Mr Darcy thought her handsome.

Mrs Bennet's ill humour had not abated, but the volume of her complaints certainly had. Elizabeth suspected that Mr Bennet's intervention deserved credit for this improvement, though he still kept to his library.

As for Mr Collins, his feelings were chiefly expressed not by embarrassment or dejection or by trying to avoid Elizabeth, but by stiffness of manner and resentful silence. Oddly enough, he had gone out for his own morning walk that day, though considerably later than hers. Elizabeth looked forward to his further absence to bid farewell to his Hertfordshire acquaintances. In another indication of her father's clever avoidance, Mr Collins had been given free use of the carriage, and he availed himself of it immediately following luncheon. His first destination: Netherfield. Elizabeth smiled to herself with the thought of Miss Bingley entertaining him. Would Mr Darcy entrust Mr Collins with a letter to his aunt? Or perhaps one to his cousin? The latter possibility nettled Elizabeth. *One of the handsomest women of his acquaintance.*

The other residents of Longbourn were now able to resume their various pursuits in blessed quiet. Mary made extracts quite enthusiastically. Kitty suggested they walk into Meryton, only to be met with indifference from her sisters. She testily resigned herself to trimming a bonnet, complaining every so often that she lacked the right colour of ribbon to do it justice.

Kitty's persistent grumblings were enough to finally convince Lydia—but only after at last finishing *Robinson Crusoe*—to agree to the desired trip into the village. They would visit Aunt Philips and the millinery shop and hopefully happen upon some of the officers. As the certainty of the excursion increased, Mary expressed a need for some exercise. The trio set out together shortly thereafter.

Elizabeth was thus left happily to the company of Jane, who seemed to be suffering some melancholy in Mr Bingley's absence.

"When will Mr Bingley return so that you might stop pining for him, dear Jane?"

Jane smiled. "He returns Friday. Are my moods now so very easily deciphered?"

"In a way. You have gone from completely impossible to read, to only slightly more scrutable."

"I am a little ashamed to admit it, since I saw him only yesterday, but yes, I miss him terribly. I never thought my happiness could be so entirely dependent upon another person. It is a little frightening."

"You have no reason to be afraid. I am sure Mr Bingley returns your feelings. Very soon, I think Mama will forget about the last marriage proposal and instead be entirely overjoyed by one with a somewhat more felicitous outcome."

"I shall not indulge your teasing." Jane looked at her earnestly. "It is one thing to think you are in love; you very well may be. But to confess it and then to stake your happiness on the hope that your feelings are returned, well, that is a decision that takes much courage. In short, you must allow yourself to trust someone else entirely."

"And you fear your trust in Mr Bingley will be misplaced?"

"No. I trust him, but he is not perfect. We must accept each other's faults along with the virtues."

"I suppose it is a very risky business," Elizabeth replied. "But I think in this case *you* take on all the risk. You see, you are a collection of nothing but virtues."

"Someday you will not be able to make light of such weighty matters. You will fall in love and embrace it with all your heart, for you certainly do not lack courage. I only hope the man you choose deserves you."

"Oh, I am sure he will be a paragon of virtue. Someone who can discuss Fordyce with Mary. Perhaps the clergyman for a parish of no mean size."

Jane laughed. "Lizzy, you are quite absurd!"

"I may be, but you are no longer sulking and sighing into your needlework, so I consider my absurdity amply rewarded."

"I do not sulk!"

"Very well. You only pine prettily. Or languish delicately. Or brood—"

"Enough! Have mercy. I pray the man you eventually choose is made of stern enough stuff to withstand your impertinence, else it will be a very short romance indeed."

"My teasing is a mixture of sweetness and archness; no one can be affronted by it." How had *that* slipped out? *He* had said it this morning.

"Well, I am glad you think so. It remains to be seen if others do." Jane tried to keep the banter going, but Elizabeth was too discomposed by the encroachment of her secret life into her usual one.

"Jane, in all seriousness, Mr Bingley is a good, kind, honourable man who loves you. If you trust in that, I am certain all will be well."

The two sisters were left to their own thoughts, and Elizabeth's were turbulent indeed. Tomorrow, she would meet Mr Darcy again. He wanted her advice. This pleased her more than it ought. It meant he was not simply seeking diversion and amusement through her. *He would bring his gloves for her.*

After another hour or so, Mary, Kitty, and Lydia returned. Mr Wickham had been most attentive, escorting them from the edge of the village to their aunt's house. Lydia grimaced at Kitty's glowing praises of him. The much-needed ribbon had been acquired for Kitty's bonnet along with some less-needed ribbon. But the most perplexing bit of information was that the Bennet carriage had been spotted returning from Netherfield towards Longbourn not two hours after Mr Collins had left them. Yet he had not come back.

"He must have gone to Lucas Lodge. Perhaps Charlotte is keeping him occupied, patient soul that she is," Elizabeth reasoned.

Lydia nodded. "That's what I said. I told Kitty we should not visit Maria precisely because he might be there."

"We owe Charlotte a great debt."

They all agreed, some more vocally than others, before once again taking up their separate activities. Lydia, Elizabeth, and Kitty trimmed bonnets. For Elizabeth, the simplicity of the task gave her a respite from her overwrought thoughts and an opportunity for silly conversation with her youngest sisters.

"Kitty failed to mention who else we saw in Meryton today." Lydia winked at Elizabeth.

"Who might that be?" Elizabeth turned to Kitty, who blushed a deep shade of scarlet but adhered most diligently to her bonnet.

"Henry Long," Lydia answered in a lilting voice.

"And how does young Henry Long?"

"*Much* better now that he has seen Kitty."

Kitty could keep silent no longer "Lydia! I wish you had not told me your suspicions. I shall never be able to meet him with any tolerable degree of composure again."

"Henry Long admires Kitty," Lydia said matter-of-factly.

"How can you tell?"

Lydia enumerated her reasons for suspicion. "He stares at her, he blushes and stutters when in her presence, yet he seeks her above all others, and he all but admitted it to me at the ball."

"Well, it is nothing to be ashamed of, Kitty. You can hardly control who fancies you. You must always be polite but do not give encouragement if you do not wish his attentions to continue. And do not let Mama know about any of this. Imagine her making up excuses to visit the Longs for the purpose of constantly throwing you into his path."

Kitty's eyes widened in horror. "Lydia, you will not say anything to Mama, will you?" she pleaded.

"If you give me a scrap of that ribbon, I shall be silent as the grave."

The ribbon in question was promptly and enthusiastically handed over.

"What is wrong with Henry Long?" Elizabeth asked, only to be answered by a shrug. "Is he not bound for Oxford? There's no point in spurning him quite yet. He may forget all about you. Or you may find him much more appealing after he returns."

"I remember how much more handsome John Lucas looked after his first year at Cambridge," said Lydia.

Elizabeth laughed. "But you were too young to notice such a thing."

"I had eyes."

"Well, just imagine how well he will look after two years spent at sea and exotic ports of call." Elizabeth allowed her sisters to imagine a newly dashing John Lucas while keeping her own thoughts to herself. *He will not have developed dimples though.*

The afternoon wore on into evening, and still, Mr Collins did not appear. They ate dinner without him, a circumstance that caused little hardship but much interest. The curiosity excited by his long absence burst forth in very direct questions upon his return to Longbourn soon after the meal concluded. He replied simply that he had made several calls during the day, ending at Lucas Lodge, where he was asked to dine. His new reticence was a delightful alteration to Elizabeth's mind.

As he was to begin his journey too early on the morrow to see any of the family, the ceremony of leave taking was performed when the ladies removed for the night, and Mrs Bennet, with great politeness and cordiality given the situation, said how happy they should be to see him at Longbourn again.

"My dear Madam," he replied, "this invitation is particularly gratifying, because it is what I have been hoping to receive, and you may be very certain that I shall avail myself of it as soon as possible."

With proper civilities, the ladies then withdrew. To say that they were all astonished would scarcely give credit to the dismay they felt to find that he meditated a quick return.

The five girls gathered in Kitty and Lydia's room. Kitty whispered, "Mary must be next."

Mary's stoic countenance cracked with alarm. Elizabeth could not tell who started giggling first, but Mary certainly was the last to join in.

A Faithful Narrative

Elizabeth rose the next morning in a state of agitated impatience, which only grew as she waited behind her closed door while Mr Collins's trunk was carried downstairs and loaded onto the chaise. She slipped out the back of the house before he departed and was therefore required to stay off the road lest she be spied. She kept to the smaller paths instead. The sounds of the stream and her arrival from an unexpected direction caused Mr Darcy to be taken quite unawares. His startled breath escaped him in a visible puff.

"Perhaps I should wear a bell around my ankle," she said with a smirk, referencing their first clandestine meeting nearly a month ago.

"Or simply stomp your feet." He grinned, and she felt lightheaded at the sight of those dimples.

"I took a more circuitous route to avoid being seen by Mr Collins as he leaves," she blurted, hoping to get herself under better regulation. Just then, they heard the sounds of a carriage from the road.

"So the good parson has retired to Kent to lick his wounds, has he?"

"Would you believe me if I told you he wishes to visit with us again? And soon?"

"No, I would not believe you."

She laughed. "I assure you, he avows a desire to come again as soon as may be. Mary is feeling apprehensive about the whole affair."

"I would imagine so. What can he mean by being so tiresome as to be always coming here?"

He sounded so exasperated that Elizabeth had to laugh again. "Surely you will depart Hertfordshire before he returns, and therefore be spared more of his civilities." She immediately regretted mentioning his impending removal. It was not a subject that brought her much satisfaction and that, in and of itself, was disturbing.

Mr Darcy made no reply but reached into his coat. He pulled out a pair of gloves and approached her. "For your comfort," he said quietly.

"Thank you," she murmured, happy for some object to tear her eyes from his. The gloves were, quite simply, the most exquisite article of clothing she had ever touched—fine leather lined with fur. She wished to rub them against her cheek but somehow managed to stop herself. "Shall we walk downstream today?"

He motioned for her to lead the way. She tried out the borrowed gloves as she walked. A good inch of floppy leather was left at the end of each finger and a similar length of her coat sleeve was covered up. She held her hands out in front of her. "They certainly are warm."

He laughed at her wiggling, flapping fingers, and she revelled in the sound of it. Then she blurted again, "My younger sisters saw Mr Wickham in Meryton yesterday."

Mr Darcy immediately sobered. "Did he say or do anything unseemly?"

"No. Lydia and Mary are already distrustful of him, while Kitty thinks him quite amiable."

"Will you tell me what else he said to you about me and my sister, aside from his grievance over the living?"

"He repeatedly pronounced you abominably proud and pompous. He also said that Miss Darcy had become too much like you in that respect, overly proud. That was the substance of it."

"He said nothing else?"

"No." Elizabeth lied, not able to bring herself to repeat the other accusations nor the rumoured engagement. She quickly added, "But I must boast of Lydia's set down. She really was marvellous that night."

Elizabeth proceeded to tell him about Lydia's defence of him and his sister and of Mr Wickham's stunned reaction.

He chuckled at it. "Sometimes I wish my sister could have a little more boldness like Miss Lydia."

"You *must* be joking."

"Georgiana is painfully shy, and what happened last summer has only aggravated her insecurity."

"What happened to the poor girl?"

"In short, George Wickham." He looked at the ground and took a deep breath. "I must go back to the death of my father to explain fully. My sister was left to the guardianship of my cousin Colonel Fitzwilliam and myself. Mr Wickham requested a sum of money in lieu of the living bequeathed to him, for he claimed a desire to pursue the law. I was happy to oblige; unlike my father, who had been unaware of Mr Wickham's want of character to the last, *I* knew his character was sadly lacking for a career in the church. He then returned a few years later after having wasted all the money on gambling and who knows what, only to demand the living he had agreed to give up. When I refused, he bitterly swore revenge upon me."

Mr Darcy stopped walking and glanced at Elizabeth, who listened in rapt attention. Sighing, he continued, "Less than a year ago, Georgiana was taken from school and an establishment formed for her in London under the care of a Mrs Younge. Last summer, they went together to Ramsgate, and thither also went Mr Wickham, undoubtedly by design for there proved to have been a prior acquaintance between him and Mrs Younge, in whose character we were most unhappily deceived. He was able to meet with Georgiana and take advantage of her trusting heart and childhood memories. He convinced her that she was in love with him. She is but fifteen, which must be her excuse. I shall not go into the painful details but shall only say that I foiled a planned elopement with just a day to spare. "

Elizabeth gasped but said nothing. Mr Darcy began again, staring down at the water. "Georgiana, unable to support the idea of grieving and offending a brother whom she looked up to almost as a father, acknowledged the whole of it to me. Obviously, Mr Wickham was after her fortune, which is thirty thousand pounds; but it was clear from our confrontation that revenge was also his motive. And his revenge would have been complete indeed. Georgiana was devastated, and both of us felt our share of guilt for what happened. The episode was kept secret to protect her. Besides the four directly involved, only Colonel Fitzwilliam knew of it."

"I shall never betray your confidence."

"I know."

"Does Miss Darcy still suffer from her ill-advised attachment?"

"She still suffers, but I do not know whether it is because she continues to harbour tender feelings...for him or because she feels she has disappointed me. She will not discuss it with me nor her new companion. You must understand that she has always been shy." He paused and looked at Elizabeth with a small smile. "We have that in common, I suppose."

"But now she is even more withdrawn?"

"Her letters are so timid. Mrs Annesley, Georgiana's companion, writes to me that she has had little success in bolstering Georgiana's self-assurance. I do not know what to do."

"If..." Elizabeth paused, not knowing how best to continue. "If she sees you more as a father than a brother, as you say, then she will feel even less able to confide in you about such matters. Does she have anyone else to confide in? A family member, preferably a younger female?"

"She corresponds regularly with my cousin Anne, who is about ten years older, but has not divulged anything to her about Wickham."

Elizabeth tried not to be distracted by her own concerns upon hearing the last. "It occurs to me that the poor girl is surrounded by much older people, people she no doubt feels intimidated by or at least wishes not to disappoint. She must be perpetually afraid of doing something wrong. She has no one with whom she can be silly and giggle, no one with whom she can act her age."

He searched Elizabeth's face for an uncomfortably long moment. "It has unfortunately been so for most of her life."

"Aside from intimacy with a young female friend or family member, I can only recommend patience and reassurance. Your sister likely needs to know that her family loves her unconditionally and merely wishes her to be herself, not some impossible ideal."

He again turned a searching gaze towards her. She chafed under it. "I am afraid I have little useful advice to give."

"On the contrary, you have been very helpful. I fear my guardian-ship of Georgiana has been inadequate."

"No, you must not think so. Children at that age are bound to make mistakes, sometimes grave mistakes, as they struggle into adulthood."

"Your younger sisters are very fortunate to have you as an example."

"Me? Hardly. Jane was patient and nurturing to all of us as we grew up, something we needed very much with parents such as ours."

"I am sure Miss Bennet nurtured you all admirably, but you—you give encouragement to your sisters to better themselves without the sting of real criticism. You make them wish to improve and believe that they can."

Elizabeth laughed nervously. "You mean I nag and tease and scold. By all means, turn it into a virtue. You will hear no objections from me."

He smiled at her but continued his unreadable staring.

"I must go. No doubt Charlotte will visit after breakfast today. I again owe her much gratitude for her saintly intervention with Mr Collins over these last two days."

They had not walked very far, but Mr Darcy offered his arm for the return trip. They walked in silence, and when they arrived at the clearing, she handed his gloves back to him. "Thank you, even my fingers stayed quite warm."

He took them, looking down. "I...I shall continue to carry them with me on my morning rides in case we should meet again."

"No doubt we shall. You are owed several amusing stories for your trouble." Elizabeth could hardly believe her daring.

His dimples made a sudden appearance. "Indeed. How could I forget? Until tomorrow, then?"

"Yes," she croaked, nearly stumbling away. "Farewell, Mr Darcy." She did not look back as she hurried towards the road and back to Longbourn.

She found all her family but Mrs Bennet in the breakfast room. They greeted her, and Jane and Mr Bennet looked at her curiously as she ate in silence.

She would see him again tomorrow. The prospect made her happier than it ought. *Foolish, foolish, foolish!*

As she had predicted, Charlotte arrived after breakfast and sought a private conference with Elizabeth.

"My dear Lizzy, I have some news I wish to share with you personally: Mr Collins and I are engaged."

Elizabeth's astonishment was so great as to overcome the bounds of decorum, and she could not help crying out, "Engaged to Mr Collins! Impossible!"

Charlotte calmly replied, "It is true, I assure you. Marriage has always been my object, though I thought my chance had long since passed. Now, I am engaged at the age of twenty-seven without having ever been handsome, and I feel all the good luck of it."

"Was this your motive then, all the time you helped distract my cousin from Jane?"

Charlotte bristled at the accusation. "I asked you multiple times whether you were certain Jane did not desire the match. I would never have positioned myself as a rival to either you or Jane. I was happy to help regardless of any secondary outcome."

There was a long silence between them.

Charlotte took on a conciliatory tone. "Do you care to hear how it happened? He dined with us Thursday night, you know. The next morning, I spied him from an upstairs window and went to meet him in the lane. But little had I dared to hope that so much love and eloquence awaited me there. In as short a time as Mr Collins's long speeches would allow, everything was settled between us to the satisfaction of both."

Elizabeth's face betrayed her shock and disappointment at Charlotte making light of such a matter, but she said nothing.

"Why should you be surprised? Do you think it incredible that Mr Collins should be able to procure any woman's good opinion because he was not so happy as to succeed with you?"

"But he does not *have* your good opinion, Charlotte," she replied quietly.

"I am not romantic, you know. I never was. I ask only a comfortable home, and considering Mr Collins's character, connexions, and situation in life, I am convinced that my chance of happiness with him is as fair as most people can boast on entering the marriage state."

"It is beyond me that you should expect to find happiness with a man you find ridiculous and irksome!"

"I knew you would judge me harshly. This is why I kept my plans from you. I could not expect support but rather lectures and disapproval. Not everyone agrees with *your* way of thinking. I know my own mind, and I ask you to respect my decisions." Charlotte sighed. "I shall go now and allow you to think about it. I shall see you at service tomorrow, and I hope you will have reconciled yourself to be happy for me. This is what I want, Lizzy."

❧

To say that Darcy looked forward to hearing any humourous tale Miss Elizabeth Bennet wished to tell him would be a drastic understatement. To say that he was happy when she voiced this plausible excuse for them to continue meeting would do injustice to the joy he had felt at that moment. He had considered claiming there was even more to reveal about Wickham, but to stretch such a subject over three days seemed a bit much. So he would not contradict her when she claimed she "owed" him some amusing stories. If anything, he owed her for the insightful advice about Georgiana, but he would gladly listen to her recite laundry lists if she so desired.

After his delightful morning stroll, Darcy spent another tortuously long day at Netherfield avoiding Miss Bingley. Reginald Hurst proved to be an undemanding companion. He napped and drank and napped some more. He wrote letters, no doubt to his mother, while drinking, before dozing off again. In the course of several hours spent together in Netherfield's library, they had shared just one conversation of any substance: about how much Hurst liked his newest rifle. As a result, they had made plans to go shooting. It would be a good way to ensure Darcy did not encounter Miss Bingley for several hours.

But at present, Darcy had a much more appealing outing in mind. It was early morning again and a certain impertinent, kind-hearted, beautiful young lady with dainty hands awaited near a sparkling stream. Before going to the stables, he slipped his spare gloves into his coat, wishing the day was cold enough to necessitate their use. He had to laugh at himself. Two days ago he had cursed the cold, and now he wished for it to return. He loved seeing Elizabeth wear his gloves.

When he arrived at Oakham Stream, he thought his handkerchief might be more needed. There would be no joyful embrace today nor even a witty greeting. She looked despondent as she paced and twisted her fingers before her.

"What has happened?" he asked with anxious bewilderment.

She looked up at him. "Charlotte is to marry Mr Collins." Her declaration was flat, but he could tell there was great emotion behind it.

He was stunned for several moments. "I thought Miss Lucas such a sensible young lady."

"Yes, eminently sensible—cunning, really. Charlotte's kindness extended further than I had any conception of; its object was nothing less than to engage Mr Collins's addresses towards herself. The possibility of Mr Collins fancying himself in love with Charlotte *had* occurred to me within the last day or two, but that she could encourage him seemed almost as far from possibility as that *I* could encourage him myself!"

She continued pacing, greatly agitated, before stopping and facing him directly. "Am I terribly judgmental and severe? Do I act as if I know better than anyone else?"

"No and no." The reward for his certainty was the barest upturn of one side of her mouth.

She shook her head and started pacing again. "I am. I am judgmental and sanctimonious and stubborn in my opinions. I expect everyone to live up to some impossible standard—*my* standard, not theirs."

He wished to take her by the shoulders to prevent her frantic pacing, but instead he simply said, "Did you quarrel with Miss Lucas?"

"Not quarrelled exactly."

"Tell me about it," he coaxed.

She shot him a glance as she paced, considering. Finally, she began, "Shortly after breakfast yesterday, she came and sought a private audience with me..."

She recounted a tense exchange that was left unresolved. "I am a dreadful friend! And still, I cannot bring myself to be happy for her. I rather expect her to be miserable in the lot she has chosen."

"You want better for Miss Lucas than she wanted for herself."

"It seems I want better for everyone than they want for themselves: Jane, John, Charlotte, my father. I judge and scold and try to arrange their lives to my liking. What claims to wisdom or experience have I that I should presume to know better for them than they do for themselves?"

"I am sure they understand you only want the very best for them."

"John did not; he and I argued bitterly before he left. And although Charlotte fully expected my reaction yesterday, it still injured her. She knew I would disapprove, which is why she did not share her scheme with me. You see? Judgmental and sanctimonious!"

Darcy longed to ask about her quarrel with John Lucas, but he checked himself. "I see nothing of the sort. She knew your opinion on the matter was as deeply held as hers, and did not wish it to cause strife between you before it was necessary."

She ignored him, pacing again. "And Charlotte has never judged any of my reckless actions. She has always been supportive even if she disagreed. When I told her about"—she motioned between Darcy and herself—"our arrangement after the picnic, she only asked how she could help. That day in Netherfield's garden, she hinted at her plan for my cousin; I realise it now. She told me marrying for security was a common enough occurrence. Then she gently chastised me for clinging too strongly to my opinions about what was best for others."

Darcy thought she would wear a rut in the ground the way she was pacing.

"What am I to do? How can I act the supportive friend and keep her from sensing my censure and condemnation? She has been the truest friend to me; I owe her this."

He finally had to act. He placed himself in her path and lightly grasped her arms to halt her. "Hush, Miss Elizabeth. All will be well."

She stood there looking up at him, and he thought she might begin to cry. He could not bear it if she did. "Let us put ourselves into Miss Lucas' shoes, shall we? As sensible and practical as we know her to be, is it not safe to say that she has no illusions about her choice? She therefore must have had sufficient reasons. Perhaps you can be reconciled to her choice if you think about it from a new perspective."

She nodded weakly.

"Miss Lucas is twenty-seven?" Another nod. "It is likely she has been considered a spinster for a few years now."

Elizabeth sighed. "She never let that sort of malicious gossip bother her before."

"Perhaps she was only putting on a brave face." Elizabeth shrugged in reluctant acknowledgement.

He continued, "She also said marriage was always her goal and that she wanted only a comfortable home."

"She could *have* a comfortable home at Lucas Lodge without marrying a fool. John would never abandon her."

"Be that as it may, she would be relying on the charity of others, and it would not really be *her* home." Elizabeth looked sceptical. "Try to think of it from her point of view."

She sighed again. "Charlotte always said she wanted her own establishment."

"Based on what we know of Mr Collins and my aunt, I can only predict that Miss Lucas's good sense and kindness will be greatly appreciated by his parishioners in Kent. Can you imagine them coming to her for assistance rather than to Mr Collins? And she will, in her own quiet way, see that they get it without anyone knowing she interfered."

Her troubled expression began to ease a bit. "She will be a great help to those people. She is patient, shrewd, and modest—just the sort of person who can work discreetly for their best interests."

"Now, has Miss Lucas ever indicated that she wished to have a family of her own?"

Elizabeth looked down at the ground. "Yes," she whispered. "Charlotte is wonderful with children. When we were younger, she always talked of having a family. But she began to avoid the subject later." She broke from Darcy's grasp and turned her back. Her voice was tremulous when she continued, "I have been an insensitive beast! How could *I*, another woman and her so-called friend, not see it when *you* so easily understood her dearest aspirations?"

If not crying already, she was on the verge of tears. Desperate to comfort her, he stepped around her, offering his handkerchief. "Shh, please. If she did not share her sorrows with you, you could not expect to read her thoughts."

She took the handkerchief and wiped at her eyes. "Had I not been so wretchedly blinded by my own conviction, I might have shown just the slightest bit of sympathy for her troubles. I offered nothing but criticism when my dear friend told me of her upcoming marriage! How shall I ever make it up to her?"

"It is very simple. You will offer your sincere congratulations and good wishes for her future life. You will show her she has not sunk in your opinion. As her friend, you know best how to do it."

"With Charlotte, I probably need only wink at her in church today, and she will forgive and understand all."

"Would that all disagreements could be resolved with a little wink."

She let out a shaky laugh, "The world would be much more pleasant, I suppose." She was quiet for some moments as she examined Georgiana's stitch work on his handkerchief—his initials and a vine pattern. "I would offer to launder this for you, but I am afraid I could not explain its presence to the servants."

"It is no matter. You barely used it."

She held it out for him. "Thank you for calming an overwrought female. You have been most considerate. I am sure your expectations for this meeting were rather different."

"No thanks are required, and there's always tomorrow." As he took the handkerchief, their gloved hands touched and she finally raised her gaze up to his. So powerful was the urge to pull her towards him, he thought he must be shaking with it.

She blinked and took several steps away. "Tomorrow, I promise to tell you my most diverting story. Until then, Mr Darcy." She dropped into a curtsey, and he was desperate to keep her there just a little longer.

"Does the rest of your family know about Miss Lucas's betrothal?" he blurted.

"Yes. Sir William appeared in the afternoon, sent by his daughter to announce her engagement to the family. Initial reactions ranged from incredulous to positively uncivil. My mother protested that he must be entirely mistaken. Lydia disputed that any man could make two marriage proposals in as many days. Kitty exclaimed how relieved she was that somebody had finally accepted him, thus *she* need never receive his addresses."

Darcy had to laugh at this unfolding, and Elizabeth started to laugh too.

"Nothing less than the complaisance of a courtier could have borne without anger such treatment; but Sir William's good breeding carried him through it all. I finally felt it incumbent upon me to relieve him from so unpleasant a situation. I confirmed his account and, as earnestly as possible, offered my congratulations. Jane readily joined in, and shortly thereafter, he left us. My mother's feelings soon found a rapid vent; do you care to hear them?"

"Absolutely. I should not wish to be deprived of knowing them."

She smirked and held out her hands as if to count on her tiny fingers. "In the first place, she persisted in disbelieving the whole of the matter; secondly, she was very sure that Mr Collins had been taken in; thirdly, she trusted that they would never be happy together; and fourthly, that the match might be broken off. Two inferences, however, were plainly deduced from the whole: one, that *I* was the real cause of all the mischief, and the other, that my mother had been barbarously used by us all. On these two points, she principally dwelt during the rest of the day. Nothing could console or appease her, not even Jane."

"Did you not confide in Miss Bennet about your difference of opinion with Miss Lucas?" Darcy now thought it odd that Miss Elizabeth should be so very distressed this morning when she could have discussed her problems with her sister.

She coloured. "Jane...Jane only sees the good in people, even Mr

Collins. I cannot have an honest discussion with her about the faults of others, least of all mine."

Darcy felt ridiculously pleased at such an admission. She came to *him* first to discuss this problem. They stood for some minutes in silence, for he knew not what to say.

"And now," she said, "I really must go if I am to keep my winking appointment today."

He bowed and bid her farewell. On the ride back to Netherfield, not even the impending luncheon with Miss Bingley could keep him from ruminating fondly on the agreeable prospect of being winked at by one Miss Elizabeth Bennet.

Schemes of Felicity

Sunday

Franklin was certainly better than Frank or Francis, though none were particularly appealing. Could it be Felix? Heavens, no! Fenton, Fletcher, Fraser, Forester? Surely not. It must be something strong and steady. Frederick Darcy sounded very well. It simply must be Frederick.

Such were Elizabeth's thoughts as she waited for the Lucas family to arrive at church. Which story should she share with Mr F. Darcy tomorrow? Preferably one that would make him laugh generously. The story of Gussy Goulding's missing tooth would no doubt suffice. He was far too good-natured to have such a rascal for a brother. Jowly Jacob knew his brother could never balance on that fencepost let alone cross from one to the next. Gussy was so terribly awkward at that age he might topple over on level ground.

Between the pitifully short interval Gus kept his balance, his graceless descent teeth first into the ground, Jacob's swooning at the sight of the blood, and young Elizabeth's suggestion that they shove the tooth back into place, only straighter this time—surely that story would earn a few guffaws, several chuckles and a generous helping of dimples. It was a rather unique scale on which to measure success, but a challenge Elizabeth was eager to undertake.

"Why on earth are you grinning so, Lizzy?" asked Lydia from beside her in the pew.

Elizabeth was nonplussed that she had been caught ruminating on a certain gentleman yet again. She shushed Lydia and shook her head.

In the next moment, she spied the Lucas clan entering. Charlotte's eyes immediately met hers, and Elizabeth winked for all she was worth.

§

Monday

Elizabeth looked on triumphantly as her audience of one doubled over with laughter.

Mr Darcy finally settled. "Has Jacob Goulding's character improved as he aged?"

"No, unfortunately. He is as mean spirited as an adult as he was as a child. As I am sure you have heard, Jacob Goulding eloped with his half-sister's governess just a few months before you arrived in the country, and I must say, every young lady breathed a sigh of relief at the news."

"Why is that?"

"As heir to the Goulding fortune, he thought himself quite the catch, and he let us all know it. He would especially single out a girl on her first night 'out,' making what was already a terrifying night thoroughly unpleasant. Jane, Kitty, and Maria were all his victims."

"And how did you escape this rite of passage?"

"I had a protector. John intervened when Mr Goulding approached me at the opening of my first assembly. John performed a similar service for Mary, and he would have done so for Kitty and Maria had he been in the country. So you see? You were not the first to shield me from the unwanted attentions of a pompous gentleman at a ball, though you *were* much more subtle than John."

Mr Darcy said nothing. Such a grave silence surely detracted from her earlier successful tally of chuckles and dimples. "Oh! I have just thought of the next story I shall tell you: the saga of Lady Lucas's gown for Maria's coming out dinner last winter."

"I am quite ready to hear it."

"Not today, I am afraid." She reluctantly removed his gloves from her hands.

"Tomorrow, then?" he asked as he took them.

She nodded, "Tomorrow."

He gifted her with a generous smile. It quite made up for his earlier silence.

§

Tuesday

" ...Thus a second emergency trip to London was made for alterations. I do believe this was my mother's intention when she continued bringing Cook's pies and cakes over to Lucas Lodge." He laughed, and Elizabeth's thoughts jumbled. "My mother...you see, she resented that Maria should have such a grand introduction. None of *us* ever had one except Jane, for my mother rushed us so. The moment we turned fifteen, any invitation to dinner would do for our coming out."

She glanced at him and nearly lost her train of thought again. "Maria waited until she was sixteen, and word had recently come from John of very successful business ventures, allowing Lady Lucas to overdo the entire affair. She wanted to bring Kitty and Maria with her to London for that last alteration. Kitty was, in fact, her real object, for through all this she had become Lady Lucas's trusted fashion consultant. I must admit, Kitty does have a great eye for colour and cut. She voraciously reads any fashion magazines she can get her hands on. And of course she desperately wanted to go to the renowned modiste in town, even as an observer, but my mother forbade it.

"As it turned out, it was very good she did not go, for the next day she came down with a fever and horrible cough. We feared she would be unable to attend Maria's party, but she recovered in time. As per the Bennets' usual custom, we arrived late to the gathering, and most of the other guests were already gathered in the drawing room. Lady Lucas came to greet us, and she was very happy to see Kitty after her illness. And now, Mr Darcy, we come to the part that makes listening to all this talk of fashion worth your trouble. Kitty said, far too loudly, 'I knew that style of gown would suit you, Lady Lucas. It makes you look ever so much thinner than you really are!'"

They laughed together for a few minutes.

"How did Lady Lucas react?" he asked eventually.

"I am sure it chafed, but she could hardly be affronted. Kitty meant it quite innocently. I told her later that the phrase she must use is simply, 'That gown flatters you,' or something similar."

He chuckled and shook his head. "Yes, that would be preferable, no doubt."

"Kitty really is thick in such matters. I believe there is little time between the forming of a thought in her mind and its speedy pronouncement by her lips. She has an uncanny talent for saying exactly the wrong thing, and she has no idea she has done so, for on top of all that, she is woefully inept at reading people's facial expressions."

"I confess, I have thought her tactless at times."

"Yes, so she would appear, and sometimes she is. A comment such as the one she made to Lady Lucas could be construed as quite mean-spirited, but it was the furthest thing from it. When people laugh at her or act offended, she does not understand, and it only makes her more peevish. Jane and I have tried to help. For example, she now knows she is not to speak about any romantic entanglements in company. If she has such questions, she is to come to us privately. Thus, she can at least avoid some of the most sensitive subjects."

It began to drizzle as they stood together next to Oakham Stream. Elizabeth thought it quite unfortunate. "It seems time to return indoors."

"What new tale will you have for me tomorrow?" he asked with an enthusiasm that made her ridiculously pleased.

She laughed. "I shall think of something."

Wednesday

Cursed, cursed rain! This was no drizzle or mist; this was a cold, heavy downpour. Even if Elizabeth ventured into it, which she was sorely tempted to do, she could not expect Mr Darcy to be so foolish. There would be no point in getting soaking wet by herself.

❧

Thursday

"Do you know anything about the family that owned Netherfield prior to its being let out?"

"No, though Bingley and I have speculated about it. There is a framed drawing of a boy and girl."

"That is Julia and Teddy Murray. The Murrays had a storied history in and around Meryton, even longer than the Bennets. Jane was best friends with Julia Murray. They were the perfect pair: Jane all fair and blue-eyed and Julia with raven hair and bright green eyes. They were always perfectly attired and smiling some secret smile to each other. I felt quite shabby in comparison, for I was always muddy and dishevelled, most likely with twigs rather than ribbons in my tangled hair."

Elizabeth glanced over at Mr Darcy and her next words died in her throat. Before he looked away, she could swear she saw a strange tenderness in his expression. Perhaps she had said something to remind him of his sister? She knew so little about his life, for she was always prattling on about hers, and he never seemed inclined to offer any information about himself.

She shook her head to regroup her thoughts. "The Gouldings were new to the neighbourhood, and they wished to be regarded as a family as prominent as the Murrays. So the Goulding boys occasionally spent time at Netherfield. One day, Jane came home covered in mud nearly from head to toe. Jacob Goulding had pushed her down after saying Julia's dress was so much better that it mattered little if Jane's got muddy."

"When my mother heard of this outrage, she went straight to Haye Park. Though she may criticise and scold us herself, she is fiercely protective of her daughters against an outsider's insults. This is why she took a rather intense dislike to *you* at the assembly despite your enviable wealth and convenient bachelorhood." She grinned at him, and he rolled his eyes.

"My mother was brought to Mr Goulding, who is haughty and mean-spirted like his eldest son. He initially belittled her, calling her a hysterical female.

"My mother was most displeased. 'Everyone knows my Jane is an angel, and everyone knows your Jacob to be a horrid fiend. If you do not make him apologise, I shall call on every family in and around Meryton to tell them about his nasty behaviour.'

'Madam,' he replied, 'I find your threats rather empty. The Bennets are nothing to the Gouldings in fortune or consequence.'

'Mr Goulding,' she said, 'that may very well be, but you delude yourself if you think people *here* will value such things over the word of the Bennets. The Murrays are *especially* fond of Jane.

'We hysterical females do enjoy a good bit of gossip. You can become the even-handed patriarch in this story, or the callous shirker of responsibility. Which should you prefer?'

"Mr Goulding had lost his complacency. Naturally, he chose the former. The next day, Jacob presented himself at Longbourn to grovel before Jane and my mother. From then on, Mr Goulding always showed my mother the greatest respect, and she never once encouraged any of us to pursue Jacob Goulding even though he was the richest, most eligible bachelor in the area."

Mr Darcy smiled and kept walking next to her. Elizabeth wished she had chosen a different story to tell him today. "This tale is not particularly humorous, but if you knew Jowly Jacob, you would think it eminently satisfying."

"Your descriptions of Mr Goulding remind me a bit of young Wickham. So I do find it satisfying."

Here was a chance to learn more about Mr Darcy. Elizabeth seized it eagerly. "Were you playmates growing up?" He nodded. "What sort of mischief did he cause?"

He sighed. "I prefer not to talk about Mr Wickham."

"Of course." They walked in silence for some minutes as Elizabeth swallowed her disappointment. Dimples and laughter were all well and good, but she did not even know his full name.

"What happened to the Murrays?" His question startled her.

"That is a tragic story. Julia and little Teddy died of scarlet fever. In his grief, Mr Murray turned to drink and gambling and he soon followed his children to the grave, leaving many debts behind. Netherfield Park was sold to pay them off, and Mrs Murray returned to her family a broken woman.

"I remember very clearly bursting into Jane's room perhaps a week after Julia's death to find her weeping. This was the first time I realised that Jane hid her emotions from others. I comforted her as best I could and loved her all the more for her quiet sorrow. I must admit that up until that point, I rather resented Jane's perfection, for I could not possibly measure up. But we became much closer after that, and how could I not improve with such an example as Jane?"

They had returned to the clearing where Mr Darcy's horse waited. "I hope for Jane's sake that Mr Bingley's return from London is not delayed. I have never seen her so restless."

"He is very eager to return, I am sure. He will not be delayed."

"That is a relief. I do not know how many more of Jane's delicate sighs I can endure." He smiled. "Lydia is also increasingly impatient for his return."

"Why should Miss Lydia wish for Bingley's return?"

"Is it not obvious? His return allows for the possibility of seeing *you* socially, and Lydia is quite keen on the prospect." He looked rather alarmed. "I *told* you not to smile at her at the ball."

"I did not! Well, not fully. I was very aware of my...of, well, my..." He trailed off as she laughed at him. "Teasing, teasing girl," he said in mock reproach.

"I delight in vexing you."

He took her gloved hand and bowed formally over it. "I look forward to being further vexed tomorrow, Miss Elizabeth." When he rose, he had a wicked glint in his eye. He held onto her hand as his smile grew, until she was gaping up at his dimpled cheeks.

She nodded and blinked stupidly, and then he laughed. "I never knew these could be such a weapon."

She shook herself, snatching her hand away. "One should always be careful with a weapon; it could misfire if used improperly." She turned towards the road.

"Thank you for the warning," he called after her.

She walked along the road until it curved out of sight, and then she leaned against the nearest tree with a hand over her pounding heart. "Weapon indeed," she whispered.

Friday

"Mr Bingley returned last night ahead of schedule, and he is currently readying himself for a much-too-early call at Longbourn," Mr Darcy informed Elizabeth as they walked along the stream together, her hand on his arm.

"Excellent! Perhaps I should get back home."

"You have at least an hour. Bingley spends a ridiculous amount of time primping, even more so where Miss Bennet is concerned."

"Are you calling your friend a dandy?"

"I am calling him a besotted fool."

"We are all fools in love, are we not?"

"Yes, we are," he said quietly, and Elizabeth found herself unable to look away from his eyes. He finally averted his gaze and slowed their pace. "If you had rather go..."

"If I see Jane looking so melancholy, I shall be tempted to tell her the news, and how shall I explain my prior knowledge?" He only nodded, not meeting her eyes.

"You must be quite weary of my silly stories by now."

"No, not at all. I enjoy them thoroughly. But perhaps you are weary of telling them."

"There is nothing I like better than the sound of my own voice." He smirked, and Elizabeth was happy the strange awkwardness had gone. "But I wonder that you should care to hear so many silly stories about people you have never met, like Jacob Goulding or John Lucas."

He shrugged.

"Oh! How could I forget? Mr Collins returns to Hertfordshire on Monday!"

"No! So soon? You must be teasing again."

"It is the truth. He stays only until Saturday, less than a week. The Netherfield party should be expecting an invitation to dinner at

Lucas Lodge on Thursday night in celebration of Charlotte's engagement. My cousin is the guest of honour of course."

"Of course. I suppose Lady Lucas will don her flattering red gown for the occasion."

Elizabeth laughed. "It does not fit her anymore."

"That is unfortunate. I should like to see this splendid garment."

"One thing to look forward to, however, is your ability to completely ignore and avoid Mr Collins! You have no secret agenda, no damsel in distress to guard from his attentions."

He laughed. "That will be a welcome change. Every conversation I had with him was rather painful."

Elizabeth furrowed her brow. "But, I thought you must get some amusement out of manipulating him. At the ball, if it was a punishment to you, why did you...?" She could not finish the question in any satisfactory manner.

"Because I knew he interfered with *your* enjoyment of the ball."

"Thank you," she said simply. They had reached the small cascades, and they stood together for several minutes in silence, looking upon the water.

"This is a picturesque spot," he finally said. "It reminds me of one of the streams in Pemberley Wood."

"You have more than one stream on your estate?"

"Yes, several. It is a rather large area."

"I would love to hear about it."

He turned to her and searched her face. "Would you?"

"Very much."

And so he told her about Pemberley's woods, meadows, fields, ponds, and streams. His descriptions were so vivid, she felt like she could see it all; his voice was so rich, she felt she could listen to it forever. She forgot about the cold or that Mr Bingley was most likely visiting Longbourn or that she had not yet broken her fast.

"I am afraid I have kept you out too long again. You are chilled," he said as they stood in the clearing. Elizabeth did not remember walking back.

She shook her head. "I had not noticed. But I must return home."

They parted, and when Elizabeth arrived at Longbourn, Kitty, Lydia, Mary, and Mrs Bennet stood outside the breakfast room door.

"La! Lizzy, wherever can you have been walking for so long? You have missed some great fun," Lydia whispered. "Mr Bingley came over quite unexpectedly and Mama invited him to share breakfast with us. Then she kept winking at us all, and Kitty, being so dense about such things, asked her 'What is the matter Mama? What do you keep winking at me for? What am I to do?' Lord, how I laughed!"

Kitty was indignant. "You did not need to pinch me so hard, Lydia."

"*Someone* had to get you to stop eating and leave the room, and Mama was being far too subtle." Elizabeth doubted that was the case.

As Kitty and Lydia argued over winks and pinches, the door opened. Mr Bingley grinned at them all and went to the library, while Jane stood, glowing, in the breakfast room.

Elizabeth went to her immediately.

"How shall I bear so much happiness!" Jane cried as they embraced.

The commotion that followed was full of giggling and squealing, and Elizabeth could not help herself from participating in it. Jane was engaged to Mr Bingley. This meant that even after Mr Darcy left Hertfordshire in a fortnight, Elizabeth could reasonably expect to see him again. Yes indeed, today was a joyous day.

27

Jealousy and Cowardice

Darcy stared out at the night passing through the carriage window, seething with jealousy. Bingley's face *still* had not lost its blissful expression, even four days after his engagement. Darcy doubted *he* would ever know such happiness. His mornings had been happy enough lately, but he could not ignore his impending departure any longer. Could he leave her? Just nine more mornings remained with her, assuming he spent none of those mornings soaking wet and alone, as he had once before.

Jealousy had become a more and more common emotion for Darcy of late, but he was hoping to bury it for the night at least. The entire Netherfield party was to dine at Longbourn, a uniting of the families to signal the future union. It would be the first time he and Elizabeth met socially since they had resumed their morning interludes. He knew not what to expect.

When they arrived, Darcy assisted Mrs Hurst and Miss Bingley from the carriage, for Bingley and Hurst were too preoccupied with what awaited them inside the house to do so. The former thought only of his betrothed, the latter only of the upcoming meal. Hurst had told Darcy more than once that Mrs Bennet set a good table and Bingley could have done much worse than Jane Bennet.

They entered and were announced, but Miss Bennet was not in

the room with her mother and sisters. Bingley hesitated in the doorway, clearly lost and unsure. Elizabeth crossed to him with a laugh. "Do not look so sad, Mr Bingley. Jane and my father will be along any second."

Bingley chuckled. "I thank you for setting my mind at ease, Miss Elizabeth."

"As my future brother, you may as well call me Elizabeth. In fact, you ought to call me Lizzy, for you are already one of my favourite people in the world for making my dear sister so happy."

Darcy moved through the greetings in a haze of jealousy. Bingley had leave to call her by the name Darcy longed to use. How many times had he thought of her in his heart as "Lizzy?" *His* Lizzy.

He shook himself from his brooding. Nothing would be served by it. Indeed, the rest of the night turned out to be delightful, in part because Elizabeth was lively and open and gracious as ever, often coaxing him to join in the conversation with a small smile and raised brow. His natural reserve could not stand against such an assault.

In the greatest surprise of all, he found himself enjoying the company of his hosts. Over the last fortnight, he had listened as Elizabeth shared her memories of her family, and he had begun to see them through her eyes: imperfect but lovable.

Her parents were perhaps the most difficult to look upon fondly. On the one hand, her mother was fiercely loyal to her daughters and singularly dedicated to pursuing their future security through the only means at her disposal: advantageous marriage. He could not blame her for being a woman of mean understanding. But he found it harder to overlook her clear favouritism towards her other daughters, not to mention her disruptive temper and uncouth behaviour, both sources of distress for a certain young lady. Tonight, however, Mrs Bennet excelled in her role as proud mother and adept hostess, though she was still playing the matchmaker, seating Darcy next to her youngest daughter again.

Mr Bennet was another matter. His failures towards his family were grave, and he could not possibly claim that he did not know any better. The power of checking Mrs Bennet's inappropriate behaviour rested with him alone, and he had neglected and avoided this duty. Still, Darcy could not help but admire Mr Bennet's sharp wit, so vividly and fondly related in Elizabeth's stories, and on full display as he discussed Miss Lydia's latest book, *Evelina*, with Darcy, Elizabeth, and, of course, a jubilant Lydia. Mr Bennet had helped shape Elizabeth into the delightful woman she was today by encouraging her study and her wit, and she loved him dearly despite his faults.

Miss Bennet was of course the easiest to respect. Darcy had already admired her protective care of Elizabeth when they had stayed at Netherfield. He now knew her to be the kindest soul, even if she was a bit naïve. He recognised a bit of himself in her concealment of her deeper emotions. It was understandable indeed, with the personalities of her parents, that she should hide her feelings, not only to protect herself from exposure but also to provide a foil to those parents. She had been trying to set a better example for her younger sisters in the only way she could. Tonight, however, her emotions were evident. The satisfaction of Miss Bennet's mind gave a glow of such sweet animation to her face as made her look handsomer than ever. Her love for Bingley could not be concealed.

Darcy had come to look fondly upon Miss Catherine as well. The poor girl was at a disadvantage, it seemed, when interacting with others. Darcy could sympathise with her social awkwardness. The difference between them was that *she* did not hide behind a proud mask. She interacted with people and she sometimes suffered for her efforts, but she did not become intimidated. In fact, she bluntly asked him about Georgiana's gowns, and he answered with as much detail as he could. She was pleased and excited, asking many subsequent questions that he could not answer to her satisfaction, until finally, Miss Lydia demanded she stop "pestering Mr Darcy."

The youngest Bennet was also impossible to intimidate. Miss Lydia was undeniably selfish and overly bold. She enjoyed being the centre of attention. But she was still a child and, according to Elizabeth, had begun to mature over the last month or so. She needed constant entertainment and therefore would make up all manner of silly games—like the linking of hands to reach around the ancient oaks. Miss Lydia had a cheerful disposition, never sinking into melancholy even when she was disappointed. She also always tried to cheer others when she thought them depressed; in this, she was similar to Elizabeth.

Finally, there was the mysterious Miss Mary. He had wondered about the middle Bennet ever since the Netherfield ball, and it seemed Elizabeth was growing increasingly curious about her quiet sister as well. They spoke about her the next morning at Oakham Stream.

"I must confess to doing something dreadful," Elizabeth said. Darcy had come to cherish her intimate confessions most of all. The amusing stories were charming of course, but she shared them with everyone. In their secret place here, she felt at liberty to tell him deeply personal information about herself. And he loved it.

"What dastardly deed have you committed now?" he asked as he offered his arm.

"Let us cross the stream and walk deeper into the woods today. It is mild and dry, and all this walking back and forth is getting rather repetitive, is it not?"

He agreed, and she pointed out the best place to cross. He preceded her and helped her across. "How chivalrous!" she said. "John never worried about keeping my boots dry."

Darcy's mood fell considerably with the knowledge that she had come here with John Lucas too. Perhaps this was not *their* secret place together, but rather, Darcy was the substitute, the temporary replacement. The thought that she would continue these meetings with another man when Darcy had gone made him sick to his stomach.

"Are you quite well, Mr Darcy?" she asked with obvious concern.

Blast! He had let his torment show on his face. "Yes, perfectly well. You mentioned a confession."

"Oh, it is nothing really. I was simply being melodramatic. If you would rather talk about something else I...I am very willing to listen."

"Thank you, but I merely remembered an item of business I must write to my steward about." He despised lying to her. "Please continue."

She searched his face, her brows drawn slightly together, before speaking again. "Yesterday I looked into Mary's papers while she left the room for a few moments."

"That is quite dreadful; how will you live with yourself?"

She glared at him. "Would *you* like your sister to rifle through your papers?"

Darcy considered; before sending his latest letter to Anne several days ago, it had been in the desk drawer, full of secrets about his L. as well as a full accounting of the Wickham saga, which he had not shared with Anne previously. "No, you are right, of course. So what drove you to commit such an invasion of Miss Mary's privacy?"

"No one can possibly make so many extracts from Fordyce. She should have rewritten the entirety of the text several times over at the rate she scribbles."

"Could she be writing a novel?"

"That was precisely my suspicion!" she exclaimed. "How did you know?"

"It was a guess. But I know Miss Mary to be an avid studier of the human character. Perhaps even more so than you. You interact, she observes."

"Yes! She is so subtle about it, and she never gossips. Most people do not notice her watching and listening."

"Have you confirmed your suspicions?"

"No, unfortunately. The top sheet seemed to be a long passage about charity. I could not read it carefully enough to know. I also saw a second sheet that rambled on about obstinacy. I do not recall such a passage from Fordyce, but it has been many years since I bothered to read it."

"Perhaps she does not write a novel, but her own morality essays?"

She snorted. "I would *much* rather she write a gothic novel. It would be so much more exciting. In any case, my prying yielded no great answers, and I shall no doubt be tempted to pry again in the future."

"Should you not just ask her?"

"Oh no," she looked up at him with a mischievous smile, "that would spoil all the fun of this little mystery."

Later that afternoon, Darcy retreated to his room to avoid Miss Bingley while Charles visited the Bennets yet again. He should have been glad of his friend's happiness, but instead he was envious and surly. He felt an urgency, a desperation that his time at Netherfield—his time with Elizabeth—was drawing short.

A knock on his door interrupted his brooding. When he answered, a servant handed him a letter. He recognised the handwriting as that of Roger, the trusted servant Darcy had sent to work at Rosings. A reply from Anne was enclosed. He sat down to read it immediately.

Dear Fitzwilliam,

Mr Collins departs from us soon again to visit his 'dear Charlotte.' He will not be carrying any letter from Mother for you. She still rereads your last letter and grumbles over it every now and then. But she will not share it with me. What did you tell her?

Your last letter to me *contained all manner of shocks to which I must now reply. First, thank you for finally telling me about Georgiana's folly. It elucidates some of her more puzzling letters over the last months. Had I known earlier, I would have urged her confidence. I shall do so now. Between the two of us, cousin, we shall restore her spirits and self-assurance.*

I understand why you could not write to me of the ordeal before. The fact that you have shared it with your L. is only further proof that you should marry her. Imagine what a more mercenary woman would do with such information! You obviously trust L. completely.

And now I must berate you. I have never been more disappointed in your behaviour; I never thought it possible. You have claimed multiple times that you will not offer for L.; that duty, society forbid it. Yet you indulge in weeks' worth of assignations in the woods with her merely because you are too weak to resist? Do you not realise that your actions, in addition to risking your own heart and happiness, risk hers as well? Do you wish to injure her, Fitzwilliam? How can you have so little care for her feelings, not to mention, her reputation? What if you are discovered?

I know what you are thinking. If you <u>were</u> discovered, you would do the honourable thing, and the decision would be taken out of your hands entirely. That is the coward's way. L. would be regarded as the scheming country chit who finally trapped the great Fitzwilliam Darcy. Is that your desire? She deserves a proper courtship. She deserves a husband who enters into marriage willingly and with no reservations. She has already proven, through her refusal of a certain parson, that she wishes to marry for love, not security, and certainly, not due to scandal.

She deserves to be happy. If you feel you can best make her happy, for God's sake, stop your cowardly hesitation and confess your love to her. If you cannot do that, cease this behaviour at once and leave her be. Leave her be, Fitzwilliam.

You know I am correct. I hope you will act as you ought to have acted from the beginning. Seize your happiness, dear Cousin. So few people ever have a real chance at it. And yes, I shall follow my own advice somehow. Recognising your behaviour for what it is has clarified what my own should be with regards to C.

Good luck to us both.

Yours,
Anne

Darcy read the letter over, feeling more and more ashamed of himself. He had behaved reprehensibly. He had found the most amazing woman—she was kind, witty, lovely, and full of integrity, and she was his perfect match. But he had denied and denigrated this powerful connexion, measuring her against some foolish society standard and finding her situation wanting even as he selfishly indulged his craving for her company. He had wished her to suffer just a fraction of what he was suffering when, all the while, the power to end any suffering was his alone if he would just abandon his stupid prejudices and court her. What a selfish fool! He had been proud, arrogant, and unfeeling.

Tomorrow morning, he would confess his deeper feelings. He would apologise for putting her reputation at risk, and he would profess a desire to court her publicly and properly if she would allow it. The engagement party at Lucas Lodge tomorrow night would be the perfect opportunity to make his intentions known to her family and the neighbourhood. By God, he *would* seize his happiness. Only her rejection could prevent it.

Darcy paced along the bank of Oakham Stream feeling a combination of fear and anticipation. How would she react? Would she be surprised, relieved, disgusted? She must know at least to some degree that he admired her. Did she return his admiration?

In this perturbed state of mind, with thoughts that could rest on nothing, he paced on, but it would not last. He heard a strange sort of cry come from the road. It was Elizabeth's voice, but...was she injured? He rushed towards the road. But he soon heard her laughter and was much relieved. He stood for a moment, listening to the delightful sound. He ought not go out onto the road lest someone see them together. But then he caught a glimpse of her through the branches. She was not alone.

Elizabeth Bennet stood laughing in the embrace of a young man.

28

Particularly Intimate

Elizabeth slipped out the back door just as the sun rose. She had been leaving very early this week for fear of running into Mr Collins on his way each morning to visit Lucas Lodge. She wondered why he did not just stay there, for surely even *he* could feel the loss of Mrs Bennet's enthusiasm for his presence. Elizabeth suspected that no polite invitation to return would be uttered *this* time when he took his leave. In any case, when the Gardiners came, there would be no room for Mr Collins at Longbourn, even if he did somehow wheedle another invitation.

The vicar had expressed his profuse congratulations when he was informed of Jane and Mr Bingley's engagement. "What a relief it must be," he had said at dinner the night of his arrival, "that one of your daughters had the good sense to be grateful and humble when Fortune smiled upon her."

"Indeed," Mr Bennet had replied, "I feel the full measure of my good fortune. Mr Bingley will be called my son. I do pity fathers when their daughters choose to marry halfwits and jackanapes." Elizabeth could barely keep her countenance, and Lydia nearly choked on her soup.

On Tuesday night when the Netherfield party was to dine at Longbourn, Charlotte had insisted Mr Collins dine at Lucas Lodge. It was a welcome relief indeed. The dinner had been a rousing success despite Miss Bingley's now slightly less overt disapproval. Elizabeth did not even mind Mr and Mrs Hurst, for the latter was making an effort to be kind to Jane, in her way, and the former treated everyone in the same manner—as second fiddle to his meal.

But Elizabeth's attention that night had been on Mr Darcy. How differently he had behaved towards the Bennets compared to before the picnic! To see him discussing the latest London fashion in reticules and turbans with Kitty was a shock indeed. He had seen Elizabeth gaping at him during that conversation, and he merely smirked and shrugged.

Now, as she walked towards Oakham Stream, her thoughts were full of him. Could it be that he finally accepted her family; that he finally saw them for real people, not merely players in his entertainment? Could it be that he saw *her* as more than a diversion?

"I cannot tell you how comforting it is to know some things will never change, Lizzybits," came a voice from behind her on the road.

Though startled, she immediately recognised the appellation and its speaker. "John!" Her squeal was largely unintelligible as she launched herself at him.

He laughed as he swung her around, and a thousand childhood memories rushed back to her. They nearly toppled over in their enthusiasm.

After he steadied them he said, "I take it this means you have forgiven me."

She laughed, feeling giddy and silly. "Yes, it pains me to admit, but it turns out I might have been wrong. Though it was still *most* disagreeable of you not to follow my recommendations on the proper course of your life to the very letter."

He dramatically wiped his brow. "What a relief! Here I thought you would insist I return to Cambridge immediately to finish my education."

She pursed her lips. "It is not a bad idea, John." But she could not keep her stern countenance and began laughing.

"By God, I have missed your laugh!" He hugged her again. "Now let me look at you. You look exactly the same, Lizzybits." He touched her nose.

She swatted his hand away. "And you are far too tan. My good-ness! Did you row the ship across the Atlantic yourself?" she said, eyeing his solid frame.

He laughed, his green eyes crinkling in that familiar way. They stood looking at each other, loosely embraced, for few moments as they laughed at nothing in particular.

"Were you going to Oakham Stream? I am anxious to see it again."

Elizabeth stepped back, shaking herself. Mr Darcy was most likely waiting at the clearing. She was suddenly nervous. She wanted John to like him, and she wanted him to like John. "Yes, I was on my way there."

"Perfect. It is as if I never left. Come along then." He dragged her towards the path but suddenly stopped when he saw Mr Darcy there. "Oh, hallo!" John said.

"Mr Darcy! I had heard that you take morning rides." Elizabeth stepped towards him, hoping he understood. "It seems I am doubly surprised on my walk this morning. Mr Lucas took me quite unawares. You have no doubt heard much of my wayward neighbour since you have been in Hertfordshire. May I present Mr John Lucas, recently returned from parts unknown. This is Mr Darcy, who has been visiting Mr Bingley, the new occupant of Netherfield."

Mr Darcy bowed stiffly. "Mr Lucas."

John was not so formal. "Ah! It is very good to meet you, sir. Char-lotte has been keeping me informed of all the goings-on in the neigh-bourhood, so I am not unfamiliar with you or your friend."

Elizabeth wondered exactly what Charlotte had told John about Mr Darcy. She blushed at some of the more mortifying possibilities before the tense silence prompted her to try easing the two men into conversation. She desperately hoped Mr Darcy would not return to his grave, reserved demeanour.

"When did you arrive, Mr Lucas?"

"Yesterday evening. But you must not tell anyone, Li—Miss Eliza-beth. It seems my mother has learned a certain flair for the dramatic from Mrs Bennet, and she wishes me to make a grand, shocking entrance at the engagement party tonight. She does not even know I have left the house."

"I certainly will not spoil Lady Lucas's moment of triumph, and Mr Darcy will not breathe a word of your return to anyone. He is most reticent. Is that not right, Mr Darcy?" She tried to tease him into a better humour.

"I shall not mention it." Nothing but impenetrable gravity.

"There's a good chap," said John. That manner of address momentarily cracked Mr Darcy's reserve, but John did not notice. "Charlotte wrote to me that you—I say! That is a fine animal!" John stepped around Mr Darcy to examine his mount, which waited on the path just off the road.

Elizabeth took the opportunity to move closer to Mr Darcy. He stubbornly would not meet her eyes. She finally poked his arm, and his eyes flew to hers. She mouthed, "I'm sorry," and shrugged with a smile. His expression softened but his eyes remained intent, those gold flecks seeming to shine at her. She did not know he had reached for her hand until she felt him squeeze it through her glove. She gasped.

"I plan to indulge in a good bit of horseflesh and spend some of my newfound fortune," John was saying, still admiring the horse. "Do you have any suggestions on where I might find one like yours, Mr Darcy?"

Mr Darcy released Elizabeth's hand with one last squeeze. "If you seek variety, I would suggest going to Bath. There are several quality horse traders there."

"Now would my parents not love a trip to Bath? Perhaps we can persuade some of the Bennet ladies to accompany us. What say you, Lizzy?" John added sheepishly, "Pardon me, Miss Elizabeth."

"It is not my decision. I should think Maria would like to take Kitty. I imagine there are a multitude of fashionable bonnets to be seen in Bath. And of course Lydia would not rest until she was invited as well."

He laughed. "How is the little imp?"

"She is hardly little anymore as she will proudly tell you. She is the tallest of all her sisters now."

"Surely not! Taller than Jane, even?"

"Taller even than Jane."

"Oh! But I have been remiss. I offer my congratulations on Jane's engagement. I seriously doubted anyone could be good enough for her, but Charlotte has put me at ease that this Mr Bingley fellow may be just right."

"He most certainly is, as you will soon learn. And I offer my heartfelt congratulations to you on Charlotte's engagement as well. Did you meet your future brother last night?" She smirked at him.

John glanced at Mr Darcy. "I did."

Elizabeth laughed. "You need not worry about offending Mr Darcy. He is the soul of discretion. Speak your mind."

John heaved a sigh of relief. "I did feel compelled to seek reassurances from Charlotte that she knows what she is about. She need not marry at all if she does not wish it. She said you told her the same thing."

"Yes, I did. But she has her own goals in mind, it seems, and I can only support her. Though I needed some expert convincing." She smiled at Mr Darcy who smiled back, finally.

John replied, "She *is* determined. I wish...well, it is done now, and the entire neighbourhood will offer its congratulations tonight, no doubt."

"Oh yes, tonight. Will that be before or after you induce all the young ladies of the neighbourhood to swoon at your grand entrance?"

He rubbed his hands together with a wicked grin. "Any admirers must first pay proper respects to Charlotte. Only then shall I bestow my favour upon them." He winked.

Elizabeth laughed. "You are more ridiculous than ever. Gussy is very eager for your continued antics."

"Gus! How splendid it will be to see him without his loathsome brother jowling about."

Again, she laughed. Every time she stopped, he would utter some new inanity. "I believe you have invented a new verb. Mr Goulding jowled himself right into an elopement with the help."

"His father must have *loved* that. But we are being terribly rude, speaking about all these unknown people in front of Mr Darcy."

"Actually, I am well-informed about the Gouldings. Miss Elizabeth has shared some stories with me." Elizabeth beamed at him.

"Lucky fellow! I have missed your stories, Li—Miss Elizabeth. You must have some new ones from the last two years."

"I am convinced they are nothing in comparison to *your* stories, Mr Lucas. Surely you have had many adventures."

"I suppose I have," he said as a strange cloud passed over his eyes. He blinked it away and continued. "I shall promise to tell you one of them if you promise to dance the first with me tonight. We must make everyone terribly jealous."

"Oh! I had not expected dancing tonight," she stalled. It was silly of her to think Mr Darcy might wish to... She could not help but glance at him, only to find his gaze steadfastly upon her. She nearly gasped again

"Certainly, there will be dancing," John said, "if we can prevail upon Mary to abandon her concertos and play some music fit for the pursuit."

Elizabeth tore her gaze from one gentleman to answer the other. "Mary will no doubt assent. I suppose I shall have to endure the envious glares of the neighbourhood girls and dance the first with you. But you must dance with Kitty and Lydia as well."

"Ah, all is as it should be again. You are bossing me about. But of course no Bennet lady will escape standing up with me. I may even dance with your mother." He winked again.

She could not help but laugh. "Oh dear, I am not sure that is the wisest course of action."

"When have I ever followed the wisest course?"

Elizabeth made a great show of racking her brain. "Never."

Both of her companions laughed, and she silently rejoiced.

They heard the sounds of a carriage around the bend in the road. John retreated farther back onto the path. "I really ought not be on the road—my mother's surprise will be ruined."

Mr Darcy gathered the reins of his fine animal and faced Elizabeth. "I regret I must return to Netherfield." Elizabeth did not wish him to go, and he made no move to leave. "Since you have ensured that there will be more than one dance tonight, Miss Elizabeth, might you favour me with one?"

"Yes, I would be delighted," she answered a trifle too enthusiastically. "I hope no one asks me how my dance card was so mysteriously full upon my arrival."

John laughed. "You will find some way to evade any prying inquiries. I can hear the stream," he said excitedly. "I simply must see it! Shall we, Miss Elizabeth?" He held out his arm for her.

She looked between the two of them, torn. It did not seem right that she should walk on John's arm along Oakham Stream. But it was a ridiculous thought, for the stream actually ran through *his* property. She went to John's side. "I look forward to our dance tonight, Mr Darcy."

"As do I, Miss Elizabeth." He bowed to John. "Mr Lucas."

"A pleasure to meet you, Mr Darcy." John replied.

Elizabeth watched as Darcy mounted his horse and rode away. She and John walked to the water, and then he turned to her, "What was that all about?"

"What do you mean?"

"You were meeting him here, weren't you?"

"Do not be ridiculous!" He shook his head at her feigned outrage. "I believe I mentioned this," she motioned towards the stream, "as a picturesque spot to visit when he dined with us the other night."

"So it was a pure coincidence that you were both here soon after sunrise on a Thursday in December?"

"It was a coincidence that *you* were here too."

"No, it was not. I came to look for you specifically."

"Oh," she said dumbly. He continued his suspicious inspection of her face. She never could lie to John. "Whatever Charlotte has told you..."

"Does Charlotte have anything to do with it?"

Elizabeth turned towards the water. "No. And there is no 'it.'"

He shrugged. "If you say so. But I shall soon charm my way back into your confidence, so you might as well just tell me."

"Gah! You are just as infuriating as ever!"

He laughed. "It is good to see you too, Lizzybits." He touched her nose.

"Stop that, you dolt!" She crossed her arms over her chest and stared at the stream in ill humour. This was all wrong.

"What's wrong, Lizzy? You know I shall keep any secret you wish, even from Charlotte."

She sighed. "I know, John." But she could not speak of Mr Darcy to anyone. She was too confused about him. "I...I feel like you went off and had this grand adventure. Now you have come back and I am exactly the same as when you left, with nothing new or exciting to share."

He put his arm around her shoulders. "That's not true. You are much prettier than when I left."

She smiled. "Perhaps, but still not as pretty as Jane."

"Peter and I are of a different opinion on that matter than most." He looked back towards the road. "Though I think Mr Darcy may be of similar mind."

She snorted. "Fools, all of you. Peter must be so happy to see you!"

He allowed her to change the subject. "Peter is a fine lad, as is Walter. I cannot tell you how glad I am to be back with my family and loved ones again. You know you are among the very dearest to me, do you not?"

She had a lump in her throat, so she only nodded. They stood together in silence for some minutes.

"Now," he said as if clearing the air, "tell me whether I should wear my blue or my red waistcoat tonight. What will the ladies prefer?" He stood posing like a drawing in a fashion plate.

She burst into laughter. "Have you become a fop as well? You look best in green, if you must know." He had always been handsome, but now he looked the picture of masculine health, his skin tanned, his brown hair lightened by the sun, and his physique shaped by constant activity. Indeed, John would set hearts aflutter when he appeared tonight. But not Elizabeth's. No, she realised now, only one man had ever set her heart aflutter. Perhaps she was not as confused as she had thought.

"Ah, green. I have just the ensemble. And what about you? The two most eligible bachelors in the area both wish to dance with you. You must look the part."

"This is Charlotte's night," Elizabeth scolded, though she was already devising her best options. She would ask Kitty to arrange her hair again. She had done a splendid job for the ball.

"Quite right, quite right. You see, it is just like old times; you are already reminding me of propriety."

"*Someone* ought to do it. I must go now, John. I shall keep your secret from all except Jane, I think. Do you mind?"

"Not at all. Until tonight then, Lizzybits." He took her gloved hand and made a big smacking sound as he kissed it.

She laughed as she turned away, and she arrived at Longbourn just as Mr Bingley did. "Good morning, Lizzy," he said with a grin.

"Good morning, Charles," she returned. "You are before your time today."

"I have come early so as not to interfere with preparations for the party at Lucas Lodge tonight. I understand it is quite an undertaking when all six of you Bennet ladies must prepare yourselves for such an affair."

"A very wise choice, sir. You do not wish to hear Lydia carry on when she thinks Kitty has had the mirror too long."

They entered the breakfast room together to enthusiastic greetings. Jane said, "Did you meet Lizzy on her walk today, Charles?"

"No, we met just in the yard here. I believe Darcy comes in this direction more often than not for his morning rides. Have you never run into him, Lizzy?"

To be nearly discovered by two different people in the course of one morning was surprising indeed. "There are so many paths around here, that it is unlikely two people should meet by accident." She carefully avoided both lying and actually answering the question, and Mr Bingley was content to turn his undivided attention to Jane.

Elizabeth thought about Mr Darcy as she ate her toast. His taking of her hand despite the possibility of John seeing, his request for a dance—these were very deliberate signs from one so reserved. She dare not put a name to it, but something had changed in her and in him. They had changed each other. Tonight would be different.

29

Once More Into the Breach

Tonight would be different. Tonight, Darcy's dream would end differently. He was determined that it should, and when Fitzwilliam Darcy made such a determination even the dream world yielded. Tonight, she would not slip from his grasp on the balcony, or if she did, he would leap immediately to her side, no matter who else called her. He had learned his lesson about hesitation.

John Lucas had returned, and although Darcy's every instinct told him to retreat from the torture of witnessing another man's familiarity with Elizabeth, he had remained. In eight and twenty years, Darcy had only ever loved one woman. Now that he had admitted to himself, he could never leave her, and he was not about to shrink away from a little competition. He may have flinched at every slipped "Lizzy" falling from John Lucas's lips, he may have roiled and seethed when Lucas asked her for the first dance of the evening, he may have felt like crying when the pair stood together ready to walk along Oakham Stream as if it were the most natural thing in the world, but one precious comfort remained for Darcy: she had wished to set him at ease. She had come to him and made him look into those fine eyes, and he had understood that she did not forget him, that he still had a place in her life.

But he did not know what that place was. She had been shocked when he grasped her hand. She had not rebuffed him, but that could have merely been a result of her discretion. Witnessing the ease with which John Lucas elicited her laughter was, in truth, the most discouraging of all. They were completely comfortable with each other, a consequence of their long shared history. They knew and cared for each other's families and friends and concerns, and it was all effortless. How could Darcy compete with that?

He took extra care with his appearance that evening, leaving Higgins a bit surprised, though he hid it well. Darcy was never one to ruminate on the appearance of another man, but he could not help but wish John Lucas was not quite so handsome. He did notice that Mr Lucas lacked one thing Elizabeth had mentioned: dimples. Darcy intended to use them to his best advantage tonight. It was a novelty indeed that he should, for the first time in his life, consciously and deliberately woo a young lady. He wished they could be afforded some privacy to speak, so he could tell her plainly his intentions, but he had wasted all his previous opportunity. Now he must show her with the distinct possibility that others would notice, and he needed all his charms for the task.

The Netherfield party arrived at Lucas Lodge before the Bennets did. Darcy greeted his hosts and congratulated Miss Lucas and Mr Collins on their engagement. Mr Collins was profuse in his thanks. "I am particularly gratified by your kind words, Mr Darcy. Lady Catherine, too, upon hearing of my choice, so heartily approved my marriage that she wished it to take place as soon as possible. Though I shall be called from my amiable Charlotte on Saturday, the pain of separation may be alleviated by preparations for the reception of my bride, as I have reason to hope that shortly after my next return into Hertfordshire, the day will be fixed that is to make me the happiest of men."

Darcy made no special effort to continue the conversation. His mind was much too occupied to have the patience for the chore. He attempted to take his leave of them, but Miss Lucas spoke to him, "Mr Darcy, I hope I do not presume too much when I say that I shall look forward to seeing a familiar face when you next visit your aunt in Kent."

"Not at all; your presence will be a welcome addition during my yearly visit." Just then he heard some frantic whispering from one of the doorways. Peter and Walter Lucas had stuck their heads out and were beckoning Miss Lucas to come to them.

"I am sorry, Mr Darcy, but I am wanted by my brothers. I'm sure *you* can imagine the excitement in the Lucas household tonight." Darcy took her meaning. Apparently she knew he had already met John Lucas that morning. He could not clarify, however, for she left him to join her young brothers, and Darcy quickly retreated from Mr Collins.

Darcy wished to silently stalk the edges of the room and gather his thoughts, but he did not want to stray too far from Bingley, who naturally was chatting amiably with everyone in the drawing room. Once the Bennets arrived, Bingley would of course greet his betrothed, and Darcy planned to be close behind him. So he suffered through stilted conversation with the Longs, Philipses, Gouldings, and Colonel Forster and his insipid wife, all the while witnessing the joyous anticipation of Maria Lucas and her young brothers, not to mention the elated pride of their parents.

The Bennets were announced. They entered in order of precedence, and Mr and Mrs Bennet went immediately to Sir William and Lady Lucas. Bingley strode purposefully to Miss Bennet, and Darcy took his opportunity to follow.

Elizabeth curtseyed and he bowed over her hand, never breaking eye contact with her. "Miss Elizabeth, I am exceedingly pleased to see you, but I find I must contradict one of my earlier statements to you."

She arched her brow at him as Miss Catherine dragged Miss Lydia past them towards Maria Lucas. "I am all anticipation to hear what has caused you to make such a grave error, Mr Darcy."

"It was indeed a grave error. I once said you were one of the handsomest women of my acquaintance. In fact, you are *the* handsomest, and I have been remiss for ever having conveyed otherwise."

She blinked and her hand trembled slightly as she retracted it. Then she met his eyes again and smiled brilliantly. "You are forgiven, sir."

"You are too kind. But I do not think my mistake can be so easily remedied as that. If you will allow me, I intend to atone for it over the course of the evening."

"It is not necessary, but just out of curiosity, how do you intend to make amends?"

"By laughing at your every quip, heartily agreeing with your every assertion, and otherwise hanging on your every word. No doubt you will think me quite a nuisance."

She laughed, and he thought he was off to an admirable start. "It is unlikely that I should ever think so, though if we discuss literature I shall be very disappointed if you simply agree with everything I say. Such a change would surely make our debates much less lively."

"I would by no means suspend any pleasure of yours," he warmly replied.

"Ladies and gentlemen, my friends and neighbours," called Sir William from the centre of the room. "Now that our dearest friends have arrived, tardy as usual,"—he winked at Mrs Bennet—"I wish to begin the evening with an announcement. Our dear girl, Charlotte, will be leaving us and starting a new life."

Darcy had by this time positioned himself beside and slightly behind Miss Elizabeth. His arm brushed hers, and he thought she leaned slightly into him. It was all he could do to comprehend Sir William's continued speech.

"Although this is to be expected, every parent feels a mixture of sorrow and pride on such an occasion. In this instance, however, my wife and I know our sorrow will be brief, for Charlotte has chosen a fine young man for a husband, one already connected to our dear friends, the Bennets. We expect all the benefits of a closer connexion between our houses. So join me in wishing Mr Collins and our Charlotte every happiness for their future life together."

The guests broke into applause and a few raucous exclamations. Mr Collins bowed in several directions, very pleased with the attention.

Sir William held up his hands to indicate he had more to say. "Now, my friends, our Charlotte is not the sort of girl to resent sharing her special night with one of her siblings. Indeed, in this case, her contentment might be incomplete were I not able to make the following announcement. As you know, my eldest son has been away these last two years making his way in the world. Some of you may have heard that he is to return to us very soon." He swept his arm towards the door. "Lady Lucas and I are proud to announce that our dear boy John is home to share in Charlotte's happiness this very night."

Peter and Walter, a pair of grinning foot guards, flanked the indicated doorway. The assembled guests turned in anticipation. Into this scene stepped John Lucas. A great gasp went up from the room upon seeing his smiling face. "Ah," he said, "you are all properly awed. A job well done, Mother and Father."

The room broke into a mixture of laughter, squeals, and more than a few raucous exclamations. Then Mr Lucas was engulfed by friends, though he was taller than most and therefore remained visible. Miss Elizabeth watched it all with a sweet smile on her face. "A flair for the dramatic, indeed," she said as she shook her head. "*My* mother never orchestrated such an entrance."

Her mother was at that moment frantically motioning for Elizabeth to join her. "Excuse me for a moment, Mr Darcy."

"Isn't it marvellous?" Mrs Bennet cried, fanning herself when her daughter arrived. "Such a handsome and amiable young man! Oh, Lizzy, you must be so happy to see him. I understand you better now, my clever girl! How indeed could you accept addresses from another when you knew John Lucas would be coming home?"

"Mama!" came the mortified reply from the love of Darcy's life, though he could not hear her next words, for she, unlike her mother, had some conception of the volume of her own voice.

Bingley joined Darcy, and they watched the Bennet ladies gather together. Misses Catherine and Lydia shared their mother's unbridled enthusiasm for the events of the evening. Miss Lydia was even jumping up and down slightly. "Well, Darcy," said Bingley, "I feel quite the outsider now. I simply must meet this Lucas fellow."

The sequence of events had been a bit worse than Darcy had anticipated, but he was by no means ready to give up his quest. "It appears as if a queue is forming for that purpose. I am sure Miss Bennet will make the introductions."

"Excellent plan, Darcy. Shall we?" They joined the Bennet family, which had somehow become the beginning of a parade of well-wishers. Darcy made certain to place himself at Elizabeth's side.

Mr and Mrs Bennet and Sir William and Lady Lucas exchanged handshakes and congratulations or embraces and exclamations, respectively. Then Bingley and Miss Bennet followed. As they waited, Elizabeth looked up at Darcy. "Are you ready to conquer that bashful reserve, Mr Darcy? Once more into the breach and all that?"

He grinned. "With you by my side I shall be quite brave."

She leaned in to whisper, "Have no fear; I promise to rescue *you* from Mr Collins this time."

By this time, they were standing directly in front of Sir William and Lady Lucas. Elizabeth greeted Sir William warmly, expressing her pleasure at their good fortune. As Darcy shook Sir William's hand, she moved on. "You have outdone yourself this time, Lady Lucas. My mother will not stop talking about your grand surprise for weeks."

Lady Lucas smiled at Elizabeth fondly and grasped her hands. "I think after we Lucases, you must be the person happiest to see our John again. You have been a true friend to all my children, and I say now without any impertinence or presumption, and as sincere as may be, I hope to one day call you more than a friend to them."

Elizabeth coloured and stammered. Lady Lucas patted her cheek. "I do not mean to embarrass you, child. Truly, do not think me meddling, only hopeful. Now go along and welcome John home. He is most desirous to speak to you."

Darcy began to doubt the wisdom of having positioned himself thus, to so easily hear all of this. He went through the motions of congratulating Lady Lucas and soon joined Elizabeth in front of Mr John Lucas himself. "Miss Elizabeth," Mr Lucas said as he bowed formally over her hand, "I cannot tell you how happy I am to *finally* see you again. You look very well."

She rolled her eyes at him but was by no means displeased. "Allow me to introduce Mr Darcy," she said, motioning towards Darcy.

John Lucas grinned. "Ah! Mr Darcy! A pleasure to make your acquaintance, sir. I had been wondering who that great, tall fellow could be."

Darcy returned an awkward greeting but Elizabeth interrupted, "Mr Lucas, you must not tease Mr Darcy. He is not accustomed to it."

Mr Lucas looked between them, "Is he not?"

She blushed, and Darcy had no idea how to correctly interpret this exchange. He redirected the conversation. "You made quite an entrance, Mr Lucas."

"Oh yes, my mother is savouring her success. But it is *she* who will be surprised when I make my own announcement at dinner."

Darcy remembered from his dance with Miss Lucas at the ball that her brother had purchased a house in town as a surprise for his family. "How long were you in London before coming to Hertfordshire?"

Mr Lucas raised his eyebrows in surprise and then glanced at Elizabeth, who was even more confused by the abrupt question. Darcy realised his mistake, but the other man smoothly covered it. "About a fortnight. Mr Gardiner sends his regards, Li—Miss Elizabeth."

"You saw my uncle?" she asked with delight.

"Indeed, I have invested with him and expect much success. He is a shrewd businessman. I also saw your aunt and young cousins. They are very excited to see you."

"Oh, I cannot wait to see them!"

"What a Christmas we shall all have together: the Lucases, Bennets, and Gardiners."

"It will be wonderful, but do not forget Mr Bingley. You just met my future brother, did you not? What do you think of him?"

"An exceedingly pleasant chap, indeed. And he has made Ja— Miss Bennet very happy, so of course I approve. We already have made great plans for sport."

"Oh dear. I hope Mr Bingley has been sufficiently warned about you."

"If he has not, no doubt *you* will take it upon yourself to do so."

"Well, I *am* rather fond of him. There's no telling what calamity might befall him if he follows you into the countryside with loaded weapons."

Mr Lucas rolled his eyes. "Look at how you have engrossed my attention, Miss Elizabeth. The other guests wait impatiently for you to move along."

"Come, Mr Darcy, we shall not keep Mr Lucas from his adoring public any longer."

As they began to move away, Mr Lucas leaned in to Elizabeth. "I am still counting on that dance, Lizzy," he whispered. Then he turned away and exclaimed, "Miss Mary! You are just the young lady I wished to speak to about the possibility of some dancing tonight."

Never had it been so apparent how very important the Bennet and Lucas families were to each other. Darcy watched as Miss Elizabeth and Miss Lucas warmly embraced and exchanged greetings.

"Mr Collins," Elizabeth then said, "I again congratulate you on your engagement, and I thank you, for you have made possible that I may call Charlotte my dear cousin as well as my dear friend."

If Mr Collins harboured any ill will towards Elizabeth, surely this sincere and gracious speech must have ended it. He bowed to her. "Dear Cousin Elizabeth, you are very kind. The Bennets' acceptance of my olive branch, and your gracious welcome when I first came to Hertfordshire, have restored me to my own family and gifted me with a new one. We must never let silly quarrels come between dear relations again."

"You may depend upon it, Mr Collins."

Mr Collins turned to address Darcy then, but Elizabeth intervened, "Mr Darcy, I see we are wanted by Jane and Mr Bingley. Excuse us, Charlotte, Mr Collins." Proper bows and curtseys were exchanged, and then they were away from the receiving line.

"You amaze me," Darcy said.

"How so?"

"You know just what to say to charm everyone, from servants to pompous parsons."

She smiled up at him. "Would you like to know my secret?"

"I would indeed."

"A combination of sweetness and archness, or so I am told." She winked. *Good God, she winked at me.* He inhaled sharply, and she laughed.

The next quarter of an hour was spent in conversation with Bingley and Miss Bennet, while the Lucases continued to receive their guests. Darcy could barely keep his eyes from Elizabeth, and he barely tried. More often than not, she returned his gaze with a small smile. Then the Hursts and Miss Bingley joined them as well as Miss Mary. Conversation flowed pleasantly between them all, the only hitches caused by Miss Bingley on occasion. But even she could not distract Darcy from his purpose—a singular focus on a certain young lady.

Miss Lydia soon appeared, briefly greeting everyone but her own sisters. To Darcy, she said, "I am sorry I did not greet you sooner, Mr Darcy. I have been quite overset by Kitty and Maria, and the excitement of the evening."

He was spared replying when Sir William exclaimed, "Capital! Capital!" to his eldest son. Then to the room, he announced, "Ladies and gentlemen, we shall pass the time before dinner with dancing," which was much to the delight of his guests.

"Oh Mary! I am sent by John to make sure you play now. Come along." Lydia pulled Mary towards the pianoforte.

In the next moment, John Lucas crossed the room under the eager eyes of every young lady and every hopeful mother to bow before Elizabeth. "May I have this dance?"

"You may," she answered.

Darcy watched with clenched fists as they walked away. Several other couples followed—Bingley and Miss Bennet, Mr Collins and Miss Lucas, Henry Long and Miss Catherine, Colonel Forster and his wife, and Miss Lydia and Gus Goulding. Miss Mary played a lively air, and the dancers made a jolly display, except for Mr Collins of course. Miss Elizabeth laughed through much of the dance, gazing upon her partner with a fond expression that made Darcy's chest tighten. He comforted himself with the thought that the next dance would be his, though it was cold comfort in the face of such joy.

When the dance ended, everyone applauded. Darcy approached the dancers to claim a certain young lady, but before he arrived he saw Peter Lucas entreat Elizabeth for a dance. She sought Darcy with her eyes but accepted. He knew she could not refuse the lad, so he had to wait through a reel. Bingley joined him as Miss Bennet was standing up with John Lucas, and the two men watched the two sisters like the lovesick whelps that they were.

When the second dance ended, dinner was announced. John Lucas went to the pianoforte. "I hope you will be amenable to a few more songs after dinner, Miss Mary, for I have yet to dance with all your sisters." He offered his arm and escorted Miss Mary into the dining room. Darcy went to Elizabeth and did the same.

The seating arrangements were not to his liking at all. Elizabeth was seated next to John Lucas near one end of the table, while Darcy was placed near the opposite end. Throughout the meal, he managed scant conversation with Bingley and Miss Bennet, but his attention could not be shaken from the laughing couple at the other end of the room. Only the thought of his upcoming dance—and Elizabeth's frequent smiling glances at him—kept him from sinking into despair. John Lucas made his announcement between courses, and everyone was much impressed. Sir William and Lady Lucas veritably glowed with pride and pleasure, and Elizabeth seemed truly shocked.

The final course was cleared, and the ladies returned to the drawing room while the gentlemen enjoyed port and cigars. Most of the gentlemen enjoyed them, that is, but one spent his time impatiently stalking the edges of the room. Finally, John Lucas suggested they re-join the ladies.

Darcy immediately sought Elizabeth out, and was welcomed by her smiling face. He forgot all about his worries at dinner. Coffee and tea were served and enjoyed amidst multiple conversations. Eventually, John Lucas approached. "Miss Elizabeth, it has been far too long since I have had the pleasure of hearing you play and sing. Will you honour us with a performance?"

"How can I deny such an earnest entreaty? I doubt my performance will live up to your memory. I am bound to disappoint."

"I do not believe that possible."

She made her way to the instrument and began a song from memory. Darcy stood entranced by her unaffected manner, her ringing voice, and the sheer beauty of her. Amidst the applause, John Lucas went to her side and leaned down to whisper something. She laughed and nodded. He then turned and stalked towards Miss Mary. "Your sister and I have plotted against you, Miss Mary. Now you simply must dance with me."

So another dance commenced, this time with Elizabeth playing.

When it was over, Mary quickly made her escape to the pianoforte, offering to play again for the other dancers.

Elizabeth had hardly risen from the bench before Darcy was at her side. "You are unusually eager to dance tonight, Mr Darcy."

"I am only eager to dance with you, Miss Elizabeth."

She put her hand on his arm, and he led her to her place. They soon were joined by John Lucas and Miss Lydia. Before the music started, Elizabeth looked significantly towards another younger sister, partnered with a young captain but staring at John Lucas in wide-eyed awe.

"Is there something amiss with my attire, Miss Catherine?" John Lucas asked.

"No. Nothing at all is amiss. I like your green waistcoat very much."

"I thank you. I was told once green suits me."

"Oh yes, it does. But you should avoid my mother tonight, I think. There's no telling what she will say about your legs."

Miss Lydia laughed heartily, and Elizabeth, although clearly embarrassed, fought laughter as well. Her mirth lasted well into their dance, and when it ended, Darcy crossed to her. "You look flushed, Miss Elizabeth. Might I escort you to the balcony for some fresh air?"

"Ah, yes. I am rather warm after such a lively dance."

As soon as they were through the door, they burst into laughter. "Poor Kitty! Poor John!" she exclaimed as she turned to face him. "Oh, but I must be amused, else I should be mortified."

They laughed together for a few minutes as the sound of the next dance drifted to them, and then the mood silently yet perceptibly shifted. They no longer laughed. Darcy's back was to the door and the light of the drawing room. Before him stood Miss Elizabeth Bennet, the woman he loved. She looked up at him in the dim light, and he thought he saw that *look*; that look she reserved only for her dearest loved ones. He stepped closer, and she did not retreat. He stepped closer, improperly close, and still she looked at him in that way. His breathing was shallow, and he could not have spoken even if he knew what to say. He took another step. *A kiss; a kiss will tell her what I cannot say.*

"Lizzy! I must speak with you this instant!" Miss Lydia testily called from behind him. "If Mr Darcy will spare you, that is."

Elizabeth exhaled and stepped away from him. The spell had been broken. "Forgive me," she whispered as she went to her sister.

Darcy remained on the balcony, gripping the railing and trying to compose himself.

30

The Fish She Lost

"Kitty!" Lydia yelled. "You have had use of the mirror quite long enough! Let me have it now!"

"Oh, stop your fussing. Your precious Mr Darcy does not care what colour ribbons you wear in your hair tonight."

Lydia kicked the leg of Kitty's chair. "*You* are fussing more than usual tonight. Could it be for Henry Long's benefit? Perhaps I will tell Mama of his interest after all."

Kitty quickly relinquished the much-coveted chair, which was quickly occupied by a smug Lydia. This Henry Long situation might prove to be very useful indeed.

But Kitty's assertion about Mr Darcy's lack of interest certainly chafed. Lydia had only seen him once since the ball, when he dined at Longbourn. He was less taciturn in general that night, but his new penchant for conversation was directed at everyone *but* Lydia. She had discussed her new book with him, but Lizzy and Mr Bennet were more prominent players in that conversation than she. Mr Darcy's behaviour towards her was what it always had been: civil, and even friendly at times, but nothing more. When would she be rewarded for all of her hard work? *Tonight.* Lydia decided tonight would be different.

When they arrived at Lucas Lodge, Lydia bemoaned this silly idea of precedence, for she could not see into the drawing room while she was trapped behind her parents and older sisters.

They were announced, and Lydia waited impatiently for her turn to enter. When she did, she saw Mr Darcy was already speaking to Elizabeth. *Perfect!* She need not seek him out. She approached them, but her arm was suddenly wrenched in another direction. "Kitty!" she whispered furiously, "What on earth are you doing?"

"Maria motions for us quite desperately. And you cannot leave me alone—Henry Long is right over there," Kitty whispered back with real fear in her voice.

"I thought you liked him now," Lydia began, but they had reached Maria, who was positively bouncing with excitement.

"Oh! You both look very pretty. There is a splendid surprise tonight. You will never guess! It will be all the talk of Meryton tomorrow!"

"What is it?" Lydia asked, hoping to learn the secret and then go back to Mr Darcy.

"No, no, I shan't tell you. You will know soon enough. Oh, but it is just the most splendid surprise!"

"Now that Kitty is safely accompanied by you, I must go greet Mr Darcy." This time her arm was wrenched back by Maria. "Why is everybody pulling me about?"

"Forgive me," Maria giggled. "But you must stay right here. This is the best place to view the surprise. I promise you will thank me."

"Ladies and gentlemen, my friends and neighbours," called Sir William. "Now that our dearest friends have arrived, tardy as usual, I wish to begin the evening with an announcement. Our dear girl, Charlotte, will be leaving us and starting a new life."

Lydia preferred not to think about the "new life" Charlotte would be starting with that ninny of a parson. She shuddered and decided not to listen any further. Instead she perused the guests as Sir William continued on.

Lizzy and Mr Darcy were still standing together at the opposite end of the room, near where they had entered. Mr Darcy looked exceedingly handsome in his golden waistcoat with his dark hair falling just so. He was so tall, his shoulders so broad! Lizzy was small in comparison, but something in the way they stood together looked very natural despite this disparity. They looked as natural together as Jane and Mr Bingley did.

Lydia tore her eyes from the pair, unnerved. Had Sir William just mentioned the Bennets? She looked around the room. Henry Long was staring at Kitty, and Kitty was desperately trying not to stare back.

The guests suddenly broke into applause and a few raucous exclamations. Mr Collins bowed in several directions, very pleased with himself. Lydia shuddered again.

Sir William was still speaking about Charlotte. Maria suddenly poked Lydia, shaking with excitement and whispering, "Very soon now!" Kitty and Lydia exchanged shrugs, and then looked towards the door Sir William had just indicated. Walter and Peter stood on either side, grinning like mad.

"Lady Lucas and I are proud to announce that our dear boy John is home to share in Charlotte's happiness this very night," said Sir William.

John Lucas stepped through the door, smiling just as Lydia remembered him. She gasped. "Ah," he said, "you are all properly awed. A job well done, Mother and Father."

Lydia squealed; she could not help herself, but the undignified sound was largely covered by the other raucous cheers in the room. Maria laughed, jumping up and down and clapping, "I told you so!"

Lydia must concede: it *was* a splendid surprise.

John shook the hand of a very happy Gussy Goulding. Lydia tried to get through the crowd that surrounded him, but then she was again yanked in another direction. "What now?" she nearly yelled.

"Mama wants us," Kitty answered.

Mrs Bennet fanned herself, exclaiming when all her daughters were gathered about her, "My dears! Is he not just as handsome as you remember? Handsomer, even!"

Lydia bounced and giggled. "He looks very well. Oh! How exciting!"

Mrs Bennet gathered her daughters closer into a huddle and leaned in, lowering her voice, "We must do all we can to make sure he remembers what Lizzy meant to him before he left."

"Mama!" Elizabeth huffed in exasperation. "Might we please just welcome home our friend and neighbour tonight and leave the matchmaking for another day?"

"Another day? But look at the way Mrs Long is eyeing him for her meek nieces. You must re-establish your prior relationship as soon as may be. We Bennets will be the first to properly congratulate the Lucases. Mr Bennet! Mr Bennet!" she called.

Before John left, Lydia had always thought he and Lizzy would wed someday. Of course it would be the same now that he had returned. He and Elizabeth would always be together, laughing, bickering, and laughing again. It was not fair. Why should Lizzy catch the handsomest, most agreeable gentleman with the easiest smile and heartiest laugh? As Lydia stared at said agreeable gentleman, lamenting the inequity of it all, another handsome gentleman crossed her vision.

Mr Darcy! She had forgotten about Mr Darcy, who was currently speaking to Sir William as Elizabeth spoke to Lady Lucas. Lydia had not even greeted him yet.

"Lydia," said Kitty suddenly, "will you stay with me through all these greetings and congratulations? I am afraid I shall say something daft."

"Very well. Keep by me, and I shall do the talking." Lydia cursed precedence again as she and Kitty moved through the queue after Mary.

To Sir William and Lady Lucas, Lydia said, "You are the very picture of proud parents tonight, as you should be."

She wanted to move on as quickly as possible, for John was next! But then he followed after Mary, saying, "Do you still avoid dancing, Miss Mary? Surely you will make an exception for me."

Mary retreated hastily, pretending she had not heard. The order of the receiving line was thus changed, forcing Lydia to greet Charlotte and Mr Collins first. She could hardly concentrate with John looking on.

"Mr Collins," she began, "You are very fortunate in your choice of bride. Charlotte is kind and sensible. I do not know how we shall get along without her." Kitty nodded in agreement.

"Thank you for your good wishes. I must agree about my amiable Charlotte..."

Just what Lydia needed—yet another long Mr Collins speech. She kept herself from wincing, though at the earliest opportunity, she turned from him and leaned towards Charlotte, lowering her voice, "Charlotte, I commend you. You have silenced the sharp tongues of every nasty gossip who ever predicted you would be a spinster."

Charlotte grinned and winked in reply and then looked towards Mr and Mrs Philips. This left Kitty and Lydia standing directly in front of one Mr John Lucas.

He bowed. "Miss Catherine! You are looking ever so lovely! And who is your friend?"

Lydia beamed while Kitty replied, "You cannot have been gone that long, John. Do not tease. You know who she is." Then she added uncertainly, "Don't you?"

He laughed. "No, I cannot believe this tall, elegant young lady is little Lydia Bennet. Impossible!"

"I have grown taller than all my sisters since you left, but no one has ever called me elegant. If you are going to say such wonderful things, I insist you never leave again."

"Now there's the bold little imp!" he touched her nose, and Lydia's heart fluttered in her chest. "I could not recognise her when she carried herself with such poise and said the most courteous things."

"One mustn't blurt out one's real thoughts all the time; even Kitty is learning that."

He threw his head back and laughed heartily. "Clearly, Miss Lydia has altered the most in my absence," he said to Kitty. "Now, I expect to dance with each of you tonight. Do not try to escape me as Mary has."

Kitty snorted, "Neither Lydia nor I would ever try to escape dancing. Well, except with Jowly Jacob or Mr Col—"

Lydia interrupted, "Kitty! You were doing so well!"

"Oh, sorry." Kitty replied sheepishly. John watched the exchange with a delighted expression on his face.

"You need not worry about my disapproval, Ki—Miss Catherine," he said. "Now about those dances. Miss Mary agrees to play some lively Scotch and Irish airs for us, but who will we get to play so that *she* may dance?"

"Lizzy can do it. Or perhaps Miss Long." Lydia wrinkled her nose. "But you had much rather have Lizzy play, I am sure."

"Excellent! When all this silly business is over," he motioned towards the queue waiting to greet him, "please fetch Mary to the pianoforte as soon as may be. Will you do that, Miss Lydia, even if I cannot break away to remind you?"

"You may depend upon it!"

Just before he turned towards Mr and Mrs Philips, he said, "There's my determined imp," with a wink. Lydia suddenly wished she had her mother's ever-present fan, for she felt rather flushed. Soon Kitty and Maria again pulled Lydia towards another group. Captain Carter and Colonel Forster greeted them cheerfully, and then the colonel introduced his new wife. She appeared to be Kitty's age, or perhaps Mary's. The colonel had married just after the ball and had been away for a se'nnight for the occasion.

"May I introduce my bride, Mrs Harriet Forster, to you? My dear, this is Miss Catherine Bennet and Miss Lydia Bennet, and you have already met Miss Maria."

Curtseys were exchanged, and before either Kitty or Lydia could offer congratulations on the colonel's marriage, Mrs Forster began, "Oh! You are the Bennet sisters I have heard so much about? I am happy to make your acquaintance. Denny and Saunderson and Wickham and, well, all the officers, really, have nothing but praises for you. Mr Wickham entreated me to pay his especial regards to you tonight."

She looked at Lydia with a knowing smirk. Lydia did not know what to make of it. She doubted Mr Wickham had complimentary things to say about *her*, though the few times they had met since that night at Aunt Philips's, he had treated her as if nothing had happened. Indeed, he had been overly polite.

Mrs Forster continued, "Oh, but I do hope we shall be particular friends. I need some female companionship in the worst way. In just a few days, I have grown accustomed to being the centre of attention for every redcoat in the area. My head has grown quite large, I am afraid. You simply must visit us any time you wish, to give the officers additional objects of admiration. It is a pity more of the officers are not here tonight." She looked around with a sigh.

Maria blushed, "My parents wished to invite more of the neighbourhood for John's return."

"Oh dear! Pay my silly ramblings no heed. Of course your brother would wish to be welcomed home by his friends and not a bunch of strangers. My, but Mr Lucas is handsome! He would look splendid in regimentals, don't you think?"

Kitty agreed enthusiastically, but Lydia thought he looked perfect as he was. She had no patience for Mrs Forster's silly blather. Lydia's attention wandered back to the infernal receiving line. Only about a half dozen people remained.

Now, where was Mary? Lydia scanned the room, once again catching Henry Long staring at Kitty. She jerked her head at him with a smile, and he approached hesitantly. Lydia made the introduction. It was a welcome break from Mrs Forster's giddy dialogue about officers. Kitty went silent and red, but after a few minutes, she smiled at Mr Long.

John Lucas was at last greeting the final guest. He caught Lydia's eye and nodded. She turned to her companions. "I must fetch Mary now so that the dancing may begin!" She located Mary, along with Lizzy, Jane, Mr Darcy, Mr Hurst, Mr Bingley, and his ghastly sisters.

Lydia reached them and briefly greeted anyone she had not yet seen already. To Mr Darcy she said, "I am sorry I did not greet you sooner, Mr Darcy. I have been quite overset by Kitty and Maria and the excitement of the evening." Perhaps she could dance with Mr Darcy *and* John Lucas tonight! She could not imagine a better way to spend an evening.

Sir William suddenly exclaimed, "Capital! Capital! Ladies and gentlemen, we shall pass the time before dinner with dancing."

"Oh, Mary! I am sent by John to make sure you play now. Come along." Lydia pulled Mary towards the pianoforte.

"Must you grip my arm so firmly?" Mary asked.

"Ha! You have no idea how sore my arm is from Kitty and Maria!"

"You had best go find yourself a partner, Lydia. I can begin any time."

Lydia turned to see where John and Mr Darcy were. *Drat!* Of course John would dance with Lizzy first. And Mr Darcy was watching from all the way across the room. He did not appear inclined to dance.

"May I have this dance, Miss Lydia?"

"Yes, thank you, Mr Goulding." Dancing with Gussy would be better than not dancing at all. He was a good dancer despite his reputation for clumsiness.

They joined the half dozen couples lining up, including Henry Long and a madly blushing Kitty. Mary played a lively air. Lydia could hear Lizzy and John's laughter nearly through the whole of it.

When the dance ended, everyone applauded and laughed. John quickly sought a second partner in Jane, which would have been a disappointment to Lydia if Mr Darcy had not approached. He meant to dance! But then he stopped at the periphery and simply watched. Henry Long asked Lydia to dance, and she was obliged to accept.

When the second dance ended, dinner was announced. John Lucas offered his arm to Mary and escorted her into the dining room. *Drat!*

Maria came with Kitty, saying, "I asked my mother to seat us near each other and near John for dinner." Lydia was grateful indeed. She looked up to see Mr Darcy escorting Lizzy into the dining room. *Drat!*

Conversation flowed easily at dinner, though Lydia most enjoyed it when John and Lizzy did not talk and laugh privately with each other. Gussy was eager to hear of John's travels, which suited Lydia's fancy perfectly. Every so often, she thought she saw Mr Darcy—who sat far at the opposite end of the table near Jane and Mr Bingley—looking in her direction, but she could not be sure.

Mrs Forster was extremely talkative again. "Mr Wickham mentioned playing cards with you last night, Mr Goulding," she said, and Lydia wondered whether it was a proper subject for dinner.

Gussy chuckled. "I can imagine he did, considering the amount he won from me. John, you should join me when I next play with the officers. But watch out for that Wickham fellow. He distracts you from the game with all manner of stories. Some of them are rather...colourful."

"Gus, I have played with pirates, ruffians, and scallywags, and I have a few colourful stories of my own. Perhaps I can distract this Mr Wickham and allow you to win back some of your coin."

Lydia interjected, "Mr Lucas, you would do well not to underestimate Mr Wickham's devious tactics." Mrs Forster looked at Lydia across the table with a quizzical expression.

John nodded. "Thank you, Miss Lydia. I try never to underestimate anyone."

After the course was cleared away, John stood up to speak. "Ladies and gentleman, I thank you for being here tonight, not only for your good wishes for my dear sister, Charlotte, and her Mr Collins, but also to welcome me home. It is precisely the sort of homecoming I would wish for: old friends"—he patted Gussy's shoulder— "and lovely young ladies." He motioned towards Lizzy, who rolled her eyes as everyone laughed.

"I do sincerely thank my parents for this wonderful celebration. They played a great joke on all of you, and now I have a surprise for *them*." He looked at Lady Lucas and then down to the other end of the table where Sir William sat. "I wish to announce that you will all soon be fortunate enough to hear many more stories about St. James Court from my father, since his trips to town will no doubt increase now that the Lucas family owns a house in London."

Good lord! Just how rich had John Lucas become in two years? Lydia could hardly believe it. Maria sat open-mouthed, staring at her brother. Lady Lucas covered her open mouth with her napkin, crying, "Oh! John!" over and over. Sir William rose and traversed the length of the table, grasping his son's hand with tears in his eyes. Mrs Bennet fanned herself.

The commotion died down as the next course was served, and John and Sir William returned to their seats. John was immediately deluged with questions about his house. It was not a very grand house but well kept. It was not in the most fashionable part of town but not too far either. "And just think," he said, "between the Gardiners' house and our new house, all the Bennets and Lucases may stay in London at the same time. There will not be a scrap of ribbon to be had within miles."

After dinner, the gentlemen enjoyed port and cigars while the ladies returned to the drawing room. All conversation revolved around John Lucas, which made Lydia even more impatient. Finally, the gentlemen re-joined the ladies.

Lizzy performed on the pianoforte at John's request. Afterwards, he turned and stalked towards Mary. "Your sister and I have plotted against you, Miss Mary. Now you simply must dance with me."

So another dance commenced. Lydia hoped Mr Darcy would ask her, but instead Captain Carter did. Mary quickly retreated to the pianoforte when the dance was over, looking relieved; Lydia wondered how *anyone* could dislike dancing with John Lucas. Then she saw Mr Darcy and Lizzy stand up together. *Blast it all!*

Suddenly John Lucas was by her side. "I hope you did not forget my vow to dance with all the Bennet sisters tonight, Miss Lydia."

"I would never dream of foiling your grand design, Mr Lucas."

"Excellent! Now, tell me all about your life in the last two years. We have a few minutes before Mary plays again."

She laughed. "What do you wish to know? Mama still devotes herself to marrying us off and has only recently gained any success in that venture. Some of us are more willing than others, you see. Papa still spends most of his time in the library, escaping from Mama's nervous fits. Very recently, he has begun to invite me into that sanctuary, for I have become a great reader."

"The imp is a booklover? I cannot believe it. Is this Lizzy's influence? She was always pestering me to read her poets and philosophers. I could not abide them." He screwed up his face in disgust.

She giggled. "Yes, in part, it is Lizzy's influence. She chooses the books I am to read, and I must say I trust her tastes completely. But really, I am attempting to fulfil my mother's quest. I aim to impress a certain gentleman with my literary acumen and thus catch a husband."

"You? But you are far too young to be married. Besides, a husband ought to accept you for the delightful girl you already are. Who is this severe gentleman who expects such scholarship in young girls?"

"He does not expect it. I merely observed that the surest way of coaxing him into conversation was to mention literature. He is most taciturn, but he and Lizzy have had some very lively debates about books. I wanted my part in the conversation."

"Taciturn? Surely he must have some charm."

"He is very handsome and very rich. And he plays cricket wonderfully."

Mary prepared to play the next song, and John offered Lydia his arm for the dance. "Cricket? Well, perhaps he is not as bad as I thought. Who is this paragon, so that I may put in a good word for you?"

"He is Mr Darcy."

John was truly shocked. "Mr Darcy? Do you mean to tell me that you are pursuing Mr Darcy for the purposes of marriage?"

"Yes. I have already put in ever so much effort. Do you think it very unlikely that I may catch him?" Lydia had been discouraged by her prospects of late, and Mr Darcy would soon leave the county.

"I can hardly say," John replied. Soon his smile returned. "But let us enjoy our dance now, shall we?"

Lydia wholeheartedly agreed. She had never enjoyed a dance so much. John was the handsomest, jolliest partner she could ever hope for. She looked forward to many future opportunities to repeat the act, even if she would never be his first choice of dance partner.

When the dance ended, he bowed to her, "Thank you, Miss Lydia. You are an excellent dancer. Now I must find Miss Kitty." He made his way through the couples, leaving Lydia near the pianoforte.

"Cousin Lydia," Mr Collins said from behind her, "might I have a word?"

If Lydia could count on it only being one word, she might be more inclined to agree. But this was Mr Collins, after all. "Oh, I was just on my way to my mother."

"This will only take a moment. I could not help but overhear your conversation with Mr Lucas before the dance." He looked terribly disapproving, though Lydia could not remember having said anything untoward or overly bold. "I must warn you against any attempt to 'catch' Mr Darcy for a husband."

"Oh, is that all? I am certain Mr Darcy is pursued wherever he goes. I am as free to try for him as the next girl."

"If it were so simple, I might not warn you off. But Mr Darcy, as it turns out, has already been caught. He is engaged to marry Miss Anne de Bourgh."

"What?" she nearly yelled. "It cannot be."

"It is true, I assure you. I offered my suggestions on the official announcement last week. Lady Catherine says I have a flair for composition, and she was most eager for my advice on it." Mr Collins was insufferable as ever while he boasted. Then he recalled himself and looked at Lydia again. "I am sorry if this news injures you. Mr Darcy and Miss de Bourgh have long had an understanding to unite their estates. Until recently, Miss de Bourgh's poor health had prevented the fulfilment of their mothers' mutual dreams. Now all is settled. If you thought Mr Darcy gave any encouragement to you, I am certain you were mistaken. I understand how one such as yourself might be awed by one such as Mr Darcy."

Lydia straightened her back and said icily, "Thank you for your concern, Mr Collins. Now I really must take my leave of you." She curtseyed and walked away.

Mr Darcy engaged all this time? Could it be true? Oh, who might know the truth of it?

"Where is Lizzy?"

"I believe she is on the balcony."

Lydia made her way across the room, weaving through happy guests on her way to the balcony. There, she saw not only her sister, but Mr Darcy. His back was to her. As Lydia squinted into the darkness, she could just make out that Lizzy was indeed there, almost entirely blocked from view by Mr Darcy's broad back.

"Lizzy! I must speak with you this instant!" Lydia called out in no good humour. "If Mr Darcy will spare you, that is."

31

Disappointed Hopes

Elizabeth was almost positive Mr Darcy would kiss her. Moreover, she was sure she would let him. She knew very little of such matters, only what she had glimpsed of Jane and Mr Bingley, but she knew she *wanted* him to kiss her. He had been so different tonight; he made her feel beautiful and clever, and...essential. As she stood on the balcony looking up into his dark eyes, she finally admitted the truth to herself: she had fallen in love with Mr Darcy. Her eyes had adjusted to the darkness, and as she gazed at him, some of the gold flecks in his disappeared into blackness. He was so close, and she was entranced by the warmth of him, the smell of him, and the enormity of this moment.

"Lizzy! I must speak with you this instant!" Lydia called. "If Mr Darcy will spare you, that is." She sounded annoyed.

Elizabeth stepped back and let out the breath she had been holding. Perhaps it was better that she and Mr Darcy should resolve this tomorrow morning, alone. After all, this had started on the banks of Oakham Stream. They had no privacy to speak here, though he did not seem inclined to speak.

"Forgive me," she whispered as she went to Lydia. Before leaving the balcony, she looked back at him one last time. He faced away from her into the darkness of the night. Lydia pulled her through the door into the drawing room.

"What on earth is the matter, Lydia?"

"Oh, Lizzy! I have heard the most dreadful news! Mr Collins..."— she looked around her to make sure no one was near—"Mr Collins tells me that Mr Darcy is...has long been engaged to Miss de Bourgh!"

Elizabeth felt as if she had just fallen off the plow horse again, like when she was seven. She had been afraid of horses ever since. "It cannot be true," she whispered, for she had only sufficient breath for whispering.

"Do you think it could be false?" Lydia asked with great hope in her voice.

Elizabeth's mind was a muddle. "We must find Mary, and ask her what she thinks."

"Why should Mary know anything more than you?"

"Mary sees and hears more than any of us, and she remembers everything."

Lydia seemed sceptical but willing to proceed. "She's over there!" She pulled Elizabeth towards the far wall where Mary, once again relieved from her duty at the pianoforte, stood and watched the room.

"Mary, we must ask you something," Lydia said.

Mary waited, looking between the two of them. Elizabeth began, "Lydia, tell us exactly what Mr Collins said, and please be mindful of the volume of your voice."

Lydia nodded. "I was speaking to John about why I started reading books—you know, to catch Mr Darcy? And then we danced, and when it was over, Mr Collins came to me in a very scolding manner. He overheard what I said and wished to warn me off Mr Darcy. Well, of course I said there was no reason not to try. Then he said that Mr Darcy has already been caught! He is engaged to marry Miss de Bourgh!"

Mary's eyes widened but she showed no other reaction. "Did Mr Collins say anything else?"

"Of course he did. He cannot help but say too much every time he opens his mouth," Lydia complained before returning to the subject at hand. "I did not believe it, but Mr Collins said he had seen the official engagement announcement Lady Catherine prepared for the papers just last week. He said Mr Darcy and Anne de Bourgh were long expected by their families to unite their estates, but that her health had prevented it. But now everything is settled and surely Mr Darcy had not given me any encouragement, for that would be impossible."

Elizabeth leaned on the back of the nearest chair, for fear she might faint.

"Well?" Lydia asked of Mary. "Do you think it is true? Is there some chance Mr Collins is mistaken?"

Mary smoothed her skirt. "I never heard anything to confirm nor deny the truth of what he says. I do remember that Miss Bingley always appeared out of sorts whenever Miss de Bourgh was mentioned. But if the engagement were known by her, surely Miss Bingley would not chase after Mr Darcy the way she does."

"That tells us nothing," sulked Lydia.

"Lizzy, what about the letter you mentioned?" Mary asked.

"What letter?" Lydia demanded.

The letter! Elizabeth had nearly forgotten about it. "When...when Jane and I stayed at Netherfield, Mr Darcy spent one afternoon writing a letter to his cousin Miss de Bourgh."

"Why did you not tell me? I could have saved myself all this trouble. Surely what Mr Collins says is true then."

"Not necessarily," interrupted Mary. "Mr Collins was completely ignorant that they exchanged any letters. Remember, Lizzy?"

Elizabeth tried to gather her thoughts. She knew coming to Mary would be the right thing to do. "Yes, but secretly exchanging letters would seemingly confirm rather than deny that they have an attachment."

"But they are cousins. Perhaps they kept their correspondence a secret to avoid raising suspicions or expectations about the nature of their relationship."

Elizabeth let herself feel a little better at the possibility. She and John did not exchange letters for the same reason, but if they could have done so in secret, they would have. Then reality intruded again. "Mr Collins got confirmation from Lady Catherine herself, and he read the announcement that is to go in the papers," she said in a quiet voice.

"Perhaps the mistake originates with Lady Catherine," Mary replied. "Mama had you married off to two different men this autumn already, and now a third. I do not doubt that Mr Collins believes what he says, but perhaps the source of his information is wrong. Our cousin may be many things, but he is not a liar."

As the word liar reached her ears, Elizabeth suddenly remembered the last thing Mr Wickham had told her at Aunt Philips's. She shook her head, "I just remembered. Mr Wickham...that night, after Lydia left us, Mr Wickham told me that Mr Darcy and Miss de Bourgh had a prior arrangement to unite their estates."

"Why did you not tell us?" Lydia yelled.

"I thought we had determined that nothing *he* said could be believed. It seemed so unlikely that Mr Darcy would come into an area secretly engaged when an engagement could prove very useful in fending off unwanted interest. It *is* true that Mr Darcy never gave encouragement to any young lady in Hertfordshire." *Except tonight.*

"That is not true!" Lydia sputtered. "The picnic! He carried me!"

Mary added quietly, "He carried Lizzy too."

"Obviously neither instance denotes anything more than his helping an injured person," Elizabeth said.

"He...he offered to send for his physician from London for me!"

"What's all this commotion, ladies? Must I break up one of the famous Bennet sister quarrels on my first night back in Meryton?" John joined them at the edge of the room.

"Oh John! It is awful!" cried Lydia. "We have just learned that Mr Darcy, the gentleman I have been trying so hard to catch for weeks, is already engaged to his sickly, rich cousin."

John's eyes were immediately on Elizabeth. "Is this true?"

Mary answered, "I am afraid it must be true. The rumour has been confirmed by two very disparate sources, Mr Collins and Mr Wickham."

"But not by Mr Darcy himself," John said. "Lizzy, did he never say anything to you?"

Elizabeth could do naught but shake her head, for she feared she would cry at any moment.

John came to stand near her. "Someone must ask him."

"*I* shall ask him, depend upon it," said Lydia, ready to confront Mr Darcy.

"Lydia," Elizabeth hissed, "do not cause a scene tonight. This is Charlotte's and John's night. You must not spoil it for them. I believe it is safe to say that the engagement is true, but for whatever reason, Mr Darcy does not wish to discuss it. If he wanted us to know about it, he would have told us. Let him have his secrecy. It is no concern of ours."

"But it is not right that he should come into the country raising expectations when none of us ever had the slightest chance with him!"

"He never did anything to raise expectations. In fact, he did his best to discourage any interest."

Lydia's renewed protests were silenced when Jane, Mr Bingley, and Mr Darcy himself joined the group. Elizabeth dared not look at him, but she could feel his eyes upon her. John stepped closer to her. She thanked heaven for his quiet support. Lydia made excuses and left in a huff to find Kitty. Elizabeth could not concentrate on Mr Bingley's cheerful conversation but was spared having to participate for John and Mary kept up their ends of the conversation admirably. All the while, Elizabeth felt those dark eyes on her. Sometime during this ordeal, she had begun clutching John's arm.

Jane said, "Lizzy, are you quite well? You look distressed."

"I am well, Jane. Thank you."

"Perhaps you could use some fresh air, Miss Elizabeth," John said. "Allow me to escort you." He swept her away, and she had never been more grateful.

They arrived on the balcony where not half an hour earlier... Elizabeth could not finish the thought without weeping. Standing beside her as they both looked out into the night, John said, "You are in love with him."

"Yes," she whispered, though he had not really asked for confirmation. "Has there ever been anyone as foolish? I was warned at every turn. And still I...I let myself—" Now she did cry.

He put his arm around her shoulders. "I am so sorry, Lizzybits."

She laid her head against him, and thus they stayed for several minutes as she composed herself.

"How much do you know?"

"Charlotte told me everything she knew, and I have guessed even more since this morning."

"How could I have been so stupid? How could I have let this happen?"

"I believe *he* must take the blame. How dare he? I've a mind to confront him myself."

"No. The mistake was mine, and so must the remedy be. I shall do what I ought to have done long ago: I shall end it. But not tonight. I cannot face him yet, John."

"I shall not leave your side until you are safely in the carriage with your family."

"Thank you."

They made their way back into the drawing room. Mr Darcy was standing near the doorway, apparently waiting. Elizabeth still refused to meet his eyes, but John paused there while she stared at the floor, and then he led her away.

"What happened?" she asked.

"He will not approach you for the rest of the night," was John's only answer.

John was right. Mr Darcy did not approach her until the Bennets left about an hour later. He came with Mr Bingley to see them into the carriage. John came too, as promised.

When Mr Darcy bowed to Elizabeth, she finally looked him in the eyes. "Until we meet again, Mr Darcy." The steadiness of her voice impressed her, especially upon seeing his stormy expression. But he understood she intended to meet him in the morning. That message had been conveyed.

John handed her first into the carriage. When they were away, Lydia informed everyone in dramatic fashion of what Elizabeth and Mary already knew. "Oh Mama!" she cried. "My heart has been broken tonight! Mr Darcy is already engaged to his cousin Miss de Bourgh!"

Mrs Bennet was incredulous at first, claiming there must be some mistake, but when Lydia explained everything, outrage ensued, "What a dreadful man! How dare he come into our house under false pretence! Lizzy, we were right about him on that first night at the assembly. He is a most disagreeable, horrid man; I quite detest him!"

Lydia began bawling loudly. Mrs Bennet embraced her, cooing comforts into her hair. Mary patted Elizabeth's knee, and Jane protested that there must be some misunderstanding or some reason for the secrecy. She would ask Mr Bingley about it the next time she saw him.

"What does it matter whether he is engaged already?" Kitty asked, tired of the subject. "Lydia never had a chance with him anyway." Lydia sputtered in outrage before Kitty added with a smirk, "And you read those books just for him! What a laugh!"

"As if *you* did not simper and smile at Henry Long all night long!" Lydia yelled.

"Lydia! You promised!"

Elizabeth turned away from their continuing argument and spent the rest of the carriage ride watching the black night pass by through the window. She longed to crawl into bed and leave this awful night behind her.

When they arrived at Longbourn, she was the last out of the carriage. Mr Bennet held on to her hand after she was safely on the ground. "Lizzy, are you...may I do anything for you?"

She swallowed, trying desperately not to cry. "No, Papa. I merely want to sleep."

He sighed. "Very well, child. I shall make sure to end the disagreement between Lydia and Kitty so that you may have some peace."

The next morning as the sun began to rise, Elizabeth struggled to get out of bed and listlessly performed her toilette. She had never been so reluctant to take her morning walk, certainly not in the last fortnight. She put on her boots in the back hallway, wishing the day was not so lovely. It was a stark contrast to her spirits. She dreaded what she must do on the banks of Oakham Stream today. Just last night, she had had very different expectations for what this walk, this day, might bring. How deluded she had been.

She could think of only three possibilities to explain Mr Darcy's behaviour. First, he had been toying with her the entire time, as Mr Wickham had suggested. She refused to believe it. He was not heartless. Second, he found her a good distraction from his worries as he had said during their first meeting together. He enjoyed the entertainment she provided, and that was all. Thirdly, he had come to care for her but was not free to do anything about it.

Whether the second or third alternative was true, last night he had merely been swept up in the moment, a moment of weakness to which she had nearly succumbed as well. Through her foolhardy behaviour, she had risked her reputation and lost her heart. And now, she must end it. She must keep this meeting brief, else she might let him see how he had hurt her. There could be nothing more mortifying. He must never know how she felt about him. She did have *some* pride left.

She arrived at the clearing where Mr Darcy paced.

32

Saying as Little as Possible

The previous night...

Why would Elizabeth not look at him? Darcy might know what to think if she would just look at him. But she stood there, silently grasping John Lucas's arm, and she kept her gaze stubbornly lowered as the conversation went on around her. He must apologise for his behaviour on the balcony. Once again, he had put her reputation at risk without knowing her feelings and without confessing his. Yet another opportunity wasted to his inarticulate hesitation.

John Lucas suddenly swept her away before Darcy could even offer. He tortured himself by watching them cross the room together and exit onto the balcony.

At the earliest opportunity, Darcy made his escape. "I shall have another cup of coffee," he said, but he went not to the coffee but towards the balcony.

As he neared the doors, he also neared Mrs Bennet, who was speaking to Mrs Philips. "Did you see them go onto the balcony? I am sure everything will be just as it should be very soon. It was silly of them not to formalise an engagement before he left."

"Of course," said Mrs Philips, "I always knew they were meant for each other. No wonder you had such problems matching her with others. You ought to have saved yourself the trouble."

"You know, I considered it, but Lizzy would never talk about him in his absence. I think perhaps they fought when he left. No doubt she wanted him to stay. She can hold quite a grudge, my Lizzy. But it was better that he *did* go, for now he is much richer! And now they can be perfectly happy together, and so near to Jane and Mr Bingley!"

Darcy made himself ignore their continued raptures about the splendid match. He now stood in the doorway of the balcony. John Lucas had his arm around Elizabeth's shoulders. Darcy could not bear the sight of it. He stepped back into the drawing room. His breath was much more laboured than it should have been. They could have easily heard him.

Some moments later, Elizabeth came back into the drawing room with her eyes lowered. Darcy began to approach but was immediately halted by a ferocious glare from her companion. Darcy had only ever seen John Lucas with an open, amiable expression; the transformation was stark indeed. Darcy considered his options. He could insist on speaking with her, causing a scene, or he could wait for a more discreet opportunity. Under the circumstances, he must choose the latter.

Darcy was forced to watch the pair for the next hour. John Lucas returned to his cheerful demeanour amongst his neighbours, but Elizabeth never seemed to regain her spirits fully. She never once looked in Darcy's direction, and she never strayed from her protector's side. Clearly, she regretted what had almost happened between them. Darcy truly despaired that he had ruined everything.

The guests began to leave, and when the Bennets went to their carriage, Darcy made sure to follow Bingley to see them off. Bingley and Miss Bennet were occupied with each other, leaving Darcy to bid farewell to the rest of the Bennets under the watchful eye of John Lucas. He hardly knew what he said when he bowed to each of them.

Finally, he stood before Elizabeth, praying for some sign from her. She met his gaze as she curtseyed. He could not read anything in it, as if she were purposefully controlling her expression. It made his heart sink.

"Until we meet again, Mr Darcy," she said.

Thank God! She intended to meet him in the morning as usual.

Everything might be set right if he could speak with her. It must be. He did not know what he would do if...

John Lucas handed her into the carriage. Mr Bennet shook his hand, saying, "It is very good to have you back, my boy. Please do not think you require a formal invitation to Longbourn. We are happy to have you any time."

"Thank you, sir. I shall be sure to take advantage of your hospitality as soon as may be and as often as possible."

"Then you will certainly see Mr Bingley very often indeed, for he seems to take every meal with us."

Bingley laughed. "I come for both the food and the company," he said as Mr Bennet climbed into the carriage.

The Bennet carriage pulled away, leaving the three men standing together near the front door.

"Well, I suppose I shall call for our carriage now that there's no reason for me to stay any longer. No offence to the Lucases, of course," Bingley said.

"I quite understand. Miss Bennet deserves such devotion. They all do," John Lucas replied as he walked past Darcy and climbed the stairs. "There is nothing I would not do for those girls."

Darcy knew those parting words were a warning of sorts. Obviously, Elizabeth had regretted their near-kiss and confessed something of it to John Lucas, who then took up a protective stance against Darcy. In the morning, he must convince her *not* to regret it. He must win her.

Back at Netherfield, he eschewed the temptation of drowning his worries in brandy so that he might have a clear head in the morning. Instead, he thought of what he wanted to say to her. He would never make a more important speech.

⁂

Darcy halted his pacing the moment Elizabeth came into the clearing. She curtseyed and he moved to greet her. "Miss Elizabeth, you must allow me—"

"Mr Darcy," she interrupted. "I cannot stay long today, and I must tell you something of import." Her face and eyes were guarded.

"I shall hear anything you wish to say."

"Yes, you have listened to me much over the last month. I know my stories diverted you, but I only have a finite number of tales to tell. Continuing to meet in this manner puts both of our reputations at risk, especially now that Mr Lucas is home. He is an avid walker, like myself, and this spot is on his property. He nearly discovered us yesterday, and though there is nothing improper going on, obviously we would wish to avoid a scandal. In any case, you are leaving in a few days…"

Pain and jealousy made Darcy forget his planned speech. "Since it will only be a few more days, I see no harm in continuing as we have been."

She raised her chin. "I see great potential harm in it. My gratitude to you cannot possibly justify the scandal that would ensue if we were discovered, not to mention the pain caused to those we care for who might misinterpret our…relationship."

Gratitude? Misinterpret? "Why the change, Miss Elizabeth? Those we care for might have misinterpreted our relationship all along. Now, suddenly, you are overly concerned with your reputation?"

"You are only a visitor here, Mr Darcy, but *I* shall most likely live here for the rest of my life. Your reckless behaviour might be forgotten or forgiven when you go back to your life. But I have no delusions about how *my* behaviour would be scorned." Her voice had risen in anger during the course of her speech.

He took a slow breath, trying to rein in his emotions. "You are right, and I apologise. We, both of us, were behaving recklessly. I should have had more care for the risk to your reputation. But you must know I—"

"Thank you," she said hastily. "If it were only the two of us involved…but there are others who might be injured by a scandal— our families, our…prior attachments." She looked at her hands as she picked at the seam in one of her gloves.

"Prior attachments," he repeated stupidly, feeling a desolation of spirits he had not experienced since his father died. He must pull himself together. She must never know the true extent of his love for her. Surely she guessed after last night, but he would not confirm her suspicions. He did have *some* pride left.

She smoothed her pelisse and spoke in a businesslike manner. "I hope to see you in company before you leave Hertfordshire, and we are bound to meet in the future when Jane and Mr Bingley..." She trailed off. "I truly am grateful, more grateful than you will ever know. I have come to value your friendship greatly." She looked up at him with moist eyes.

Gratitude and friendship—Darcy despised them. "I do not wish for nor expect your gratitude." He found it difficult to speak, but at least his countenance was composed now.

"I know. I wish...I wish every happiness for you and your family in the future, Mr Darcy." There was great emotion in her voice and in her eyes. He was nearly undone again, looking into the fine eyes that had haunted him from the first night at the assembly. They would never look upon him as he wished. Her loving looks would be reserved only for her family and for...Darcy could not finish the thought.

He broke eye contact. "Miss Elizabeth, I have truly enjoyed our time together, not because you entertained me, which you did, but because you are intelligent, generous, and altogether delightful. Any man would be lucky to call you his own." He barely managed to control his voice. He bowed, whispering. "God bless you," and turned away towards his horse.

For the first time, Fitzwilliam Darcy left the clearing before she did.

❧

The first thing he did when he returned from Oakham Stream was destroy the letter he had half-written to Georgiana asking her to come to Netherfield before Christmas. It was a bitter reminder of his dashed hopes. The second thing he did was write a letter to Anne about his heartbreak, his failure. After sealing, addressing, and leaving it to be sent in the post, he turned his attention to his third goal: drinking the contents of the two decanters in his bed chamber. He missed luncheon while undertaking this task.

Now those bottles were empty, and Fitzwilliam Darcy was drunk, but he needed to be drunker still. He stumbled from his chamber, bound for the library and the next available bottle of port, brandy, whiskey, anything to numb this unbearable ache.

The library was occupied by Hurst and Bingley. Darcy went straight to where the libations were kept, grunting his greetings. Hurst whistled.

"Good God, Darcy. It is two in the afternoon!" Bingley pointed out the obvious. "Is this why you skipped luncheon?"

"Were you even here, or were you at Longbourn yet again?"

"I was here, but I am going to Longbourn momentarily. I was about to invite you to come with me. I have reconsidered."

"Well, go along, then. Your angel awaits."

"You had better finish your binge today. Hurst and I were just making plans to hunt tomorrow. You should take advantage of the country for what little time you have left in it."

Darcy made no reply but took a swig from his glass while leaning unevenly on his other arm.

"I've a mind to ask that John Lucas to join us. I suspect I may see him at Longbourn today. In any case, I pass near Lucas Lodge every day—"

Darcy groaned belatedly. "Please do not invite him. Wait until I am gone."

Bingley clucked his tongue. "Do not tell me; let me guess. He smiles too much. No, he enjoys dancing too much. No, he has low connexions."

"You have covered some of my thoughts."

"Well, I quite like the chap, and as he is to be an important neighbour to me, I plan to pursue a friendship. You cannot always be lowering yourself to visit me in unfashionable Meryton."

"No, I cannot."

"My, but you are a surly drunkard. Hurst, I leave him in your capable hands. Keep him away from Caroline for his own good."

Hurst laughed. "Indeed."

Bingley crossed to the door, shaking his head at Darcy. "Gentlemen, my angel awaits," he said with a flourish as he left.

"Well, old boy, what has you in it?" Hurst motioned for Darcy to sit down.

Darcy lunged for the nearest chair, the contents of his glass sloshing as he did so.

"Hmmm...perhaps you should go back up to your room while you still have the use of your legs."

Darcy waved his hand at Hurst in dismissal.

"Oh, do not worry, I shall join you and bring up some of those bottles with me. I know when a man is determined. It is better to let him drink his fill than to argue with a surly drunkard."

"You are a bit of all right, Hurst."

He smiled. "That's what my mother always tells me. Now let's get you upstairs before Caroline discovers you."

Darcy hefted himself out of the chair, coherent enough to see the wisdom in Hurst's plan.

33

Why is Not Everybody as Happy?

Charles Bingley shifted uncomfortably under the eyes of everyone in the room. Blast Darcy for being drunk and not coming here to answer these questions himself! Bingley had been accosted the moment he walked in the door, and he had barely had time to greet Jane, who was looking particularly fetching today. *Blast Darcy!*

"Miss Lydia, if Mr Collins says he saw the announcement, then I am sure he did. But again, I have no knowledge of an engagement between Darcy and any young lady." Bingley knew the rumour must be false, but with Mr Collins standing not three feet away and completely convinced of his information, well, what could Bingley say?

"You see, my young cousin, I am in a better position to know the truth of it. I have it from Lady Catherine herself. As I said, Mr Darcy was hesitant to announce the engagement due to a deep concern for Miss de Bourgh's health. But through Lady Catherine's wise choice of physician and the utmost attention to details of diet, schedule, temperature, and the like, Miss de Bourgh is vastly improved and able to fulfil her most fortunate lot."

"But if it is all settled, why hasn't Mr Darcy confided in his closest friend?" Lydia looked between Bingley and Mr Collins suspiciously.

"That is a question only Mr Darcy can answer." Bingley said, hoping to put an end to the discussion. This rumour might be the most successful means of discouraging Miss Lydia's pursuit of Darcy. Therefore, though it painted Darcy in a rather negative light, it was not really harmful if they believed it for a short while until Mr Collins left. Darcy would be livid with his aunt, no doubt.

"We could have asked him if he had accompanied you today." Mrs Bennet took over the inquisition.

"Mr Darcy was unable to join me, unfortunately." It was not exactly a lie.

"And when will he be *able* to tear himself from Netherfield?"

"Mama! Leave poor Mr Bingley alone. He has no control over Mr Darcy's actions nor his confidences," Elizabeth said in exasperation. Bingley tried to give her a grateful look, but she had crossed to the window to look up at the blue sky.

Lydia huffed and flounced to the chair Elizabeth had just vacated next to Mr Lucas. "Lizzy, tell John the story of Lady Lucas's red gown for Maria's coming out. He was away for all that."

"No, Lizzy," groaned Kitty, "please do not tell that one."

Elizabeth remained silent at the window, but Lydia responded. "Why not, Kitty? Is it because, as usual, you blurted out something rude and injured another person's feelings?"

"Will you start crying and carrying on again, due to your very deep and abiding love for Mr D—"

"That is quite enough, girls." Mr Bennet sounded like a man at the end of his tether.

"She started it," Kitty muttered.

Lydia wished to finish it as well, "We cannot all be as lucky in love as you are, Kitty. There's only one Henry Long, thank goodness." Kitty turned a deep shade of red.

Mr Bennet raised his voice. "Behave or remove yourselves! Your petty bickering is not nearly as enjoyable as you think."

Bingley looked towards Jane in question. Her answering look told him she would explain later. When would they be alone and able to speak freely? Moreover, how much time would he spare for speaking as opposed to other pursuits when such an opportunity arose? Privacy was indeed a precious commodity to the newly engaged.

"Perhaps I shall invite Mrs Long over for tea tomorrow," Mrs

Bennet said to no one in particular. Kitty stood and rushed from the room, followed by Maria Lucas. Lydia snickered.

Mrs Bennet continued as if nothing was amiss. "Tis a pity you are leaving us so early in the morning, Mr Collins." She did not sound the least bit regretful "But of course, Mr Bingley and Mr Lucas, you must come to take tea with us."

"Then I suppose I must, Mrs Bennet," John Lucas said.

"Oh," Mrs Bennet said with a shake of her finger, "you are a joke-ster, Mr Lucas. And what about you, Mr Bingley?"

Bingley felt rather awkward. "I apologise, but I have plans with Hurst and Darcy for shooting. Hopefully the fine weather will hold, and we shall make a day of it. We wish to give Darcy some country sport before he must go back to London. Mr Lucas, I had meant to ask you to join us..." *Blast Darcy.*

"I am already engaged, it seems. The two of us will have many more opportunities for sport, I hope, when your friend is gone."

"Yes, I look forward to it." That worked out better than Bingley had imagined.

Lydia fidgeted in her chair. "But you must hear that story about your mother's gown, Mr Lucas. It is ever so funny! Lizzy, you simply must tell it. Kitty will not mind *now*; she cannot hear you."

Elizabeth was still standing at the window, silent. Her attitude reminded Bingley of his taciturn friend and his habit of standing apart, removed from conversation. It was a stark contrast to how he had last seen Darcy, inebriated, surly, and a trifle pathetic. What could have set off such a binge? *Blast him!* Bingley would be worried about him all day.

John Lucas cleared his throat. "You need not concern yourself with my entertainment, Miss Lydia. There will be plenty of time for me to hear all the stories I have missed. But now I must tell you all something. I have written a book."

Elizabeth turned from the window. "A book? You do not even read books; now you are writing them?"

"As it turns out, I *do* read books. I read books about real things, not all that nonsense you tried to force on me. Give me a good taxo-nomic monograph over useless poetry or drama any day." He smiled charmingly.

Elizabeth put her hand over her mouth to stifle her laughter. "'A good taxonomic monograph?'" she mimicked. "Pray tell, is that what you have written?"

"I suppose it cannot be classified as a monograph, strictly speaking. But it is a description of medicinal plants used by the people who live on the various islands in the Caribbean Sea."

Elizabeth sat down across from him. "I suppose you always did have an interest in botany, in your way. But to think that you should do something useful with it..."

He grinned. "Does my industry surprise you, Lizzy? In truth, a fortuitous meeting with an extraordinary man inspired me to make more of my hobby. I am convinced we shall hear much of Mr von Humboldt in the future."

"Will you attempt to publish your tome?" Mary asked.

"Perhaps, when it is finished."

"Mr Gardiner has had some dealings with a publishing house in London," offered Mr Bennet, "should you decide to pursue it."

"That is very lucky, for I would have had no idea how to begin! But it still needs some work before such a step could be taken. And I should like to show Kitty my sketches."

"I should like to see them too," Lydia said.

"Have you developed an interest in either botany or art while I was away, Miss Lydia?"

"Well, not really. But if you drew them, I wish to see them."

He smiled, "Then I shall show them to both you and Kitty, but you must promise not to bicker anymore."

She pouted. "I am not sure I can promise such a thing, though I shall try if she will."

"I suppose that's all I can ask."

Mr Lucas then fell into easy conversation with Jane, Elizabeth, and Mary about numerous topics, with Bingley, Mr Collins, and Lydia sometimes participating. Bingley noticed that Mr Lucas appeared perfectly comfortable with the whole family, and also very familiar. He used the given names of all the Bennet girls. Perhaps what had been whispered over and over last night was true: perhaps there *was* an attachment between him and Elizabeth. Bingley would have to ask Jane about it.

At the thought of his angel, Bingley lost track of the conversation as he watched her, longing for just a little privacy. How sweetly she smiled! How he wished to kiss those sweet lips!

"Mr Bingley," Mr Collins interrupted Bingley's rather inappropriate train of thought. "I hope you will convey my apologies to Mr Darcy. I could not make the time to visit him and offer to convey any letters to Rosings. Perhaps I might stop by Netherfield tomorrow morning as I leave, but it would be very early indeed."

"I do not believe Mr Darcy has any letters to send his aunt at the moment, Mr Collins. You need not concern yourself."

"But perhaps he would appreciate the opportunity to send a missive to Miss de Bourgh without having to trust such tender sentiments to the post."

Lydia rapped her fingers on the arm of her chair in impatience, and Bingley prayed this exchange would not bring up *that* subject again. *Blast Darcy!*

"I highly doubt Darcy has anything to send that he would not trust to the post. In any case, he will be leaving soon himself."

"Oh yes, I expect to see him at Rosings very soon."

Elizabeth stood and went to the window again. "Is it not beautiful out, Lizzy?" said Jane. "Shall we not take a turn in the garden?"

Bingley could think of nothing more welcome at this moment. He stood and extended his hand to Jane. "What a splendid idea! Shall we?"

"Oh yes! You young people must take a turn in the garden before dinner. Perhaps Mr Lucas will escort Lizzy and tell her more about his...studies in botany," Mrs Bennet suggested.

"I shall be happy to."

"I wish to hear about your studies too, John," said Lydia.

"Do not be silly, Lydia. You could not care less about botany." Mrs Bennet winked not very discreetly at her youngest daughter. All pretended not to notice.

"Very well," she sighed. "I shall walk with Mary."

They moved into the entryway to don their coats, hats, and gloves. Bingley cursed the cold for necessitating the use of those gloves. His skin still tingled where he had held Jane's bare hand to help her rise. To ensure a modicum of privacy, Bingley stalled so that they might be the last pair walking out. He then led Jane to the cover of some tall hedges in the opposite direction of the others.

"Charles, must you be so very obvious?" Jane laughed.

"Yes, I must, when there are always so many people about." He turned and, without more tiresome words, took his angel into his arms. She did not protest. "Ah, my Jane," he whispered as he kissed her cheekbone, her jaw. "Now my day has vastly improved."

"Has your day been so very terrible?"

"Any day in which I am kept from your undivided attention for so long is a terrible day. How shall I bear tomorrow without seeing you?"

"I daresay you will survive." Then her lips brushed his, and all thought left him for a few minutes as instinct took over.

The sound of Lydia's laughter penetrated the haze, which was perhaps a good thing considering the strength of his ardour. He peered around the hedge. "Are Lizzy and Mr Lucas willing participants in your mother's matchmaking? They seem very close."

"They are very close. I had thought they were merely friends, but Lizzy has been acting strangely since last night. I intend to force her to confide in me tonight when I sneak into her room after everyone retires."

The thought of Jane in her bedclothes, with her hair down and lit by candle glow, reignited some of Bingley's barely cooled ardour.

"How do you manage to drive every rational thought from my head?" he whispered. He took off his gloves and then removed one of hers. With his finger, he traced the ring he had given her. How he loved to see her wearing it! Then he began drawing circles on her palm.

Her breath was short as she whispered, "Charles."

If not for the sound of Mr Collins's voice passing nearby, Bingley would have again engaged in what the newly engaged often engage in. Instead, he exhaled shakily. "Perhaps we should think about setting a wedding date, dearest Jane."

She blushed as she pulled on her glove. "Perhaps that would be wise."

After righting themselves, he offered his arm, and they stepped out onto the path to join the others. "What's all this about Henry Long and Kitty?" he asked while they were still out of earshot.

"Oh, Mr Long has shown some interest in Kitty, which she seems to return now that she has had time to consider. But she did not want my mother to know for obvious reasons." He nodded, and she continued hastily, "Last night, at the height of Lydia's tantrum over learning of Mr Darcy's engagement, she revealed Kitty's secret to my mother. They have been quarrelling ever since."

They were rather more like Bingley's sisters than he had realised.

"Now, now, Jane," said Mr Lucas, "we, none of us, will abide your whispered secrets." He winked.

Elizabeth elbowed him. "Do not tease Jane or Mr Bingley, or you must answer to me."

Jane went to Elizabeth with a laugh, leaving Bingley standing with Mr Lucas, who rubbed his elbowed ribs. "I hope, Mr Bingley, that you do not take offense to my using Miss Bennet's Christian name here. It occurs to me how odd it must seem to you. But she is like another sister to me."

"I assure you, Mr Lucas, I did not take offense. I noticed you address them all familiarly."

He sighed, "I suppose I should take more care, but it is very difficult to refer to people I have known all my life so formally. Now, you must drop this 'Mr' business, and simply call me Lucas. I imagine we shall be seeing a lot of each other from now on."

"I shall be happy to if you will do the same for me."

They went back into the house and were re-joined by Kitty and Maria. They passed the time pleasantly until dinner, which was, as usual, excellent. They had the added bonus of the enthralling tales of John Lucas's travels. Elizabeth, who would usually be the one to amuse them with stories, deferred to her friend and watched him with a sort of fond pride. The only hitch in the evening's gaiety came from Mr Collins. He felt some dim-witted compulsion to constantly mention Lady Catherine, Miss de Bourgh, and Mr Darcy, causing palpable tension in the room.

Added to this, Bingley could never free himself of the niggling worry about Darcy and his intemperate drinking. He would not have believed his friend capable of such behaviour if he had not witnessed it himself. So Bingley, though reluctant to leave his angel, cut short his stay after dinner, claiming he must be well rested for hunting in the morning.

When he arrived back at Netherfield, he looked for Hurst in his usual haunts without success. He went up to Darcy's room and found his friend sprawled diagonally across the bed, fully dressed but for his boots and cravat. Hurst was slumped in one of the armchairs by the fire, snoring loudly. Bingley shook him, exasperated upon seeing the many empty bottles in the room. Hurst had not sobered Darcy up; he had merely joined him in intoxication.

Hurst snorted awake, blinking. "Bingley, you have returned."

"Yes, and what have I returned to but two drunken fools rather than one?"

"Oh, I can handle my liquor well enough, and a man in *his* state should not drink alone." Hurst motioned to Darcy.

Bingley was relieved to find Hurst coherent. "Did he say anything about *why* he is in such a state?"

"Nothing discernible. He kept talking about a stream in Pemberley Wood. I could not understand one whit of it. I have never seen such a lovesick fool in all my days."

"You think Darcy is in love?"

"Obviously," he said in a tone that made Bingley feel quite dense. "What else could send an otherwise reasonable man into such turmoil?"

"But who can she be, and why does he not pursue her?"

"The only thing I can think is that he is in love with your angel."

"No, no. I once asked him as much before I pursued her myself, because he was acting strangely then too. He is not in love with Jane, I am sure of it."

Hurst shrugged. "One of those other Bennet girls then. The one who is always going on about books perhaps."

"Elizabeth!" Hurst startled at Bingley's declaration. "Of course! She stayed here with Jane. She makes Darcy talk and laugh more than anyone!"

"I would not know about all that, but it may explain his intense dislike of the Lucas fellow."

Bingley slumped into the other chair, "It must have been awful to watch Lucas's homecoming and hear all the talk of an attachment between the two. So he drowned his sorrows."

They looked towards Darcy, who twitched and mumbled in his sleep.

Bingley furrowed his brow. What could be done? Perhaps he would know more after Jane talked to Elizabeth. If Elizabeth and John Lucas *were* attached, it would be better for Darcy to leave as planned and try to move on with his life. If they were *not* attached, there was no reason for Darcy to suffer. But nothing could be done until Bingley knew more and bringing it up would only torture Darcy further.

"Will he be recovered enough to shoot tomorrow, do you think?"

"I should say so. He has been asleep since dinner. Oh, Caroline is very angry that neither of us dined in company, I should warn you." Hurst smirked at Bingley's cringe before continuing, "As long as he has a good breakfast... The distraction will do him good, probably."

Bingley nodded, "And will *you* be capable of operating firearms tomorrow morning, Hurst?"

He snorted. "You should know me better than that, old boy."

"Well, let us get some sleep then. We must outsmart the coveys."

Bingley removed any remaining spirits from the room, and they left Darcy to his fitful slumber.

34

Misery of the Acutest Kind

"Oh Lizzy," Jane said, stroking Elizabeth's hair. This was far beyond the normal trials and tribulations for which Jane often offered comfort to her younger sisters. She did not know what else to say. Elizabeth hardly ever cried, but Jane felt the wetness of tears through her nightdress as Elizabeth lay on her lap. It made Jane angry. "How could he behave in such a manner?"

"If you must chastise someone, chastise me," Elizabeth sniffed. "I should have known better. I *did* know better, but I still behaved recklessly. Engaged or no, Mr Darcy could never choose someone like me. He was always going to return to his grand life."

"Perhaps you were reckless, but he...he was almost cruel. You risked everything, and he risked nothing."

"I think he suffers. If you had seen his face this morning... He is fond of me a little."

"I hope he suffers more than a little for what he has done."

Elizabeth sat up and wiped her cheeks. "No. I owe him—we owe him. Your current happiness could not have happened without his help. He is so clever, Jane. He is the cleverest man I know and the most honourable. He could never break his engagement to his cousin even if he wished to. And if Miss de Bourgh's health was at all uncertain...well, I can see why they kept the betrothal a secret."

Jane shook her head, "I always knew that when you fell in love you would do so wholeheartedly. Here you sit defending his good character to me of all people."

Elizabeth smiled wanly. "I remember a rather different discussion on the night of the picnic. We took opposite sides then." Her smile disappeared as she looked down. "The next morning I met him at Oakham Stream for the first time."

"Lizzy, are you certain he would not break his engagement? Did you ask him?"

"Absolutely not! I could never ask such a thing. I should hope both of us have more honour than that."

"But does he know how you feel? Did you tell him you love him?"

She shook her head. "I would rather he did not know. It would not change anything. But he must suspect."

"He will regret you."

Elizabeth sighed. "Perhaps. We cannot all be as lucky as you in this business of courtship and love."

"Apparently luck had very little to do with it." Jane embraced her. "Thank you for everything you did to ensure my happiness with Charles. I wish you had not paid so great a price."

"Jane, you must promise not to tell Charles."

"I do not know whether I can promise that."

Elizabeth looked alarmed. "But if Charles knows, he will tell Mr Darcy. Please, I wish as few people to know about my folly as possible."

Jane sighed. "I promise I shall not bring it up, but I also will not lie to Charles if he asks me about it." Elizabeth nodded. "How many people *do* know?"

"Charlotte knows some of it, John knows most of it, and you know all of it. Papa and Mary may suspect as well, but I am not certain."

"I am a bit ashamed of myself for having no inkling whatsoever. I have been truly self-absorbed."

"Not self-absorbed. You have been Charles-absorbed." Elizabeth smirked as she climbed under the covers. It was a vast improvement from her earlier tears.

"Tomorrow, I shall devote my entire day to you and you alone." Jane said as she tucked Elizabeth in and moved towards the door.

"That's because Charles will be off shooting and not available to you! You will be pining prettily again."

"No, I will not!" Jane turned back. "Well, perhaps a little. We shall cheer each other."

"Yes, we shall. And if we fail, John will cheer us both. Good night."

"Good night, dearest Lizzy."

§

Saturday

Walking with Elizabeth and John in the garden, Jane heard Lydia giggle behind them. It was another clear, sunny day, though rather cold, and Mrs Bennet had suggested the young people walk out. Of course her design was to pair Kitty with Henry Long and Elizabeth with John. Mary, Lydia, and the two Miss Longs were left to the four officers who were visiting—Lieutenants Denny, Wickham, Saunderson, and Pratt. Jane received a pointed look from her mother when she insisted on joining John and Elizabeth, but Jane had vowed to devote her day to cheering Elizabeth. Mrs Bennet's pointed looks were thus ignored.

Elizabeth held her face up to the sun as she walked between her two companions. "It is a lovely day, though I wish for Jane's sake the weather would turn. We certainly will not see Mr Bingley when it remains like this."

"Men must have their sport," John said. "Where did you walk this morning, Lizzy? Did you happen to run into my future brother before he left for Kent?"

"I did not walk this morning. I adopted Lydia's schedule and slept to a ghastly late hour." Elizabeth's tone was light and cheerful, too cheerful. Jane shot John a glance over her sister's head.

He furrowed his brow. "Perhaps we may walk out farther than the garden right now."

"That is a splendid idea! Do you not think, Lizzy?"

Elizabeth only shrugged in reply.

Jane spoke to John. "Elizabeth becomes quite disagreeable when she does not get her exercise. You must convince her, or none of us will be able to abide her tonight."

"Now Lizzy, we cannot have you starting any more fights with your sisters. The situation is precarious enough between Kitty and Lydia. Where shall we walk?"

Mary joined them suddenly. "Are you walking out somewhere? You must let me come too; I cannot listen to any more of Lydia's unabashed flirting. Her heartbreak was superficial indeed."

Jane turned her head to observe Lydia prancing on the arms of both Mr Denny and Mr Wickham. "She does seem to be enjoying the attention of her two escorts. Anything that improves her peevish mood is welcome, though I thought she disliked Mr Wickham."

"It seems she is willing to forget her earlier opinions," Mary said with a hint of disgust. "Shall we walk to the stream?"

"No!" said Jane and John in unison. John continued, "That is, I have already seen Oakham Stream since my return. Perhaps Oakham Mount, or is that too far?"

Mary and Jane assured him it was not.

"I shall inform Mama of our plans."

Jane returned quickly to the house before Elizabeth could beg off the outing. She went to the sitting room where her mother still entertained Mrs Long and Aunt Philips. "Mama, Mr Lucas has expressed a wish to see Oakham Mount. Mary, Lizzy, and I shall accompany him."

"Oh yes, it is a fine day for walking," Mrs Bennet said as she came towards Jane. Then she added in a low voice, "You and Mary will tire before you reach the top, and Lizzy and Mr Lucas will continue on, no doubt." She winked.

Jane re-joined John and her two sisters, and they set off. Jane sensed that both Mary and John were as determined as she to cheer Elizabeth. Their concerted efforts and the wonderful view at the top of Oakham Mount succeeded somewhat. Upon their descent, Mary and Elizabeth walked ahead arm in arm, chatting.

"How much do you know?" John asked.

Jane looked up at him. "Everything. She confided in me last night the whole of it."

"Good. I could tell you were ignorant of her troubles, and I was quite bewildered by it. I thought you two shared everything."

"Normally we do. In the beginning, she wished not to worry me.

Then she feared my disapproval. I was too absorbed in my own concerns to notice anything was amiss."

"You cannot blame yourself. You and I both know who must bear most of the blame. Thank goodness for your mother's timely invitation yesterday. Otherwise, I would have had no excuse to decline Mr Bingley's day of sport. Honestly, Jane, I could not vouch for my behaviour if forced to spend the whole day with *him* after seeing how she suffers."

"I had a similar reaction when I learned all. But Elizabeth defends him, and Charles has unwavering faith in his friend's good character. I keep thinking there must be some horrible mistake, some dreadful misapprehension."

"But *why* does he not come explain himself?"

"I do not know," Jane answered sadly.

❧

Sunday

Jane and Elizabeth waited outside the church for the rest of the Bennets. Jane was disappointed that Charles had not joined them. He did not always attend services with her at Longbourn parish, but she thought he would have done so today since they had not seen each other since Friday.

"I believe the weather is about to turn," Elizabeth said, watching the clouds roll across the sky. The air was strangely thick with moisture and the leaves swirled around them in the gusting wind.

Charlotte and John approached. "Reverend Woods is deafer than ever," John said.

"Yes, and his thunderous sermons will make us all deaf someday," Elizabeth quipped.

"Lizzy," Jane said in reproach, but she was relieved to hear Elizabeth joking again.

John clutched his hat against a strong gust of wind. "We had better return home, Charlotte. I fear the sky is about to open up."

"Will we see you tomorrow, John?" Jane knew that John had been the most successful in cheering Elizabeth.

"Probably not. I am to spend the day with Gus, and then we have an engagement to play cards with some of the officers tomorrow night. That Wickham fellow was quite adamant that I join them."

Elizabeth and Charlotte said nearly simultaneously, "Be wary, John."

"Good lord! I am more than capable of holding on to my fortune in a card game. Do not worry so." He bowed formally to Jane and Elizabeth, "Always a pleasure, Miss Bennet, Miss Elizabeth. Shall we, Charlotte?"

Lydia arrived. "John! Are you not coming to Longbourn today?"

"I cannot ignore my family for another day, no matter how diverting the company at Longbourn. They have just got me back, after all." He indicated his parents and siblings waiting nearby.

She sighed. "I suppose. But it is ever so much more fun when you are there." He smiled and tipped his hat before leading Charlotte away. Lydia added quietly, "Especially with Kitty not talking to me."

Only Jane and Elizabeth heard the last part. "Perhaps you should try to make amends, Lydia," said Jane.

They walked towards Longbourn behind Mary, Kitty, and Mr and Mrs Bennet. "Me? But she is the one who was so cruel."

"You know she does not mean it when she says such things, and your retaliation was much worse because you *knew* what you were doing."

She pouted. "Nobody takes my part. None of you care that I am suffering."

"You seemed happy enough when the officers visited yesterday," Elizabeth pointed out.

"Why should I not enjoy their attentions? They talk to me and listen to me."

"As long as you recognise their attentions for what they are and nothing more. Do not go fancying yourself in love after a few smiles and compliments."

Lydia glared and spoke over the wind. "Because that is all Mr Darcy ever gave me, is that what you mean? Of course I was a silly, deluded fool to think someone like him could ever care for me."

"If we never discuss Mr Darcy again, it will be too soon."

Lydia was taken aback by the uncharacteristic fierceness in Elizabeth's tone, but not for long. "That's right. Why should any of you give a second thought to my injured feelings when you are all so happily matched with your own suitors? Jane has Mr Bingley, Lizzy has...has John, and even Kitty has Henry Long now! It is not fair! *I* wanted to be the first of us to wed—or at least the second."

Jane interjected in her sternest voice, "Enough, Lydia. If you only think of love in terms of rivalry and competition with your own sisters, clearly you know nothing of love."

Lydia ran off ahead of the rest of the party as large drops of rain began to fall.

§♣

Monday

The storm had raged all night. The wind died down in the morning, but the rain continued, sometimes falling as tiny ice drops as the temperature hovered near freezing. From the window, Jane could see downed branches and rivulets of running water everywhere. Surely the roads were impassable. She would not see Charles for the third day in a row. John coming to visit was also unlikely.

She looked towards Elizabeth, who sat at the other window, staring out into the rain. Kitty sat near the fire sketching. Lydia had gone up to her room immediately following breakfast. She was not speaking to any of them, and Jane could not be sorry for it. Lydia continually brought up Mr Darcy's name, and Elizabeth's composure was strained. Jane knew not what she could do to comfort her dear sister. She had never felt more powerless.

Jane turned back from the window to take up her handiwork when she caught sight of Mary standing in the doorway, looking positively shocked. "Jane, may I see you in the kitchen?" Her steady voice revealed no hint of alarm

Neither Kitty nor Lizzy paid any heed as Jane left the room. Mary pulled her to the kitchen where Mrs Hill and Thomas, Longbourn's long-time groomsman, were seated.

"What is the matter?" Jane asked.

"There is news from Netherfield. Dreadful news. Becky usually attends Longbourn parish with her family on Sundays and then spends the whole day here with them. Yesterday, however, she

335

returned to Netherfield immediately following the service. She knew she was needed. The situation is very dire there."

Mary paused, and Jane felt an awful panic rise up in her. "Has something happened to Charles?" she managed to whisper.

Mary shook her head. "No, not Mr Bingley. Thomas, tell her, please."

"My girl tol' me there were a shooting accident on Saturday. Mr Bingley's gentleman friend—his gun misfired and, well, there were burns to the face."

"Oh no, Mr Darcy? But he lives?"

"As of yesterday, he lives. The real worry is infection, I expect. Mr Jones was sent for immediately, and riders were dispatched to Mr Darcy's physician in London as well as to his family. Becky said the whole house was in an uproar. I hope the physician was able to make it through the storm. No one can use these roads now."

"Mary..." Jane and Mary stared at each other. How could they tell Elizabeth?

Thomas added, "I mean to send my boy to see Becky in the mornin.' He don't mind the mud. Becky is a might upset at the whole thing. She always said the men o' the house were good fellows— much kinder than those two high-and-mighty ladies. I'll be keepin' the gentleman in my prayers."

"Thank you, Thomas. I wish to send a note tomorrow with Tommy, if I may."

"Of course, miss."

Jane and Mary stood together in the hallway for several minutes.

"She must be told. We cannot keep this from her," Jane finally said.

"Yes, but I certainly do not wish to be the one to do it."

"I shall do it. I will take Lizzy to my room where no one will see. But you must tell Kitty and Lydia."

"Very well. Though I shall have little stomach for Lydia's theatrics."

They nodded and entered the sitting room.

"Lizzy, will you come to my room?"

Dinner was a strained affair. Three sets of eyes were focused on Elizabeth, who said nothing and ate less. Mrs Bennet was completely focused on Lydia, who wept periodically, crying out "Dear Mr Darcy!" Kitty did not know what to say or do.

Elizabeth retreated to her room even as the last course was being cleared. Jane hurried to follow, but was halted by Mr Bennet's hand on her arm. He whispered, though no one would have heard him over Lydia's wailing, "Jane, stay with her. I am sadly lacking in sympathetic words. I fear I can offer little to her now."

"I shall stay with her all night, Papa." Jane hurried to her sister's room and entered without knocking. Elizabeth sat at the vanity, staring blankly at herself in the mirror. Jane unpinned her hair and began to brush it, the only sound in the room that of the rain pelting the window pane.

Mary entered after softly knocking. She sat in a chair near the bed but said nothing.

"You two do not have to follow me around as if on eggshells."

"You ought not be alone now." Jane plaited Elizabeth's hair. "But let us go to my room. It is warmer, and the bed is more comfortable. There are advantages to being the eldest."

Elizabeth made no protest when Jane tugged on her arms to make her rise. As the three of them crossed the hallway, they heard Lydia's cries from downstairs. "...marred by burns! What about his dimples?!"

Jane shut the door behind her, relieved that it was thick enough to block out further lamentations. "Perhaps Mary will read to us. Would you like that, Lizzy?"

Elizabeth climbed listlessly into the bed.

"I have just the book in my room," Mary said. "Let me retrieve it."

She moved towards the door but stopped in her tracks when Lydia's voice could be heard through it. "I want Jane! Where is she?"

Lydia burst into the room and threw herself into Jane's arms. "Oh, Jane! May I stay with you tonight? Kitty is being horrid!"

Kitty stood in the doorway. "I did not say anything!"

"That's just it! You offer no words of comfort while my Mr Darcy is dying!" Lydia bawled.

"Calm yourself. We are all very worried about Mr Darcy. But Lizzy is staying with me tonight." She motioned towards Elizabeth.

"But *I* am the one who is upset!"

"We are all upset, Lydia," said Mary. "But not all of us are as vocal about it as you are."

"Lizzy never even liked Mr Darcy because he said she was not handsome. She is probably glad this happened!"

Just as Jane was about to reprimand Lydia, Elizabeth threw off the covers and ran from the room, knocking Kitty out of the way. She slammed her bedroom door behind her.

Jane followed Mary into the hallway. Kitty stood with her ear to Elizabeth's door. "I think I hear her crying," she whispered. "Lizzy never cries."

Jane tried the doorknob; it was locked, as she suspected. She had a key, but she dare not use it with Lydia near. "That's it. Everyone goes to bed in their own rooms. Now."

"Why should Lizzy be crying?" Lydia demanded. "I am the one who suffers through such a tragic loss."

"Lydia," Mary hissed, "if you were not so stupidly selfish, you might for once in your life think about someone other than yourself."

Lydia ran to her room and slammed the door.

"Kitty," Jane said to her stunned sister, "you may stay in my room tonight. I am staying with Elizabeth."

Jane retrieved the key to Elizabeth's door. "Mary, I think I had better go in alone."

"Wake me if you feel I can help."

Jane nodded and turned the key in the lock. "Good night to both of you."

Tuesday

My dearest Charles,

We are all so very distressed by the tragic events at Netherfield. You must be overset with morbid worry and obligations. Do not hesitate to call on Longbourn if we can help in any way. My love, you are,

*as always, foremost in my thoughts. I pray the next news we have
from Netherfield is happier than the last.*

Yours always,
Jane

Jane sealed the note and went to the kitchen. She handed it to
Tommy. "Thank you so much for braving such a long walk in the
mud and for carrying my note to Mr Bingley."

Tommy looked up at his father, who nodded in encouragement.
"It is no trouble, Miss Jane."

"You be sure to come back here to warm up after your return. We
will have your boots cleaned and Cook will have a special treat for
you."

He grinned. "Thank you." Then he bundled himself up and went
out the back door. He sank an inch into the mud with each step. The
sun was finally out, and it was bitterly cold again. Jane hoped that the
mud would either freeze or dry out enough to allow travel. Until it
did, they must wait for Tommy's return.

She went into the sitting room where all her sisters were gathered
save one. Lydia was upstairs with their mother. Elizabeth stared out
the window, Kitty stared at Elizabeth while fiddling with a bonnet,
and Mary wrote an extract, though not with her usual vigour.

An hour later, Hill summoned Jane and Elizabeth to the kitchen.
John Lucas was standing just inside the kitchen door with horribly
muddied boots.

"Come in, John."

He held up his hand. "Jane, Lizzy, I had planned to spend the day
with you all until I met Tommy on my way here. What precisely has
happened at Netherfield?"

Jane proceeded to tell John everything she knew.

John nodded as he glanced at Elizabeth. "I have seen such
injuries before. If I had known sooner... There are herbal remedies,
effective remedies. I need some time to prepare the ingredients. But

then I shall go to Netherfield to offer my help. Lizzy, do you wish to come with me?"

Elizabeth jerked her head up. "Come with you?"

"You will regret not speaking with Mr Darcy if..." John trailed off, leaving the worst unspoken.

"I shall have a lifetime of regret no matter what happens. But it is not my place. I am nothing to him."

"I have seen the way he looks at you. You are most definitely *something* to him."

She shook her head and whispered, "It is not my place. His family should be there. I keep thinking of his poor sister. Oh, John, you must help him! His physician may not have arrived before the roads became impassable."

"I promise I shall do anything I can. Are you sure you do not wish to come with me?"

"I am not sure of anything anymore."

John embraced her while looking helplessly at Jane. "Now that you mention his family, I may have news on that front. Last night when I was with the officers—yes, Gus and I braved the mud for a card game—I heard tell of a very grand carriage passing through Meryton. It carried three fine ladies, and the driver asked for safe direction to Netherfield."

"It must be Lady Catherine, Miss de Bourgh, and Miss Darcy. That is as it should be."

Jane asked, "How did the carriage successfully manoeuvre on these roads yesterday?"

"I suppose they knew the urgency of the situation and risked getting mired somewhere along the way. The worst of the mud is here, because we are nearer the stream. The roads in the village are not as bad." John put on his hat and bid them farewell.

As he walked away, Jane saw he did not sink as much as Tommy had. Perhaps the mud was freezing. Perhaps the roads would be passable soon.

35

A Report of a Most Alarming Nature

Lydia spent the morning with her mother, not wishing to face any more chastisement from Jane or Mary. Their words would not leave her mind, no matter how much she cried in Mrs Bennet's arms. What did Mary mean—think about someone else? Think about Lizzy? What Kitty had said was correct: Lizzy never cried. So why was she crying?

Lydia could not imagine ever wishing to cry again if she had been assured a life with John Lucas. In truth, *he* was the real reason for much of Lydia's behaviour of late, though she could never admit it to anyone. She resented that three of her sisters now had suitors before she did. Lydia was rather mortified by the strength of her jealousy. It had made her behave terribly to Kitty, it had made her flirt shamelessly with Mr Wickham of all people, just so John would see, and it had made her lash out cruelly at Lizzy last night.

The Mr Darcy situation was merely an excuse for her to release her emotions. Of course learning of Mr Darcy's engagement had been a great shock and disappointment, and now she worried for his well-being. It would be dreadful for such a handsome young man in the prime of his life to meet such an end. And what of his orphaned sister? Lydia could not imagine having her entire family taken from her.

"Shall we join your sisters for luncheon, my dearest?" Mrs Bennet said, stroking Lydia's hair.

"Yes, I suppose." She must begin to make amends. But how Lizzy would receive her? There was only one way to find out.

Lydia and Mrs Bennet made their way to the sitting room where the others were gathered. Elizabeth was sitting at the window, staring out into the garden. Lydia went to her. "Lizzy?"

She turned her face towards Lydia, revealing the dark circles under her eyes. Lydia swallowed. "I am sorry I said such an appalling thing to you. I know you would never wish ill on anyone." Elizabeth turned her face back towards the window. "Perhaps...perhaps I underestimated your friendship with Mr Darcy. You did stay at Netherfield with him, and you did have all those literary discussions with him. You...you do not dislike him at all, do you?"

Lizzy shook her head with her eyes closed. Lydia took her hand. "I keep thinking of poor Miss Darcy."

"As do I." Two tears trailed down Elizabeth's cheeks.

"Oh Lizzy, do you think he will recover?"

She wiped at her eyes and took a deep breath. "Tommy did not bring good news from Netherfield, though he only spoke to the servants. He said the fever has set in, and it is in God's hands now. Mr Jones and Mr Darcy's physician from London attend their patient round the clock."

"The same physician he offered to send for when you hit a cricket ball at my head and knocked me senseless?"

Elizabeth almost smiled. "The very one."

"I hope Miss Darcy can be with him soon."

"We have reason to believe that she is with him already. John told us of a carriage—"

"John was here?" Lydia beat back her jealousy again.

"Only briefly. He said a grand carriage conveying three fine ladies passed through Meryton yesterday on its way to Netherfield."

Hill announced luncheon.

Elizabeth sighed. "I am not hungry."

Lydia pulled on her hand. "You must eat something. Now tell me what else John said."

Lydia apologised to all her sisters over the course of the afternoon. Kitty was the most reluctant to forgive her, but she was eventually won over. Lydia had even been able to coax Lizzy from the window when she asked for another book recommendation.

And so it was that no one saw the carriage coming slowly up the lane. The first clue they had that there were visitors was Hill's very formal announcement, "Lady Catherine de Bourgh and Miss de—"

An impressive lady in great finery pushed into the room before Mrs Hill could finish. A younger woman in a more understated yet just as fine gown stood in the doorway surveying everyone in the room. She smiled slightly. No similar gesture softened Lady Catherine's mouth.

Mrs Bennet rose with a shocked, "Oh! Lady Catherine. Forgive us; we had not expected—"

"You have a very small park here," Lady Catherine said before any greetings or introductions were exchanged.

"I'm sure it is nothing in comparison to Rosings, my lady; but it is much larger than Sir William Lucas's."

"This must be a most inconvenient sitting room for the evening in summer; the windows are full west."

Mrs Bennet assured her that they never sat there after dinner in the summer and then added, "May I take the liberty of asking your ladyship whether you left Mr Collins well? He arrived back in Kent well before the storm, did he not?"

"Yes, he is well. I saw him the day before last. The weather in Kent is far superior to the weather here." Lady Catherine sat in the nearest chair; her daughter claimed a seat near the door.

Elizabeth asked the question they were all thinking, "Do you bring news from Nether—"

Lady Catherine interrupted again. "I have come to speak with Miss Lydia Bennet, whichever of you that may be." She rose up and peered around the room.

Everyone turned to look in Lydia's direction, and she was momentarily stunned. Had Mr Darcy asked for her? No, that was a ridiculous thought. "I am she."

Lady Catherine turned her full attention to her. "You? But you are a mere child!" Then she composed herself and spoke in a more civil voice. "You can be at no loss to understand the reason of my journey hither."

Lydia gulped. "Indeed, you are mistaken, madam. I have not been at all able to account for the honour of seeing you here. No doubt you are much more needed at—"

"Miss Bennet," interrupted her ladyship, "I am not to be trifled with. My character has ever been celebrated for its sincerity and frankness, and in a cause of such moment as this, I shall certainly not depart from it. A report of a most alarming nature reached me two days ago. Mr Collins told me that you, that Miss Lydia Bennet, not only brazenly schemed to catch my nephew, *my own nephew*, for a husband, but that you then doubted the truth of his long-standing betrothal to my daughter! Though I know he would never give even the slightest encouragement to one such as yourself, though I would not injure him so much as to think it possible he would ever consider you an acceptable choice, I instantly resolved on setting off for this place that I might warn you to abandon all your deluded hopes in that quarter."

Lydia stood so that she need not look up to this horrid woman any longer. "If I have leave to be equally frank, Lady Catherine, I must tell you that your nephew behaved abominably in keeping his betrothal a secret from all of us." Her Ladyship gasped. "Of course all the single young ladies would pursue him! What do you think happens when a rich, handsome young man comes to a place like Meryton? If he did not wish to endure the aspirations of one such as myself, he ought to have been honest from the start."

"How dare you—"

"I was not finished! I must question your priorities at a time like this. I do regret speaking ill of Mr Darcy, today of all d—"

"I shall not be interrupted. Hear me in silence. Do you know who I am?"

Lydia snorted, about to answer that she had certainly heard enough about Lady Catherine to last a lifetime, but Miss de Bourgh finally spoke. "That's enough, Mother!" Her tone of voice belied her somewhat meek exterior. "If you do not wish to be interrupted, perhaps you ought not interrupt everyone else. Mrs Bennet, Miss Lydia, all the rest of you Miss Bennets, I am sorry we have not been properly introduced, and I apologise for my mother's behaviour today. She has been rude beyond comprehension."

"Anne!"

"Mother, you have had your part of the conversation. Now I shall have mine." Lady Catherine stood in stunned silence while Miss de Bourgh spoke to Lydia. "You must not think my cousin dishonourable in any way. He was never dishonest with any of you. We are not engaged."

"Not engaged?!"

"Anne! From your infancy, you have been intended for each other. It was the favourite wish of his mother as well as of yours. While in your cradles, we planned the union."

"I have heard it all before, Mother. You did as much as you could in planning the marriage. Its completion depended on others who do not wish as you do. I am neither by honour nor inclination confined to my cousin nor is he to me. Why, then, is he not to make another choice? And if one of these fine young ladies is his choice, why may not she accept him? I have accepted someone of my own choosing."

"No more of this Christopher Grantly nonsense! I shall not allow it!"

"How many times must I tell you—I do not need your permission!" The two were yelling at the top of their voices.

"You *will* marry Darcy! If you do not, you will be censured, slighted, and despised by everyone connected with me. Your alliance will be a disgrace; your name will never even be mentioned by any of us."

"These are heavy misfortunes," replied Miss de Bourgh. "But as the wife of Mr Christopher Grantly and the *sole* heir of Lewis de Bourgh's Rosings Park, I must have such extraordinary sources of happiness necessarily attached to my situation that I shall, upon the whole, have no cause to repine."

"Obstinate, headstrong girl! I am ashamed of you! You and Darcy are formed for each other. You are descended, on the maternal side, from the same noble line—"

Kitty stood up and yelled, "What does any of this matter with Mr Darcy on his deathbed? He most likely will not live to marry anyone!"

"Kitty!" admonished Jane.

Lady Catherine and Miss de Bourgh gaped at Kitty. "What do you mean?" they demanded in concert.

Jane asked, "Have you not come from Netherfield where you saw Mr Darcy?"

Miss de Bourgh answered, "No, we came directly from Kent. We spoke to Mr Collins on Sunday and left early Monday morning, though we were delayed for several hours during the storm and the rest of the journey was very slow going."

"But the rider—did no express rider arrive on Saturday night or perhaps Sunday morning?"

"No. Please tell me what is going on."

"I am very sorry to tell you, but there was a shooting accident on Saturday. Mr Darcy's gun misfired, and he suffered powder burns. The storm and the mud have made it difficult for us to keep contact with Netherfield, but today, we heard he has developed a severe fever, likely from infection."

"Mother, we must go this instant!"

"Yes, the carriage! The carriage!" Lady Catherine fled from the room, demanding the carriage the whole way down to the front door. The others followed her.

When Lydia arrived outside, Thomas was having words with the driver. "The wheel is weakened. It is not safe to take this carriage out on those roads again."

A quarrel ensued with Lady Catherine herself, who insisted on leaving immediately. Finally, Thomas offered to ready the Bennet carriage for their use and to ride along to give direction for the safest route to Netherfield. It was, by necessity, a longer route that bypassed the main road along Oakham Stream.

Mrs Bennet said to the assembled ladies. "Let us return indoors while the carriage is readied. There is no need to remain in the cold."

They returned to the sitting room where Lady Catherine, with much improved civility, thanked Mrs Bennet for the use of her carriage. The two began a strained conversation near the door. Miss de Bourgh came into the room where Lydia and her sisters sat.

"I must take this opportunity before I go. Forgive my forwardness. Which of you is Miss Elizabeth Bennet?"

She followed everyone's gaze towards Lizzy, who blinked and swallowed. "I am she."

"Miss Elizabeth, may I tell you something?" She approached and sat near Lizzy.

"Of course you may, Miss de Bourgh."

"My cousin and I, we secretly exchange letters with the help of trusted and discreet servants. We are very close, he and I. We were brought together at a young age when each of us lost a parent. Since then, we have been like brother and sister, and we *never* could have fulfilled my mother's wishes for us. Do you understand?"

Elizabeth nodded. Miss de Bourgh continued, "Fitzwilliam's recent letters were—"

"Fitzwilliam?" Elizabeth whispered.

"Fitzwilliam is Mr Darcy's given name. His recent letters, ones he wrote to me from Netherfield, were filled with some very interesting revelations. Do you care to hear them?"

Elizabeth nodded silently again. "He wrote me of a young lady who had touched his heart. He called her only L."

Kitty gasped. "Can it be true? Did he really fancy Lydia all that time?"

"Quiet, Kitty," ordered Mary. All of them were as eager for Miss de Bourgh's next words as Lydia was.

Miss de Bourgh continued, "He struggled against his feelings for several weeks because of society's expectations. You must understand that Fitzwilliam has always taken his duty as the master of Pemberley very seriously. Despite his misgivings, he met his L. on a series of morning walks where he fell even more in love with her."

"Morning walks? That sounds more like Liz— Oh!" Kitty voiced her enlightenment only a moment after Lydia made a similar conclusion silently. *Mr Darcy in love with Lizzy?* Elizabeth, her sister, meeting Mr Darcy in the woods every morning? Lydia only half-listened to the rest of the conversation, so great was her mental distraction.

"These were not assignations," Miss de Bourgh added. "They started innocently with a specific purpose. His last letter to me was quite despondent. You see, he had decided to court L. properly, for he could not imagine himself ever loving any woman as he loves her. But then he discovered that she was already attached to a long-time family friend who recently returned to Hertfordshire."

"That must be John!" By this point, everyone ignored Kitty's exclamations.

"If I could speak with this young lady, this L., I would tell her how very much my cousin loves her." Miss de Bourgh's voice faltered. "If... if Fitzwilliam is really on his deathbed, a visit, a few kind words from her, the knowledge that she returns his feelings even in the slightest degree—I am convinced he would cherish these things beyond almost anything on this earth."

Elizabeth looked down at her trembling hands, blinking furiously. Miss de Bourgh leaned forward and grasped them gently.

"You must go, Lizzy," Mary finally said.

Elizabeth rose unsteadily. "I must go."

"Come with us in the carriage," Miss de Bourgh said.

"It will be faster to walk. To run!"

"Put on your boots and coat at least," said Jane, as Elizabeth hurried for the door.

"Where on earth is Lizzy going?" Mrs Bennet asked, halting her conversation with Lady Catherine.

"She has been confined indoors too long," Mary replied.

"She is going for one of her walks *now*? I shall never understand that girl!"

Lydia heard the kitchen door slam. Lizzy was going to see Mr Darcy! She had stolen Mr Darcy away from her own sister! Lydia was walking towards the door before she even knew it.

Mary followed her into the hallway. "Do not cause any more trouble, Lydia. Think of what has happened over the last month. Think very carefully."

Lydia pulled on her boots and tied them. "I shall not listen to your scolding, Mary. She is the one who... How *dare* she! She cannot have John Lucas *and* Mr Darcy!"

She pulled on her coat and gloves and ran from the house into the muddy cold.

36

The Smallest Hope

Bingley read Jane's note again. It was the one small bit of comfort he had had over the last few days. She did not chastise him for neglecting her even though she had only heard of the accident through the servants. He had not even had a chance to send her a reply, for the note made its way through various servants to reach him, and then Tommy was already gone.

Bingley needed no chastisement; he felt guilty enough already for letting either of them go shooting after such a night of intoxication. Why had he listened to Hurst's assurances? He would never forgive himself if...

"Mr Lucas," announced Mrs Trent.

Bingley looked up to see John Lucas with a bundle under his arm, shoeless. "Mr Lucas! Please come in."

"You are to call me Lucas, remember? Forgive my appearance. I thought it easier to simply remove my boots than to spend the time scraping the mud off. I wished to see you right away."

Bingley smiled, "Of course you are welcome, and I do not mind your lack of footwear."

"Did Mr Darcy's physician successfully travel from London through the storm and mud?"

"Yes, he was offered an exorbitant amount of money to do so. His name is Robertson."

He nodded. "Has the fever broken?"

"No," Bingley replied sadly.

"How long has it lasted?"

"Since yesterday morning."

Lucas sighed. "I ought to have come sooner, but I only just learned of it. Is Mr Jones here?"

"No, he has returned home for a short respite. Why?"

"He knows me well and would take my part. No matter. You heard me mention my interest in herbal remedies, did you not?"

Bingley indicated that he had.

"I have prepared a febrifuge, or fever reducer. I have seen it work wonders when taken as a tea. Do you think Mr Robertson will hear me, that I may convince him to try it? Some people do not set much store in herbal medicine."

Bingley brightened considerably. "We shall convince him together! We must try something." He rang for Mrs Trent, who appeared almost immediately.

"Mrs Trent, please ask Mr Robertson to come to the library."

When she left them, Lucas added, "I also have a poultice for the burns. A salve would be more effective, but it takes more time to prepare. I have started one at home and will return when it is ready."

"You are very kind."

"No, it is the least I could do."

Mr Robertson entered, and Bingley made the introductions. "Mr Lucas is an authority on herbal medicine. He has been kind enough to prepare...what was it? A tea to reduce fever and a poultice for the burns? I think we should try them."

"I have no objections at this point. Nothing else is working. I thank you, Mr Lucas."

Lucas smiled. "I have written out directions for proper preparation and administration. Shall we go to the kitchen to have it brewed?"

The three men made their way towards the kitchen, where confused servants eyed them.

"Becky!" Lucas said. "How wonderful to see you."

"My brother told me you were back. But where are your shoes?"

He smirked. "Waiting for me safely at the door. Would you rather I track mud all over the house where you would have to clean it?"

"Most people wouldn't give it a thought."

He shrugged. "How are you at following directions, Becky?"

"Good enough, I expect."

"Let me show you how to make this into a tea; it will bring down a fever." Lucas set his bundle on the counter and began to unwrap it.

She watched as he produced a small packet of dried leaves. "Is that so? Where did those come from?"

"Cuba. Here, smell." He held them up to her nose.

She recoiled after one whiff but recovered quickly. "Ghastly. Do you need boiling water?"

"That is precisely what I need."

In addition to Mr Robertson and Bingley, a small audience of servants gathered to watch, partly out of curiosity and partly because John Lucas was a most engaging lecturer. The result of the demonstration was about two cups worth of a vile-smelling tea. Lucas handed a slip of paper to Mr Robertson. "Here are the directions."

"Thank you, though I think everyone in the kitchen now knows how to make it." He turned to Becky. "Can you prepare a tray to bring this up to our patient? I shall see you up there."

"Yes, sir."

Bingley motioned for Lucas to return to the library with him. "You have lifted our spirits. We were most disheartened before you brought a little hope. Let me offer you something—a brandy, perhaps."

Lucas waved it off. "I really should not stay too long. Longbourn will be most anxious for news. Will you call for my horse while I show Mr Robertson how to apply the poultice?"

They had arrived outside the library door. "I shall see to it. And perhaps I may send a note along with you for Jane?"

"Yes, of course."

Bingley caught Mrs Trent on her way somewhere. "Will you have Mr Lucas's horse readied?"

He turned into the library. Before he even reached the desk to write his note, Lucas bounded back through the doorway. "Bingley, can you tell me... I thought perhaps Mr Darcy might wish to convey a message to Longbourn as well. Is he lucid?"

"Lucid?"

"If I spoke to him, would he be able to respond coherently?"

Someone cleared his throat from the far corner of the room. "Of course I am lucid. What sort of question is that?" Darcy rose from his chair, scowling at the two men.

"What the devil!?" Lucas pointed at Darcy and demanded of Bingley, "What is the meaning of this?"

"I do not understand."

Darcy approached as Lucas gaped at him.

"Is this some sort of sick joke? For a man whose gun exploded in his face four days ago, you look remarkably well, Mr Darcy."

Darcy tried to glare fiercely, but his eyes kept sinking to John Lucas' stockinged feet. "I believe *you* are the one playing a sick joke. Bingley, what is he doing here? You hardly have time to entertain guests."

Now two great, tall fellows glared at Bingley fiercely. "I am not entertaining him! He brought herbal remedies for Hurst."

Lucas blinked. "Mr Hurst? Mr Hurst is the one who lies upstairs with powder burns and a fever?"

"Yes. Did you think it was Darcy?"

"Yes! Everyone thinks Mr Darcy is on his deathbed."

"Everyone?"

"Well, everyone at Longbourn."

"But how could that have happened?"

"I think Thomas was the one who—Blast! It does not matter now!" He turned to Darcy, "*All* the Bennets believe you to be suffering from a life-threatening fever."

"All the Bennets," Darcy repeated. He paled and his eyes searched Lucas's face.

"Yes. All of them," Lucas said urgently. "It is imperative that she— that they learn the truth as soon as possible."

Bingley took Lucas's meaning. "You are referring to Elizabeth? Hurst and I recently formulated a theory about Darcy's feelings for her. Of course I will explain this misunderstanding in my note." Bingley moved around the desk. Then he remembered what else they believed about Darcy at Longbourn. "Darcy! Everyone at Longbourn also believes you are engaged to wed your cousin!"

"What?!" the taller fellow shouted.

"Miss Lydia and Mrs Bennet were most agitated by something Mr Collins had said. He claimed to have seen the betrothal announcements. Your aunt asked him to edit the text or some such before it goes in the papers. He went on and on about the splendid match when I was there on Friday."

Darcy glared at him. "And did you tell them it is not true?"

Bingley shrugged. "Well, not exactly. I was not about to call Lady Catherine a liar right in front of Mr Collins. You know how he would have reacted."

"But why did you not tell *me* about it afterwards? Do you know what you have done?"

"Me? Blast it, Darcy—you are far too reticent for your own good! I might have known how important it was at the time had you confided in me rather than drink yourself into a stupor!" Bingley's ire rose. "Besides, you ought to have ended your aunt's aspirations long ago, but you have found the rumours useful for your own purposes. And you *know* we have not had five minutes to spare for conversation since the accident. For God's sake, take some responsibility; this misunderstanding is *your* doing, not mine."

Darcy paced, running his hand through his hair. "I am sorry, Bingley; you are correct."

"Am I to understand," Lucas said, "that Mr Darcy is *not* engaged to Miss de Bourgh?"

"No, he is not."

Darcy crossed to the door. "I must go to Longbourn."

"Just a moment," Lucas called. He approached and stood toe to boot with Darcy. "What are your intentions?"

They locked gazes. "I shall marry her tomorrow if she will have me."

After a long moment, Lucas nodded once and said, "Take my horse. He is already saddled and waiting out front."

Darcy stared at him, his brow furrowed. "You have no objections to my marrying her?"

"That is her decision."

Darcy offered his hand, which Lucas shook. "How will you get home?"

Lucas grinned. "I shall borrow *your* fine animal. What the devil are you waiting for?"

With one last handshake and a rushed "Thank you," Darcy went into the hallway. A moment later, they heard the front door shut.

John Lucas stood staring towards the door for a few moments. Bingley did not know whether he should speak or not. Finally, Lucas turned back, "Well, let me see to that poultice for Mr Hurst."

Bingley slapped his shoulder. "I shall take you up myself, Lucas."

Bingley jolted awake in the library. He must have fallen asleep after Lucas left. He had not been getting much sleep since the accident. He wondered how Darcy had fared.

"Where is my nephew? I demand to see him immediately!"

Bingley rubbed his eyes. So he had not been dreaming that angry voice. He stood and walked towards the door, only to see Mrs Trent standing there. "Sir, a Lady Catherine de Bourgh is here asking for Mr Darcy."

Lady Catherine pushed into the room, tracking mud all over the floor. "You must be Mr Bingley?"

"Yes, it is a pleasure to see you here, madam."

"You can surely understand my abruptness under the circumstances. I insist on seeing my nephew."

She walked back out into the hallway and Bingley followed, where he saw another lady speaking with Mrs Trent. Bingley smiled, about to introduce himself and welcome this newcomer.

"Where is my nephew? What room?" Lady Catherine said as she went to the stairs.

"Mother—"

"I assume he is in your best room, Mr Bingley. Where is that?" Lady Catherine asked over her shoulder as she began climbing.

Bingley was relieved to see Caroline coming down the hallway. "Mr Darcy is not in his room at present, Lady Catherine. Allow me to introduce my sister, the mistress of the house. She will see that your wait is a comfortable one."

"It is an immense pleasure to meet you, Lady Catherine," Caroline said smoothly. "We have heard so much about you—"

"What do you mean, not in his room?" Lady Catherine ignored Caroline completely. "Mr Bingley, I am not accustomed to repeating myself. I demand to be taken to my nephew this instant!"

"Mother—"

"He is not here, Lady Catherine. If you will come into the drawing room, we shall gladly explain."

"Not here!? You have allowed him to travel in his condition, on these roads? Does no one have any sense but me?"

"Mother, come down and stop interrupting every—"

"I shall not waste my time being polite to these fools, Anne! How can you be so calm?"

"Lower your voice!" Mrs Regina Hurst boomed from the top of the stairs.

Lady Catherine sputtered as she swung her head around. "How dare you? Do you know who I am!?"

"I do not care who you are!" She came halfway down the staircase. "*I* am Regina Hurst, and my son lies upstairs fighting for his life. Shut your unruly mouth, or I shall throw you out into the mud myself!"

Lady Catherine backed down two steps, shocked into silence.

"Mrs Hurst, please forgive my mother," Miss de Bourgh said. "She was under the mistaken impression that her nephew, Mr Darcy, was ill, not Mr Hurst. Naturally, she was very upset. She will not disturb you nor your son any longer. Come down here, Mother. This is the last time I shall smooth over the offenses given by your rudeness."

Lady Catherine rather meekly descended the stairs. Mrs Hurst looked to Anne, "I shall overlook this instance as long as it does not happen again, Miss-?"

"I am Miss de Bourgh, and this is my mother, Lady Catherine de Bourgh."

Mrs Hurst nodded to her and glanced briefly at Lady Catherine. "I am also inclined to forgive you both as we owe a great debt to Mr Darcy. He sent for me, as well as his own physician, immediately after the accident, thus ensuring we were able to reach Netherfield before the worst of the storm."

"My cousin always keeps his head about him in a crisis. I am glad he was of service to you and Mr Hurst. Now, Mr Bingley, Miss Bingley, you mentioned retiring to the drawing room..."

"Yes, please follow Caroline."

Caroline led their guests away, and Bingley started to follow.

"Mr Bingley," Mrs Hurst said. "What is the name of the young man who brought the tea?"

"Mr John Lucas."

"When Mr Lucas returns, my mother, my sister, and I wish to thank him personally. Will you inform us as soon as he arrives?"

"Indeed, I shall be happy to."

She thanked him and ascended the stairs. Bingley hurried to reach the drawing room, where he found Caroline conversing with a much subdued Lady Catherine.

"Mr Bingley," Miss de Bourgh said quietly. "Can you tell me where my cousin has gone?"

"He went to Longbourn. He had just learned...some news. I assume Longbourn is where you heard the erroneous rumour?"

"Yes, we came from there. But when did he leave?"

Bingley pulled out his watch. "About an hour and a half ago."

"That is perfect," she said to herself, "for that is just after Miss Elizabeth left. No doubt they met along the way." She beamed, then recollected herself. "I probably do not make much sense to you."

"No, you make perfect sense. It's high time those two cleared up all these misunderstandings."

37

When One Has a Motive

Darcy splashed through muddy puddles as he raced towards Longbourn. He had no idea what he would say or do when he got there, but all that was secondary to his need to see Elizabeth. Their dreadful parting might have been a huge misunderstanding. She had believed he was engaged to Anne, which he certainly was not. Perhaps, just perhaps, she was not in love with John Lucas. He had to know one way or the other. He would confess his love and throw himself at her mercy. If he were not rushing towards the most important moment of his life, Darcy would have laughed at how low he had fallen.

How much farther until he reached her? Two miles? Perhaps less. It seemed an interminable distance. As he rounded another turn, he was arrested by the sight before him. Elizabeth Bennet stood, breathless and in shock, her hem six inches deep in mud. She was the most beautiful thing he had ever seen.

Darcy was out of the saddle and stepping towards her before he realised it. He opened his mouth to speak without knowing what he would say, but in the next moment, the wind was knocked out of him as she launched herself into his arms. Without thinking, he embraced her tightly. She trembled—was she crying, or just cold? He held her closer and breathed deeply.

Her face was buried in his coat. "Thank God. Thank God," she gasped.

She pulled back slightly, and he reluctantly loosened his grip. But he would not release her hands, loath as he was to break the contact between them. She wore no gloves.

Her eyes travelled intently over his face. "You are not shot."

"No, I am not." He cursed his stupidity for uttering such an absurd answer. As he expected, she seemed to recall herself, and whatever unguarded mood she was in ended.

"Good. Lydia would hate to see either of those dimples lost to scars."

Her attempt at levity would not distract Darcy. He was steady to his purpose. "And you? Would you hate to see me scarred?"

Her eyes softened again. He held his breath as she brought her hand up to the side of his face. "Of course. I could not bear it."

He cradled her hand to his cheek, relishing the feel of her bare skin against his. After a few moments, she retracted her hand, and he said, "I am not shot, and I am not engaged."

She looked down. "Yes, Miss de Bourgh corrected our misapprehension on the latter count."

"Anne?" he asked, confused. But he interrupted when she tried to answer. "It matters not, as long as you know the truth. While we are clearing the air, I must confess something." He waited until she looked up at him again. "I love you, Elizabeth Bennet, ardently and absolutely. I know that your heart may already belong to another. But I want no further misunderstandings between us. If there is any chance to win you, I shall do whatever I must. I shall spend my life proving myself worthy of your regard."

It seemed an eternity as she gathered herself to reply. "What a waste of your life to spend it proving to me what I already know or attempting to win that which you already possess. For my heart belongs to you, utterly and irrevocably."

The happiness this reply produced was such as he had probably never felt before, and an expression of heartfelt delight diffused over his face. But then he remembered one more issue he must confront. "But what of John Lucas? Do you not love him?"

"I love John as I love Jane. I can never give up his friendship. It is a part of me—will always be a part of me. Perhaps, under other circumstances, I might have been happy trying to make a life with John. But not anymore."

"Why not?"

"Because I fell hopelessly in love with another man, a man who is not remotely like a brother to me."

Darcy swallowed. "Please tell me I am that man."

She laughed. "Yes of course, you fool. Who else could it be?"

Darcy pulled her into his arms again, and the sense of rightness nearly overwhelmed him. "Then I beg you to marry this fool, Elizabeth. I love you beyond reason. Please say you will be my wife. Please say you will spend your life with me."

She stiffened and began to pull away. In desperation, Darcy blurted, "Or if you think this too sudden, if you need more time to decide, will you consent to a formal courtship? Let me prove my constancy, my devotion to you." He waited in agony for her answer.

"Fitzwilliam," she said softly, and he was comforted by the sound of his name on her lips. "What of the great differences between our stations? What of my low connexions, my vulgar mother, and ridiculous sisters? Society will not approve of me—and certainly not of them."

He took off his gloves and reached for her hands. How could he explain? "I must tell you that Mr Hurst's gun, not mine, misfired on Saturday. It is Hurst who battles for his life now."

"Oh no! Poor Mr Hurst! It must have been terrible." Her compassion always moved him, and this time it moved him to lift one of her hands and kiss her bare knuckles. She allowed it.

"It *was* terrible. And do you know what was the very worst of it? Hurst never once asked for his wife; he asked only for his mother. If that is the sort of marriage society would approve, then I want no part of it. The concerns you mentioned before—I dwelled on them from my high horse for far too long, and I nearly lost my perfect match. I do not care, should never have cared, what society will say about you. I have long loathed high society! Why should I now let its precepts dictate the most important decision of my life? Anyone who comes to know you will understand, nay approve, my love for you. And I have come to care for your family too. It only took seeing them through your eyes instead of my own, dearest, loveliest Elizabeth! What do I not owe you! You rescued me from my lofty perch and gave me the courage to interact with people for the sheer delight of genuine camaraderie."

"Oh, Fitzwilliam." Her face, her eyes, and her voice—they all expressed what Darcy had long wished for: unconditional love. Despite all his faults, despite the pain he had caused her, Elizabeth loved him. This witty, brave, lovely country miss was in love with Fitzwilliam Darcy! He sank to one knee and felt the cold mud oozing around his leg.

"Are you daft? Get up out of the mud!" She tugged on his hands to no avail.

"Elizabeth June Bennet, I love you. Nothing would make me happier than spending the rest of my days with you by my side. Will you do me the very great honour of becoming my wife?"

She took breath to reply. "I love you, Fitzwilliam Darcy, and I shall marry you!"

Darcy rose and swept her into his arms, swinging her around. Her laughter and the distant roar of Oakham Stream filled his ears. He put her down and took her hands again. "Your hands are freezing. Where are your gloves?"

"I rushed from the house thinking you were on your deathbed. I am lucky I remembered my boots!"

"Here, wear mine." He handed them over and watched, elated, as she pulled them onto her delicate hands.

"Oh! Fitzwilliam, your aunt and cousin now believe you to be gravely ill. They came to Longbourn, and we spread our poor information to them. You must find them and set them at ease. To avoid the stream, they were to take the high road and reach Netherfield from the north."

"Do you wish to be rid of me so soon? Bingley will explain the misunderstanding to them, I am sure."

"But they were very worried. Miss de Bourgh told me how you exchange letters with her. Why did you never tell me?"

"There are many things I should have told you, but I was perfectly content just listening to you. You have no idea how much I love the sound of your voice and the expression on your face when you speak of your loved ones."

"And *I* should have told you the nature of my relationship with John. But really, I mentioned him so often and shared so many improper details with you about my friends and family, you should have just asked me."

"I was petrified that you would reveal a secret engagement."

"And I was crushed when I learned of *your* secret engagement."

He shook his head. "I should be furious with my aunt, but I must admit that Anne and I left her just enough hope to avoid a confrontation all these years. We were cowardly."

"Well, Lady Catherine and Miss de Bourgh have certainly had that confrontation now—in Longbourn's sitting room, no less. Your cousin revealed that she is engaged to a Mr Christopher Grantly."

"Engaged! She wasted no time once she made up her mind. That is just like Anne. But why are they come to Longbourn?"

"Lady Catherine came to demand Lydia give up her aspirations to catch you for a husband." He would have laughed, but she worried her brow. "Lydia is no doubt feeling betrayed by me and by you. She overheard everything Miss de Bourgh told me about your letters and what you wrote about me. I must make amends to Lydia somehow. She will be hurt and angry. We lied to everyone, Fitzwilliam."

"I shall speak to her if you wish."

"No, I must do it."

"Fancy meeting you here, Miss Elizabeth, Mr Darcy." John Lucas ambled up alongside them. "It is a very fine day for walking, is it not?"

"John! Why do you have Mr Darcy's horse?"

He dismounted. "Did he not tell you? We are trying an exchange for the day. From the look of Mr Darcy's trousers and your poorly fitting gloves, I am to wish you joy, Lizzybits."

She went to him with a laugh, and they embraced. Darcy found he was no longer jealous of John Lucas. He wondered, though, whether the gentleman's easy smile hid deeper feelings for Elizabeth. Darcy supposed he would never know—he certainly would not ask such a question. Whatever John Lucas felt for Elizabeth, it was clear he wanted only her happiness. Darcy was much more inclined to like him now.

"Thank you, John. Did you have a hand in sending Mr Darcy to Longbourn?"

"I did, once I realised *you* were completely wrong, and *he* was neither dying nor engaged. You two seem prone to dreadful misunderstandings, but I am glad they have been cleared up to everyone's contentment." Lucas offered Darcy his hand. "You are a lucky man."

Darcy shook it. "Luckier than I deserve."

"Well, I was about to go to Longbourn, but I imagine they are not yet aware of your happy news."

Elizabeth answered, "No, they are not."

"Then I shall go home instead. Such joyous news should come from you, though I may not be able to resist telling Charlotte." He swung himself up into Darcy's saddle.

"Oh yes, tell Charlotte she was right about Mr Darcy all along."

He laughed. "She usually is." He tipped his hat to each of them. "I shall see you both soon, no doubt. Mr Darcy, you know where to retrieve your fine animal."

Darcy smirked, "I do."

Lucas moved past them, but then stopped. "You had better move off the road to continue your...conversation. As unlikely as it seems, footprints here indicate there are other people about today." He urged Darcy's mount into a trot and was gone.

Darcy looked around them. A more private locale *would* be desirable at present. He pulled Elizabeth off the road in the opposite direction of the stream.

"You must tell me how Mr Hurst fares," she said.

"I shall tell you, but right now, we have some unfinished business."

"Unfinished business?"

"Yes, I have been greatly regretting that we were interrupted on the balcony the other night."

She blushed. "Oh."

He took her face in his hands and caressed those blushing cheeks. She held his gaze steadily. He moved his thumb over her bottom lip.

She closed her eyes and sighed. He could not resist any longer. He stooped to brush her lips with his.

Her lips were softer than he had imagined. Her kiss sweeter, more exquisite than any dream could be—and he had had plenty of dreams. But now he wanted to kiss her again and again. And again. And not just on those sweet lips, but everywhere. Better to stop while he had some measure of control.

He pulled back barely an inch and looked upon her. She waited, her face tilted up, her eyes closed, her lips slightly parted. How many times had he dreamt of her like this? How many times had he prayed for the strength to resist the temptation of that sweet mouth? Now he only prayed the strength of his ardour would not frighten her.

38

A Tale of
Two Kisses

She had not expected his lips to be so soft. Nor had she expected the kiss to be so simple. Having come unnoticed upon Jane and Mr Bingley in amorous embrace before, Elizabeth knew there was more to it than this. What was he waiting for?

She opened her eyes. His face hovered above her, and she began to better understand all the times he had stared at her in their early acquaintance. It was *not* disapproval. It was instead a mixture of rapt admiration, perhaps fascination, as Charlotte had once conjectured, and restraint—though right now the former almost completely eclipsed the latter. Elizabeth very much wished him to surrender at last; she wished to finally feel the full force of what he had been hiding: his love for her.

He exhaled and pulled her closer. She went up on her toes and wound her arms around his neck. He lifted her off the ground and kissed her repeatedly, and not at all softly. She had no idea what she was doing. But Elizabeth was, as ever, eager to learn new skills and accomplishments, and he seemed to appreciate her efforts.

After some minutes spent in avid pursuit of accomplishment, he groaned. She felt it before she heard it, pressed as she was against his chest. Then he pulled his lips away. Her protest died in her throat, for those same lips were suddenly on the column of said throat. His harsh breath was hot against her skin as he kissed her and murmured words of love long repressed. Elizabeth threw her head back with a sigh. "Fitzwilliam..." She did not recognise her own voice.

He came back to her mouth and kissed her with less fervour than he had before. He lowered her to the ground, and she did not trust her legs to hold her upright, yet somehow they did. He took her face in his hands and devoured her features with eager eyes.

"How you tempt me, Elizabeth."

"If you had done *that* on the balcony, I think we both could have avoided several days of heartache."

He smiled. "I shall never hesitate to kiss you again."

"I shall depend upon it." She felt giddy at seeing his dimples again.

"May I escort you home now, Miss Eliz—"

They heard screaming—dreadful, terrified screaming. "That sounds like Lydia!"

Elizabeth ran for the road and, upon reaching it, turned to run towards the commotion.

Darcy caught her arm. "We will ride. It is faster."

"I do not ride!" She was frantic to get to Lydia.

He grasped her shoulders. "Do you trust me?"

Looking up into his eyes, she did. "Yes."

He lifted her onto John's horse, and before she could panic, he swung himself up behind her. They galloped for perhaps half a mile before spying Darcy's riderless horse on the road.

§

Half an hour earlier...

It took less than two dozen steps into the mire for Lydia to regret leaving the house. But her boots were quite covered in mud, so she kept running. She tried to keep her dress hem from getting muddied by hiking her skirts up indecently high, but it only slowed her down more. Lizzy always could run the fastest, but Lydia was not one to give up so easily. She followed her sister's footprints in the mud. If Lydia could not catch up, she would go to Netherfield and confront Lizzy there. She plodded along, becoming angrier with every new mud splatter on her dress. This was all Elizabeth's fault!

She began to recognise which sections of road were frozen, thus avoiding the deepest mud. She passed the lane for Lucas Lodge, where she noted another set of footprints.

Lydia heard voices up ahead, but she could not make out the words. She continued on, coming around a turn to discover her sister and Mr Darcy. He was kneeling in the mud! Lydia could not see Lizzy's face, but *his* looked absolutely adoring.

"Elizabeth June Bennet, I love you. Nothing would make me happier than spending the rest of my days with you by my side. Will you do me the very great honour of becoming my wife?"

"I love you, Fitzwilliam Darcy, and I shall marry you!" Her voice trembled with great emotion.

He rose and swung Elizabeth around as they both laughed. Lydia had never seen Mr Darcy giddy, but that was the only way to describe him now. They looked truly happy. Lydia was glad they did not see her. She must look a perfect disaster, and she felt like one too. She could not let Lizzy see her like this: pitiably defeated.

Lydia turned and stormed towards Longbourn without seeing anything around her, her forgotten hem left to swing in the mud. How could Elizabeth do this to her own sister? How could she steal Mr Darcy away when she knew Lydia wanted him? How could she do this to John?

A friendly voice startled her. "Why such haste, Miss Lydia?" Mr Wickham stood on the road in front of her.

She curtseyed quickly. "Mr Wickham, good day. Why are you out on the road today?"

"I had some business with Mr Lucas, but he was not at home. I am glad to have happened upon *you* though, for now my trip was not wasted."

Lydia barely heard his explanation or his flattery. She was too distracted. "Pardon my brevity, but I must go home. Good day, Mr Wickham."

"You are quite distraught, Miss Lydia. I cannot leave you alone." He fell into step beside her.

"Very well," she huffed, "just be sure to keep up."

"Whatever has you so troubled?" he asked with great sympathy.

Perhaps *here* was someone who would condole with her, for she doubted any of her sisters would. "My horrid sister Elizabeth has stolen—stolen!—him away. Oh, she is devious. They have been meeting secretly all this time and now...now he has asked her to marry him! She will get everything that should have been mine! But I shall never call her Mrs Darcy! Never!!"

Mr Wickham gripped her arm, dragging them both to a stop. "Are you telling me that Darcy and Miss Elizabeth are engaged to be married?"

"She just accepted his proposal. They were so involved in their scandalous behaviour that they did not know I was there to see them," Lydia spat.

"Oh, Miss Lydia, I see now why you are distressed. You have done nothing but champion Darcy, and now he has betrayed you with your own sister. You poor, dear girl."

At seeing the pity in his hazel eyes, Lydia blinked furiously to keep the tears from spilling out of hers. Anger had been a better feeling than *this*.

"I wish to go home now." She turned and resumed walking.

Mr Wickham still had his hand on her arm. "You have been treated abominably ill. You cannot let them succeed in their betrayal!"

"But what can *I* do? Mr Darcy does as he pleases, and everyone will congratulate Lizzy on making such an excellent match."

"I know a way we can stop the marriage."

She stopped and peered at him. "What way is that?"

He glanced around them. "It is a delicate matter. Let us go somewhere a bit less exposed before I explain further."

Lydia hesitated. Lizzy deserved to have her hopes dashed the way her own had been. She and Mr Darcy had been deceiving Lydia all this time! Mr Wickham was waiting for her decision, looking straight in her eyes. He had showed such sympathy, such kindness today. Perhaps she had been deceived about his character as well. But was she really prepared to break up the couple? They had looked very happy.

There was no harm in hearing Mr Wickham's idea; she need not agree, after all. "I shall hear what you have to say."

He led her away from the road into the woods to an area sheltered by some evergreen trees. He turned towards her and stood quite close. "This is private enough."

She stepped back. "I should think so. Please explain your meaning. What is it you have to say, Mr Wickham?"

He smiled and took her hands. "I should very much like it if," he paused and bit his lip. But, rather than finding it endearing, Lydia thought it feigned modesty. He continued, "If you would consent to elope. Think of the fun we could have together."

"Ha! You must be joking."

"I thought we had made a new start. I thought you were beginning to like me. I like you *very* much."

His words were innocent enough, but something about him made Lydia wary. She wished to return to the road. "I...thank you for the sentiment, but your proposed solution would only create more problems. I must refuse."

"That is a pity. But I have another option."

His smile turned into a leer. He leaned towards her and put his hand on the back of her head. Lydia's heart pounded in her chest. His lips came down upon hers roughly. She was too shocked to react. He thrust his tongue into her mouth—his tongue! She could think of nothing but his unpleasant taste and smell. Tobacco and...the way Kitty's breath smelled in the morning before cleaning her teeth.

For some reason, the thought of Kitty snapped Lydia from her stupor, and she pushed against Wickham with all her might. It was enough to break his hold on her. She staggered backwards, wiping her mouth with the back of her arm. "What are you doing? Do not touch me again!"

He held out his hands, the very picture of innocence. "But this is how we stop Darcy's marriage, Miss Lydia. Is that not what you wish to do?" All of the innocence left his expression.

Comprehension crashed upon her. "You are going to ruin my entire family by ruining...me! Then none of us will make respectable marriages."

"Now you begin to see the advantages of my plan."

He was upon her again, and she thrashed violently to get away, but he caught both her arms. His foul mouth hovered near hers as his body pressed against her. "Oh, Miss Lydia, you do not disappoint. I like a girl with spirit. Georgiana would have been far too timid. This will be a more satisfying way to avenge myself on Darcy. If you relax just a little, I promise we can both enjoy ourselves."

Lydia drew breath to scream, but she barely got out a whimper before his mouth silenced her. She could *not* submit. She kept struggling, but he was too strong. She stopped resisting his kiss for a moment. He took advantage by shoving his tongue into her mouth. Lydia bit down as hard as she could and tasted blood. She brought her knee up. He doubled over in pain, groaning and swearing.

Lydia turned and stumbled in the direction of the road. She ran faster than she ever had before, screaming the whole way. A low branch whipped her across the face; her feet caught on roots and branches, not to mention the mud. But she did not stop. She could hear him behind her, uttering terrible, vulgar oaths. Lydia looked over her shoulder, grateful she did not see him. Suddenly she crashed into a solid torso and felt strong arms surround her. *Oh God!* How had he caught up to her? A desperate shriek rose in her throat.

The arms were shaking her. "Lydia! What is wrong?"

She looked up into alarmed green eyes. She stopped screaming and began crying into her rescuer's chest. "John, John! Do not let him near me! Please!"

He held her away from him and examined her. They heard Mr Wickham approaching. "I will catch you, Miss Lydia," he taunted.

Lydia let out a frantic sob and John's face suddenly changed from confused alarm to rage. She had never seen him look so...fearsome. He pulled her against him, cradling her head to his chest. "He will never touch you again. Shh."

She gripped his coat in her fists and sobbed like a child.

"Compose yourself a little, Liddy. Do not let him see you like this. I promise you have nothing to fear now." She nodded and sniffed, wiping her face. "Stay behind me," he said as he repositioned them.

Lydia peeked around John's back. "Wickham, I suggest you stop where you are," he said.

Wickham obeyed, a false smile on his face. "Lucas! You were just the man I was looking for when I ran into Miss Lydia."

"You had better tell me what business you have with me before I render you unable to speak."

Wickham laughed nervously. "I wanted to give you some of what I owe you from our card game last night."

"Keep it." John moved towards Wickham, leaving Lydia feeling exposed.

Wickham held up his hands. "Lucas, I do not know what she told you, but you know how young gentlewomen are. They are very eager until their good breeding takes over, and then they begin to protest." He pointed at Lydia, "You saw how she flirted with me the other day. Miss Lydia came into the woods with me for one purpose, I assure you."

"You disgusting liar!" Lydia screeched, but she need not have bothered. Wickham was already falling in a heap into the mud. John stood over him with clenched fists.

Now that she was no longer frightened, the full measure of her wretched mistake struck Lydia. "How could I have been so stupid? He will tell everyone and I shall be ruined. I've ruined us all!" She sobbed, this time out of guilt. Poor Jane! Poor Lizzy! They had found good, honourable men who loved them, and Lydia had condemned them all to shame and misery. Even Kitty would lose Henry Long!

Wickham groaned and sat up. "We could have at least had some fun out of it. It will surely be the last time any man shows an interest in *you*. You should have enjoyed it."

Lydia put her hands over her ears while John punched him in the face. Wickham collapsed onto the ground again. "That will keep the filthy lecher quiet so I can think."

"It is no use," she whispered with her head lowered.

John came to her and lifted her chin. "Lydia, I am sorry I must ask, but it may be...necessary. What did he do to you?"

She tried to look away, feeling shamed, but he held her chin. He looked so worried, not disapproving at all. "He tricked me into leaving the road with him. I...I ought to have known better, but I was so angry. Then he grabbed me and kissed me. He smelled ghastly. I tried to fight him but...he had my arms. He kissed me over and over, and then I bit him and ran away. I was so frightened, John!"

"That is everything that happened?"

"Is that not enough?" she cried.

He tenderly wiped the tears from her cheeks. "Shh. You were very brave, Liddy. Very brave."

Lydia's heart pounded in her chest again, but this time it was rather...different.

"Lydia! Lydia!" Elizabeth called frantically from the road.

Lydia sank down onto a fallen log. She dreaded having to explain how she had spoiled everything. She had come into the woods with Mr Wickham for the sole purpose of ruining her sister's happiness. And now she had ruined *all* of her sisters' futures. How could any of them forgive her? How could she forgive herself?

39

Discharging Debts

Mr Darcy dismounted and eased Elizabeth down. They left the road, making their way through trees and bushes. Elizabeth caught a glimpse of John. "There!" she pointed.

She was puzzled by the scene before her. John stood while another man—an officer from the look of his mud-covered coat—lay in a heap to one side. To John's other side, Lydia sat on a log. Her dress was muddied to her knees, and even one of her coat sleeves was dirtied to the elbow. She had a puffy scratch on one cheek, and she had clearly been crying. "Liddy?" Elizabeth said as she went to her.

"Oh Lizzy!" Lydia sobbed into Elizabeth's coat.

"What has happened?"

She had trouble making out the words, but Lydia repeated them over and over. "I have ruined everything. I am so sorry."

Elizabeth looked towards John. "What is the meaning of this?"

"I heard screaming and followed it. Lydia was running towards the road quite distraught, chased by Wickham." He pointed towards the heap of redcoat and then ground out, "He tried to force himself on her. But she got away on her own, thank God."

Elizabeth held Lydia tighter. "But why would he do such a thing? Did he not expect her family, her friends, to retaliate?"

John shook his head while Lydia cried, "It is my fault!"

"This cannot possibly be your fault, Liddy."

She wiped her face, composing herself as best she could. "It is. You will hate me when I tell you. You will all hate me."

"Impossible. I could never hate you." Elizabeth gave her a tender smile. "Just please tell me what happened."

Lydia looked down at her hands, twisting her fingers. "I followed you from the house to...to confront you about Mr Darcy."

"I never meant to deceive you."

Lydia shook her head, still refusing to look up. "When I caught up to you, you were with Mr Darcy, and he was...I saw him propose. I turned around to go home, angry and jealous. Then Mr Wickham was there on the road. He saw I was upset and offered to walk me home. I was only too happy to share my troubles, and when he heard that Mr Darcy proposed to you, he said...he said—"

Mr Darcy interrupted. "You need not say any more, Miss Lydia. Clearly, this is my fault. He dragged you off the road when he knew hurting you would hurt me. I ought to have dealt with him long ago."

"He did not drag me," Lydia whispered. "I went with him! I was so stupid! How can any of you forgive me?"

Elizabeth rubbed her back. "But why did you go with him?"

"He said he knew a way...a way to prevent Mr Darcy from marrying you. He would explain in a more private setting. First he said we should elope, but when I refused, he..." She shook her head, hardly able to speak. "He meant to ruin all of us by compromising me. Through me, he would have his revenge."

Elizabeth was horrified. "Is that what he said to you when he... when you were alone with him?"

She nodded. "He said he would avenge himself on Mr Darcy."

"Oh Lydia, you were very foolish, but angry people are not always wise. This is *my* fault for not telling you what I knew of Mr Wickham."

Lydia finally met Elizabeth's eyes. "How can you say that when *I* have brought ruin upon us all purely out of a bitter, selfish desire to hurt you and Mr Darcy?" She began to sob again, and Elizabeth embraced her, murmuring words of comfort.

"If you are all done blaming yourselves for Wickham's actions," John said, "it is time we deal with Mr Wickham himself. He stirs."

Mr Wickham rubbed his jaw. He eyed John warily before turning to Mr Darcy. "If circumstances were different, I might wish you joy, Darcy. 'Tis a pity about the Bennets. All those lovely young ladies left unmarried. No one will have them after hearing of Miss Lydia's wanton behaviour."

John struck him in the face, and Elizabeth never thought she would be so pleased to see violence done to another human being. Mr Wickham groaned and struggled to rise again.

"Lucas, I ask that you refrain from hitting him," Mr Darcy said. Elizabeth recognised his controlled exterior for what it was: a façade.

"Oh, sorry." John did not sound the least bit sorry. "I will let you hit him the next time."

"I shall look forward to it, but right now, I need him coherent. Mr Wickham and I have matters to discuss."

Mr Wickham pulled himself upright once more and tried to wipe the dirt from his clothing. "I would much rather deal with you, Darcy. At least *you* are reasonable. This one"—he indicated John—"is more like that hot-headed cousin of yours." He gave up his fruitless efforts at making himself presentable. "I had meant to simply ruin your happiness by making marriage to Miss Elizabeth impossible, but now I see another option. Do you care to hear it?"

"Tread carefully, Wickham, or you may find me rather more like Mr Lucas."

Mr Wickham smirked. "I am very fond of Miss Lydia's pluck. I might be willing to marry her, given the right financial inducement."

Lydia shuddered in Elizabeth's arms.

"Think of it. You could still marry where you wish, old friend. We will be brothers."

"You cannot seriously consider this!" John spoke what Elizabeth was thinking.

Mr Wickham glanced over at Lydia and Elizabeth, leering. "I shall be very happy to become better acquainted with all my new sisters, including the future Mrs Darcy."

John moved in to punch Wickham again, but Mr Darcy was faster, hitting him in the gut. Mr Wickham doubled over, choking out, "And let us not forget dear Georgiana—she always was affectionate and pleasing and extremely fond of me."

John spoke to Mr Darcy, "Enough of this nonsense. I do not know what is between you two, but I will marry Lydia myself before I let that blackguard near her!" Lydia went very still.

John added angrily, "I call you out, Wickham."

"No!" Lydia gasped. "If anything happens to John because of me...!" She looked anxiously at her sister. "Lizzy, Mr Darcy, do not let him do this!"

"I can certainly best *this* poor excuse for a man," John sneered.

Mr Darcy stared icily at Mr Wickham. "You have gone too far. The time has come for a more permanent solution to your long perfidy. It is time I demanded repayment for purchasing all the debts you left in Lambton. I am the only reason you have not been hounded by debt collectors."

Mr Wickham became a bit less complacent. "Do not be a fool. Do you really wish to lose your chance at happiness? I shall ruin the Bennets, and while I am at it, I shall ruin Georgiana. I shall have my revenge."

Mr Darcy clenched his fists but spoke calmly. "You must owe quite a few tradesmen in Meryton as well. Perhaps I shall settle your debts with them. I imagine the total will be several hundred pounds when all is done. You remember my uncle, the judge, do you not?"

Mr Wickham laughed nervously. "You always were a good mathematician, but you are forgetting the matter of Miss Lydia's reputation. Threatening me with debtor's prison certainly will not persuade me to keep quiet."

Lydia shook off Elizabeth's arms and approached him. "But who will believe *you* over the four of us, especially when you are rotting in prison?"

"It will merely take a hint, a suggestion, of scandal to throw suspicion upon your family, you little chit," he spat.

She kicked him in the shin. "*That's* for making me get mud all over my dress!"

While Mr Darcy roughly restrained Mr Wickham, John chuckled

and pulled Lydia back towards Elizabeth. "My favourite imp is recovering her spirits already."

"I have made my decision, Wickham," Mr Darcy said with finality. "Now, I will leave you in Mr Lucas's capable hands for a few hours while I visit the shopkeepers in Meryton."

John grinned. "I find myself at leisure this afternoon."

Mr Wickham lost all his smugness. "Wait, Darcy. I see I have pushed you to your limit. But think of the Bennets. You have the power to keep that family's reputation unblemished. If you send me to America, rather than to debtor's prison, I promise not to utter one word defaming Miss Lydia."

"No!" John said vehemently. "He is barely held in check by society now. I have seen what men like him are capable of when unleashed in the New World."

Mr Darcy considered. "Mr Lucas is correct."

"Then I will be sure to give a very detailed account of my time alone with Miss Lydia. I will even embellish it, for who can really know the truth of such private encounters?"

John was about to hit him again, but Mr Darcy held up his hand. "I do have something to offer you, Wickham. Do you care to hear it?"

After receiving no reply, he explained. "As your principal creditor, I shall have considerable influence on where you will be sent and the conditions under which you will be held. Certainly you have heard some of the more harrowing accounts of foul, crowded cells shared with violent criminals. You might buy yourself some comfort and some safety with your silence."

Mr Wickham swallowed as Mr Darcy leaned towards him. "If I hear *one word* from anyone against Miss Lydia's reputation, or any of her sisters—or my sister, or Mr Lucas' sisters—I shall ensure you are kept in the vilest conditions imaginable. Even if I must bribe the prison guards, I shall spare no expense. You will pray for some disease to take you, rather than spend your days in pain and filth. Do you understand?"

He nodded, all hints of overconfidence and belligerence gone.

"Mr Lucas, will you help me escort Mr Wickham to Colonel Forster?"

John slapped his back. "Most happily. I like your methods more and more, Darcy." Then he turned to Mr Wickham, saying jovially, "Come along, I will tie you to my horse."

Mr Darcy went to Elizabeth and Lydia, his mask giving way to open concern and remorse as he approached. "How can I ever atone for what you have endured, Miss Lydia?"

Lydia gaped. "I...it was not your fault. Can you forgive *my* stupid, selfish actions, which nearly cost you your happiness?"

"I could hardly blame you for being ignorant of his true character. I should have warned the good people of Meryton rather than let Wickham move like a wolf amongst you."

Elizabeth interjected, "You two will not quarrel for the greater share of blame annexed to this afternoon. I must have my part too." They both smiled at her weakly. "Oh Liddy, are you quite well?"

"I am well. But we must invent some excuse for my appearance."

"The truth is excuse enough. We shall all dote on you for weeks, especially Mama."

"No! I do not wish anyone else to know!" She looked intently between Elizabeth and Mr Darcy. "I cannot expect Mama to keep such a secret. She would not *mean* to tell anyone; she just cannot help herself. And I would rather Jane, Mary, and Kitty not know of such things. There's no need to spoil their...to worry them so. Please, do not tell them."

"Of course; I shall do as you wish. And Mr Darcy and John can be trusted with any secret." She and Mr Darcy exchanged a look. "Only we four shall know."

Lydia nodded, relieved. "May I be the first to wish you joy, then?"

"I think you might justly hate me instead."

"No. I was as blind as Kitty to not have seen the truth sooner. Besides, catching Mr Darcy for a brother is even better than catching him for a husband. I may play cricket with him and dance with him, but I will not be expected to read so many books."

Elizabeth hugged her. "Thank you, Liddy. You are remarkably gracious."

"Even I must improve under such influence as you and Jane."

"You may depend upon me asking for a dance any time the chance arises, Miss Lydia."

"I shall hold you to that. And you, Lizzy, owe me a story—a love story."

"I owe all my sisters a full explanation. But let us get you home and out of the cold."

They made their way to the road where John waited with the horses and a subdued Mr Wickham. "Lizzy, Mr Bingley gave me this note for Jane. You had best take it. I have a full afternoon ahead of me." He indicated Wickham.

"Oh! Mr Darcy is not shot!" Lydia exclaimed.

Mr Darcy smiled, "No, I am not. Your sister will explain everything to you." When he turned his gaze to her, Elizabeth's breath hitched.

Lydia moved several steps away, in the direction of Longbourn, giving the couple some privacy. Mr Darcy took immediate advantage.

"I fear I shall not see you again today, as I have much to accomplish."

Elizabeth nodded. "You were magnificent. But do not forget your aunt and cousin in all this unpleasant business. They have had a dreadful fright today. Shall I see you tomorrow?"

"Do you really need to ask? I am extremely eager to speak to your father and just as eager to see you again." He leaned in close. "I love you, dearest Elizabeth."

"And I love you, Fitzwilliam." Elizabeth's heart overflowed with love and admiration. She tried to think rationally. "Take your gloves back; you need them more than I."

"But you must walk home in the cold."

"It is not far. You must resume carrying your spare pair from now on."

"There is much I shall resume," he said in a low voice that made her tingle all over. She was caught in the intensity of his gaze before he broke it to take the gloves. He pulled one on. Then, with his bare hand, he took her hand in his. "Until tomorrow." He kissed her hand, then turned towards the waiting horses.

"Come on, Lizzy," Lydia said. "We must come up with a plausible explanation for my appearance."

Jane, Mary, Kitty, and Lydia hung on Elizabeth's every word. She had finally confessed everything to them, beginning with the picnic. Jane already knew most of it, but today's events were new even to her. "Then he kneeled down—"

"In the mud!?" Kitty asked from her bed, shared with Mary and Jane.

"Yes, one knee right in the mud. I saw this part," bragged Lydia, who was sharing her bed with Elizabeth. "He said, 'Elizabeth June Bennet, I love you. Nothing would make me happier than spending the rest of my days with you. Will you do me the very great honour of becoming my wife?'"

"How did he know your middle name?" Mary asked. Elizabeth could not remember how he had learned it. She certainly never told him.

"*That's* all you have to say after hearing such a declaration?" an incredulous Kitty asked of Mary.

Mary shrugged. "No one ever uses Elizabeth's middle name."

Kitty turned back to Elizabeth. "And you accepted him."

Elizabeth could not keep herself from beaming. "I accepted."

"Then what happened? Is that when Lydia fell in the mud? Why did he not come to speak with Papa immediately? Did he kiss you?" Kitty had too many questions to wait for any answers.

Elizabeth felt Lydia stiffen beside her. "We agreed he ought to return to Netherfield to set his family at ease."

"But Mr Darcy will come tomorrow?" Kitty asked.

"Yes, he will."

"Oh, Lizzy, it is a wonderful story. Probably your best story ever, yet you cannot share it with many people. What a pity."

"But I can share it with *you*, which is what matters most. It is an enormous relief not to keep secrets from my dear sisters any longer. I am truly sorry for deceiving all of you."

"I am more than willing to forgive you if I may accompany you when you shop for your trousseau!"

Elizabeth laughed. "For Kitty, forgiveness is obtained through fashion. How shall I get back into my other sisters' good graces? I know Jane can never be angry with me; what about you two?"

"I wish to shop with you as well," Lydia said.

"And so you will. The poor modiste will have no idea what she is getting into. Mary, what say you?"

"I have no need to shop with you, but I shall think of something else."

"Very well, I am at your disposal. Now, it is time to sleep."

Jane and Mary extracted themselves from Kitty's bed, hugging themselves against the cold. With a parting "good night," they disappeared out the door.

Elizabeth bid good night to Kitty then turned to Lydia, whispering, "Good night, Liddy. Sleep well." She kissed her brow.

Lydia embraced her tightly. "Good night."

Elizabeth shut the door to Kitty and Lydia's room and snuck across the hall to her own. She doubted she would be able to find slumber easily. Her emotions today had gone from the depths of despair to the pinnacle of elation. Mr Darcy was well and unharmed, and he loved her. They were engaged!

But then there was fear and worry over Lydia. Elizabeth had never seen her youngest sister so distressed yet so reluctant to show it. Usually, when Lydia suffered some injury or insult—or merely an inconvenience—everyone heard about it, whether they wished to or not. They could not be expected to offer sympathy and attention if they were ignorant of her troubles, after all.

But today, Lydia had insisted that everyone remain ignorant of what happened with Mr Wickham. Even Elizabeth did not know exactly, though she could guess in generalities. Lydia's appearance and demeanour were telling, especially after Elizabeth's own experience alone with a man in the woods. What a contrast her first kiss must have been to poor Lydia's frightening ordeal.

"Lizzy? Are you asleep?" Lydia's whisper broke the stillness of Elizabeth's bedroom.

"No."

"I cannot sleep either. May I stay with you?"

"Of course." Elizabeth gasped at the cold blast of air as her sister pulled back the covers.

"Sorry," Lydia muttered, settling herself in the bed.

"Why can't you sleep? I should think you exhausted."

"I had a bad dream."

"Do you wish to tell me about it?"

"No. I wish to hear again about your secret morning meetings with Mr Darcy."

"Very well. The first time we met, I did not hear him approach…"

40

The Very Great Pleasure

Her eyes. Darcy kept coming back to her eyes. Of course her skin was exquisite, her graceful throat, delicious, and her lips—her lips were a revelation. But it had always been her eyes, and his mind was full of them for the rest of the afternoon, even as he completed his unpleasant tasks. Likewise, he thought of her eyes on his ride back to Netherfield (restored to his own mount), during his bath, and throughout dinner with far too many people, none of whom were her. Now, Darcy tried to keep his mind more agreeably engaged, sitting silently through Anne and Lady Catherine's incessant bickering. Alas, some voices cannot be easily ignored.

"This is not to be borne. Darcy, I insist we announce your betrothal to Anne immediately, thus putting an end to the ambitions of every low-born country miss you encounter, not to mention Anne's ridiculous notion of marrying Christopher Grantly."

Now he *must* speak. "Let me declare the impossibility of your aspirations for us once and for all. Anne and I shall never marry. I wish my cousin much joy with Mr Grantly, as should you. He is a good man."

She made a dismissive gesture. "Nephew, you are to understand that I came here through all this mud with the determined resolution of carrying my purpose. I have not been in the habit of brooking disappointment."

"That will make your situation at present more pitiable, Mother, but it will have no effect on Darcy, nor me." Darcy suspected Anne was enjoying herself just a bit too much.

Lady Catherine acted as if Anne had not spoken, still addressing Darcy. "You and Anne are destined for each other by the voice of every member of your respective houses, and what is to divide you? The upstart pretensions of the second son of an obscure gentleman farmer without family, connexions, or fortune? Will he, rather than you, be master of Rosings Park? Is this to be endured?" She turned suddenly to Anne, "It must not, will not be! If you were sensible of your own good, you would not wish to quit the sphere in which you have been brought up."

"In marrying Mr Grantly, I should not consider myself as quitting that sphere. He is a gentleman, I am a gentleman's daughter; so far we are equal. The same can be said of Miss Bennet and Mr Darcy." Anne used to possess more subtlety than this; Darcy braced for his aunt's reaction.

Indeed, Lady Catherine's suspicions began to awaken. "Why do we speak of Miss Lydia Bennet again? What has *she* to do with any of this? She may *be* a gentleman's daughter, but who was her mother? Who are her uncles and aunts? Do not imagine me ignorant of their condition."

"Whatever her connexions may be," said Darcy, his anger increasing with every word, "if *I* do not object to them, they can be nothing to you."

"Has that insolent girl actually drawn you in? Have her arts and allurements made you forget what you owe to yourself and to all your family. Have you taken leave of your senses? I am ashamed of you! Heaven and earth! Of what are you thinking? Are the shades of Pemberley to be thus polluted?"

They were interrupted by an insistent knock on the door of the sitting room they had borrowed for this pleasant little family discussion. Louisa Hurst entered, "I am terribly sorry to interrupt, but I feel it necessary to warn you. You must lower your voices. Mrs Hurst—my mother-in-law—is of a mind to come speak to you herself, but I convinced her to let me instead."

Lady Catherine inhaled sharply, looking alarmed. Perhaps she had already had the misfortune to rouse that great lady, Regina Hurst, in defence of Mr Hurst. From the look of Anne's hidden smile, that was precisely what had happened.

"I apologise, Mrs Hurst. We shall mind our voices henceforth," Darcy said. "How is Mr Hurst?"

"He is a little better, I think. Mr Robertson is pleased with his progress."

"I am very glad to hear it."

"I never thanked you, Mr Darcy. I have never been much use in a crisis, and seeing Reginald that first day... Well, I thank God you were here. You were much more valuable to him than I."

Darcy heard the regret in her voice. Perhaps this misfortune would be a new start for the Hursts. "I may have been of service during those chaotic hours after the accident, but you will be the most important to him during his recovery, Mrs Hurst."

"That is my hope. Now, I shall leave you to your...discussion. Mother and Grandmother promised to tell me childhood tales of Reginald."

She left them, and Darcy turned back to Lady Catherine. "Where were we, Aunt? Oh yes, I believe you were accusing me of losing my senses."

"Nephew," her tone took on a forced sweetness wholly incongruous with her character, "I am almost the nearest relation you have in the world. Will you promise me never to enter into an engagement with Miss Bennet?"

"I shall make no promise of the kind. I am my own master and shall marry where I wish."

Her mask fell, but she was careful to keep her voice low. "I am shocked and astonished. I expected to find you more reasonable. You have no regard, then, for the honour and credit of your family! Unfeeling, selfish fool! Do you not consider that a connexion with Lydia Bennet must disgrace you in the eyes of everybody?"

"Lady Catherine, I have nothing more to say. You know my sentiments."

"You are then resolved to have her?"

"I have said no such thing. I am only resolved to act in that manner, which will, in my own opinion, constitute my happiness."

"You refuse, then, to oblige me. You refuse to obey the claims of duty, honour, and gratitude. You are determined to ruin yourself and become the contempt of the world, by marrying not only a girl of inferior breeding and fortune, but a mere child! Why, she is younger than Georgiana!"

He finally had to concede this much. "I have no intention of marrying Miss Lydia."

Lady Catherine was the very picture of relief. She moved to speak again, but Darcy held up his hand.

"You will do well, however, to remember the kindness that so-called inferior family, the Bennets, offered to you and your daughter today, after enduring what I can only imagine was the most insulting behaviour conceivable from you. I have come to learn there is much more to 'good breeding' than family and fortune. There is kindness, grace, and compassion, and let us not forget humility, Aunt. Every one of Mr Bennet's daughters possesses these fine qualities in excess of you, no matter your title." She sat, open mouthed, while Anne smirked.

"Now, Lady Catherine, I expect you to speak only complimentary things of the Bennets for the remainder of the night, as my friend— your host—Mr Bingley, is engaged to marry Miss Jane Bennet. When we visit Longbourn tomorrow, I further expect you to thank the Bennets for their kindness to you and behave in a manner in keeping with *your* good breeding."

She snapped her mouth shut. "Naturally, I must thank them for the use of their carriage, yes."

"Very good. Shall we join Mr and Miss Bingley now?" Darcy was eager to be away from her. He wanted to blurt out that he would marry Elizabeth—no one but Elizabeth. However, since he had not been able to ask Mr Bennet's consent, he thought it better not to mention their understanding yet. Anne directed several curious looks at Darcy, but they could not speak freely. He must thank her a thousand times for her intervention today.

The three of them made their way to the drawing room, where

Bingley and Miss Bingley waited with coffee. Miss Bingley, eager to impress her most distinguished guest, proceeded to engage Lady Catherine in conversation. She soon learned precisely the right combination of subtle agreement and unabashed flattery. It took less than a quarter of an hour under this manner of treatment for Lady Catherine's spirits to be restored.

Darcy took advantage of the distraction afforded by the forging of this new friendship by seating himself at the writing desk. He had just begun to request Georgiana join him at Netherfield before Christmas when Anne came to him.

"Fitzwilliam, I gave you ample opportunity to tell Mother of your engagement. Did you not meet Miss Elizabeth today?"

"Yes, thank you for sending her running out into the cold without her gloves." He did not mean that sarcastically at all. Really he did not.

"Well?" she asked impatiently. "Did you not *finally* ask her to marry you?"

"Yes, I did."

"She could not have refused you. I shall not believe it—not after speaking with her today."

"She accepted me." Darcy was powerless to keep the raw enthusiasm out of his voice.

Anne grinned, then said in a scolding manner, "Then *why* did you not tell Mother? She is directing all of her ire at me for *my* engagement. You must have your fair share."

"I am sorry, Anne. I have not yet spoken to Mr Bennet."

"But you were gone so long today. Whatever were you— Fitzwilliam! You could not have been doing *that* for so long out in the mud and cold."

"Please." Darcy winced, not wishing to think about what Anne knew of *that*, nor to discuss it with her. "There were some unexpected complications. I shall speak to Mr Bennet tomorrow and then happily inform Lady Catherine."

"Oh, Fitzwilliam, you have set up a very wicked joke. Mother will learn your happy news at Longbourn! Though she sorely deserves the mortification, I do not think the Bennets deserve her temper."

Darcy was far too preoccupied to have considered it. "Do you think she will cause a terrible scene?"

Anne shrugged. "Most likely. I shall try to mitigate her outbursts, if I can."

"We must impress upon her beforehand the need, the expectation, to be civil."

Anne gave him a dubious look, then eyed his letter. "To whom do you write?"

"Georgiana. I hope she will join me here before Christmas. I suppose I should ask Bingley though."

"He looks as though he would appreciate being called away from Mother's monologue. I shall sacrifice myself and send him over."

She did as she promised, and Bingley was only too happy to break away. "Darcy, your aunt is rather..."

"Opinionated?"

Bingley cleared his throat and sought some means to change the subject. "You are no longer planning to leave us in two days' time, are you?"

"No, I wish to extend my stay if I may."

"Of course; I shall be pleased. It goes without saying that Caroline will be delighted as well, though perhaps when she learns what I suspect is the cause of your change in plans, she will be far from delighted." Bingley grinned at Darcy like a fool, and Darcy grinned back like a bigger fool.

"Will you extend your hospitality to Georgiana as well? I wish her to come before Christmas."

"We shall be doubly delighted."

"Please do not mention it to Miss Bingley until tomorrow, though, after I have spoken with Mr Bennet."

"Ah, the interview. Do not expect him to make it easy for you."

"I never presume to know what to expect from any of the Bennets."

"Then you are well prepared. Hurry up and finish your letter so that you may join in the fascinating conversation."

Bingley re-joined the ladies, leaving Darcy to finish writing to Georgiana. He hoped Lady Catherine would be fatigued after her journey; he was hardly in a state of mind for social niceties. He also fully expected to have some very satisfying dreams tonight. Indeed, he was feeling rather fatigued himself.

§❧

Darcy paced back and forth as much as his hiding spot behind Long-bourn would allow. He hoped—very, very much—that Elizabeth planned to walk this morning. So here he was, before sunrise, skulking behind the house where he might catch sight of the back door through the trees.

He tried to think of all he must tell her. She would wish to know how Hurst fared, and he must remember to tell her about Mrs Regina Hurst and her sister, Mrs Piper, not to mention their mother, Hurst's grandmother, Mrs Fenton. Darcy knew Elizabeth would delight in his descriptions of those three formidable ladies. He supposed he must also tell her about Wickham, though he loathed bringing up that unsavoury subject. She at least must know that all went according to plan. He must warn her that Lady Catherine would probably behave rudely to her family, no matter how much he and Anne wished otherwise. He must tell her that Georgiana would be coming to Netherfield. Similarly, he must ask her how Miss Lydia fared.

As he catalogued the subjects to be covered, he heard a door shut. He barely caught a glimpse of Elizabeth as she sprinted through the garden, for she was already on the path that cut towards the road. He intercepted her, startling her in the process.

"Fitzwilliam! You frightened me!"

"I apologise. It is too muddy at Oakham Stream. I wanted to save you the walk."

"You are forgiven. I hoped to see you this morning; I was unsure if you would ride today."

Darcy found it very hard to remember what he wanted to say. "You need never doubt I would ride anywhere at any time for the slightest chance of seeing you."

"How you flatter me," she said as she smiled up at him sweetly.

Her eyes—always those fine eyes. He simply was not strong

enough to resist their lure. The list of subjects to be covered must wait; he had forgotten it all anyway. With a reverently whispered, "Elizabeth," he took her into his arms and lost himself in her again.

41

The Silliest Girl in England
Part 2

Lydia had feigned sleep when Elizabeth slipped out the door to meet Mr Darcy in the pre-dawn light. She found she was barely jealous. After yesterday's terrifying ordeal in the woods, she saw the people around her with greater clarity. The way Mr Darcy looked at Elizabeth! She should have known he was in love with her sister at the ball, possibly even before that. All this time, Lydia thought herself more astute, more observant than Kitty, but in the case of Mr Darcy, she had been completely blinded by self-interest. Not once had she ever truly given a thought to how Mr Darcy might be feeling—as if *his* feelings were not even a consideration!

In truth, she had not truly given much thought to her own feelings. She sought a prize—that of a handsome, rich husband—without considering what would happen after she won it. Would she spend the rest of her life with a man of whom she knew so little? Did she really want to leave her mother, her father, her sisters, and her friends so soon?

When John had proclaimed *he* would marry her, rather than let her marry Wickham, Lydia had been so very tempted to accept. As Mrs John Lucas, she need not leave her family and friends at all. But she knew John did not love her, not in the way a man ought to love his wife. Oh, he cared for her in a protective, brotherly sort of way. It might be enough, if not for the possibility that he was in love with Elizabeth, a thought Lydia wished not to dwell on more than she must.

But while Lydia may have been selfish enough to let John rescue her reputation through marriage, she would never forgive herself if he was hurt, or worse, in a frightful duel. Thank heaven, Mr Darcy was so clever and resourceful. No one need marry her to save her reputation now.

This morning, she would begin to repay Mr Darcy the only way she could: by lessening some of the mortification and confusion he and Lizzy must face when their secret was finally revealed to Mrs Bennet.

Both Mr and Mrs Bennet were surprised to see their youngest daughter join them at such an early hour. Mr Bennet looked up from his book as Lydia poured herself a cup of tea and sat next to her mother.

"You look much improved this morning." Mrs Bennet nodded her approval. "I should hope you have learned not to follow Lizzy's example and go about walking all over creation no matter the weather."

Yesterday's misadventure was the very last thing Lydia wished to discuss. "Isn't it wonderful news about Mr Darcy, Mama?"

"Indeed, my dear; he is neither injured nor engaged. Perhaps you may still catch him."

"I am sure Mr Hurst is thrilled to be so accommodating of your matrimonial schemes," Mr Bennet said with a grim frown.

"Papa," Lydia remonstrated, "of course I am very sorry Mr Hurst has suffered this terrible accident. But *he* does not have an orphaned sister to care for."

He gave Lydia a long look. "No, he does not," he agreed before turning back to his book.

"Mama, about Mr Darcy, I no longer wish to catch him."

"Why ever not? He is just as handsome as before—he will not have any scars like Mr Hurst."

Lydia winced. Had she ever sounded so small-minded? "I do not wish to marry so soon. Besides, I am younger than Mr Darcy's sister. He would never think of me as a potential bride."

"Of course you wish to marry—all girls do. You must keep at it. The biggest fish cannot be caught so easily, Lydia. If you want him, we shall keep trying to get him for you."

"I do *not* want him."

Mrs Bennet gave Lydia a conspiratorial smile. "I see. Someone else has caught your eye. Is it that handsome and gallant Mr Wickham?"

Lydia gripped the arm of her chair as the blood rushed in her ears. Her mother was still speaking, "I do understand, but you are much better off with Mr Darcy. He is so rich, and you are fond of him still, aren't you? Remember his dimples."

"I...I esteem Mr Darcy. I think he is clever and honourable. But we have very little in common. I do remember his dimples. I also remember that I have been an appalling failure at making him smile. It should not be such a difficult task, not if we were really meant to be together."

Mrs Bennet sighed in resignation. "I warned you he was very dour. You did not seem to mind it after the picnic."

"I mind it now, Mama." Here was Lydia's chance to rouse her mother's suspicions. "Have you noticed," she began as she spread jam on her bread, "that Elizabeth has had the most success in making Mr Darcy talk and laugh?"

"Elizabeth?"

"You remember the lively discussions they have had together here?"

"Lizzy is always going on about books. But as I recall, *you* were also a part of those discussions, following all your effort at reading. And your father was as well." Mrs Bennet motioned towards Mr Bennet, who no longer held his book but rather peered at Lydia over his coffee.

She ignored him, hoping to get back to her object. "I did participate a little. You know, Lizzy told me that she and Mr Darcy have very similar taste in books. When she stayed at Netherfield, he loaned her several from his personal collection because Mr Bingley's library is so meagre."

"That was very kind of him."

It was clear Mrs Bennet was already tiring of the subject and remained entirely oblivious to what Lydia meant to imply. "I imagine they had several lively discussions over the course of her stay there and became much better acquainted with each other while Jane and Mr Bingley were falling in love."

That did it. "Better acquainted," Mrs Bennet murmured to herself. "But he does not think her handsome."

"Remember what John used to say of Lizzy's beauty? One does not see it just by looking at her, but by speaking with her. Mr Darcy has spoken with her many times now."

Mrs Bennet gulped. "Yes, many times."

"Perhaps he has reconsidered his first impression. She was the only one he asked to dance at Lucas Lodge, was she not?" Lydia knew perfectly well that she was.

"Yes, now that I think of it. I was so focused on Lizzy and Mr Lucas that... Mr Lucas! What about him?" Mrs Bennet looked between Lydia and Mr Bennet.

"Perhaps, Mrs Bennet, you should set aside your matchmaking schemes. Our daughters have the matter well in hand, it seems."

"Lydia, you really do not wish to catch Mr Darcy any longer?"

"No, Mama. I do not wish to catch anyone. I would rather someone care for me the way Mr Bingley cares for Jane."

Mr Bennet gave one slow nod. Mrs Bennet was kept from replying by the appearance of Mary in the breakfast room, who greeted them all, giving Lydia an appraising glance before sitting across from her. Mrs Bennet, with much on which to ruminate, ate in silence for some time. Jane and Kitty joined them soon, and the typical breakfast conversation resumed.

Just as Lydia was about to take her leave, Elizabeth returned, ebullient. She greeted them all in turn and took her seat.

"How was your walk, Lizzy?" Mary asked, and Lydia nearly laughed aloud at her blank expression. Lydia would not be fooled by Mary's feigned disinterest any longer.

"Splendid," Elizabeth said before recalling herself. "That is, most of the mud has dried. The road is much improved."

"Thank goodness. I must visit Mrs Philips today," said Mrs Bennet.

"Oh, Mama, that would be ill advised. I...chanced upon Mr Darcy on his morning ride. He said—"

"Mr Darcy?!" Now Elizabeth had her mother's full attention.

"Y-yes, Mr Darcy. He said he planned to call on you today with his aunt and cousin to thank you for the use of our carriage and to inquire after theirs."

Mrs Bennet pushed back from the table. "Then I certainly shall not go out! There is much to be done. I must speak with Cook. And Hill. And, oh dear, what did Thomas say about the de Bourgh carriage?" Her voice faded away down the hallway.

"Well, Lizzy, I hope you are satisfied. Your mother will be occupied with nothing but getting fish on the unlikely chance that Lady Catherine accepts an invitation to stay for dinner," Mr Bennet said. "Lydia, have you finished your meal?"

"Yes, Papa."

She rose, wondering what he might wish to say.

"Let us go to the library."

When they reached their destination, he closed the door and indicated that she should sit. He leaned against the front of the desk. "I get the distinct impression that 'walks' taken by my daughters involve a bit more than walking. Should I know anything in particular about yesterday?"

Lydia shrugged. "You may wish to speak to Lizzy as she is the one who takes all the walks."

"Indeed I shall ask Lizzy, if you send her in when you go. But first, I have a few more questions for you to evade."

Lydia leaned forward, taking a quill off Mr Bennet's desk. She needed something to occupy her hands while under his scrutiny.

"I trust you meant what you said to your mother. You have relinquished any aspirations of marriage involving Mr Darcy?"

"Yes." She ran the quill between her fingers over and over, hoping he would lose interest.

"You do not wish to elaborate? That is rather unlike you. Perhaps you were scared off by his gruesome aunt?"

She dared to meet his eye. "Papa! You are teasing me!"

He chuckled. "I am. But in all seriousness, it is heartening to see you give more deliberation to such a weighty matter as marriage.

There is no need to rush, Lydia. You are young and growing less and less silly every day, it seems."

"Am I no longer one of the silliest girls in England?"

"No. Kitty is the sole boaster of that title now."

She tried not to laugh. "Papa, it hurts a girl's feelings to hear her father say such things."

"I suppose the only remedy is to find some way of making Kitty less silly. Do you think we might persuade her to read and discuss books with us too?"

"She will likely only agree to read gothic novels, which means *you* would have to read them too, if they are to be discussed."

He grimaced. "Perhaps Kitty and I can work out a bargain. For every horrid gothic novel I read, she will read two books of worth."

"You may propose it, but she will hold fast to a more equitable exchange."

"Each of my daughters is obstinate in her way." He sounded rather proud of it. "Well, if you will procure Kitty's favourite novel for me, I shall read it and astonish her one night by singing the praises of the dashing hero."

Lydia laughed, "What a fine joke! I shan't spoil it."

He took the quill from her, saying quietly, "You are a good girl, Lydia."

She rose hastily to leave, swallowing the lump in her throat. Then, on an impulse, she embraced him. He returned the gesture rather awkwardly but not reluctantly. Lydia could not remember the last time he had hugged her. "Thank you, Papa," she whispered before exiting the library.

※

Kitty was the first to spy the Bingley carriage coming up the lane that afternoon. Upon this discovery, frantic orders to straighten skirts and pinch cheeks were given to all present.

Kitty kept them informed on the view from the window. "They are getting out of the carriage now. It is Mr Darcy! And Mr Bingley! Now they are helping Lady Catherine out of the carriage. And now Miss de Bourgh."

"Come away from the window," Mrs Bennet cried. "Now, girls, make yourselves look respectably occupied. Kitty, my dear, try not to say too much. Mary, for goodness sake, child, must you constantly have fingers stained with ink? There's no time to clean them now; you must hide them. Jane, you sit here, yes. Now Lizzy..."

Mrs Bennet arranged them to her liking until Hill finally announced, "Lady Catherine de Bourgh, Miss de Bourgh, Mr Darcy, and Mr Bingley."

"What a splendid surprise! You are very welcome, Lady Catherine..."

As Mrs Bennet fawned over her distinguished guests, Lydia wondered that Lizzy did not melt under Mr Darcy's fervent gaze. Soon though, Mrs Bennet had gushed long enough over Lady Catherine and Miss de Bourgh. "Mr Darcy, we are so very pleased to see you well! And we cannot apologise enough for alarming your dear relations yesterday. We were quite misinformed."

"It was an innocent misunderstanding. Your man, Thomas, explained that he was most likely the source of the confusion. But enough of that, I believe I have some introductions to make." Mr Darcy proceeded to introduce Lady Catherine and Miss de Bourgh to each of them by name. There were curtseys and smiles exchanged, though not by Lady Catherine. She merely inclined her head.

"And this young lady is Miss Lydia Bennet," Mr Darcy concluded.

"Mother and I had the pleasure of speaking briefly with Miss Lydia yesterday. Is that not so, Mother?" Miss de Bourgh said as she curtseyed.

Lady Catherine paused and inclined her head again before Mrs Bennet insisted everyone sit.

"How is Mr Hurst?" Jane asked of Mr Bingley, who of course had taken a seat next to his betrothed.

"He seems to be recuperating. Today he begged me to pour some brandy into what he called 'Lucas's revolting swill.' Luckily, Mr Lucas was not offended."

The Bennets laughed. "No, he would not be," said Elizabeth. She turned to Lady Catherine and Miss de Bourgh. "Thomas took your carriage into Meryton this morning. The wheelwright promises that it will be ready for your use within two days."

"That is much sooner than we had expected. Is it not, Mother?"

Lady Catherine nodded once. Her ladyship's attention, more often than not, was squarely on Lydia, who was amused rather than intimidated by it.

Miss de Bourgh continued, "You must thank Thomas for acting so quickly. He took prodigiously good care of us. Did he not, Mother?" Miss de Bourgh's inquiry was met with yet another inclination of the head.

Thus progressed the conversation for a number of minutes. Eventually, the combined efforts of Jane, Lizzy, Mr Bingley, Miss de Bourgh, and Mrs Bennet coaxed Lady Catherine into participating more. Lydia suspected this was by design, for Mr Darcy soon stood and exited as discreetly as possible. She was overset with panic that he might feel duty bound to tell Mr Bennet of her ordeal with Mr Wickham. She followed, somewhat less discreetly if Lady Catherine's gaze was any indication, and caught up to Mr Darcy just as he was about to knock on the library door.

"Mr Darcy!" she whispered.

He startled, then whispered, "Yes?"

"You will not tell my father *everything* that happened yesterday, will you?"

"I gave my word that I would not."

She exhaled in relief. "Yes, of course. I am sorry to bother you." She smiled. "Carry on."

"Wait, Miss Lydia, are you well?"

She knew his concern was genuine. "Yes. I am simply ashamed of my behaviour."

"Ashamed? But it was not your fault."

"I am not blameless." He began to protest, but she held up her hand. "Please let us never discuss it again. Besides, you have important business with my father."

He looked towards the door. "Have you any advice?"

"Do not let him fool you. Your visit is not wholly unexpected."

The door in question suddenly opened. "I thought I heard voices, though I had little notion of their belonging to the two people who now stand before me."

"Papa, Mr Darcy wishes a word with you. I showed him the way to the library."

Mr Bennet had a telling twinkle in his eye. "But Mr Darcy has been in my library before—on the day of the picnic, if I recall. What was it we discussed then?"

Lydia made her escape, returning to her seat in the drawing room. Lady Catherine certainly took notice but said nothing. In fact, for the next quarter of an hour, Lady Catherine had no part in the conversation at all. She spent this time with her eyes fixed either on Lydia or on the door, the very one that so often drew Elizabeth's gaze. At the conclusion of this interval, two came through it: Mr Bennet and Mr Darcy.

"Mr Bennet, allow me to introduce Lady Catherine de Bourgh, my aunt, and Miss de Bourgh, my cousin."

In the ensuing conversation, Mr Darcy was all nervous energy except when he and Elizabeth locked gazes from across the room, then he was all dazed grin. Finally, Mr Bennet came to the announcement all save two in the room were expecting.

"As distinguished as our illustrious guests are, today is auspicious for another reason. With five lovely daughters, perhaps one day such announcements will feel commonplace. But I must admit, I remain rather stunned with the novelty of it all." He held out his hand. "Elizabeth, my dear, please join me."

A flushed Elizabeth crossed the room and took Mr Bennet's hand. He patted hers as he began again, "Today, Mr Darcy has requested, and been given, my consent and my blessing to marry our Lizzy."

Reaction was immediate and varied: cheers, laughter, squeals, tearful embraces, hearty handshakes. But the aforementioned two in the room were rather more subdued. Mrs Bennet sat and blinked, looking around the room from person to person. Lady Catherine sat and stared, unblinking and unseeing.

Mrs Bennet recovered first. "My dear Lizzy! I had not the slightest inkling until this morning! And then I feared giving any encouragement because you are always so contrary whenever I set to matching you!"

Elizabeth laughed. "Not this time, Mama. This time I am most compliant."

"Oh, but you will have a grand life! And Mr Darcy—so tall and so handsome! What a fine pair you make!"

"Mother, it seems you have two weddings to attend in the near future. Will you not join me now in wishing Fitzwilliam joy?" Miss de Bourgh asked the last with much uncertainty in her voice.

The room quieted.

"Nephew, as you said last night, you are your own master. I wish you joy—for myself and for my dear sister, your mother, whose dearest wish was for her children's happiness."

After a short silence, Mrs Bennet proclaimed, "You must all stay for dinner!"

42

Such a Conclusion to Such a Beginning

Fitzwilliam Darcy was a man distracted. To most observers, this was not unusual; he often seemed distracted when in company—staring out a window, appearing deep in thought. But before, he merely wanted to avoid the attentions of the fortune hunters, social climbers, or other unsavoury characters who often sought to ingratiate themselves to him.

This time, as he stood in Netherfield's drawing room on Christmas Eve, a fortnight after his joyous engagement, his mind was more agreeably engaged by the woman he was to wed in three months' time. She sat on the floor with a group that ranged in age from six to seventy. It consisted of the four Gardiner children, along with Lydia Bennet and the three Lucas brothers. But the eldest person taking part in the merry games on the floor was Mrs Fenton, Hurst's grandmother. Nearby, Mary Bennet played Christmas tunes from memory on the pianoforte. Bingley, Jane, Miss Bingley and Miss Lucas were conversing near the fireplace. Opposite them, Mrs Bennet, Mr and Mrs Philips, and Sir William and Lady Lucas were gossiping and boasting to Mrs Gardiner, who had arrived with her family from London several days ago.

Darcy stood with Mr Bennet and Mr Gardiner at the edge of the room, but he only caught parts of their conversation, distracted as he was by a certain young lady. Mr Bennet directed amused glances at him. Though Darcy was not of a disposition in which happiness overflowed in mirth, he had come to accept that he must constantly appear the besotted fool, at least to Mr Bennet. He could not help it, nor would he wish to return to those days of hiding his regard for Elizabeth and being aloof and detached from the happiness around him. How could one maintain grave silence in company such as this? These people might not be fashionable or boast of great connexions; some of them were even vulgar. But they were genuine, they cared for one another, and a number of them would soon be his family.

His family. It would grow to include not just two lonely siblings, but all these sisters, cousins, aunts, and uncles. Darcy heard Georgiana laughing as she sat with a group gathered around a fashion magazine. Mrs Regina Hurst and Mrs Piper pointed out their preferences to Kitty, Maria Lucas, and Georgiana.

Georgiana appeared happy and was surprisingly chatty. Elizabeth had been correct—his sister needed female companions and confidantes nearer her age. How fortunate that his betrothed had a bevy of sisters and friends to offer! In securing his own happiness, Darcy had secured Georgiana's as well. Her joy at his impending marriage could not be contained. When he had finally introduced her to his betrothed, Elizabeth had overcome Georgiana's initial timidity and, as usual, set her at ease with the same kindness and liveliness that charmed everyone.

Seeing and hearing the good cheer all around him, Darcy could imagine his Christmases to come, gathered in another drawing room at Pemberley. Many of those present today would be there, but so would others: his own cousins, aunts, and uncles, and, hopefully, his own children. Pemberley would be filled with the laughter of family again, and he owed it all to Elizabeth. He could never express, never repay, all she had given him, though he would make his best attempt at it.

Bingley was the first to notice Mrs Hurst enter the drawing room. "Ah, Louisa. We are so glad you have joined us." Everyone else added their welcome.

"Thank you all. Reginald is fatigued and requires some rest. He bade me to partake in the festivities for a while and to bring him an eggnog when I return." Hurst was sounding more and more like himself.

Mrs Hurst made her way over to watch the Gardiner children in their game, where Mrs Fenton vociferously invited her to join them. Elizabeth took advantage of the resulting repositioning to excuse herself. She went to one of the windows, catching Darcy's eye on her way. Eager to join her, Darcy turned towards Mr Bennet and Mr Gardiner. "If you will ex—"

"We shall certainly grieve for the loss of your contribution to the conversation, Mr Darcy." Mr Bennet waved him away with a chuckle. Darcy could only smirk apologetically before striding to the window.

A certain young lady awaited. "You are taciturn tonight, Mr Darcy."

"I am simply beguiled by my betrothed."

"Then you will not mind answering some rather forward questions for her?"

"Not at all."

"When did you learn my middle name?"

He had not expected such a question. "When did I— Well, it was when you stranded yourself on the staircase after your sprained ankle. Jane called you by your full name when she scolded you."

She nodded. "And when did you fall in love with me? How could you begin? I can comprehend your going on charmingly when you had once made a beginning; but what could set you off in the first place?"

"I can fix on the precise hour, the exact spot, and the specific look when I knew that I loved you, though I suspect the moment when I actually fell in love with you precedes them by several days."

His certainty surprised her. "Indeed? And will you not share these love-inducing events? I shall advise my unattached sisters how to duplicate them and catch their own rich husbands."

He turned back towards the room. "You sat in that very settee with your legs up. Your mother had just mortified you by scheming to match Lydia with me, and your father had finally checked her behaviour. The way you looked at him... I knew I wanted you to look upon me with such love. I knew I loved you."

She grasped his arm as they turned back to look out the window. A few large snowflakes fell in the dusk. "And when do you suspect you actually fell in love with me?"

"It must have been at another window, only I lurked outside of it, peering in at a woman of such integrity and strength of character as I had never imagined."

She leaned into him, squeezing his arm. "Thank you, my love," she whispered, full of emotion.

"To what do these questions tend?" he asked.

"Oh, this will sound strange, but Mary wished me to ask."

"Mary?"

"It was she who first wondered how you knew my middle name. She also asked me several questions about our...well, what you might call our courtship, in retrospect. I promised all my sisters some form of recompense for having kept such secrets from them. Kitty and Lydia's retribution took a more material form, but Mary only wanted information. She will not reveal our private affairs to anyone."

"Yes, I know. Would you...may I ask you the same question? When did you first love me?"

"It has been coming on so gradually that I hardly know when it began. But I believe I must date it from our first dance."

Darcy recalled that dance, how they had moved in perfect unison. "It *was* an exceptional dance. And when did you realise that you loved me, if not then?"

"I finally admitted it to myself on the balcony at Lucas Lodge."

Darcy sighed. "And then I almost let you slip away. I wonder how long we might have continued in our mutual misunderstanding. Hurst's injury had certainly great effect, for it lured Mr Lucas here to lend assistance. What becomes of the moral if our comfort springs from a tragedy? This will never do."

"You need not distress yourself. The moral will be perfectly fair. Lady Catherine's unexpected visit and Anne's open disavowal of your rumoured betrothal were the means of removing all my doubts. We are not indebted for our present happiness to Mr Hurst's injury. I would have certainly spoken to you directly upon our next meeting, whenever that may have been."

"Lady Catherine has been of infinite use, which ought to make her happy, for she loves to be of use. But I think the true moral must be that we ought to always speak openly and freely with each other and never hesitate to share our thoughts."

She looked up at him warmly. "You are indeed the cleverest of men, Mr Darcy."

"I shall be the happiest of men on the day you become Mrs Darcy, and every day thereafter. March first seems a very long way off," he grumbled.

"Yes, but with Charlotte and Anne to wed in the interim, it is the earliest date that allows us all to attend each other's happy days. Just imagine how much longer we should have waited if Jane and Charles had not agreed to a double wedding."

Elizabeth Darcy shifted carefully in the bed, trying not to disturb her...husband. She could not help her mental pause at the thought, for it was the second day of March, her first morning with a new name and a new husband. A new life.

Yesterday, she had said goodbye to her parents, her sisters, and the only home she had ever known. The most difficult parting was of course with Jane, but Elizabeth had been surprised by the poignancy of some of the other farewells too. She had grown closer to her younger sisters over the last few months, possibly because they all realised their lives would soon be forever altered.

Likewise, her relationship with her father had deepened and become richer since confronting him at the picnic. How strange to think that very act of defiance had begun both her and Jane's journeys towards their current married state.

After the wedding breakfast, she and John had said their goodbyes as well. "You look beautiful—the perfect bride," he had said.

"Have I fooled even you in my finery? Surely not. In a moment you will touch my nose and call me Lizzybits."

"I think not, Mrs Darcy," he had replied.

With those few words from her childhood friend, Elizabeth suddenly felt the full magnitude of the transformation her life had just undergone. Gone forever were her carefree days of tree climbing and reckless dares and so many hours of fun that she could not begin to tally them. Henceforth, she would only return to her childhood home as a visitor. It was different for a man, an heir. John had gone off and had his adventure, but there had never been a doubt, barring some tragedy, that he would return to live his life in his boyhood home.

"Oh John." She had reached for his hands. "I have great plans for epic cricket matches at Pemberley. You must come this summer."

He had laughed. "Your Mr Darcy has already requested my participation."

Then she had felt "her Mr Darcy" at her side, supporting her elbow. "The carriage is ready. Are you ready to depart, Mrs Darcy?"

"Quite ready, and I do enjoy being addressed thus."

He had smiled, revealing those much-heralded dimples. "Not nearly as much as I enjoy addressing you thus, Mrs Darcy."

Elizabeth's recollections were halted when her Mr Darcy shifted in bed behind her. Sharing her bed was not a new experience, not with four sisters—but her sisters were never so warm, so large, so... naked. Last night, their state of nudity had seemed, if not perfectly normal, then exceedingly necessary. Indeed, at a certain point, any remaining garments were a *most* irksome impediment. But that was last night. To find herself naked next to an equally naked man in the light of morning was another thing entirely.

A forearm worthy of ogling stole around her waist. She waited, too embarrassed to turn over and face him. His deep voice made her shiver when he said near her ear, "Good morning, Lizzy."

It was the first time he had ever called her Lizzy. During their engagement, she had been Elizabeth. Yesterday, she had been Mrs Darcy. Today, she was Lizzy. She turned over onto her back, her nakedness forgotten.

He was propped up on his elbow, looking down at her with a mixture of admiration, tenderness, and wonder. Oh, but he was handsome, his hair disheveled, a hint of beard growth on his jaw. He took her breath away.

Finally, she broke their silent communion. "Say it again, my love," she whispered, placing her hand against his rough cheek.

He kissed her palm before lowering his face to hover just above hers. "Good morning, Lizzy." He kissed her. "My Lizzy."

And she was.

ABOUT THE AUTHOR

KC Kahler lives in northeastern Pennsylvania and works in online education, after having dabbled in sandwich making, bug collecting, and web development. She discovered Jane Austen fan fiction in 2008 and soon began dabbling in writing her own. KC's first novel, *Boots & Backpacks*, was published in 2014. *A Case of Some Delicacy* is her second novel.

KC blogs about Austen and other pop culture topics. In 2015 and 2017 her popular Austen + The Onion Headlines meme was featured in *The Atlantic*, *Flavorwire*, and *AV Club*. In 2017, she made the requisite pilgrimage to Jane Austen country, where she took the waters in Bath, walked the lanes of Steventon, didn't fall off the Cobb in Lyme Regis, and stood awestruck in Chawton.

For more information about new releases, sales and promotions on books by KC and other great authors, please visit www.QuillsAndQuartos.com.

ALSO BY KC KAHLER

Boots and Backpacks-Pride & Prejudice on the Appalachian Trail, Roughly

William Darcy counts down the last few months to his 30th birthday with dread. Orphaned as a child, his parents' will includes a bizarre clause: Darcy must get married by his 30th birthday in order to inherit the family fortune. To make matters worse, the press knows about this deadline, as do the hordes of women chasing him in the hopes of becoming Mrs. Darcy. His family legacy hangs in the balance, but Darcy has little faith in the fairer sex. Will he find a woman he wants to marry, and quickly?

Elizabeth Bennet is determined to pursue her education and career without letting a man get in the way. When her traveling companion drops out, her planned hike on the Appalachian Trail is jeopardized. She meets the spoiled, snobby William Darcy just when he is desperate to escape the spotlight. No one will suspect that the Prince of Manhattan has gone backpacking! Darcy and Elizabeth form a tenuous partnership and begin a 300-mile journey that will transform them both.

In classic romantic comedy tradition, Boots & Backpacks follows our reluctant partners as they build trust, friendship, and even more. Six weeks together on America's most famous hiking trail may turn out to be just what these two need!